FIRE
AND
ASH

JONATHAN **MABERRY**

SIMON & SCHUSTER

First published in Great Britain by Simon & Schuster UK Ltd, 2013
A CBS COMPANY

This edition published in 2015
Published in the USA in 2013 by Simon & Schuster Books for Young Readers,
an imprint of Simon & Schuster Children's Division, New York

1 3 5 7 9 10 8 6 4 2

Simon & Schuster UK Ltd
1st Floor, 222 Gray's Inn Road
London WC1X 8HB

www.simonandschuster.co.uk

Simon & Schuster Australia, Sydney
Simon & Schuster India, New Delhi

A CIP catalogue record for this book
is available from the British Library

PB ISBN: 978-1-4711-4491-2
Ebook ISBN: 978-1-4711-1796-1

Printed and bound by CPI Group (UK) Ltd, Croydon, CR0 4YY

MIX
Paper from
responsible sources
FSC® C020471

Simon & Schuster UK Ltd are committed to sourcing paper
that is made from wood grown in sustainable forests and supports the Forest
Stewardship Council, the leading international forest certification organisation.
Our books displaying the FSC logo are printed on FSC certified paper.

This one's for the peacemakers.
For the brilliant young writers in my Experimental Writing for
Teens class: Rebekeh Comley, Nathan Zalesko, Zach Baytosh,
Sarah Buschi, Carl Hall, Mei Peng Rizzo, Maxwell Cavallaro,
Will Perkins, and Archer O'Neal Odom.

And—as always—for Sara Jo.

ACKNOWLEDGMENTS

Special thanks to some real-world people who allowed me to tap
them for advice and information. My agents, Sara Crowe and Harvey
Klinger; my film agent, Jon Cassir of CAA; my editor, David Gale, and
all the good people at Simon & Schuster Books for Young Readers;
Nancy Keim-Comley; Tiffany Fowler-Schmidt; Michael Homler of
St. Martin's Griffin; Dr. John Cmar of Johns Hopkins University
Department of Infectious Diseases; Carl Zimmer, author of *Parasite
Rex* (Simon & Schuster); Alan Weisman, author of *The World
Without Us* (Thomas Dunne Books); M. Burton Hopkins Jr., Sam
West-Mensch, Chris Graham, David Nicholson, and John Palakas of
the History Channel documentary *Zombies: A Living History*; U.S.
Army helicopter pilot Samuel C. Garcia; Mason Bundschuh; the
crew at First Night Productions—Louis Ozawa Changchien, Paul
Grellong, and Heath Cullens; and Robert Kirkman, creator of *The
Walking Dead*.

Part 1

The Hinges Of Destiny

"Changing is what people do when they have no options left."

HOLLY BLACK,
Red Glove

BENNY IMURA SAT IN THE DARK AND SPOKE WITH MONSTERS.

It was like that every day.

It had become the pattern of his life. Shadows and blood. And monsters.

Everywhere.

Monsters.

THE THING CROUCHED IN THE DARKNESS.

It stank of raw meat and decay. A metal collar was bolted around its neck and a steel chain lay coiled on the bottom of the cage, looking like the discarded skin of some great snake.

The thing raised its head and glared through the bars. Greasy black hair hung in filthy strings, half hiding the gray face. The skin looked diseased, dead. But the eyes . . .

The eyes.

They watched with a malevolent intensity that spoke of a dreadful awareness. Pale hands gripped the bars with such force that the knuckles were white with tension. The thing's teeth were caked with pieces of meat.

Benny Imura sat crossed-legged on the floor.

Sick to his stomach.

Sick at heart.

Sick in the depths of his soul.

Benny leaned forward. His voice was thick and soft when he spoke.

"Can you hear me?"

The creature's lips curled.

"Yes, you can hear me," said Benny. "Good . . . can you understand me? Do you know who I am?"

A fat drop of bloody spit oozed from between the creature's teeth, rolled over its bottom lip, hung for a moment, and then dropped with a faint *plash* to the floor.

Benny leaned closer still. "Do you recognize me?"

After a long moment, the thing in the cage leaned forward too. Its face underwent a slow process of change. Doubt flickered in its eyes; the lips relaxed over the teeth. It sniffed the air as if trying to identify Benny's scent. The doubt in its eyes deepened. It bent closer still, and now the lips seemed like they were trying to shape a word.

Benny pushed himself even closer, trying to hear what sound that word carried.

"Huh," murmured the creature in a rasping croak, ". . . huh . . . hun . . ."

"Go on," Benny encouraged. "Go ahead. You can do it. Say something. . . ."

The creature rested its forehead against the inside of the bars, and Benny leaned all the way forward.

". . . hunh . . . hunh . . ."

"What is it?" whispered Benny. "What are you trying to say?"

The creature spoke the word. It came out as a whisper. A full word. Two syllables.

"Hungry!"

Suddenly it lunged at Benny; gray hands shot between the bars and grabbed Benny's shirt. The creature howled with triumph.

"HUNGRY!"

Wet teeth snapped at him. It jammed its face between the bars, trying to bite him, to tear him.

To feed its hunger.

Benny screamed and flung himself backward, but the creature had him in its powerful hands. The teeth snapped. Saliva that was as cold and dirty as gutter water splashed Benny's face.

"Hungry . . . hungry . . . hungry!" screamed the thing.

Behind Benny a voice shouted in anger. The soldier, moving too slow and too late. Something whistled through the air above Benny's head and rang off the bars. A baton, swung by the soldier with crippling force.

The creature jerked backward from a blow that would have smashed its jaw and shattered its teeth.

"No!" bellowed Benny, still caught by the thing's hands, but squirming, fighting it and swinging his arms up to block the soldier.

"Move, kid!" snarled the guard.

The baton hit the bars again with a deafening *caroooom!*

Benny bent his knees and forced his foot into the narrow gap between him and the bars, then kicked himself backward. The creature lost one handhold on his shirt, but it grabbed the bar to brace itself so it could pull even harder with the other. Benny kicked out, once, twice, again, slamming his heel into the hand holding the bar, hitting knuckles every time. The creature howled and whipped its hand back from the bars. Its screech of agony tore the air.

Benny's mind reeled. *It can still feel pain.*

It was the strangest feeling for Benny. That thought, that bit of truth, was a comfort to him.

If it could still feel pain . . .

It was still alive.

"Out of the way, kid," roared the soldier, raising his stick again. "I got the son of a—"

Benny kicked once more, and the whole front of his shirt tore away. He collapsed backward against the soldier, hitting his legs so hard the man fell against the concrete wall. Benny sank onto the cold floor, gasping, shuddering with terror.

Inside the cage, the creature clutched its hands to its gray flesh and let out a high, keening cry of pain and frustration.

And of hunger.

The soldier pushed himself angrily off the wall, hooked Benny under the armpit, hauled him to his feet, and flung him toward the door. "That's it. You're out of here. And I'm going to teach this monster some damn manners."

"No!" shouted Benny. He slapped the soldier's hands aside and shoved the man in the chest with both hands. The move was backed by all of Benny's hurt and rage; the soldier flew backward, skidded on the damp concrete, and fell. The baton clattered from his hand and rolled away.

The creature in the cage howled and once more lunged through the bars, trying this time to grab the fallen soldier's outflung arm. The guard snatched it out of the way with a cry of disgust. Spitting in fury, the soldier rolled sideways onto his knees and reached for the baton.

"You made a big damn mistake, boy. I'm going to kick your ass, and then you're going to watch me beat some manners into—"

There was a sudden rasp of steel and something silver flashed through the air and the moment froze. The soldier was on his knees, one hand braced on the ground, the other

7

holding the baton. His eyes bugged wide as he tried to look down at the thing that pressed into the soft flesh of his throat. The soldier could see his own reflection in the long, slender blade of Benny Imura's *katana*.

"Listen to me," said Benny, and he didn't care that his voice was thick with emotion or that it broke with a sob. "You're not going to do anything to me, and you're not going to do anything to—"

"To *what*? It's a monster. It's an abomination."

Benny pressed the tip of the sword into the man's skin. A single tiny bead of hot blood popped onto the edge of the steel and ran along the mirror-bright surface in a crooked line.

"It's not a monster," said Benny. "And he has a name."

The soldier said nothing.

Benny increased the pressure. "Say his name."

The soldier's face flushed red with fury.

"*Say it*," snarled Benny in a voice he had never heard himself use before. Harsh, cruel, vicious. Uncompromising.

The soldier said the name.

He spat it out of his mouth like a bad taste.

"*Chong.*"

Benny removed the sword and the soldier started to turn, but the blade flashed through the shadows and came to rest again, with the razor-sharp edge right across the man's throat.

"I'm going to come back tomorrow," said Benny in that same ugly voice. "And the day after that, and the day after that. If I find even a single bruise on my friend, if you or any of your friends hurt him in any way . . . then you're going to have a lot more to worry about than monsters in cages."

The soldier glared at Benny, his intent lethal.

"You're out of your mind, boy."

Benny could feel his mouth twist into a smile, but from the look in the soldier's eyes it could not have been a nice smile.

"Out of my mind? Yeah," said Benny. "I probably am."

Benny stepped back and lowered the sword. He turned his back on the soldier and went over to the cage. He stood well out of reach this time.

"I'm sorry, Chong," he said.

Tears ran down Benny's face. He looked into those dark eyes, searching for some trace of the person he'd known all his life. The quick wit, the deep intelligence, the gentle humor. If Chong was alive, then those things had to still be in there. Somewhere. Benny leaned closer still, needing to catch the slightest glimpse of his friend. He could bear this horror if there was the slightest chance that Chong was only detached from conscious control, if he was like a prisoner inside a boarded-up house. As horrible as that was, it suggested that a solution, some kind of rescue, was possible.

"C'mon, you monkey-banger," Benny whispered. "Give me something here. You're smarter than me . . . *you* find *me*. Say something. Anything . . ."

The thing's gray lips curled back from wet teeth.

". . . hungry . . ."

That was all the creature could say. Drool ran down its chin and dropped to the straw-covered floor of its cage.

"He's not dead, you know," Benny said to the soldier.

The soldier wiped at the trickle of blood on his throat. "He ain't alive."

"He's. Not. Dead." Benny spaced and emphasized each word.

"Yeah. Sure. Whatever you want, kid."

Benny resheathed his sword, turned, and walked past the guard, out through the iron door, up the stone stairs, and out into the brutal heat of the Nevada morning.

Three weeks ago we were in a war.

I guess it was a religious war. Sort of. A holy war, though it seems weird to even write those words.

A crazy woman named Mother Rose and an even crazier man named Saint John started a religion called the Night Church. They worshipped one of the old greek gods of death, Thanatos. Somehow they got it into their heads that the zombie plague was their god's deliberate attempt to wipe out all of humanity. They considered anyone who didn't die to be a blasphemer going against their god's will.

So, the people in the Night Church decided that they needed to complete Thanatos's plan by killing everyone who's left. They trained all the people in the church to be really good fighters. They call themselves the reapers.

When that's done, they plan to kill themselves.

Crazy, right?

According to our new friend, Riot, who is (no joke) Mother Rose's daughter, the reapers have killed about ten thousand people.

Ten thousand.

A lot of reapers were killed in a big battle. Joe killed them with rocket launchers and other weapons we found on a crashed plane. Joe's a good guy, but seeing him kill all those killers . . . that was nuts. It was wrong no matter what side I look at it from.

But then . . . what choice did he have?

I wish the world still made sense.

MILES AND MILES AWAY . . .

The man named Saint John walked along a road shaded by live oaks and pines. The trees were unusually dry for this time of year, victims of a drought that was leeching away the vital juices of the world. The saint did not mind, though. It was another way that his god was making it impossible for life to continue in a world that no longer belonged to mankind. Saint John appreciated the subtlety of that, and the attention to detail.

His army stretched behind him, men and women dressed in black with white angel wings sewn onto the fronts of their shirts and red tassels tied to every joint. Each head was neatly shaved and thoroughly tattooed with flowers and vines and stinging insects and predator birds. As they marched, these reapers of the Night Church sang songs of darkness and an end to suffering. Hymns to an eternal silence where pain and indignity no longer held sway.

Saint John did not sing. He walked with his hands behind his back, head bent in thought. He still grieved for the betrayal of Sister Rose. But his spirits were buoyed by the knowledge that Sister Sun and Brother Peter—two of his

Council of Sorrows who would never betray him—were working tirelessly to serve the will of their god. They would light the fire that would burn away the infection of humanity.

While they labored back in Nevada to start that blaze, Saint John led the bulk of the reaper army through deserts and forests, across badlands and into the mountains in search of nine towns—nine strongholds of blasphemy and evil. Until yesterday he did not know the way. But they had met a traveler who was willing to share all that he knew of those towns. He was reluctant at first to share, but with some encouragement he was willing to scream everything that he knew.

The first of the towns was named Haven. As unfortunate and naive a name as Sanctuary.

The second town was a place called Mountainside. . . .

He listened to the songs of the reapers, a dirge lifted by forty thousand voices, and Saint John walked on, content.

Out in the dark, beyond the ranks of the reapers, came a second and much larger army. One that did not need to be fed, one that never tired, one that required only the call of dog whistles to drive it, and the presence of the chemical-soaked red tassels to control their appetites.

Yet, in their own way, they too sang. Not hymns, not anything with words. Theirs, lifted by tens of thousands of dead voices, was the unrelenting moan of hunger as the army of the living dead went to war under the banner of the god of death.

THE SUN WAS A SPIKY CROWN OF LIGHT RESTING ON THE MOUNTAINTOPS to the east. Benny closed his eyes and turned his face to the light, soaking in the heat. The holding area had been too cold. Benny had never dealt with air-conditioning before, and he wasn't sure he liked it. The sunlight felt good on his face and chest and arms. By this afternoon he would be hunting for even a sliver of shade, but for now this was nice.

We're going to save Chong, said his inner voice.

"Yes we are," Benny growled aloud.

A shadow crossed over his face, and he looked up to see a vulture glide through the air from the top of the six-story hospital blockhouse. It flapped its big black wings as it came to rest atop a parked jet that stood still and silent two hundred yards away.

The jet.

It had drawn Benny, Nix, Chong, and Lilah away from Mountainside. It was supposed to answer all their questions, to make sense of the world.

It sat facing the distant mountains, windows dark, door closed. But around that door were blood smears, arterial splashes and one handprint, faded now from crimson to brown. The metal stairs sat a few yards away. There was blood on every step, and trails of it along the ground heading toward the row of massive gray hangars beyond the blockhouse.

The first time Benny had seen the blood, he'd asked his escort monk, Brother Albert, about it. "Did the zoms attack the crew?"

Brother Albert flinched at the use of the word "zom," and Benny regretted using it. The monks always called the dead the Children of Lazarus, and they believed that these "Children" were the meek whom God intended should inherit the earth. Benny was pretty sure he didn't agree with that view, though it was a lot more palatable than the more extreme apocalyptic thinking of the Night Church.

"No," said the monk, "the sirens called the Children away while the jet landed."

The military people used a row of sirens on tall towers to lure the zoms away to clear the airstrip or allow access to the hangars and blockhouse. Soldiers stationed in a small stone building at the far end of the field controlled the sirens. When those sirens fell silent, the dead wandered back again, drawn by the living people on the monks' side of the trench.

"Then what happened?"

Brother Albert shrugged. "Not really sure, brother. They were delivering supplies and equipment to a base in Fort Worth. Must have been an attack there." He paused. "Do you know about the American Nation?"

"Sure. Captain Ledger and Riot told us some stuff. It's in Asheville, North Carolina. Supposed to be, like, a hundred thousand people there. There's a new government, and they're trying to take back the country from the dead."

16

"That's what they say."

Benny glanced at the jet. During the big fight with the reapers, it had come swooping down out of the sky like a monster bird out of ancient legend. Impossibly huge, roaring with four massive engines, it had sailed above the battle and descended toward Sanctuary.

When they'd first seen it almost a year ago, soaring high above the mountains in California, they'd thought it was a passenger liner. They now knew that it was a C-5 Galaxy military transport jet. The largest military aircraft ever built.

"What about the crew?" asked Benny. "Are they okay?"

The monk shrugged. "Don't know. They don't tell us anything."

It was true. The military scientists ran a mostly underground base on one side of the trench, and the monks ran a hospital and hospice on the other. Except for interview sessions in the blockhouse, communication between the two was weirdly minimal.

Past the jet, at the far side of the airfield, was a huge crowd of zoms. They shuffled slowly toward Benny, though the closest of them was still a mile away. Every morning the sirens' wail cleared the way for him to cross the trench, and every evening it cleared the field for Nix to come over. Each of them spent an hour being interviewed by scientists. Never in person, though. The interview booth was a cubicle built onto the corner of the blockhouse; all contact was via microphone and speakers. The novelty of this pre–First Night tech wore off almost at once, though. The scientists asked a lot of questions, but they gave almost nothing in return. No information, no answers. Allowing Benny to see Chong was a surprising act of generosity, though Benny wondered if it was just part of a scientific experiment. Probably to see how human Chong still was.

Hungry.

God.

Every evening the monk took Nix over there. Would they let her see Chong too?

They reached the entrance to the cubicle. It opened as Benny approached. Inside was a metal folding chair.

Benny glanced over his shoulder at the zombies. The ranger, Captain Ledger, had told Nix that there were only a couple hundred thousand. The monks said that there were at least half a million of them over there. They worked with the sick and dying far more closely.

"They're waiting, brother," murmured his escort monk, and for a moment Benny didn't know whether Brother Albert meant the zoms or the scientists.

"Yeah," said Benny. "I know."

The monk pushed the door shut, and the hydraulic bolts slid back into place with a sound like steam escaping. There was only a tiny electric light that barely shoved back the shadows.

While he waited in the dark, he thought he could hear Chong's voice.

Hungry.

THE LOST GIRL WAS LOST INDEED.

Eight months ago she'd lived alone in a cave behind a waterfall high in the Sierra Nevadas. She spent her days hunting, foraging for books in deserted houses, evading zombies, and hunting the men who had murdered her family. From age twelve until just after her seventeenth birthday, Lilah spoke to no one.

The last words from her mouth before the long silence were spoken to her sister, Annie, as she knelt in the rain near the first Gameland.

Earlier that day Lilah had escaped from Gameland and then gone back for her sister. Annie was supposed to wait for her, but she didn't. She escaped from her cell only to be hunted through the storm by the Motor City Hammer. In the windy, rainy darkness Annie tripped and fell, hitting her head on a rock. A mortal injury. The Hammer left her there like a piece of trash that wasn't worth throwing away.

Lilah saw this from a place of concealment. She was twelve, emaciated, and weak. If she'd attacked the Hammer, he would have beaten her and dragged her back to the zombie pits. Knowing him as she did, he might have put

Annie in with her. That was a guaranteed moneymaking attraction.

When the Hammer was gone, she crept onto the road to where Annie lay. She tried to breathe life back into Annie's lungs, tried to push it into her chest the way George had taught her. She tried to will that fading spark to flare. She begged, she made promises to the heavens, offering her own life if Annie could be spared. But the slack form she held changed into something that did not want her breath or her prayers. All it wanted was her flesh.

Lilah held the struggling body tightly in her arms and buried her face in Annie's hair. For a long, terrible moment she wondered if she should stop fighting, if she should lie back and offer her throat to Annie. If she could not protect her in life, she could at least offer her sustenance in death.

That moment was the longest of her life. The most terrible.

"I'm sorry," she said, and reached for the rock onto which Annie had fallen. It was small, the size of an angry fist. Another half step to the right and Annie would have missed it and fallen into a puddle instead.

Lilah wanted to close her eyes so that she did not have to witness what she was about to do. But that was a coward's choice. George had taught the girls to be strong. Always strong. And this was Annie. *Her* Annie. Her sister, born on First Night to a dying mother. She was the last person on earth who Lilah knew. To turn away, to close her eyes, to flinch from the responsibility of being a witness for her sister's experience felt as cowardly and awful as what the Motor City Hammer had done.

So Lilah watched Annie's face. She watched her own hand lift the rock.

She watched everything.

She heard herself say, "I love you."

She heard the sound of what she was forced by fate and love to do. It was a dreadful sound. Lilah knew it would echo inside her head forever.

Lilah spent the next five years in silence.

There was conversation, but it was always in her head. With Annie, with George. Lilah rehearsed the words she wanted to say when she was strong enough to hunt down the Motor City Hammer. Now he was dead too. And George.

Annie.

Tom.

Lilah walked the trench, hour after hour, mile after mile. She was so much stronger now than she had been. She knew that if she could take this body and these skills and step back to that moment on the rainy road, it would have been the Hammer gasping out his last breaths in the darkness.

Lilah made sure that she was strong. Fast, and skillful and vicious.

Heartless.

That had been her goal. To become heartless. A machine fine-tuned for the purpose of slaughter. Not of zoms—they were incidental to her—but of the evil men in the world. Like the Hammer, like Charlie Pink-eye and Preacher Jack. Like Brother Peter and Saint John and the reapers. She willed herself to become merciless because if she accomplished that, then she would never know fear and she would never know love. Love was a pathway to cruel pain. It was the arrow that

Fate always kept aimed at your back. Love would interfere; love would create a chink in her armor.

No, she would never allow herself to love.

As she walked, she thought about that. That promise was as vain and as fragile as the promise she'd given Annie to return and free her.

When Lilah rescued Benny and Nix from bounty hunters in the mountains, she had stepped across a line. When she met Tom and saw that a man could be good and decent, compassionate and strong, Lilah had felt her resolve weaken. George had been the only good man she'd ever known. A total stranger who'd been the last of a group of refugees from the zombie outbreak. He'd raised Annie and Lilah. He'd loved them like a father, fed them, cared for them, taught them. And had been murdered by the men who took the girls to Gameland.

Lilah had believed that he was the only decent man left alive, that all the others were like the Hammer.

Then Tom.

Whom she fell in love with. Who refused her love in the gentlest, kindest way.

Tom . . . who died.

She stopped and let her gaze drift across the trench to the blockhouse. To where Chong crouched in the darkness.

Lilah had never wanted to feel anything for Chong. He was a town boy. Weak and unskilled in any of the ways of survival. She had not wanted to like him. Falling in love with him was so obviously wrong that sometimes she laughed at herself. And when the absurdity of it struck her, she lashed out at Chong.

Stupid town boy.

"Chong," she whispered.

What is the good of becoming strong if love bares your flesh to the teeth of misfortune? Why risk loving anyone or anything when life is so frail a thing that a strong wind can blow it out of your experience? She wanted to go back to her silence and her solitude. To find her cave and hide there among the stacks of dusty books. With the waterfall roaring, no one could hear her scream, she was sure of it.

How long would it take, how many weeks or months or years, before she could think of Chong's name and not feel a knife in her heart?

The reapers had taken Chong from her.

Forever? Or just for now?

She didn't know, and neither did the scientists in the blockhouse.

If it was forever, then a cold voice in Lilah's mind told her what the future would be—an endless, relentless hunt to find and kill every reaper. In books the heroines vow to hunt an enemy to the ends of the earth. But she was already there. This was the apocalypse, and the future was awash in blood and silence.

"Chong," she said to the desert sky, and tried to will her heart to turn to stone.

"GOOD MORNING, MR. IMURA," SAID A COLD, IMPERSONAL FEMALE VOICE through the wall-mounted speaker. "How do you feel today?"

"Angry," said Benny.

There was a pause. "No," said the voice, clearly thrown off track, "how do you *feel?*"

"I told you."

"You don't understand. Are you feeling unwell? Are—"

"I understood the question."

"Have you been experiencing any unusual symptoms?"

"Sure," said Benny. "My head hurts."

"When did these headaches begin?"

"'Bout a month ago," said Benny. "A freako mutant zombie hit me in the head with a stick."

"We know about that injury, Mr. Imura."

"Then why ask?"

"We asked if you had any unusual symptoms."

"Zombie-inflicted stick wounds to the head actually *aren't* all that usual, doc. Look it up."

The scientist sighed—the kind of short nostril sigh people do when they're losing their patience. Benny grinned in the shadows.

The next question wiped the smile off his face. "What happened in the holding cell today?"

"He . . . tried to grab me."

"Did he *touch* your skin with his *hands*?"

"No."

"Did he *bite* you?"

"No."

"Did he get any bodily fluids on you?"

"Eww. And, no."

"Are you running a fever?"

"I don't know, why don't you let me in there so you can take my temperature?"

A pause. "There is a safety protocol—"

"—in place," completed Benny. "Yeah, I know. I've heard that forty million times."

"Mr. Imura, we need you to tell us if the infected—"

"His name is Lou Chong," barked Benny. "And I wish you'd tell me what you've done to him."

A longer pause this time. "Mr. Chong has been treated."

"I know that, genius. I want to know *how*. I want to know what's going on with him. When's he going to get better?"

"We . . . don't have those answers."

Benny punched the small metal speaker mounted on the wall. "Why not?"

"Mr. Imura," said the woman, "please, you're being difficult."

"*I'm* being difficult? We gave you all that stuff we found in that wrecked transport plane, all those medical records. Why can't you do something for us?"

When there was no immediate answer, Benny tried to

shift topics, hoping that might nudge them into an actual exchange of information.

"What about that pack of wild boars that tried to chow down on my friend Lilah? Where'd they come from? I thought that only humans could turn into zoms."

"We are aware of a limited infection among a small percentage of the wild boar population."

"What does that mean? What's a 'small percentage'? How many is that?"

"We don't have an exact number. . . ."

Benny sighed. They were always evasive like this.

After a moment the woman asked, "Are you experiencing any excessive sweating, Mr. Imura? Double vision? Dry mouth?"

The questions ran on and on. Benny closed his eyes and leaned back in his chair. After a while the voice accepted that Benny wasn't going to cooperate.

"Mr. Imura—?"

"Yeah, yeah, I'm still here."

"Why are you making this so difficult?"

"I keep telling you—I'm not. I'm trying to communicate with you people, but you keep stonewalling me. What's that about? 'Cause the way I figure it, you guys owe me and my friends. If we hadn't told Captain Ledger about the weapons on the plane, that reaper army would have come in here and killed everyone—you, all the sick people, the monks, and everyone in this stupid blockhouse."

The plane in question was a C-130J Super Hercules, a muscular four-propeller cargo aircraft built before First Night. Benny and Nix had found it wrecked in the forest. It had been used to evacuate a scientist, Dr. Monica McReady, and her staff from Hope One, a remote research base near Tacoma, Washington. The team had been up there studying recent mutations in the zombie plague.

"Don't confuse heroism with mutual self-interest, Mr. Imura," said the woman scientist in an icy tone. "You told Captain Ledger about those weapons and materials because it was the only way you and your friends could survive. It was an act of desperation that, because of the nature of this current conflict, benefited parties that have a shared agenda. Anyone in your position would have done the same."

"Really? That plane was sitting out there for a couple of years—pretty much in your freaking backyard—and you had no clue that it was there. If you spent less time with your heads up your—"

"Mr. Imura . . ."

He sighed. "Okay, so maybe we had our own survival in mind when we told you about it—we're not actually stupid— but that doesn't change the fact that we saved your butts."

"That's hardly an accurate assessment, Mr. Imura. Saint John and the army of the Night Church are still out there. Do you know where they are?"

Benny's answer was grudging. "No."

In truth, no one knew where the reapers had gone. Guards patrolling the fence had seen a few, and Joe Ledger said that he'd found signs of small parties out in the desert, but the main part of the vast reaper army was gone. Saint John himself seemed to have gone with them, but nobody knew where. At first Benny and his friends were happy about that—let them bother someone else; but on reflection, that was a selfish and

27

mean-spirited reaction. An immature reaction. The reapers had only one mission, and that was to exterminate all life. No matter where they went, innocent people were going to die.

"So," said the scientist, "you can't really make the claim that you—and I quote—'saved our butts.' We might all be wasting our time."

"What's that supposed to mean?" There was no answer. He kicked the wall. "Yo! What's that supposed to mean?"

Nothing.

Then the lights came on and the door hissed open. Outside, the sirens were already blaring.

7

BROTHER ALBERT ESCORTED HIM ACROSS A BRIDGE TO THE MONKS' SIDE of Sanctuary. On the other side, Benny spotted Lilah walking along the edge of the trench. He fell into step beside her. They walked for a while in silence. Behind them the guards used a winch to raise the bridge.

Lilah was tall, beautiful, with a bronze tan and blond hair so sun-bleached that it was as white as snow. She had wide, penetrating eyes that were sometimes hazel and sometimes honey-colored, changing quickly with her fiery moods. She carried a spear made from black pipe and a military bayonet.

Every time he saw her, Benny felt an odd twinge in his chest. It wasn't love—he loved Nix with his whole heart, and besides, this girl was too strange, too different for him. No, it was a feeling he'd never quite been able to define, and it was as strong now as it had been the first time he'd seen her picture on a Zombie Card.

Lilah, the Lost Girl.

He finally worked up to the nerve to say, "They let me see him today."

Lilah abruptly stopped and grabbed a fistful of his shirt. *"Tell me."*

Benny gently pushed her hand away and told her everything that had happened. He left out the part about the soldier trying to hit Chong with his baton. There were already enough problems between Lilah and the soldiers. For the first few days after Chong had been admitted into the labs for treatment, Lilah stayed by his side. Twice soldiers had attempted to remove her, and twice soldiers were carried to the infirmary. Then on the eighth night, Chong appeared to succumb to the Reaper Plague. His vital signs bottomed out, and for a moment the doctors and scientists believed that he'd died. They wanted to have him quickly transported outside so he could be with the zoms when he reanimated. Lilah wouldn't accept that Chong was dead. Either her instincts told her something the machines did not, or she went a little crazy. Benny was inclined to believe that it was a bit of both. When the orderlies moved in to take Chong away, Lilah attacked them. Benny never got all the details, but from what he could gather, four orderlies, two doctors, and five soldiers were badly hurt, and a great deal of medical equipment was damaged in what was apparently a fight of epic proportions. The soldiers came close to shooting Lilah, and if she hadn't used one of the chief scientists as a shield—holding her knife to the fabric of his hazmat suit—they might have done it.

It was a stalemate.

And then the machines began beeping again, arguing with mechanical certainty that Chong was *not* dead. The scientist, fearing for his life and seeing a way out of the standoff, swore to Lilah that they would do everything they could to keep Chong alive, and to find some way of treating the disease that thrived within him. Lilah, never big on trust, was a

30

hard sell. But in the end, Chong's need for medical attention won out. She released the scientist. Chong was injected with something called a metabolic stabilizer—a concoction based on a formula found among Dr. McReady's notes on the transport plane. Once Chong was stabilized, Lilah was taken—at gunpoint—outside the blockhouse and turned over to Benny, Nix, and the monks. She was forbidden to cross the trench. Four guards were posted on the monks' side of the bridge to make sure of that.

As Benny described Chong's condition, Lilah staggered as if she'd been punched. She leaned on her spear for support.

"He spoke, though," said Benny hopefully. "That's something. It's an improvement, right? It's a good sign and—"

Lilah shook her head and gazed across the distance toward the white blockhouse. "My town boy is lost."

"Lilah, I—"

"Go away," she said in a voice that was almost inhuman.

Benny shoved his hands in his pockets and trudged off to find Nix.

BEYOND THE FENCE . . .

Through the long eye of the telescope, the boy with the sword slung over his back and the girl with the spear looked like they were standing only a few feet away. Close enough to touch.

Close enough to kill.

"I will open red mouths in your flesh," whispered the man with the telescope. "Praise be to the darkness."

Zoms rely on one or more senses in order to hunt. Smell is big, we know that. They can smell healthy flesh. That's why cadaverine works; it smells like rotting tissue.

Sight and hearing are just as important to them.

There has to be a strategic way to use these three senses against them. I'm going to talk to Captain Ledger about it. He seems to know more than anyone about fighting zoms.

SIX MONTHS AGO . . .

Saint John stood under the leaves of a green tree while the two most powerful women in the Night Church argued with each other.

"It's *old-world* heresy," insisted Mother Rose, who was the spiritual leader of the Night Church. She was tall and lovely, graceful as the morning, as beautiful as a knife blade. "That plane and its contents represent everything the church opposes."

"I don't dispute that," said the other woman, a frail Korean named Sister Sun. A year ago she had been athletic and strong, but over the last few months cancer had begun consuming her. By her own diagnosis she had less than a year to live, and she was determined to use that year helping the Night Church conquer the heretics. "My point is that we need to examine those materials to understand what's happening with the gray people."

"Nothing is happening with—"

"Mother, you *know* that's not true. Our people have seen case after case of gray people moving in flocks. That never happened before. There are rumors of gray people who move almost as fast as the living. Even some incidents of them picking up rocks and stones as weapons."

"So what?" countered Mother Rose in her haughty voice. "All life changes. Even un-life. It's part of nature, isn't it?"

"That's just it," insisted Sister Sun. "The Reaper Plague isn't part of nature, as I've said many times."

Saint John turned now and held up a hand. Both women fell immediately silent.

"The plague that raised the dead and destroyed the cities of sinful man was brought to earth by the divine hand of Lord Thanatos."

"All praise to his darkness," said the women in unison.

"Therefore it is part of the natural order of the universe."

"Honored One," said Sister Sun, "please listen to me. Both of you—listen. I know this plague. I studied it after the outbreak. My team was working with the Centers for Disease Control and the National Institutes of Health. No one alive knows this disease better than me except for Monica McReady."

"That heretic is dead," said Mother Rose.

"We don't know that for sure," said Sister Sun. "We sent five teams of reapers out to search for her, and two teams never returned."

Mother Rose dismissed the argument with a flick of her hand.

"If McReady was tampering with the disease—if she was trying to create a cure for it, then she might have caused it to mutate," said Sister Sun passionately. "Any possible change to the disease can have a significant impact on the predictable behavior of the gray people, and that is a danger to our church. You know it is. If you let me look at the research materials on the plane, I might be able to determine what she was doing. Maybe I can stop it, or perhaps learn enough to predict what changes are occurring so we can adapt behavioral modifications into our church doctrine. But we can't allow random changes to manifest without a response from the church. Think of how disruptive that would be, especially to reaper groups that have a high percentage of new recruits. Doubt is our enemy."

Mother Rose shook her head the whole time. "The plane is a shrine, and I have put my seal on it. It stays closed."

She turned her back and walked away.

Sister Sun gripped Saint John's sleeve. "Please, Honored One, surely *you* understand the danger."

"The shrine belongs to Mother Rose," he said.

"But—"

"It belongs to her."

The saint gently pulled his arm away and walked off under the shadows of the trees, aware that she stood and watched him the whole time. He did not let her see the smile that he wore.

THE MESS HALL WAS IN A QUONSET HUT SET BEHIND THE DORMITORY hangar. Rows of long trestle tables, folding chairs, a steam table were set up for self-service. Benny picked up a tray and a plate, slopped some runny eggs and links of what he hoped was pork sausage. It might as easily have been lizard or turtle, as Benny had already found out.

There was never a lot of food. Enough, but none to spare.

The first time Benny had come here, he'd piled his tray high. No one had said anything until he sat down across from Riot, who gave him a stern glare.

"Y'all got enough food there for a pregnant sow," she'd said to him, her voice heavy with an Appalachian accent.

"I know, right?" he said, and jammed a forkful of eggs into his mouth. "It's not even that bad."

Riot was thin and hard-muscled and very pretty, with a shaved head that was tattooed with roses and wild vines. She wore jeans and a leather vest buttoned up over nothing else that Benny could detect. "Maybe that zom knocked all good sense out your head, boy . . . but did it knock out all your manners, too? There's four people not going to eat today because y'all took enough food for five. Look around—you think there's anything close to *abundance* round these parts? Everyone here's a few short steps away from starving and here you are, stuffing your face like it's your birthday."

When Benny looked around, all he saw were the bland, accepting smiles of the monks. Then he looked down at the heap of eggs, the mounds of potatoes and vegetables, and the half loaf of bread. Without another word he got up and walked back to the steam table and placed his tray in front of the first person in line. Then he left and didn't eat anything else all day.

Now he had it down to a rhythm. A scoop of eggs, half a roast potato, a slice of bread thinly coated with butter, and a cup of well water. Always a little less than he wanted, always leaving a little extra for the next person. After the first couple of hungry days, Benny began to feel good about that. Now it was his ritual. He also spent time every day working in the bean fields and fruit groves, doing unskilled grunt labor to help. It was exhausting work, but it felt good. And there was the side benefit of approaching it as exercise to reclaim his strength and muscle tone.

He tried to get some of the monks working the fields to sing a few of the off-color work songs Morgie had learned from his dad, but that kite wouldn't fly.

Today Riot was on the other side of the mess hall, seated next to Eve, the tiny blond-haired girl Benny had rescued after they'd both fallen into a ravine filled with zoms. Eve was laughing at something Riot said, and even from that distance Benny could hear the strange, fractured quality of that laughter. The poor kid had been through too much. Reapers had raided and burned the settlement in which she'd lived and slaughtered nearly everyone. The refugees spent several mad days running through deserts and forests, only to be hunted down and sent "into the darkness." Eve had witnessed the terrible moment when reapers cut down her father and mother.

The monks worked with Eve every day, coaxing the little girl inch by inch out of the red shadows of her trauma, but even though there had been some progress, it was apparent that Eve might be permanently damaged. Benny was almost as worried about Riot as he was about Eve—the former reaper seemed to take it as her personal mission to "save" the girl. Benny dreaded what might happen to Riot if Eve's fragile sanity finally collapsed.

It made Benny both sad and furious, because the reapers were so much worse than the zoms. The dead were mindless, acting according to the impulses of whatever force reanimated their bodies; the reapers *knew* what they were doing.

In his calmer moments, Benny tried to explore the viewpoint that the reapers actually believed that what they were doing was right, that they believed they were serving the will of their god. But he could not climb into the mind-set of a religion based on extinction. Even if the reapers believed that their god wanted everyone dead, they had no right to force that belief on everyone else. They had no right to turn the life of a child like Eve into a living horror show.

No right at all.

"Hey," said a familiar voice behind him, and he turned, already smiling because a bad day had just gotten a whole lot better.

"Hey yourself," he said, and leaned across the table to give Nix Riley a quick, light kiss. She was a beautiful girl with wild

39

red hair, emerald green eyes that sparkled with intelligence, and more freckles than there were stars in the sky. A long pink scar ran from her hairline almost to her jaw, but even with that she looked young, and fresh and happy. It had been months since she looked this good. Like Eve, Nix had suffered through the absolute horror of seeing her mother murdered in front of her. Not by reapers—those killers were not yet a part of their lives—but by the brutal bounty hunters Charlie Pink-eye and the Motor City Hammer. Nix herself had been beaten and kidnapped by the pair. They were going to make her fight in the zombie pits of Gameland. Tom and Benny had rescued her, but from then on life for Nix had become a constant nightmare, running from one room in hell to another.

Nix sat down, but caught him staring at her. "What? Do I have something on my face?"

"Just this," he said, and blew her a handful of kisses.

"You are too corny for words," she said, but she was smiling. "You were in the blockhouse a long time today. What did they talk about?"

Nix's smile leaked away as he told her about Chong.

"I thought Lilah said that he was *alive!*"

"He *is* alive."

"But . . . he tried to bite you."

"Okay, so he's sick, he's messed up—but he's still Chong."

"How? How is he still Chong? He's totally infected, Benny. They're keeping him in a cage, for God's sake."

Benny's face grew instantly hot. "What are you saying? You think they should put him down like a dog?"

"Not like a dog, Benny. He's a zom and—"

"And *what*? They should quiet him?"

40

Nix sat back and folded her arms tightly across her chest. "What do you think is going to happen, Benny? Do you think that Chong is going to suddenly snap out of it?"

"Maybe he will!" Benny yelled.

"Maybe he can't."

"I can't believe you're giving up on him, Nix. This is Chong. *Chong!* He's our friend."

"Was that really Chong down in that cage? Would Chong try to take a bite out of you?"

Benny whammed the table with his fist. "He's not a zombie, Nix. He's *sick* and he needs our help."

"What help?" she demanded, her voice jumping a whole octave. "What can we possibly do for him?"

Benny had to fish for how to answer her. When he spoke, his voice was a hot whisper. "We need to give the scientists time to figure it out."

"Okay. Fine. What happens in the meantime? We go visit him like he's a zoo animal?"

"Why are you being such a bitch?"

Nix stood up so suddenly that her belt buckle caught the edge of her plate and flipped it over, flinging eggs everywhere. Surprise, embarrassment, and anger warred on her face.

"I—"

"Save it," snapped Benny as he got up and stalked away.

He made it almost all the way to the door before Nix caught up to him. He heard her coming and quickened his stride, but she ran the last few steps, caught his sleeve, and spun him around. Before he could say anything, she stuck a finger in his face.

"You listen to me, Benjamin Imura. I love Chong every bit

41

as much as you do. I loved Tom, too. And I loved my mother—but people die. In this world, people die. Everyone dies."

"Well, thank you, Lady Einstein. Here I was thinking that everyone lived forever and every day was apple pie and puppies." He glared at her. "I *know* people die. I'm not stupid, and I'm not kidding myself about how much trouble Chong's in. Maybe he can't come back, maybe he's already too sick . . . but I heard him speak today, and even though it was only one word, it proves that some part of him is still there. He's not gone yet, and I won't give up on him. Not until there's no hope and no chance at all."

"Benny, I—" she began, but he shook his head and turned away.

He pushed past some monks who were on their way into the mess hall. Behind him he heard Nix call his name, but she did not follow him outside.

11

MILES AND MILES AWAY . . .

His name was Morgan Mitchell, but everyone called him Morgie.

Morgie was big for his age, looking more like eighteen than fifteen. Beefy shoulders, arms heavy with muscle, and a dusting of beard smudging cheeks and chin.

His clothes were soaked with sweat, and his eyes were filled with shadows.

An old truck tire hung by a rope from a limb of the big oak tree. The weathered rubber was scarred by thousands of impacts from the bokken—the wooden sword Morgie held in his hands. Each blow made the tire dance and swing, and Morgie shifted this way and that to chase it, to continue hammering it, to smash at it over and over again. The force of each blow threw echoes against the rear of the house that stood vacant and silent at the other end of the yard. The bokken was hand-carved from a piece of hickory. It was his sixth sword. The first five had cracked and broken in this yard, defeated not by the tire but by the force of the hands that swung the wood, and by the muscle in arms and shoulders and back.

And by pain.

Each blow hurt. It wasn't the shock that vibrated back from the point of impact and shivered through Morgie's muscles and bones. It wasn't that at all. The pain was in his heart. And he hammered at it every day. Several times a day. The training leaned him, burning away childhood fat, revealing muscles forged in a furnace of grief and regret.

Morgie knew he was being watched, but he didn't care. It was like that all the time, almost every day. Randy Kirsch, mayor of Mountainside and former neighbor of the Imuras, sat on his porch. Two men sat with him, each of them drinking coffee from ceramic mugs.

"Two ration dollars says he breaks another sword today," said Keith Strunk, captain of the town watch.

"Sucker's bet," said Leroy Williams, a big black man sitting to his left. He was a corn farmer who'd lost his right arm in a car crash after bringing a group of people through a horde of zoms after First Night. "Kid's working on some real fury down there. He'll break that sword or knock the tire out of the damn tree."

The mayor glanced at his watch. "He's been at it for two hours now."

"Makes me sweat just watching him," said Strunk.

They all nodded and sipped their coffee.

The *thump, thump, thump* of the sword was constant.

"You ever find out what happened between him and Benny?" asked Strunk. "Heard they had some kind of fight right before Tom took those kids out of town."

The mayor shook his head.

"I heard it was over the girl," said Leroy. "Little Phoenix.

Remember, Morgie went courtin' at the Riley place that night Jessie was killed. Morgie got his head near stove in by Marion Hammer. And then seven months later Nix goes off with Benny."

"Ah," said Strunk. "A girl. That'll do it."

They all sighed and nodded.

"I don't think it's just the girl," said Mayor Kirsch. "I think it was that fight. I heard Morgie knocked Benny down."

"If they were fighting," said Leroy, "then they were fighting over the Riley girl."

They all nodded again.

Captain Strunk said, "Morgie asked me the other day if I'd let him join the town watch. When I told him he was too young, he got a job as an apprentice fence guard."

"Ugly work for a boy," said the mayor. "And he asked me for an application to the Freedom Riders. He wants to roll out with Solomon Jones and that crew."

"Thought you had to be eighteen for that," said Leroy.

"You do. But he's trying to get a special dispensation because he trained with Tom Imura."

"Ah," said Strunk.

Leroy grunted. "Maybe they should let him in. Tom trained those kids good . . . and besides, look at him. Kid's bigger and tougher than any eighteen-year-old I know."

"Tom did a good job," said Strunk as they watched Morgie hammer away at the tire. "Bet Tom would be proud of him."

The wooden sword whipped and flashed and pounded, again and again and again.

BENNY WALKED ALONG THE TRENCH—WELL AWAY FROM LILAH—UNTIL THE weight of the sun's heat slowed him to a less furious pace. Finally, drenched in sweat and feeling about as low as he could feel, he stopped, shoved his hands into his pockets, and stood there, staring across the trench at the dead. A few of them moved restlessly, but the rest stood as still as if they were the tombstones of their own graves.

Movement caught his eye, and Benny turned to see Riot as she walked Eve to the playground and handed her over to the head nun, Sister Hannahlily. Then Riot spotted him and came his way.

"Hey," she said quietly.

"Hey," said Benny.

"I saw that fuss in the dining room. You fighting with Red?"

Benny shrugged.

"This about Chong?"

"Yeah," said Benny. "I suppose."

"He's pretty messed up, huh?"

"He's sick . . . and if you want to lecture me, too, about—"

"Whoa—slow your roll, boy," she said. "Just asked a question."

"Yes," Benny said slowly. "He's in bad shape."

"Red wants to put him down, is that the size of it?"

"Yes."

"She know that Lilah'd skin her quick as look at her, right?"

"She knows."

"So, where's that leave everyone?"

Benny sighed. "In trouble."

"Life don't never get easy, does it? It just keeps getting harder in stranger ways."

They watched Lilah, who had stopped pacing and now stood as silent as the dead, staring across the trench toward the blockhouse.

"That Lilah's a puzzle," said Riot quietly. "I must'a tried fifty times to talk to her. Not deep conversation, just jawing about the time of day. All she did was tell me to go away. That's it, two words. Go away."

"Lilah's had a really hard life," said Benny.

Riot's face took on a mocking cast. "Did she now? Well, she sure don't hold the deed on grief and loss, son. We all been mussed and mauled by bad times. But that girl's done gone and shut down. I met gray people with more personality." She tapped her temple with a finger. "I'm beginning to suspect there ain't nobody home."

"She'll snap out of it once they do something for Chong."

Riot cocked her head to one side. "Y'all really think so?"

"Yes," said Benny with far more certainty than he felt. In truth he was frightened for Lilah. Any gains she had made since he and Nix had found her—wild and almost unable to communicate with people—seemed to have crumbled away. And secretly, he agreed with Riot's assessment that Lilah's personality seemed to be . . . well, *gone*. She would participate in combat training, but otherwise there was nothing.

His inner voice asked, *How deep inside your own heartbreak do you have to fall before there's no outward sign of life?*

It was a sad question, and that made him wonder what Nix would have been like if she'd dealt with her mother's murder without friendship and support.

Or what he would be like after Tom's death if it hadn't been for Nix, Lilah, and Chong.

He ached to do something. If this was an enemy he could fight, he'd have his sword in his hands, but the truth was that there were some enemies you could not defeat.

Benny nodded toward the blockhouse. "You were in there, right? A few years ago? In the lab area. What was it like?"

"Those boys didn't let me see much. They stuck me in a little room with a cot, a commode, and nothing else. Not even a good book to read. All I got to do was stare at the walls all day, every day, and that ain't even as entertaining as it sounds." She thought about it, then chuckled. "I was right happy when I heard that Lilah done busted up the place. They're good people over there, but they sure ain't nice."

Benny grunted and changed the subject. "Have you seen Joe today? I want to ask him about Chong."

She shook her head. "No. He was out at the wreck until late last night. Not sure when he got back. Saw that big ol' dog of his this morning—one of the monks was walking him."

Benny said, "What do you think of him?"

"Joe? You should ask Red," said Riot. "She thinks the sun rises and sets around that feller. Better watch out, boy—I think she's sweet on him."

"It's not like that. Nix has been pumping him for information."

"Information for what? For that silly diary of hers?"

"It's not silly and it's not exactly a diary," said Benny. "She's been collecting information on zoms."

"Like what?"

"All sorts of stuff—traps, barriers, and like that. How to fight them. She's been working out how we—people, I mean—can take back the world. It's smart, too. Joe gave her pages and pages of notes. She's been asking him how to fight the reapers, too. Like, if we settle in a town or maybe start a settlement somewhere, Nix wants to be ready to defend it against anyone, living or dead."

Riot nodded approval. "If that happens, let's put her in charge of the defenses."

He nodded.

Riot smiled. "Wow. And all this time I thought she was writing love poetry or stories about princesses and unicorns."

"You really don't know Nix, do you?"

"Apparently not. She's a . . ."

Riot's voice trailed off, and she stared openmouthed at something across the trench. When Benny followed the line of her gaze, he saw a figure that made him feel sick and sad.

It was a zombie. A woman. In life she had been beautiful, with masses of wavy black hair and a face as coldly regal as any of history's great queens. Now her flesh was gray and wrinkled, the moisture leeched away by the heat, and her hair hung in matted strings.

Mother Rose.

Once the spiritual leader of the Night Church. Once consort to Saint John.

Once Riot's mother.

Now . . . what was she?

Mother Rose stood at the edge of the trench, and in some weird and inexplicable way she must have recognized Riot. The two of them, mother and daughter, stared at each other. Benny tried to calculate all the things that separated them. Beliefs, remorse, life itself, so many things, all of them greater than actual measurable yards, feet, and inches.

Two small tears broke and fell down Riot's cheeks. "Oh God."

"Riot, don't look," sad Benny quickly. "Go back to the hangars, don't let—"

"Go away," said Riot.

"Hey, no, I just meant—"

"Just go."

Riot crossed her legs and lowered herself slowly to the ground. She sat there, staring across the trench at the thing that had been her mother.

Benny turned and slowly walked away.

13

BENNY WENT BACK TO THE MESS HALL TO FIND NIX. HE DIDN'T WANT TO be mad at her. Maybe if they talked it out she'd understand the thing with Chong.

But she wasn't there.

The breakfast crowd was mostly gone, but Benny saw the ranger, Joe, come in. The big man wore camouflaged pants, a sweat-stained gray T-shirt, and handmade sandals. His blue eyes were hidden behind dark glasses. His skin was burned to a red-gold except for white lines from scars old and new. There were a lot of scars. Although he had to be in his late fifties or even early sixties, Joe was very fit, with ropy muscles that flexed under his tough hide as he walked. Ordinarily Joe was vibrant with good humor and rapid-fire snarky comments, but today he shambled to the steam table, and it looked like he needed to use serious concentration to spoon eggs onto his plate. Joe's dog, a monster of a mastiff named Grimm, trailed along behind him. Joe thumped down into a chair at a table by the far wall; Grimm collapsed on the floor next to him. Everyone at the adjoining table got up and moved.

Benny drifted over.

Grimm lifted his head and studied Benny the way Morgie

Mitchell used to study a grilled flank steak. Joe was hunched over his food, shoveling eggs into his mouth. He didn't look up to see who was approaching.

"Buzz off."

Benny stopped. "What?"

Joe raised his head only enough to glare at Benny over the top of the sunglasses, which had slid halfway down his nose. His eyes were bloodshot and bleary. "Oh, it's you."

"Mind if I sit down?"

"Yes."

"What is it about today? Is it Tell Benny Imura to Go Away Day?"

"Sounds good to me. And in the spirit of that . . . go away."

"No, I don't think I will." He took another step closer. Grimm gave a warning growl so deep and low that it seemed to vibrate up through the floor. "Is he going to bite me?"

"Pretty good chance of it," admitted Joe.

"I'll risk it."

Joe leaned his forearms wearily on the table. "What's your deal, kid? Does 'buzz off' have a different meaning with your generation?"

"No. I get it. You want me to leave. It's just that I'm not going to."

Benny lowered himself onto a chair. The ranger watched him with a kind of bleak fascination.

"You're a weird kid," said Joe. "Most people go on the assumption that Grimm would gladly have them for lunch. You don't seem to think so. I'm not sure if you're a good judge of character or a total moron."

"Jury's out on that at the moment," said Benny.

"Okay . . . what's on your mind?" Joe sighed. "And keep your voice down. My head hurts."

Benny peered at him. "Are you drunk?"

"No, I'm hungover. There's a distinct difference. One is fun; the other is a whole lot less fun. Right now I am not having any fun, and you're not helping."

"Here's a thought—why not *not* get drunk?"

Benny was not a fan of drunks. Alcoholism and heavy drinking had been serious problems in all the Nine Towns ever since First Night. There were a lot of excuses, of course. Every adult had lost someone during those dreadful days. The apparent apocalypse had burned the faith out of a lot of people—faith in their religions, their ideologies, their expectations, their government, and their own dreams. The persistence of the zombie plague created tremendous paranoia. The world seemed to be ending, so why bother? Why not get drunk? Why not blur all the sharp edges? It saddened Benny as much as it disgusted him, because it was an acceptance of defeat. There was no fight left in it. There was no attempt to get back up and shake a fist at the universe and try again. One of Tom's favorite martial arts sayings was: "Fall down seven times, get up eight." Yet it seemed that some people just kept wanting to fall back down.

Joe sipped his coffee. "Exactly when did it become your business what I do?"

"You're a soldier, right? A ranger? Aren't you supposed to be a role model?"

"Wow, you're an obnoxious SOB today. You have a double helping of cranky flakes for breakfast?"

"No. I spent the morning down in the dungeon under the

blockhouse looking at my best friend, who seems to be turn-ing into a zombie."

"Ah," said Joe. "Yeah, that'll do it. I saw him yesterday. Shame."

"It's a 'shame'? That's the best you got? A shame? I thought those scientists were supposed to *cure* him."

"First," said Joe, pointing at Benny with his coffee cup, "stop shouting. You're hurting my head. Second, what do you think they are over there? Wizards? You think they can wave a magic wand and make everything all better?"

"Yes. After we found those records on the wrecked plane, you were all excited. You said that we saved the world."

Joe rubbed his eyes. "Yeah, well . . ."

"Well . . . what? We gave them Dr. McReady's research notes, so why can't they help Chong?"

"It's complicated. They're running into some speed bumps with those notes."

"Like what?"

"Look, kid . . . you know that Doc McReady was ready to crack this thing, right? Her lab up at Hope One was where the real cutting-edge research was being done. Out there in the field. Out where the Reaper Plague was mutating. She was sending reports back here to Sanctuary, so they were fol-lowing her lead, but they were a couple of steps back. It's not like the old days when data could be shared via the Internet. When Hope One was evacuated, the transport plane was sup-posed to bring back everything McReady had. All of it, right up to the minute so the bigger lab at Sanctuary could fin-ish her research and actually beat this thing." He paused and shook his head. "Think about that, Ben. We were that close.

We were ready to beat the plague that destroyed the whole world."

"So . . . okay, it's a shame that Dr. McReady died when the plane crashed—or maybe the reapers got her, whatever—my point is that if her research was on the plane, then how come the scientists in the blockhouse can't just, I don't know, *finish* it?"

"Because," Joe said quietly, "not *all* the research was on the plane."

If Joe had reached across the table and punched him in the face, Benny could not have been more stunned.

"I went over the cargo manifests," continued the ranger, "and there's a reference to the D series of boxes. We found series A through C. Nothing marked with a D. And based on the time Hope One was evacuated, there was nothing dated later than a month before she left."

"Did they somehow leave the stuff up at Hope One?"

"No way. The manifest says that it was packed. It *should* have been on that plane."

"Then where is it?"

"Well, gee, kid, if I knew that, I wouldn't have gotten paralytic drunk last night, now would I?"

Benny felt his face grow hot. "You're telling me there's *no* clue at all?"

Joe sighed. "I don't know. There was a single reference to Umatilla, but no notations. Nothing to say that they stopped there."

"What's Umatilla?"

"The Umatilla Chemical Depot is an army base in Oregon. They stored chemical weapons there. Stuff like GB and VX nerve agents. Bad stuff that was scheduled for destruction. The base was closed in 2015. Not sure what happened to it after that, but there'd be no reason for the transport plane to stop there, and certainly no reason to offload the D-series notes there. Whole area was overrun during First Night. I only mention it because it's the one thing in the records we can't account for."

"Are you going there?"

"Me? No. I sent word to a couple of my rangers to head up that way. It's a long shot and probably not worth the effort."

"Look," Benny said angrily, "even if you don't have that last month's worth of stuff, what we found had to put you pretty far ahead. That should be worth something."

"It is," Joe conceded tiredly. "Some of the clinical data in those boxes is responsible for your friend Chong still sucking air. The metabolic stabilizer and a few other treatments. That's what's keeping him on the happy side of being dead."

"Chong spoke to me today."

Joe cocked an eyebrow. "What did he say?"

Benny told him.

"Ouch," said Joe. "Look, this thing's gone off the rails. I was out there all day yesterday, but I couldn't find the missing notes. I got to tell you, Benny, this isn't the ending for all this I'd been writing in my head. For the last couple of years that plane's been the Holy Grail for us. It was our silver bullet. We find it and find Doc McReady's notes and *bam*, the mad scientists in the blockhouse cook up a cure and we all tell our grandkids how we saved the world. But . . . the doctors over there can't seem to figure out where Doc McReady was going with her research during those last weeks before

Hope One was shut down. There were samples of a mutagen, but there was also a reference to a workable treatment code-named Archangel. But the name's all we have. There's not one scrap of data on what Archangel is or does. Those boxes are the key, and they're missing. We lost our last chance to beat this thing."

"Don't *say* that! There has to be something else we can do. There has to be a way to find that stuff."

Joe simply sipped his coffee.

"Joe, are you going to sit there and tell me that you just give up? You? You're Captain Ledger, for God's sake. You're a hero of First Night."

"Sure, kid, it says so on a Zombie Card. It must be true."

"My friend is *dying*," growled Benny. "We can't give up."

"You think you're the only person who can feel pain?" asked Joe, his eyes old and bleak. "Before this thing started, I had a wife and a six-month-old kid. I was overseas on a mission when the Reaper Plague got loose. I called my wife, told her to get the hell out, to go to my uncle's farm near Robinwood, Maryland. It took me a week to get a flight back to the States. By the time I got to San Diego, the whole country was going nuts. No more commercial flights. The military bases were trashed too. When the people started panicking, everybody flocked to the closest base, but because so many of the refugees were already bitten and infected, those bases turned into killing fields. I stole a helicopter from a National Guard base that had become an all-you-can-eat buffet and made it halfway across the country before the army started dropping nukes on the zoms. The EMPs killed the engine, killed my cell phone and our satellite phone. Helicopter died, and we went down hard. There were ten of us on the bird. Four of us survived the landing. We split up and each tried to find our way home. It took me three weeks to make it all the way to my uncle Jack's place. But . . . there was no one there. The place had burned to the ground, so there was no way for me to tell if my wife and kid ever made it there."

Benny stared at him.

"So why am I telling you all this?" asked Joe. "I'm telling you this because everything in our world points to my family being dead. My wife, my son, my uncle. My brother, Sean, and his family in Baltimore. I never found any of them. Not a hint, not a sign in all these years. They probably *are* dead. They're probably walking around as the living dead, just like everyone else. But you know what?"

Benny said nothing. He doubted he could even speak.

Joe laid his hand on the butt of his holstered pistol. "If I *believed* that, if I actually got to the point where I believed that everyone I ever loved was dead, then I'd blow out all my own lights. But I don't know that, kid. I don't. I can't. Not even now, not even after the setback with Doc McReady's notes." He sighed. "All I got left is one slim chance that the world isn't totally broken. That's what keeps me going, and that's why I won't lay down my arms."

Finally Benny said, "Then why get drunk?"

The ranger shook his head. "Sometimes despair gets in a few good punches. Last night was a bad night. This morning sucks too. This afternoon I'll map out a search grid, and first thing in the morning I'm going to start looking under every stone, inside every cave, and up the butt-hole of every lizard in the desert. If those records are there, I will find them."

"What if they're not there?" asked Benny. "What if they're somewhere else? What if the reapers took them?"

"You ask very bad questions." Joe sighed. "Go away."

"I can help."

"In ten seconds I'm going to tell Grimm to bite something valuable off of you. Ten, nine, two . . ."

Benny left, but he wasn't going to waste the rest of the day. Tomorrow was too late to start looking for something that Chong needed right now.

He stole a quad, fired up the engine, and went rocketing toward the desert.

Yesterday Benny and I drove our quads along the inside of the perimeter fence here in Sanctuary. Only on this side of the trench, of course. Even so, it's a total of fourteen miles of fence. There are two solders at the main gate and three two-man patrols on quads. Eight soldiers to guard all those miles of fence. We had more than that back in Mountainside.

It makes me wonder if there's a problem with the security.

Dr. McReady's transport plane had crashed more than ten miles from Sanctuary. The ride to the crash site was tricky, because the soldiers once stationed at the base had used dynamite to block most of the roads, leaving only a single twisted and obscure path through the red-rock mountains. A quad could just about ease through.

Benny's quad was an ugly little machine with four fat rubber tires and a kind of saddle for the driver. Despite the horrible sound it made, Benny found he rather liked the machine. Over rough terrain it could travel an astounding twenty-five miles per hour. On a flat road, Benny had gotten his quad to go over forty miles per hour. On foot, he could manage as much as five miles an hour if he pushed it, and more often two to three because of terrain and weather conditions.

It amazed him that he could drive all the way back to Mountainside, a trip of over 470 miles, in two days. One if he didn't stop to eat or pee. That kind of speed seemed unreal. It had taken more than a month to walk that distance. Granted, a lot of the travel time had been spent evading zoms, hunting for food, searching out paths, and training with their swords.

As Benny left Sanctuary, he paused for a moment to look at the hand-lettered sign that was hung on the big chain-link fence.

SANCTUARY

GIVE ME YOUR TIRED, YOUR POOR

YOUR HUDDLED MASSES YEARNING TO BREATHE FREE

Below that the original words, sand-blasted and pale, were still visible:

AREA 51

UNITED STATES AIR FORCE

THIS IS A RESTRICTED AREA

TRESPASSERS WILL BE PROSECUTED

Benny took a long breath and exhaled through his nose, revved the engine of his quad, and headed out into the desert.

Those records were out there. Six boxes marked with a big letter *D*.

He was going to find them.

NIX RILEY COULD BARELY SEE THE BLADE.

She parried more by reflex than anything, and the spear caromed off her sword with such force that shock waves rippled up her arms. The next blow was even harder, and the next. Nix stumbled back, swinging and swinging, breath coming in painful gasps. Finally one blow caught her sword just above the guard and knocked it out of her hands. It thudded to the ground. Her attacker kicked Nix's feet out from under her, and Nix thumped down, hitting her elbows, her shoulders, and the back of her head on the hard sand. She suddenly felt the sharp tip of the spear press down between her breasts—right over her heart.

"You're dead," growled Lilah. They were on a rocky shelf a quarter mile behind the dormitory hangar. Sheer cliffs rose behind them, and all around were the shadowy clefts of deep arroyos. A few sparse cacti and Joshua trees littered the land-scape, offering no useful shade at all.

Nix couldn't really see the Lost Girl. The tears in her eyes smeared everything, removing all precision and meaning.

"Concentrate," barked Lilah as they set themselves to begin another drill.

But too many things were clattering around in Nix's mind.

She needed to apologize to Benny, but he was gone. She'd seen him drive away on a quad. She'd almost gone after him, but hadn't. This needed fixing, but Nix didn't know which words would form the glue of that repair.

So she'd gone looking for Captain Ledger, to see if he'd give her another combat lesson. He nearly sicced his dog on her.

The ranger was an enigma, one of the many things about this phase of her life that Nix didn't understand. Sometimes he was so gruff and rude that she wanted to feed him to the zoms. Yet sometimes he could be extraordinarily kind and wise. Almost like Tom.

Shortly after arriving at Sanctuary, Joe gave Nix a real sword to replace the wooden sword she'd carried from Mountainside. He'd offered one to Lilah as well, but the Lost Girl preferred her spear.

The sword Joe gave Nix was one of several top-quality *katanas* the ranger possessed. The handle and fittings were new, but Joe said the blade was ancient. Hundreds of years old.

"Isn't it fragile?" Nix asked, terrified that she might destroy so beautiful a relic.

But Joe laughed. "This sword was made by Hoki Yasutsuna, one of the greatest Japanese sword makers of all time. It's a superb blade. I'd take it into any battle without hesitation. And it has a name, *Dojigiri*."

"What's it mean?"

Joe grinned. "*Dojigiri* means 'Monster cutter.' Rather appropriate, don't you think?"

The sword did not look particularly impressive, with

plain black silk bindings on the handle and a speckled cord. However, Nix accepted the sword with wide-eyed reverence.

"*Dojigiri*," she repeated, holding it as if it would shatter in her hands. "Monster cutter. This is crazy. This must be worth a fortune."

"It's worth whatever value you place on it, Nix. No one else is looking. The whole value system is a historical footnote."

"But . . . this should be in a museum."

"Used to be," said Joe with a smile. "It was a national treasure of Japan and happened to be part of a collection of priceless artifacts on loan to an American museum. Lately, though, the only people visiting museums are zombies and scavengers, so I liberated it along with some other goodies. Not really theft, is it? Besides . . . the sword was made to be used, not to gather dust. I believe Tom was training you kids to be samurai, right? So . . . *be* samurai."

Benny drew his *kami katana* and showed it to Joe. "I have a good sword too."

The ranger gave him a tolerant smile. "Not sure how to break this to you, kid, but your sword is a good-quality modern blade, and definitely reliable in a fight, but it's not what you'd call a 'legendary' sword."

Benny was affronted. "This was *Tom's* sword."

"Sure," agreed Joe, "and he put it to good use, but the fact remains that they made about ten thousand swords just like that one. Hell, that one isn't even Tom's original."

"Yes it is!" Benny insisted.

"No, it's not. He broke his first sword a few days after First Night. He told me about it. Quite a story, too. And . . . I think he might have had another one after that. I was with him when he took this baby off one of the skull-riders who—"

"The *who*?" asked Benny and Nix together.

Joe blinked at them. "The skull-riders? The kill squad out of Reno?" He paused. "Tom never told you about that?"

"No," said Benny and Nix at the same time.

"Didn't he tell you about the time he and I and a guy named Solomon Jones took down a group of slavers up around Lake Tahoe? Or the time we teamed up with Hector Mexico, Johnny Apache, and the Beatbox Boys and cleared out the reavers who were raiding the trade route between the Nine Towns?"

"No," Benny said heavily. "Are you making this stuff up? Tom never said anything about this. He was a bounty hunter, that's all."

"That's all? Really?" Captain Ledger laughed. "How do you think Tom learned all his tricks? You think he got that good quieting zoms? Get your head out of your butt, kid. While everyone was building the towns and putting up that fence, your brother was riding with some hard-asses out in the Ruin." He paused, considered, sighed. "But . . . I guess that's Tom for you. He never was one to brag. Surprised you never asked the other bounty hunters about him."

"The only bounty hunters Benny ever listened to were Charlie Pink-eye and the Motor City Hammer," said Nix.

"Ah," said Joe. "Those two. Tom would have done the whole world a favor by putting bullets in their brainpans back when he had the chance. Would have saved the world a lot of grief." Joe suddenly stiffened and cut a sharp look at Nix, then winced. "Ahhh, jeez, I'm sorry. I forgot about your mom. I'm an idiot."

Nix wanted to cry, but she kept her eyes dry. "Benny killed Charlie. I killed Marion Hammer."

A slow smile formed on Joe's face. "Seriously?"

"Yeah," said Benny.

"Holy frog snot. You have *got* to tell me everything."

So they told him about the murder of Nix's mother and the horrors of that incident.

"I knew her, you know," said Joe sadly. "Jessie was one classy lady. Gorgeous, too. You have her eyes, Nix. And her toughness. I know she'd be proud."

Now tears rolled down Nix's cheeks, but her voice didn't break as they continued the story. When they got to the end, Joe clapped Benny resoundingly on the shoulder and kissed Nix on the forehead. "That's sweet! That's the cat's ass. You killed Charlie with the Hammer's own pipe, and then you killed him *again* in the zombie pits. Oh man, now *that's* legendary."

Nix wiped away her tears. "It didn't feel legendary at the time. It was scary and weird."

"Sure, but then all real adventures are scary and weird," said Joe. "Believe me . . . I know."

They returned to training, but Benny was clearly angry. Nix could understand why. Joe made a point of evaluating everything they'd learned from Tom, and frequently suggested some modifications. A couple of times that day Benny balked at changes in technique suggested by the ranger.

"That's not how Tom did it."

Joe's reply to each comment was a shrug. "Do it whatever way will keep you alive."

But Joe's advice had pushed too many of Benny's buttons.

"Hey, man, stop acting like you know more than Tom."

Joe smiled. It was a tolerant smile, but his patience clearly didn't go too many layers deep. "Listen to me, kid. I'm offering you the chance to learn some extra skills and about the nature of warfare. You want to learn this stuff, fine. You don't want to learn it, also fine. But understand two things about Tom. First, he was a very, very talented amateur, but he was an amateur. He was one day out of the police academy when First Night happened. He'd never served in the military. Most of what he learned about combat he picked up during the fourteen years he worked as a bounty hunter and closure specialist. And he learned a lot from me. Now . . . from what I saw when he ran with my pack, and from what I've heard since, Tom became seriously good. Good enough to spank Charlie Pink-eye and his crew, and tough enough so that Preacher Jack had to shoot him in the back rather than risk fighting him one-on-one. That says a lot. Tom was the kind of guy I'd want at my back in any situation. But here's the flip side of that. Before First Night—for a lot of years before First Night—I was the top shooter in a group that hired only top shooters. I was fighting monsters, bad guys, and terrorists before Tom was even born. Grasp that for a minute, kid. I'm not saying this to brag. This is a perspective check. I've been fighting this war in one way or another for more than forty years. Even before First Night I've seen things you wouldn't believe. Stuff that would have you screaming into your pillow every night. I led combat teams into firefights on every continent, and I've killed more people than you ever met. With hands, guns, knives, and once with a paperback book. You think I'm trying to bust on your brother by correcting the way you swing a sword? Kid, if I wanted to humiliate him or you, I'd take that sword away from you and break it over my knee. But as it turns out, I happen to respect what you and Nix can do, and I respect what Tom taught you, and I respect Tom as a fallen brother-in-arms. I respect all of that so much that I want to make sure it doesn't go to waste just because you have too much pride and ego to take some constructive criticism. So if you want to stop arguing with everything I say, then I'll teach you every dirty trick I can so you stay alive."

Benny glared up at him for a very long time. Finally, when his voice was under control, he said, "That's one thing. You said there were two. What's the other? Was there something else you wanted to say about my brother?"

Joe gave Benny the coldest smile Nix had ever seen on a human face.

"Yes," said Joe. "Tom's dead. I'm alive. After all these years, I'm still alive. That makes a statement. Learn from the survivors or go the hell home."

That had been the end of the discussion. Benny had stormed off and spent the rest of the afternoon stewing about it.

The next day he was back, with his sword, his gear bag, and his apologetic pride.

Joe never said a word about the argument, never acknowledged it. They picked up where they'd left off, and Joe drilled them mercilessly. And well.

Both of them had improved quite a lot. They were faster, trickier, stronger, and far more devious.

Now, though . . .

Nix felt clumsy and stupid. Lilah got through her guard again and again and again.

"I—I'm sorry . . . ," said Nix in a tiny voice.

"Sorry?" Lilah withdrew her spear, raised it over her head, and with a savage grunt drove it down. The blade bit inches deep into the sand right beside Nix's face, chopping off several strands of curly red hair. "*Sorry?* Are you training for combat or practicing for your own death, you silly town girl?"

Nix covered her face with her hands and shook her head.

"I'm sorry," was all she could say.

Lilah straightened and stood over Nix for a while. Then she threw her spear down in disgust and sank onto the ground beside the weeping girl.

"What is it?" Her voice was always a ghostly whisper.

Nix rolled toward her and wrapped her arms around Lilah, clinging to her as a child might. Clinging to her as a drowning person might.

They never heard the zoms coming until white fingers clamped like iron around their flesh.

16

WHEN RIOT COULDN'T BEAR TO STARE AT HER MOTHER ANY LONGER, SHE went to the playground to find Eve. They sat together on a blanket, with sewing gear scattered all around them: needles, spools of thread, balls of colored yarn, thimbles, and all sorts of fabric scraps.

As Riot watched, Eve used a pair of scissors to cut a piece of pink felt into the shape of a blouse. Almost the shape of a blouse. Currently it looked more like a blob or a three-legged pink turtle. Eve's little pink tongue tip stuck out from the corner of her mouth as she worked.

Overhead, a pair of capuchin monkeys that had long ago escaped from a private zoo in Las Vegas capered among the leaves. The nuns had named them Charity and Forbearance. The children called the monkeys Chatty and Foobear.

"There!" said Eve proudly as she held out the finished piece.

"That looks pretty," said Riot. The blouse still had three arms. "Is . . . one of those the neck hole?"

Eve considered the shirt, frowning slightly. "Oops," she said, and trimmed one of the sleeves. "Better?"

"Way better," agreed Riot. "That's as pretty as a rainbow after a spring rain."

Eve giggled.

They found some blue fabric for a skirt and little bits of brown for shoes, and Riot helped Eve glue and sew the pieces onto a burlap rag doll one of the nuns had made. As they worked, Chatty and Foobear crept down the tree and sat the edge of their blanket, watching with luminous dark eyes.

When the doll was nearly finished, Eve leaned over and began sorting through the supplies until she found a nearly empty ball of bright red yarn. She held it against the doll to examine the color, and then nodded to herself. Riot watched as Eve cut off a few small pieces and began tying them around the doll's neck. For one horrible moment Riot was afraid that Eve was making something like the red streamers that all the reapers wore tied to various places around their bodies. The streamers were symbolic of the red mouths opened in the flesh of the "heretics" that the reapers sent on into the eternal darkness. They were also dipped in a chemical mixture concocted by Sister Sun, which emitted a strong scent that discouraged the dead from attacking.

But that was not what Eve was doing.

She strung the red yarn around the doll's throat.

"What's that?" Riot asked, her smile broad and forced.

"A necklace."

"Oh . . . nice. What kind of necklace? Is it a ruby necklace like a princess would wear?"

Eve looked at the red loop of yarn around the burlap throat of the doll. Then she slowly turned her face to Riot. The smile was so bright and happy.

"No, silly," she said, "it's like the one mommy wore. Remember? Her necklace was all bright and shiny."

"Necklace . . . ?" Riot murmured. The heart in her chest turned instantly to ice.

Eve's mother had indeed worn a necklace of shining red. She'd worn it the very last time Riot and Eve had seen her. It was not a necklace of rubies, of course, or even of garnets. The reaper Andrew had cut Eve's mother down with a scythe. The blow had taken the woman across the throat, and the red that had glistened there had been her own bright blood.

Riot looked at the doll and then at Eve. The little girl smiled and smiled, bright as the summer sun, and behind those innocent blue eyes something shifted and moved.

Something very dark and very wrong.

17

THERE WAS NO TIME TO SCREAM.

Four cold hands grabbed Nix from behind and tore her away from Lilah.

The Lost Girl started to yell, but then a red-mouthed thing ran at her.

Ran.

It came so fast, hands reaching, lips peeling back from cracked and jagged teeth. The zom slammed into Lilah, caught her off guard, knocked her backward. They fell over and over down the slope, hung for a moment at the edge of a sheer six-foot drop into an arroyo, and then toppled out of sight.

There was no way for Nix to tear free of the hands that grabbed her from behind. Teeth snapped inches from her neck and shoulders and ears. The angle was impossible for sword-play, so she did the only practical thing she could: She opened her hand and let Monster Cutter clatter to the ground. Then Nix threw herself backward as hard as she could, using all the power of the zombies' pull along with the strength of her own legs. The extra momentum spoiled what little balance the awkward creatures had, and the two zombies fell hard onto the ground, with Nix's body landing slantwise across them. With humans, a fall like that would have jolted the air from their lungs, but these were dead things. Luckily, Nix made herself exhale on impact—as both Tom and Joe had taught her. The exhale relaxed her body for the impact, but the jolt was still heavy enough to explode fireworks in her head.

There was a strange, wet quality to the bodies she landed on. Were they recently dead? Were they still filled with blood and other bodily fluids? Her pants and the back of her shirt felt warm and damp.

The gripping hands were still there, so Nix raised her arms straight up, hands almost touching above her, then slammed her elbows down as hard as she could. Her left elbow hit a zom in the nose and knocked its head back against the rocky ground; her right elbow struck the second zom in the ribs. In both cases, the blows jolted their bodies and gave her a split second to pull free and roll away. She scrambled to her feet and faced the dead. One of the two zoms lay still, the back of its head smashed to a pulp. The other struggled to right itself.

"Lilah!" Nix yelled, but there was no answer. She heard scrabbling sounds from the arroyo, but it was impossible to tell if that was Lilah fighting for her life or another zom coming up the slope to join the attack.

Nix had no weapons. She'd dropped her sword, and her gun belt was hung on a tree limb up the slope. The second zom was on its feet now, and Nix saw that it was one of the recent dead, probably another of the party of refugees Riot had been leading from the destroyed town of Treetops to Sanctuary. The zom was a Latino man, not tall, but broad-shouldered and powerful-looking. There was a faint red smudge around its mouth that wasn't blood. It looked like powder of some kind. There was more of it sprinkled on its clothes. She wondered if it was some kind of pollen.

The zom moved toward her, staggering on bowed legs, his gait made awkward by the absence of one shoe. As he reached out toward Nix, she saw that his palms and forearms were crisscrossed with wounds. When she realized what they were, it sickened her. Defense cuts. The kind a person gets when they're backing helplessly away from someone trying to cut them. Had this man been unarmed against a reaper? There were similar cuts all along the insides of his arms and outer chest. Nix could imagine him backing away from a killer, arms spread in a hopeless attempt to shelter someone else. A wife, perhaps, or children. Using his own flesh as a shield, and knowing with each cut that nothing he could do, not even the sacrifice of his flesh and blood, would be enough to keep the knives of those fanatical killers from doing their horrible work.

It made Nix want to gag. This man had suffered so much. There was a final deep gash across his throat from where the death blow had been dealt, and his clothes were stained with blood that had pumped out of him with his failing heart. That heart hung still and silent within the walls of his chest, a thing that had been both defeated and broken by evil.

If Nix could have turned and run away, she would have. But there was only sheer rock behind her. The path to escape was behind the zom. There was no option left except to fight. To do more harm to this man.

A black goo dribbled from the creature's mouth, viscous

and heavy, and Nix thought she could see tiny white thread-worms wriggling in the mess.

She swiftly knelt to snatch up a fist-sized rock, and as she did so Nix saw one more thing that made no sense. The one shoeless foot was swollen and discolored, a sign of advanced decomposition. There was similar discoloration on the man's arms and chest, and some on his face. Discolored veins were visible through his skin, and some of his fingernails had even fallen off. The tissues were becoming swollen as the process of decay released gasses from the disintegrating tissues.

But . . . that was impossible.

One of the enduring mysteries of the post–First Night world was that zoms decayed to a certain point, and then the process stopped. No one knew why. The living dead did not corrupt to the point where their flesh actually fell apart. But this man looked ready to burst apart; his soft tissue was beginning to liquefy. And that did not happen. Not to any zombie. Only after a zom had been quieted did the normal process of decomposition run its full course. This was something she had never heard of. Not even in Dr. McReady's reports. Was this a new form of mutation? If so . . . what did it mean? What *could* it mean?

The zom kept moving toward her. He did not run, but it was more than a shuffling walk. Even with the advanced decomposition, he moved with more speed than a regular zom, and even more coordination.

Nix hurled the rock as hard as she could. It struck the monster in the chest with a sound like a bursting watermelon. Fetid black blood erupted from the wound. The smell was so intense that Nix staggered backward. The only thing that pungent she'd ever smelled was pure cadaverine, but that was weird, because a body only produced cadaverine when it was going through advanced decomposition. Her science class had toured the cadaverine plant in town, and they'd seen how the technicians harvested it from rotting animal flesh.

Nix took that moment to pick up two more stones as fast as she could, hurling them sidearm, hitting the thing in the shoulder and face. It staggered sideways into the rock wall, but it rebounded and came after her again. Nix scooped up a bigger stone. It was too big to throw, so she gripped it with both hands, raised it over her head, ran down the slope, and brought the stone down with all her strength.

The zom's head exploded.

Black goo splattered her face and hair and clothes. She screamed and began hysterically slapping at the wormy muck.

Behind her the zom collapsed onto the ground with a boneless, meaty thud that was entirely disgusting to hear.

"Behind you!"

It was Lilah's voice, hoarse and ghostly and urgent. Nix spun back as a third zom came running at her—fast, even going uphill. The zom was thirty feet away. Nix dove for her sword and came up with *Dojigiri* in her hands, and with no time left, she swung hard and wild.

The zombie's last running steps were confused, and the headless body puddled down onto the ground, leaking pints of black, wormy blood.

His name was Chong.

He knew that much, though the name was more of a sound, something familiar to which he reacted. He did not know what the name meant. Or if it meant anything at all.

Chong squatted in the darkness, arms resting loosely on his knees, hands dangling, head lowered, looking up from under threads of filthy hair. Every once in a while his fingers twitched, a spasm very like the motion of grabbing something. Of squeezing something that would scream.

Spit glistened on his lips and ran down his chin.

He thought about the boy who had been in here earlier. There was a sound for him, too. A word sound that triggered memory. Not memories of laughing or talking or fishing or trading Zombie Cards. Those memories sometimes flashed through his brain, but they were meaningless fragments. No, what he remembered was the smell of the boy.

The smell of meat. So much of it. So close.

As he thought about that boy, he felt his lips move. He heard his throat make a sound. Listened as the sound filled the air.

"B-Benny . . ."

Hearing the name intensified his hunger.

That meat had been so close. His teeth had almost had it. His stomach ached at the thought. He crouched there in the shadows and waited for the other boy—for the meat—to come back.

19

THREE MONTHS AGO . . .

Saint John loved the screams. They sounded like prayers to him.

With each shriek of pain, each cry for mercy that would not come, he knew that the eyes and minds and souls of the heretics were opening to the truth. The old gods, the old religions, could not protect them, because they were all false. When the blades of the reapers opened the red mouths, each mouth spoke the truth. The only salvation was oblivion.

He stood in the burning street with Sister Sun. She pleased him. The woman was brilliant by any standard, and as cold as moonlight. She kept disease from sweeping through the reaper army, though the withering winds of cancer were destroying her day by day. In the last six months she'd lost forty pounds, and soon she would be a skeleton.

If she had a flaw beyond physical infirmity, it was a stubborn refusal to let go of the science of the old world. That brought her into conflict with the more hard-line reapers, but it also provided an interesting X factor that Saint John occasionally found useful. The fact that Mother Rose hated and feared Sister Sun was another useful thing. By observing that dynamic without becoming involved in it, Saint John often learned valuable things about each of them. They were, at present, the two most powerful women in the Night Church.

Now he accompanied Sister Sun along a burning street toward the center of this doomed little town.

"What is it you wanted to show me?" he asked.

"Brother Victor was injured in the fighting," wheezed Sister Sun. "A sucking chest wound. He was taken to a gazebo we've been using as a triage center for this engagement, but he bled out. The Red Brothers were going to release him outside of town so he could wander, but . . ."

She let her words trail off as they arrived at the gazebo that stood in the village square. The structure was surrounded by members of the Red Brotherhood—the combat elite of the reapers. They were each marked by a bloodred palm print tattooed on their faces. They parted to allow Saint John and Sister Sun a better view but kept everyone else away.

As Saint John approached, he saw Brother Victor on the other side of the rail. The reaper's face was dead pale and his mouth dark with blood. He turned toward the movement of the newcomers and immediately crouched like a cat ready to spring. He bared his teeth and snarled. A black, viscous goo, thick as motor oil, dribbled over his teeth and down his chin. Small white worms writhed in the muck.

It was clear that Brother Victor had become one of the gray people.

The dead thing suddenly hurled himself at Saint John.

Four muscular Red Brothers leaped to intercept the rush, and they forced Victor back with wooden poles. The reaper retreated, but he began pacing back and forth, occasionally lunging at the rail with cat quickness.

Saint John frowned. "I don't understand this. Is he dead?"

"He is," said Sister Sun.

"But he's so fast."

"Yes. Fast and smart. Look."

The dead reaper attacked the rail over and over again, hitting different points, trying to squeeze between the guards, snarling all the while. He was so fast that once he nearly got across the rail before the men with the poles battered him back.

"He keeps trying the rail at different points," observed Sister Sun. "He's trying to find a weakness."

"You examined him? He has no pulse, no—"

"He's dead," said Sister Sun. She leaned close. "This is the mutation we've been hearing about. Now it's happened to one of our own. Honored One . . . if this spreads . . ."

Saint John said nothing. He could almost taste the fear in Sister Sun's voice, and he could see it in the eyes of the Red Brothers.

However, in his own heart, deep down in that velvety darkness, he felt quite a different emotion. And it made him smile.

UP AHEAD BENNY SAW A HAZY STRETCH OF GREEN FLOATING INSIDE A mirage.

The forest.

The very fact of the forest out here in the dry vastness of Nevada was bizarre. Before First Night, some real estate developers had come out into the hottest part of the desert and decided that this would be a wonderful place to put a golf course. They built row after row of tall wind turbines to generate electricity and pump water to irrigate the landscape, and planted trees, grass, and decorative shrubs in what was otherwise an inhospitable environment. In doing so they created the illusion of a lush forest cut with wide green lawns. The wind turbines hadn't been knocked out by First Night; however, heat and blowing sand had stilled most of them. Only a few still channeled sluggish water into the soil. Most of the exotic foliage was now dead, coarse weeds and bare dirt having replaced most of the lush grass. Lovely shrubs had been replaced by uglier, hardier foliage. When the last of the turbines quit working, the desert would kill the remaining imported trees and reclaim the land. Benny figured that within ten years there would be no trace of the golf course, no evidence that man had ever tried to impose his whims and his will on the fierce Mojave.

The four fat tires rumbled effortlessly over the rocky ground. Ahead he could see flashes of white through the green. The plane. As he drove toward it, Benny's mind churned on so many different things that he never heard the second quad come tearing toward him from behind a stand of trees. His only warning was when the other quad's engine roared to full throttle as the driver slammed into Benny's machine.

Suddenly Benny was flying into the air, arms pinwheeling, legs kicking. He landed with a thud that jolted every muscle and bone in his body. His *katana* went slithering out of its scabbard onto sandy ground. But Tom had taught him to react rather than allow himself to gape in surprise. He scrambled around, got to his feet, and came up into a crouch, confused, scared, and angry. His quad lay on its side near the transport plane, its wheels still turning, a second machine jammed hard against it, blue ethanol fumes chugging from both tailpipes.

He heard a crunch of a footfall, turned fast, and saw a glittering knife slash through the air toward his throat.

BENNY SCREAMED AND FLUNG HIMSELF BACKWARD AND FELT WIND WHIP past his Adam's apple as the blade missed him by a hairbreadth. His heels hit a gnarled twist of an exposed tree root, and Benny went down on his butt with a thump that snapped his teeth together with a loud *clack!*

The reaper grinned in obvious anticipation of an easy kill. "I bring the gift of darkness to you, my brother."

"Bite me," gasped Benny, and snatched up a handful of pebbles, hurling them at the killer. The reaper twisted away and took the stones on shoulders and hip instead of full in the face.

Benny's sword was ten feet away, the steel blade gleaming with deadly potential. The killer stood between Benny and the *katana*, so it might as well have been on the far side of the moon. The big plane lay a few yards behind Benny's back.

The reaper crouched, knife in hand, muscles bunching as he prepared to pounce. He was a tall man in his early twenties, all wiry muscle and sinew, dressed in black jeans and a muscle shirt with angel's wings hand-stitched across the chest. The man's head was shaved bald and comprehensively tattooed in a pattern of creeper vines and locusts. Strips of red cloth were tied to his ankles and wrists and looped around his belt. The cloth smelled like rotting meat—evidence that it had recently been dipped in chemicals that were used to prevent the living dead from attacking. Benny smelled every bit as bad from the cadaverine he'd sprinkled on his clothes.

Benny scooted backward on the ground, putting as much distance as he could between him and the reaper. The killer faked a lunge and then kicked sand in Benny's face; but Benny was already in motion, already scooping a handful of sand to throw at the reaper. Both masses of sand hissed through each other and struck their targets. Benny whipped his arm up to save his eyes, but he got a choking mouthful. The reaper tried to turn away and partially succeeded, so that the sand pelted his cheek and ear.

With a growl that was equal parts anger and fear, Benny drove his shoulder into the reaper's gut, exploding the air from the killer with an *oooof*. Benny's rush drove them both into the curved metal side of the gigantic transport plane. The impact tore a cry from the reaper, and he dropped his knife. Benny head-butted him, smashing the man's nose. The reaper screeched again, but a split second later he jerked his knee upward as hard as he could into Benny's crotch.

Benny staggered back, hands cupped around his groin.

The reaper moaned and sagged to his knees, blood pouring down his face from his shattered nose. "I will . . . open . . . red mouths . . . in your . . ."

"Yeah, yeah," wheezed Benny in a tiny voice as he fought against pain and nausea, ". . . open red mouths in my flesh . . . send me into the darkness . . . got it . . . *owwwww!*"

Gagging and coughing, the reaper reached for the knife. Benny kicked it away.

They got slowly and painfully to their feet. The reaper's nose was a purple bulb; his mouth and teeth glistened with red. Benny was sure that his testicles were somewhere up in his chest cavity.

The reaper sneered at Benny. "Are you really so stupid that you think you have a chance?"

"Yes," said Benny defiantly, then he frowned. "Wait, no, I mean I'm not stupid, but yes, I have a chance against you."

"I'm not talking about this fight, brother."

"Don't call me brother, you enormous freak," muttered Benny.

"The army of the Night Church will sweep away all defiance to god's will."

"Yeah, I know, you're invincible. Oh, wait, didn't you idiots get your butts handed to you by *one* guy with a rocket launcher? How's that 'sweeping away all defiance' thing working out for you?"

The reaper spat blood onto the sand. "The reapers who died at the Shrine of the Fallen were heretics and traitors to Thanatos—praise be to the darkness. They were the scum who followed Mother Rose. You have no idea what kind of army follows Saint John. Brother Peter and Sister Sun will sweep away all resistance to god's will."

"Sure. Fine. Whatever. I'm sure whoever you're quoting would be impressed. But check it out—you try and take Sanctuary again, and Captain Ledger will introduce you to Mr. Rocket-Propelled Grenade."

"You think that heretic can defend Sanctuary from us?" The reaper laughed.

"Pretty much."

"The voice of god will echo from the mountaintops and proclaim the glory of the darkness, and clouds of blood will cover the lands. Then the quickened dead will consume those who are slow to accept the darkness."

"Okay, don't take this the wrong way," said Benny, "but you're crazier than a bag of hamsters."

The knife lay ten feet from the reaper's right foot; Benny's sword was twelve feet to his left. They each looked at the weapons at the same time. At the sword, at the knife, then at each other. Then they lunged at the same time. The reaper was faster, taller, and stronger and he snatched up the knife, his fingers curling the deer-bone handle into perfect placement in his palm. Benny, a fraction slower and ten years younger, threw himself into a dive-roll and came up with the *katana* in a wide two-handed grip. He whirled and dropped into a combat crouch.

"Don't!" warned Benny, backing up a step. "We both know I'm going to win. Why push it? Just walk away."

That should have ended the fight. A knife against a sword. But the world was broken, and so was sanity.

The reaper screamed and threw himself at Benny.

"No!" screamed Benny as the moment became red madness.

The knife tumbled once more to the sand. The reaper opened his mouth and said the same thing Benny had said.

"No."

And it meant the same thing and so many different things. His knees buckled and he dropped down.

"No," he said again, as if repeating it could enforce some of his will upon the world.

The world, stubborn to the last, refused to listen. The reaper toppled forward onto his face with no attempt to catch his fall. Small puffs of dust plumed up around the man. Benny stood there, his sword still raised.

He closed his eyes.

"No," he said.

When I was eleven I played with dolls.

When I was twelve I started reading books about magic and romance.

When I was thirteen I fell hopelessly in love.

When I was fourteen I became a killer.

NIX STOOD UNDER A SHOWER OF SUN-HEATED WATER AND SCRUBBED HER skin raw. Lilah stood outside the stall, working the handle, pumping gallons of water from the big tank. The water was not pure enough to drink, but it was a million times cleaner than the bloody goo that clung to Nix's hair and skin. At one point Nix heard a weird little whimpering sound, like a small, frightened animal might make. When she realized that she was making the sound, she stopped scrubbing, closed her eyes, and leaned her forehead against the inside of the wooden shower stall. Shudders rippled up and down her body. Lights seemed to flash behind her eyes. She spent a lot of time concentrating on her breathing. Trying to remember how to do it right. Keeping it from turning into sobs. Or screams.

The water slowed and stopped. Nix heard a soft sound as Lilah leaned against the door from the other side.

"Nix—?"

"Y-yes."

"Are you . . . ?"

"I'm fine. I didn't get any in my mouth or eyes or anything."

"We have to tell them," said Lilah. "Four of them . . . four fast ones. We have to tell Joe."

"I know."

Nix leaned her cheek against the grainy wooden door and listened to the sound of Lilah's voice. It was rare to hear the Lost Girl sound so scared.

"What does it mean?" asked Lilah in her ghostly whisper of a voice.

"I don't know."

23

Benny stepped away from the man he'd just killed.

Overhead the first vultures were beginning to circle. Benny studied the dead man, wondering if he would rise from the dead—as nearly everyone did who'd died since the plague began on First Night—or if he would stay dead. Lately more and more people seemed to stay dead. No one knew why.

Stay dead, Benny silently told him.

Seconds blew past him like bits of debris on a hot wind. The reaper's fingers twitched. Then his foot. Suddenly his eyes snapped open, his lips parted, and he uttered that long, low, terrible moan of hunger that marked him as one of the living dead. It was an eternal hunger, a hunger that made no sense. The dead did not need to feed, they required no nourishment.

So why were they so hungry? Why did they kill and devour human flesh?

Why?

"*Why?*" demanded Benny.

The sound of his voice made the zom turn his head. The thing sat up slowly, empty eyes turning toward the sound, nose sniffing the air. Benny's cadaverine would keep him safe. He could let this one go.

The monks back at Sanctuary did not permit any of the zoms there to be killed.

This, however, was not Sanctuary. This was the Rot and Ruin.

Benny brought his sword up into a high guard, backing away slowly as the zom got clumsily to his feet. It stood for a moment, swaying as if taking a second to get used to what it was and how it felt about this new type of existence. That was wrong, though, and Benny knew it. The dead did not think, did not feel.

They simply *were*.

The creature moaned again. Benny listened to it, searching inside the sound for some trace, however small, of meaning, of humanity. Of anything.

All he heard was hunger. Vast, hollow, eternal.

The zombie looked at Benny and shuffled uncertainly toward him.

"Don't," said Benny, and the single word caused the zombie's head to jerk up. The glazed eyes shifted up to look directly at him. It took another step.

Benny retreated a pace, and the zom took two more steps. It was close now; one more step and it would be close enough to make a grab. Its hands rose and reached for Benny.

"Don't."

Benny slowly, numbly reached over his shoulder and slid the *katana* into its scabbard. Then his hands flopped down at his sides, hanging slack and purposeless. The zombie took another step, and now it pawed at Benny with clumsy fingers that twitched and jerked as if trying to remember their lost dexterity. Benny batted the hands aside.

The zom reached again.

Benny knew that he should end this. Here and now, quick and clean. It would be easy. After everything he'd been through, a single zombie no longer frightened him. He was sure he could break its neck with his bare hands, or easily cripple it with a kick to the knee.

He could. He probably should. As long as the plane was here, a wandering zom was a potential threat. Even to someone like Joe.

But Benny didn't attack. He backed away again, unwilling to inflict harm on this thing, even though a few moments ago it was a killer who wanted to murder him. That was different, and he knew it was different. Now everything about this creature, this *thing* . . . this former person, was different. Benny felt his heart hammering in his chest, and he wanted to do something. Scream, or throw up, or cry. Or run away.

Or die.

The zom reached again and again, and each time Benny slapped its fumbling hands away.

"C'mon, man," pleaded Benny, "*don't.*"

It kept coming. A step, a reach. Benny slapped the cooling hands away. The thing recovered its balance, brought its hands back, stepped, reached. The whole encounter was becoming a sick and sad ballet, a dance for two of the strangest kind. The moment had lost its veneer of horror for Benny and had become something else, something indefinable and surreal. It was terrifying in a nonphysical way. He felt that he teetered on the edge of some action that would damage his own soul far more than this monster could harm his body. His racing mind sought to understand it, but the truth, the insight, eluded him every bit as diligently as he eluded the zombie.

The zombie suddenly stopped, and its eyes flicked toward the forest. It took one lumbering step that way, then another, and another, heading away from Benny, heading toward the woods, following . . . who knew what. A sound, a smell?

Benny watched the zom until it vanished into the shadows under the trees. Then he bent and picked up his *katana*, cleaned the blood from the blade, and resheathed it.

The actions were performed almost without thought. His thoughts were elsewhere. They tumbled through a red awareness of what he had just done.

He'd killed a man.

A person.

A small, strange part of his mind wanted to gloat—the attacker had been older, stronger, faster, and probably more experienced, a reaper of the Night Church. In a one-on-one duel, Benny should have lost, even with the better weapon. But that part of his mind was only a fragment, and Benny prayed that it never grew to become something bigger. That part of his mind was okay with killing. It *wanted* to kill. It liked the excitement of battle, the promise of bloodshed, the rush of adrenaline.

Benny feared that part of himself. He tried to believe that it didn't belong to him at all.

Lies like that never work on your own mind, though.

The rest of him was appalled by what he had just done. Benny had killed people before—at Charlie Pink-eye's camp in the mountains of central California, at Gameland in Yosemite, and here in the Mojave Desert when the reapers tried to send Benny and all his friends into the vast, eternal darkness.

There were birds singing in the trees, and the air buzzed with insects. A small tan snake whipsawed through the brush, and off in the distance a pair of monkeys chattered as they chased each other through the boughs of a piñon tree. The desert was calm and beautiful. It was peaceful.

Benny Imura sat down with his back against a rock, set his sword aside, bent, and buried his face in his palms.

"I'm so sorry," he said. Though whether his apology was to the day, to the man he'd been forced to kill, to the monster that man had become, to the forest, or to the distorted image of himself that capered like a bent reflection in a funhouse mirror, Benny could not say.

CAPTAIN LEDGER SQUATTED DOWN BESIDE THE ZOM LILAH HAD KILLED. HE no longer looked hungover. He merely looked old and tired. And deeply disturbed.

Grimm stood nearby, looking up and down the slope at the bodies. Big and fierce as he was, the mastiff occasionally uttered a fearful whine.

"You're certain that all of them were fast?"

"Three for sure," said Nix. "The one whose head I cracked . . . I don't know about that one."

"Still," said Joe, "three out of four."

He pivoted on the balls of his feet to study the landscape. "This slope leads down to a T-road," he mused aloud. "Go right to the hangars . . . go left and it becomes a deer path that goes nowhere but up into the mountains."

"I found the tracks," Lilah told him. She nodded to the mountains. "They came from there."

"Does that make any sense?" asked Nix. "Why would zoms climb all the way over a mountain? I thought they didn't go uphill unless they were following prey. That's what Tom told us."

"Tom was right," agreed Joe.

"Could the sirens have called them here?" asked Lilah.

"I don't think so. Sanctuary sits in a kind of bowl of flat-land surrounded by mountains. Once that wail hits those mountains it bounces all over the place, and it's impossible to pinpoint the source unless you're down here on the flatland. I don't think we can sell that as the reason." He paused, thinking, then said, "No," again, very softly.

When they'd told Joe about the attack, he'd fetched a small leather valise, which now stood open beside him. He spent several careful minutes collecting samples from the zoms. Tissue and fluids. Then he took a large magnifying glass and peered through it as he bent over the head and shoulders of one of the corpses. He grunted.

"What is it?" asked Lilah.

Joe used a small brush to sweep something off the zom's blouse into a vial. When he held it up to examine it in the sun's glow, Nix saw that it was the red powder she'd noticed on the Latino man.

"Do you know what it is?" asked Nix. "Is it important?"

"I hope to God it *isn't*," he said, but he did not elaborate. Instead he got up and examined the other bodies, focusing now almost exclusively on collecting samples of the red powder. He stopped by one corpse, glanced at it, and then looked at Nix.

"Is this the one you said might not have been fast?"

"Yes," she said. "I landed on it and hit it in the face with an elbow and—"

Joe appeared to stop listening. He stood up, and his eyes roved over the scene.

"How the hell did this get here?" he murmured. Then Nix thought he mouthed a word: "Archangel."

Then Joe suddenly began packing his samples into the case.

"What is it?" asked Nix. "What's wrong?"

"Wrong?" Joe gave her a smile that might have been an attempt to reassure her. But it was ghastly. False and fragile. "It's nothing. You girls go back to the mess hall and get some lunch. Everything's fine."

He rose, clicked his tongue for his dog, and hurried away. A few minutes later they heard the sirens as Joe prepared to cross the bridge. The last thing Nix and Lilah saw of him was the ranger vanishing into the hangar next to the blockhouse. He had the valise with him, and he was running.

AFTER A WHILE BENNY GOT TO HIS FEET.

The zom had not returned, but even so Benny removed a bottle of cadaverine from his pocket and dribbled some on his clothes. It amazed him that after all this time he could still smell the stuff, and he had to dab mint gel on his upper lip from a small pot he always carried. The mint was so strong that it completely killed his sense of smell. When your clothes smell like rotting human flesh, an overload of mint is a genuine blessing.

He had a strange thought. If he died now and reanimated, would the presence of the mint gel mean that cadaverine wouldn't deter him? Probably. It was a creepy thought.

It was heating up to be another blistering day in a spring season that was already unusually hot. Even back home in Mountainside it had been a strange spring, with April temperatures in the eighties and almost no rain. Benny had no idea whether this was simply one of those years—there are hot ones and there are cold ones—or if it was an omen of something bad coming. His mood was tending toward the pessimistic view.

Maybe it is the end of the world, whispered his inner voice. *Maybe Captain Ledger is right. Maybe there are no chances left.*

"Oh, shut up," growled Benny.

He walked over to the wrecked airplane and stood for a moment at the foot of a sturdy rope ladder Joe had rigged to the open hatch.

Benny wished he'd asked Nix to come with him. He closed his eyes for a moment and thought about how she probably looked this morning, up there in the rocks, training with focused determination with the *katana* Joe had given her. Benny conjured her image in his mind and suddenly she was there, as real as something he could actually touch and hold. Her wild red hair trembling in the morning breeze that swept in from the desert, her intelligent green eyes roving over the landscape as she imagined attackers closing on her, her countless freckles darkening as her pulse rose to flush her skin. And the sword. Benny was a very good swordsman, but Nix was better. She was faster, more precise, less tentative, and far more vicious. In her small hands that powerful weapon sought its true potential. The blade became a streamer of flowing mercury, the edge cleaving effortlessly through air or straw targets or living-dead necks.

So far, though, Nix had not used that blade against the living.

Not like Benny had used his *kami katana*. Now, and too many times before today.

She had killed, though, Benny thought. Killed with knives and guns and with her old wooden bokken. She was like him in that regard. And also like Lilah, Chong, and Riot. Killers all.

Children at war.

Children *of* war.

It was so unfair.

"Nix," Benny said, just to put her name on the wind. Then he spoke her full name. "Phoenix."

Her name, either version, even now when he was angry with her, was like a prayer to him.

The first girl he had ever loved.

The first *person* he had ever loved. Aside from his parents, but that had been a remembered love from a tiny child. Not like this.

He loved Nix. She was the only girl he ever expected to love.

He would kill for her.

No, corrected his inner voice, *you* have *killed for her. And with her.*

"Shut up," Benny said again, and he turned away, as if by moving his body he could step away from that inner voice and all his melancholy thoughts.

The plane lay there. Dead. Discarded by time. And yet somehow strangely alive to him.

Waiting for him.

He found himself smiling.

Joe had expressly ordered Benny—and everyone else—to stay out of the plane. The head scientist, Dr. Monica McReady, and her entire crew had either been killed in the crash and then wandered off once they'd reanimated as zoms, or they'd been murdered by the reapers of the Night Church.

Now the most crucial part of Dr. McReady's research was missing.

In either case, the world's best hope for a cure was lost, maybe forever.

It was crazy, but three weeks ago Benny and Nix had not

known about Dr. McReady, her team, the possibility of a cure, or the fact that anyone was still left to do the research. That had been so amazing, so life-changing.

How was he supposed to suddenly discard all that hope and simply accept that there was no future unpolluted by plague and death? He didn't know how to fit that into his head. It didn't seem to fit, and Benny knew full well that he didn't want it to fit.

If hope of a cure was gone, then what did that mean for Chong? Maybe he was dead already. Maybe all hope was dead.

We lost our last chance to beat this thing.

"No," Benny said, and now that word held an entirely different meaning than it had a few minutes ago. Now it was filled with anger. With defiance, and Tom had once told him that defiance in the face of disaster was a quality of hope. "No—absolutely fricking no way."

The black mouth of the plane's open hatchway yawned above him.

Benny hooked his fingers through the rope ladder and tugged it. Sturdy and strong.

But Joe—the towering, deadly ex-special ops shooter who now ran a team of rangers in the Ruin—had said to stay out of the plane. No excuses, no exceptions.

"Well," Benny said to the rope ladder, "what can he do? Send me to my room?"

He climbed up into the plane.

The inside was a mess. Joe had apparently trashed the place while scavenging the materials and looking for the missing D-series notes. With the captured zoms removed, and all the equipment cases and boxes of records gone, the structural damage was easier to see. The plane had broken its back on landing, and the craft's metal skin was rippled and torn. The floor was littered with discarded junk. Papers, broken containers, and hundreds upon hundreds of shell casings from the automatic weapons Joe had fired when repelling the reaper assault. They gleamed dully in the streamers of light that stabbed down through tears in the ceiling. Paper trash was heaped against the walls or left where it had fallen. Benny sat down on an empty case that had once housed a rocket launcher and began digging into the paper.

He had no real idea what he was looking for. It wasn't like he expected to find a piece of paper labeled CURE.

Even so, there was an answer here. Some kind of answer, he was sure of it.

Hours passed as he went through every piece of paper, no matter how small.

There was nothing of value there.

Not a word, not a scrap.

Benny picked up the papers he'd found and hurled them as hard as he could against the wall. Pages, whole and partial, slapped against the unyielding metal and then floated to the deck, as disorganized and useless as before.

He climbed down to the ground, his face burning with anger and his whole body trembling with frustration.

That was when he remembered the quads.

The engines of both vehicles had eventually stalled out.

"Ah . . . man . . ."

He ran over to the machines. The reaper's quad was still upright and was jammed at an angle against Benny's machine, which lay on its side. Benny pushed the second quad, a Honda, back from his Yamaha. The Honda moved with a sluggish, lumpy resistance—the right front wheel was flat, the rubber exploded from the impact. Benny examined the Yamaha. The right rear wheel hung at a strange angle, and when he bent to examine it, he groaned. The axle had been snapped like a bread stick.

Benny straightened, exhaled a long, slow breath, thought of Tom's many lessons about maintaining calm in the middle of a crisis—and then spent the next two minutes screaming and kicking the Yamaha from every possible angle.

Then he spent three minutes standing there, chest heaving, both feet hurting like hell, glaring at the machine.

Finally he opened the rear compartment on the Yamaha and took out the jack and the lug wrench and took a wheel off his bike and put it onto the Honda. The wheels were the same size, and it wasn't until Benny was finished that he grudgingly accepted that as a lucky break. Not all the quads were the same size.

Then Benny tried to turn the Honda on. Nothing happened.

He tried again.

Same effect.

It hadn't stalled after the crash. It had run out of fuel.

Benny snatched up a rock and came very close to slamming it down on the fuel gauge.

Stop it! bellowed his inner voice.

It actually stopped Benny mid-smash.

He stared at the rock he held.

"Oh man," he said, and let it drop.

Find a hose, said his smarter inner voice. *Siphon gas out of the other—*

"Yeah, yeah, I know, I got it," he growled.

His inner voice shut up.

Benny dug through the compartments and saddlebags of his own quad and found nothing. Then he began foraging through the Honda.

He found a siphon hose right away. However, what he found next made him forget completely about the hose, the fuel, the quad, the residual pain in his groin, and virtually everything else.

Tucked into the back compartment of the Honda was a loose-leaf binder with the word TEAMBOOK printed on the spine and a flag embossed on the front. The flag was not the Stars and Stripes of the old United States of America. No, this was the symbol of the newer, post–First Night American Nation. It was the same symbol that was painted on the tail fin of the plane and on patches worn by dead members of the crew.

Benny flipped the Teambook open and saw that there was a double-sided page devoted to each member of Dr. McReady's team from Hope One. Each page included a color photograph of a person in either the brown-and-green uniform of the new American Nation or in the white lab coat of McReady's science team. Below each photo was basic data: name, rank, serial number, gender, blood type, height, weight, eye color, hair color, and an abbreviated service record. A lot of it meant nothing to Benny, especially in sections where there was an overabundance of military abbreviations and acronyms. Hope One had been staffed by Dr. McReady, six other scientists, ten lab technicians, eighteen soldiers, and five general staff. Forty people. The C-130 had eight additional soldiers and a flight crew of four. Fifty-two people in all.

He studied the photo of Dr. Monica McReady. She was a black woman with short hair, and a pair of reading glasses hung around her neck. According to her data, she was fifty-six years old.

"Where are you?" he asked her. "Where's your cure? I have a friend who needs you. His name is Chong and he's . . ."

Hungry.

". . . he doesn't deserve this. Where are you?"

The picture told him nothing. The book as a whole, however, did. There was blood on every single photograph in the book. Old, dried blood. Weeks old, at least, and in some cases the gore was so old that it was caked and powdery. These were not random splashes but deliberate markings. About half the photos had been crossed out with a dripped red X. Eleven others were marked with a bloody thumbprint in the upper right corner. When he compared the prints, Benny saw that they were each different, no two alike. The remaining photos were also marked by a thumbprint, but in each of these cases the thumbprint was placed over the heart of the person. The same thumbprint was used for all these.

So what did it mean?

Benny chewed on it.

The Xs seemed obvious. Those were members of the crew who had been killed, or who'd died during the crash. Two of the pictures marked that way showed men dressed as pilots, and Benny had seen those men before. On the day they'd found this plane, there had been two zoms tied to crossbars erected on the ground in front of the cockpit.

The second set, the ones with unique thumbprints, took him longer to figure out, but as he went through each picture again he spotted a face that he recognized. The face was the same, but in the photo the man had black hair.

Benny had looked into that same face minutes ago. He had looked into those eyes while the man in the photo was alive, and he'd looked into the same eyes once all traces of human life had fled.

The reaper.

According to the Teambook his name was Marcus Flood, age twenty-six, born in Kansas City. A lance corporal in the army of the American Nation.

The man he'd just killed had been a member of Dr. McReady's crew. One of the soldiers assigned to help evacuate Hope One.

But he'd become a reaper.

How?

Why?

Riot and Joe both said that the reaper army had been built mostly from people who had been given a choice: die with everyone else in your town, or join. It was a conqueror's strategy that had worked for everyone from Alexander the Great to the Nazis, so apparently it still worked. Even so . . . Benny could not climb inside the head of someone who would willingly become part of a group whose ultimate goal was to end all human life. Sure, it meant living a little longer, but the end was still going to be the same. Death.

What made someone make that choice? Did they think that somehow they'd slip through the cracks and not be sent into the darkness when Saint John thought it was time? Or did they really buy into the reaper beliefs?

The man in that photo seemed to.

There was another photo in the batch that caught Benny's attention. Another soldier. A big man, tough-looking but also strangely familiar. The sheet said that his name was Luis Ortega, and his designation was team logistics coordinator.

Whatever that meant.

Benny touched the picture.

"Where do I know you from?" he wondered aloud. Was this man another of the reapers, like Marcus Flood? If so, was he now wandering around on the airfield? Had he been one of the reapers with Mother Rose, one of those gathered a few yards from here? Benny and Nix had secretly watched that gathering. Had he died with Mother Rose or vanished with Saint John and the main body of the reaper army? Was he one of the thousands of sick people being tended by the way-station monks? Or one of the refugees Riot was guiding to Sanctuary?

The half-remembered encounter had to be recent, though, because it throbbed insistently in Benny's mind.

Because of the severity of the head wound he'd received, the monks told him there was a strong chance that he might have some amnesia. Not total, not even a lot, but some blank spots. This was one of those spots, he was sure of that. He could almost—*almost*—see the memory of this man, almost catch it. A big man in a military uniform like this. Benny had seen hundreds of other military clothes, from zoms killed during the battles after First Night. Some of the men in town had camouflage jackets from the old world. The uniforms of the new American Nation were different. The camouflage was a different pattern, with bits of dusty red mixed in with the black, tan, brown, and gray.

Then . . . something, some fragment of a memory went skittering across the back of Benny's brain, triggered by Sergeant Ortega's face and uniform. He went still, hoping to catch a glimpse of it, to discover what it wanted to tell him.

But that fast it was there and gone, hiding in the shadows under a rock in his damaged memory.

Benny flipped back through the book, this time looking at the small pieces of paper clipped to some of the pages. One note was written in round cursive by a decidedly feminine hand.

Mutations reported in California.
This needs to be checked out.
Field Team Five?

Mutations?

And . . . what was Field Team Five?

He searched the rest of the compartments and saddle-bags on the quad, but there were no more notes or papers. He found some dried meat wrapped in palm leaves, but he distrusted what the reapers considered wholesome food, so he threw that away. He found an item that seemed totally out of place among the reaper's possessions: an old, unopened package of brightly colored rubber balloons. Fifty of them. It seemed so bizarre and incongruous a thing for a killer to have. He wondered if they were used for some kind of silent signaling. Benny almost tossed them away, then decided to keep them. Eve might like them. Anything that might put another smile on the little girl's face was worth treasuring. He stuffed the package into his vest pocket.

The only other thing of apparent importance he found was a small spiral-bound notebook. Every page was filled with small, crabbed handwriting. Most of what was written there were prayers and rituals of the reapers. Benny debated tossing it away, but decided to keep it. If the reapers were the enemy, then some of Tom's advice applied: *Know your enemy. The more you know about them, the less easily they can surprise you. And by studying them you might identify a weakness or vulnerability.*

And there was the phrase Lilah had learned from George, the man who'd raised her: *Knowledge is power.*

The other reason he decided to keep the notebook was what the reaper had written on the last page. It was a kind of code:

CA/R 1: 4,522

Quad: 66

CA/R 2: 19,200

Quad: 452

NV/R: 14,795

Quad: 318

WY/R: 8,371

Quad: 19

UT/R: 2,375

Every instinct, every nerve he possessed screamed at him that this was important. This, the Teambook, and the urgent note Benny suspected had been written by Dr. McReady. Important . . . but in what way?

How?

No way to ask the reaper now, Benny thought, and he flinched at the memory of what he had been forced to do.

He put the notebook in his pocket and the Teambook into the Honda's storage bin. Then he used the rubber hose to siphon ethanol from his own crippled quad into the Honda's tank. Benny replaced the gas cap, climbed into the saddle, started the engine, and drove thoughtfully back to Sanctuary.

The people I grew up with, the folks in Mountainside, call the start of the plague First Night. It's kind of misleading, because it took weeks for civilization to break down.

Riot and the people she was with call it the Fall.

I've also heard people call it the End, the Gray Rapture, the Rising, Z-Day, Armageddon, the Apocalypse, the Punishment, the Retribution, Plague Day, War Day One, and other stuff.

Riot was dozing in a straw basket-chair when one of the nuns came to find her. She opened her eyes to see the tight, unsmiling face of Sister Hannahlily, the head nun who oversaw the children during their afternoon nap.

"You have to come at once," said the nun.

"What's wrong?" Riot demanded. "Is something wrong with Eve?"

The nun seemed to be caught in a moment of terrible indecision, as if uncertain how to answer so simple a question.

"You need to come," she said. "Right now."

Riot got to her feet and followed the nun. Sister Hannahlily did not exactly run to the tent used for the children's nap time, but she walked very fast, her body erect with tension, arms pumping.

"Oh God," breathed Riot to herself, "don't let that little girl be hurt. Don't let her be hurt. . . ."

They reached the tent, where Brother Michael, a monk who helped with psychological counseling, was waiting for them. Before First Night he'd been a radio call-in host.

"What in tarnation is going on?" asked Riot.

Sister Hannahlily looked frightened, and Riot couldn't

imagine why. There was a faint sound coming from inside the tent, a soft thudding sound that Riot could not make sense of, like someone fluffing a pillow.

"We moved the other children out of the tent," said Sister Hannahlily. "We thought it best."

"Moved them out? Why? Where's Eve?"

"Inside," said the monk.

Riot reached for the tent flap.

Eve was the only person in the tent. Riot could tell almost at once that the little girl was asleep, though she was standing and moving. Sleepwalking, in a way. In a horrible way.

The girl had gathered all the rag dolls the children had made during arts and crafts. They lay side by side on one of the cots. Eve held a pair of the pinking shears used to cut the fancy, frilly trim for the dollies' dresses. She held the shears in both hands and with slow, determined, deliberate swings of her entire body, she stabbed the dolls over and over and over again.

And she smiled as she did it.

Riot gasped, and Eve paused for a moment, turning her face toward the open tent flap. The little girl's mouth smiled, but there was no humor in her eyes. There was nothing in her eyes. No emotion, no recognition, no anger.

There was absolutely nothing.

It was as if those blue eyes looked in on a house that was empty of all light and life, a place where only dark and awful shadows moved.

Then Eve turned back to the dolls.

The shears rose and fell, rose and fell.

27

THREE MONTHS AGO . . .

Saint John came out of a long private meditation when he heard a quiet footfall nearby. "Good afternoon, Sister Sun," he said quietly, eyes still closed.

"Honored One," she said.

Saint John opened his eyes and touched her head, murmuring a small blessing. She straightened up and sat where he indicated. Sister Sun had once been a lovely woman, and she still had deeply intelligent eyes and a face that reminded him of paintings he'd seen of Ma Gu, the ancient Korean goddess of longevity. It was a bitter irony, of course, since she had so little time left in front of her. Months, not years. He never commented on the resemblance, of course, because he felt it might offend her in a spiritual sense to be reminded of a goddess from one of mankind's many false religions.

Instead he said, "You look troubled, sister."

"I am. There have been more reports about mutations. More of the gray people who can move faster than should be possible."

"How many cases?"

"Seven, which brings the total number of reliable reports to twenty-two."

"And this continues to disturb you?"

"Yes, Honored One. We will be moving the reapers back into Nevada soon, and I asked Mother Rose if it wasn't time for us to consider opening the shrine."

"What would you have us do, sister?" asked Saint John. "Use the weapons of the heretics?"

Sister Sun took a moment on that. "Honored One . . . I love my fellow reapers, but I'm not fool enough to think that all of them are with us out of an undying love of Thanatos—all praise his darkness. Some of them—maybe a lot of them—are opportunists who chose to kiss the knife rather than feel its caress on their flesh."

Saint John did not comment on that.

"But I wasn't making a case with Mother Rose for the weapons aboard that plane," she said. "I only want access to Dr. McReady's notes, samples, and clinical studies and—"

Before she could say more, her body was racked by a coughing fit that was deep and wet. It made her frail body hitch and pulse with pain, and her bird-thin bones creaked. She pressed a red kerchief to her mouth. Saint John was aware that red cloth was chosen because it more effectively hid the droplets of blood torn from her with each barking cough.

"The darkness calls out to you, my sister," said Saint John.

When she could speak, she said, "Praise to the darkness. But please, listen to me. I'm almost out of time. Look at me, Honored One. To read and process that research takes more than a healthy mind, and when my body fails my mind will go too. The Night Church will lose a valuable opportunity to understand why this plague is changing and what those changes will mean for our mission. I don't know how much longer I can do reliable work."

"The plague is the plague," he said. "It is no threat to our god's plans."

"I believe it has become a very real threat," Sister Sun said. "The pathogen that started the plague was really an amalgam of several super-viruses and some genetically engineered parasites. As you know, this was not something nature—or god—created. The Reaper Plague was a weapon of war, however—"

Saint John interrupted. "No. It was the voice of god whispering in the ears of certain people. They were told to create the plague as a way of cleansing the earth of the infection of life. The Reaper Plague was the sword of god, and it is from that sword that I took the name for the servants of god whose knives open the red mouths in the last of the sinners."

They rose and walked in silence for a while. Finally Sister Sun spoke. "Honored One, that is a theological discussion, and I defer to your holy insights. However, the matter of Dr. McReady's research is a more . . . um, mundane matter. It's science."

"Yes, I do understand that. She wants to stop the Reaper Plague," observed Saint John. "Dr. McReady is an enemy of god, and her works are blasphemy."

"No doubt," said Sister Sun quickly. "My point, Honored One, is that the pathogen may have become unstable."

"Don't all living things change?"

"Not this," she insisted. "The Reaper Plague—from everything I learned about it before kneeling to kiss the knife—was designed *not* to mutate. This is a bioweapon, a designer plague. It was designed to remain stable so that the outcome of any implementation could be precisely predicted. That means that if the plague is mutating, it isn't happening naturally. Someone is causing that mutation. And I think we both know who."

They walked well beyond the perimeter of the reaper camp before Saint John spoke. "What danger do you foresee from a mutation?"

"If the gray people mutate into something that would prey on the reapers, wouldn't that send the wrong message to our people? We tell the reapers that the gray people are like sheep and we are shepherds, but that would change. We'd become hunted. The message would get mixed, and that could hurt us. It would weaken our control. It might shake the faith of the people."

"Or," said Saint John, "it could test that faith."

"Dr. McReady's research is far too dangerous to leave unaddressed. We must act. We must find her."

"Our best guess is that Dr. McReady is somewhere in California," mused Saint John. "Or perhaps Oregon. If she's still alive, then explain to me how her experiments hundreds of miles away could be causing mutations here."

"Honored One . . . I think *we* may have caused this."

"How so?"

"When Mother Rose found the plane, there were many things aboard. The gray people she'd captured, the medical records, biological samples, and bags of some red powder. I was never allowed to examine any of this. However, I know that one of Mother Rose's reapers opened one of the bags of powder. Probably out of idle curiosity. He found nothing of value and dumped that bag out of the hatch. If I'm right, then it may have contained a mutagenic agent of some kind. It would explain the mutations that we've been seeing, because they all began *after* that bag was opened."

Saint John frowned. "That's disturbing."

"I think McReady had compounded a mutagen and was taking it to Sanctuary for development and possible mass production."

"Ah . . . Sanctuary," murmured Saint John. "The time may come when it will be necessary to burn that pestilential place from the surface of the earth."

"They have a whole army division there."

"Do they?"

"It's what our spies say."

He gave a soft grunt.

"If I had access to McReady's research," continued Sister Sun, "I might be able to do something about the mutations. Possibly stop them. Or maybe devise another kind of mutation. Something that would serve the Night Church rather than pose a threat to it."

Saint John pursed his lips but said nothing.

"Please," begged Sister Sun softly, "let me have access to McReady's research."

28

Nix sat on a swing, arms looped around the chains, toes dug into the sand so that the swing moved only a few inches back and forth. The adrenaline in her bloodstream had begun to wash out, and it seemed to be taking all her energy with it, leaving her exhausted and sad.

Seeing Eve did not make that sadness retreat one inch.

The little girl was dozing in Riot's arms, but Eve's brow was furrowed. Nix could imagine what her dreams were like.

When she closed her own eyes, Nix saw Charlie Pink-eye and the Motor City Hammer crowd her mother into a corner and begin beating her. That memory was the very last Nix had of her mother. Right after that Charlie knocked her unconscious. By the time she regained consciousness, Nix was already in the Ruin on the way to Gameland. And her mother was dead. Found too late and quieted by Tom Imura.

Would her dreams ever go away?

Nix doubted it.

She worried about it too. Grief and anger were changing her, warping her. For months she had been mean to Benny— the one person who loved her unconditionally. She felt shrewish at times, and vicious.

Only recently had that begun to change, and Nix didn't know why.

She still had her nightmares. And in her troubled sleep she probably furrowed her brow as Eve was doing now. She knew she ground her teeth—her jaws always hurt in the morning.

How does one come back from that edge? What was that saying from Nietzsche?

Battle not with monsters, lest ye become a monster, and if you gaze into the abyss, the abyss gazes also into you.

Nix wished she didn't understand what that meant.

Riot caught her looking at Eve, and for a long moment the two of them stared at each other, saying so much without words. Riot slowly nodded, and Nix nodded back.

She understands too.

And Lilah.

Benny, too, now that Tom was gone.

And Chong?

He hadn't wanted to come along on this journey. The jet didn't matter to him. He left home for love, and in the wilderness he stumbled along all the way to the edge of the abyss.

Was Chong already lost? Was he a monster?

If you fought monsters and then became one . . . could you ever go back again? Or did the abyss own Chong . . . and Eve?

And all of them?

29

Two months ago . . .

Saint John leaned against a tree, peeling a fig with a small knife, enjoying the sensation of the blade sliding just beneath the skin of the fruit. He wondered, not for the first time, if fruit could feel pain. If it could scream. Even a simple fig would taste so much better if that were the case.

Six tall, stern fighters of the Red Brotherhood stood nearby. Two watching him, four watching outward. The least experienced among them had sent a hundred heretics into the darkness. Saint John loved the Red Brothers as if they were his own children, and it was their choice, not his, that they wear the tattoo of his left hand on their faces. Brother Peter was his right hand, and they—collectively—were his left.

Inside their circle, seated on a tree stump, was Sister Sun. On the ground between her and Saint John was an old blue plastic ice chest. The lid was sealed with tape. A stack of boxes stood beside the cooler. Each of the boxes was marked with a large letter *D*.

"My sister," said Saint John, "do you know what this is?"

Sister Sun's eyes were wide as she stared at the material. She nodded, almost unable to speak.

"Do you maintain that it serves the will of god to open those boxes? To read the words of the heretic McReady?"

She tried to speak, but her voice was thick. Sister Sun cleared her throat and tried again. "I do, Honored One."

"Even though our Mother Rose believes that this is tainted?"

"Yes."

"Even though to do so would be to break faith with Mother Rose?"

Now Sister Sun raised her eyes and looked directly at the saint. "My faith is in god," she said. "I . . . I mean I love Mother Rose, but—"

"Do not apologize," said the saint. "It's unseemly."

She blushed and nodded.

Saint John cut a piece of fig, put it in his mouth, chewed it thoughtfully, then nodded to the folders.

"Mother Rose will be in Utah until next month. When she returns, she will very likely inspect the seals on the Shrine of the Fallen."

Sister Sun nodded.

"When that happens, she will find all these seals intact. Everything correct and in order."

He did not say "or else" or make any other threat. He cut another slice of fig and offered it to Sister Sun, who reached out a trembling hand to take it. She chewed it quietly while he stood there and smiled at her.

BENNY PARKED THE HONDA IN THE DAMAGED YAMAHA'S SLOT AND WENT looking for Captain Ledger.

As he passed the playground, though, he saw Riot and Eve sitting on a set of rusted swings. Benny drifted over that way. Riot's face was animated as she told a funny story involving a crazy little dog name Rosie and her adventures in an abandoned toy store. Benny thought that Riot looked deeply strained despite her animation. There was an odd light in her eyes and a detectable tremolo in her voice.

Sister Hannahlily stood a dozen yards away, pretending to water flowers, but she was clearly watching Eve. Deep lines of concern were etched into her face.

Eve's face was slack, her mouth open, her eyes dull and fixed, as if all her internal lights had been switched off. It was how she often was, drifting between moderate highs and very deep lows. Benny took the bag of balloons from his pocket, tore it open, selected a bright yellow one, and began blowing it up as he strolled over in front of the swings. Riot saw what he was doing and raised her eyebrows in surprise. Balloons were rare—like most things from the old world, they weren't made to last, and most of them were so dried out that any attempt to blow them up was a failure. The ones in the bag were wonderfully preserved, and with each puff the balloon grew and grew.

Eve's face remained slack, but after the fifth or sixth puff her eyes reclaimed a little bit of their focus and shifted toward him. The more the balloon expanded, the more awareness seemed to grow in the little girl's eyes. Riot gave Benny a grateful smile that glistened with tears.

It really must be one of Eve's bad days, Benny thought. *Riot looks like she's ready to scream.*

Finally Benny stopped and tied off the balloon.

"For milady," he said, presenting the balloon to Eve with an exaggerated flourish and bow. "I believe you ordered a big, squishy, yellow thing."

There was a moment when Eve did nothing except look at the balloon, her mouth and body still slack. Then, like the sun peering shyly through the darkest of storm clouds, a small smile formed on her lips. She glanced at Benny and blinked several times, as if she was seeing him for the first time. Which, he thought sadly, she probably was. He kept his own smile pasted onto his face while the girl struggled out of the shadows. When her tiny hand slowly rose and reached for the balloon, she took it as lightly as someone reaching for an illusion in a dream, as if she was afraid it would suddenly vanish.

Benny straightened and took two more balloons from the pack, a blue one and a green one. He almost picked a red one, but Riot gave him a quick and desperate sharp shake of the head. He stuffed the red one quickly out of sight and handed the other balloons to Riot.

"If you fly away to the land of Oz," said Benny, "make sure to send me a message via delivery Munchkin."

Eve nodded seriously, as if that was a reasonable suggestion.

Benny left, and when he looked over his shoulder, Riot was teaching Eve how to blow up the green balloon. The little girl was smiling, but the whole thing hurt Benny's heart. He was aware that the older nun, Sister Hannahlily, was watching him. He smiled and nodded to her, and she responded. A nod, no smile.

A few minutes later Benny found Joe Ledger working out in a small enclosure behind the last of the hangars on this side of the trench. Grimm, Joe's dog, opened one baleful eye, decided Benny wasn't a lunch being delivered, and went back to sleep. Even so, Benny stayed well away from the mastiff as he entered the enclosure.

Joe Ledger was stripped to the waist, wearing only camo pants and boots, and he shifted around on the balls of his feet as he worked a heavy bag. Joe barraged the leather with jabs, hooks, overhands, uppercuts, backhands, hammer blows, two-knuckle hits, corkscrew punches, elbows, and the occasional cutting palm. Then he shifted to kicks—snaps and round-house kicks, hooks and slashing knees. The bag juddered and danced as if it was being hit by continuous gunfire, and with each blow dust puffed through the canvas's thick weave.

It bothered Benny that despite Joe being at least thirty years older than Tom, the man was at least as fast. Maybe faster. And a whole lot stronger. That was annoying. It felt wrong, somehow, as if this man's superior skill was in some way an insult to Tom's memory. Even so . . . it was mesmerizing to watch.

Eventually, though, his impatience ran faster than his fascination with the display of martial arts. Benny cupped his hands around his mouth and yelled, "Hey—Joe!"

Grimm gave him a single, scolding bark.

"I wasn't talking to you," said Benny.

Benny could almost swear that the dog cocked one eyebrow in wry amusement.

Finally Joe stepped back from the bag, chest heaving, sweat running in lines down his body and limbs. His face was flushed a deeper red than his sunburn, and his eyes were bright. He no longer looked hungover.

"Hey, kid, what's shaking?" asked Joe as he took a canteen from where it rested atop a stack of cinder blocks, unscrewed the cap, and took a long pull. There was no alcohol stink, and Benny was pleased to see that the canteen was filled with water rather than any "hair of the dog" booze. Joe seemed to sense something of that and grinned. "Best way to clean the system out is a lot of water and the kind of workout that gets the blood pumping."

"Or you could stay sober."

Joe peered at Benny while he took another long pull. "You're kind of a pain in the ass, anyone ever tell you that?"

"It's come up in conversation."

"No doubt. So," said Joe as he raised the canteen for another drink, "to what do I owe the honor of your company?"

Benny said, "A reaper tried to kill me today."

Joe spat water halfway across the enclosure. "What? Where?"

"Out at the plane."

"At the plane?" Joe yelled. "What in the wide blue hell were you doing out *there*?"

"Not dying, thanks for asking," Benny shouted back.

Joe pointed a finger at Benny. "I thought I told you kids not to go anywhere near that plane."

"You did," agreed Benny. "I ignored you. Mostly because I don't remember you being the boss of me. When did that happen?"

"When you met a responsible adult," thundered Joe.

"Really?" returned Benny acidly. "Responsible adult? That's a joke. Almost every adult we've met since we left home has been one kind of psychopath or another. Bounty hunters who tried to make us fight in the zombie pits at Gameland. Nut-job loners who like putting people's heads on their gateposts. Way-station monks who think the zoms are the meek who are supposed to inherit the earth. Scientists who lock themselves in a blockhouse and won't even *talk* to us. Reapers who are trying to kill *everyone*, and you—whatever you are. Joe Action Figure. Don't lecture me on 'responsible adults.' Me and my friends— the *kids* you're talking about—we haven't started fights with anyone. We're not trying to push our religious views on anybody, and we're not trying to take what anyone else has. And just because we're teenagers doesn't mean that we can't make good decisions and take care of ourselves. We're not little kids anymore. We've had to grow up a lot in the last few months. A whole lot. We came out here to find proof that the people of *your* generation haven't actually destroyed everything that was ever worth anything. Why? Because your story might be over, but ours isn't. I just hope that when we become adults we're

131

not as vicious, violent, and destructive as most of the so-called adults we've met out here in the Ruin. 'Cause I'm here to tell you, Joe, we could use some better role models."

Joe sucked his teeth. "You finished?"

"No. The reaper who attacked me was also an adult."

Grimm gave a throaty *whuff*.

Joe shot the dog an evil look. "Who asked *you* to take sides?" He wiped his mouth with the back of his hand and said, "Okay, okay, so life's been hard for you, kid, I get it. Later on we can sit down and cry a little. Right now, though, how about you stop making speeches and tell me what happened at the plane? Actually, no. First tell me how you got away? And where's the reaper now?"

"He's dead."

"How—?"

Benny looked him straight in the eye. "I killed him."

Joe said, "What?"

"I killed him. He came at me with a knife. I . . . had no choice."

"Ah, jeez, kid." Joe sat down heavily on the stack of cinder blocks. "Look, Ben, I'm glad you're okay, and I'm sorry you had to go through that."

It was not the response Benny had expected. He thought there would be more yelling, or some booyah crap about the glory of combat. Instead Joe looked genuinely sad. It confused Benny.

"I'm pretty sorry I had to go through it too," he said.

"You sure you're not hurt?" asked Joe.

Benny shrugged. "Some bruises. A bad case of the shakes . . . and I guess a sick feeling in my stomach."

"Yeah. That pretty much comes with the job."

"Job? What job? I'm not a soldier."

"Maybe not, but let's face it, kid, we are at war. Saint John has launched a genocidal holy war, and the very fact that we're alive makes us enemy combatants in his book."

"I don't want to fight Saint John."

"Hey, I don't either."

"Besides, the reaper army vanished. You drove them off with the rocket launchers and all that."

Joe shook his head. "Be nice if that was true, kid, but the reapers I fought were Mother Rose's splinter group. The main force of the reaper army is somewhere else. Hopefully they're far, far from here, but the plain fact is they're out there somewhere."

"'Main force'? How many reapers are there?"

"Conservative guess, including the group with Saint John and a half-dozen smaller groups he could gather together if he needs . . . call it thirty-five, forty thousand."

Benny nearly fell down. *"What?"*

"Could be more."

"But . . . that's more than all the people in Mountainside and the other eight towns put together!"

"I know. It's also why Saint John keeps winning. He has too big an army to lose any fight. Even if the defenders are well armed, Saint John can keep throwing bodies at them until they run out of bullets. He's not a tactical genius, you know, he's simply willing to do whatever it takes to win."

"And people are willing to die for him . . . that's so . . ."

"You're looking at it the wrong way," said Joe. "They're not dying for Saint John, they're dying for what he's selling.

He has them convinced that death is the antidote to pain and suffering, and it's a hard argument to beat. Most religions talk about an afterlife or a paradise, right? Well, this world has been pretty much a crap sandwich for fifteen years, and it wasn't always so friggin' wonderful before that. Life is hard, people suffer, people get sick, they lose those they love. If you really believed that once you pass into the darkness, as Saint John calls it, there is no more pain, no more suffering, just bliss—if you believed that, you'd do anything to get there. Even walk into a fusillade of bullets. Especially if you believed that by dying for the cause you're ensuring the salvation and bliss of everyone else. It's a win-win situation. Saint John may actually believe this crap too, and probably does. In strategic terms, though, he's adopted an 'anything goes' approach to winning."

"Jeez . . ."

"The reason no one's beat him yet," said Joe, "is that people these days are afraid. They're fighting like whipped dogs. There's no genuine aggression left in them. They fight defensively, and that's why they're going to lose every battle."

"I thought the saying was that the best offense is a strong defense."

"You have it the wrong way around. The best defense is a strong offense. There's an adage from the Wing Chun style of kung fu that goes 'The hand which blocks also strikes.' You understand what that means?"

Benny nodded.

"It's academic, though . . . there's no one west of the Rockies with either the technical oomph or the monkey-bat crazy nerve to fight him the right way."

"What's the right way?"

Joe cocked his head and considered Benny. "I've got my fair share of psychological issues," he said. "There have been times when I've been in situations where I should have lost. I've been up against better numbers, and I've fought tougher men. You know why I'm still sucking air and they're worm food? Because when it comes right down to it, there's nothing I won't do to win. Nothing. One time when we were really up against it, a guy I worked for looked at me and said, 'I'd burn down heaven itself to stop this thing.' If you think that sounds grandiose, that's 'cause you didn't know the man. That's what he was willing to do, and I'm a whole lot crazier than him. So . . . I guess you have to ask yourself, young samurai, how far would you be willing to go to stop Saint John if he was coming after you and yours? How scary are you willing to be in order to take the heart out of the enemy? Are you willing to be the monster in the dark? Are you willing to be the boogeyman of *their* nightmares? If you can look inside your own head and see the line that you won't cross, the limit that's too far, then I can guarantee you Saint John will win. No question about it."

Until we found the crashed transport plane, we didn't know what was out there in the Ruin. We knew someone had managed to fly a jet, but that didn't tell us much.

Now we know about the American Nation.

The old government collapsed, and even though there are rumors that the president and some members of Congress went into hiding in a bunker, no one's ever heard from them again. Captain Joe Ledger told us that a big group of survivors managed to take over the city of Asheville in North Carolina. There are more than a hundred thousand people there, and at least another fifty thousand living in fortified towns near there. Joe and a bunch of soldiers cleared out the zoms, and they have teams working to clear out all the areas around the city. They took back an army base and an air force base, too, which is why they have so many weapons. And the jet. They also have Black Hawk and Apache attack helicopters. Most of that stuff is in North Carolina.

I asked him if there were helicopters and stuff in the hangars, but he didn't answer.

BENNY SAID, "I FOUND SOMETHING I THINK YOU NEED TO SEE."

"Is it a red powder?" Joe asked quickly.

"What? No. Why?"

Joe waved it away. "What've you got for me?"

Benny produced the Teambook and handed it to Joe.

The ranger stared at it for a moment, eyes bulging from his face. "Where did you find this?"

"The reaper had it in his quad. And no, I don't know where he found it. We . . . didn't really talk, you know."

"This must have come from the plane, and it definitely wasn't there when I searched it. That means it was removed before that day."

"Is that good for us?" asked Benny. "Does it mean the D-series records are around somewhere?"

"It might."

"Joe, what if the records aren't around here?"

"What do you mean?"

"I don't know . . . it just seems strange to me that one complete set of records is all that's missing from the plane. So far we haven't found that stuff, and none of the zoms was Dr. McReady. What if she was never onboard that plane?"

"The whole point was to evacuate her, kid."

"I know, but maybe something else happened. Would there be any kind of record of that?"

Joe grunted. "It's possible but unlikely. Once the plane left, McReady wouldn't have had any way of getting out of there, and my rangers have been to Hope One. She didn't stay behind."

"Are there other places she could have landed? Other bases like Sanctuary?"

"Not like Sanctuary, but there are a million places she could have landed. No way to know unless it was recorded, and I've been over every inch of that plane. . . ." His voice trailed off.

"What is it?" asked Benny.

"I might be jumping the gun here. We actually *don't* know if the plane landed anywhere else or not. There was no flight log in the cockpit, at least none that we could find. I knew all those guys. Only Luis would know, and we never found his body."

"Who?"

"Luis Ortega, the logistics coordinator. He would have maintained a record of everything. Luis was detail-oriented like that. You sneeze and he has a record of the time, the date, and the air-speed velocity. He never missed a trick."

"Wait . . . I know that name."

Benny flipped to the picture of Sergeant Luis Ortega and showed it to Joe. "Is this the guy you're talking about?"

"That's him. Luis was a big ol' boy, looked like a line-backer but he had the heart of an accountant. He was exactly the kind of miss-nothing guy you'd send when you wanted to evac a research facility. He'd bring back every last paper clip." Joe cocked an eye at Benny. "How is it you picked up on him so fast?"

Benny explained about how he'd thought he recognized the man but couldn't remember from where. "Is he here?" he asked. "I mean, is he maybe one of the zoms over on the airfield?"

Joe thought about it. "No, I don't think so. Last time I saw him was when they were loading the plane to fly up to Hope One. But . . . let me know if you remember where you saw him. If those D-series records weren't onboard, or if Doc McReady planned any other stops, maybe to drop some of her research and cargo anywhere, then Ortega would defi-nitely be the one to know all the details. That's his job." Joe grunted again.

"What?"

"I kind of wish he *was* over at the airfield. Being the logistics guy, he'd have a notebook with every detail of every movement of every person, every box, every piece of pocket lint. Ortega was totally anal-retentive. He was always mak-ing notes about stuff and shoving them into his shirt. Added them to his duty log at the end of the day."

"I also found one little notebook, but I don't think it's a duty log." Benny handed it over.

Joe leafed through it and gave a dismissive grunt. "Reaper prayer book. Might be useful as toilet paper, that's about it."

"No," said Benny, "look at the last page."

Joe flipped it over and scanned the list, and his face made an ugly shape. "Oh . . . crap."

"What's it mean?"

Joe held out the book and pointed to the first lines.

CA/R 1: 4,522

Quad: 66

CA/R 2: 19,200

Quad: 452

"R stands for reaper. CA is California."

"How do you know that?" asked Benny.

"Because there are abbreviations for Nevada and Wyoming, too. NV and WY." Joe sighed. "These are head counts of reaper armies. Looks like there are two in California, one of 4,522 and a much bigger one of 19,200. Then you have 14,795 in Nevada, 2,375 in Utah, and 8,371 in Wyoming. You were asking about how many reapers there are. This is your answer."

Benny did the math in his head. "That's 49,263. Oh my God."

"Yeah, well, we already knew we were in big trouble."

"What are the rest of those numbers? The quads . . . those are how many bikes they have?"

"Yup, and the good news is that they don't have a lot of them. Sixty-six for one group and only 452 for the big army."

"That's good news?"

Joe sighed. "Actually, come to think of it, it's not. Saint John is probably using quads to pull equipment and food wagons, but push comes to shove, he'll detach those and use the quads like light cavalry."

Benny had hoped this stuff might help Joe find the D-series notes, but instead it was quickly crushing Benny's own optimism. He almost didn't give the ranger the last piece.

"I also found this," he said reluctantly. "It's a handwritten note, and I think it's from Dr. McReady."

Joe read the note.

Mutations reported in California.
This needs to be checked out.
Field Team Five?

"What's it mean?" asked Benny.

The ranger gave him a brief, bleak stare. "It means that we have more questions than answers." Joe clicked his tongue for Grimm, who lumbered to his feet. "Listen, kid, I want to go show this to Colonel Reid. Maybe she can make something out of it."

"Who?"

"The base commander. She's my boss."

"How come I never met her? You never told me anything about—"

"There's a lot you don't know, kid, and there's a lot I'm not authorized to tell you. Now's not the time to play catch-up. Go find your girlfriend and Lilah. Let them tell you *their* story."

"Why? What happened? Is Nix okay?"

"She's not hurt," said Joe evasively. "Talk to her, talk to Lilah, and then maybe we'll all have a conversation later. I'm going over to the blockhouse. You have to promise me—swear to me—that you won't leave Sanctuary again. Not unless I'm with you."

"Sure," said Benny, though he was pretty sure he was lying to the man.

Miles and miles away . . .

"Heads up and eyes forward," called the guard in the tower. "Trade wagon's coming in."

The three fence guards glanced up at him and then followed the direction of his outthrust arm.

"Trade wagon?" wondered Tully, the oldest of the guards. "This time of day?"

His shift partner, Hooper, lifted the binoculars that hung around his neck on a leather strap and stared through the fence. The sun was almost down, and the slanting rays painted the big field and the distant tree line in shades of bloodred, vermilion, and Halloween orange.

"Trade wagon, all right," he said. "Half a day late and . . . wait . . . I think something's wrong."

The youngest of the three, a fence guard trainee, raised his own binoculars. They were an old but expensive pair that had once belonged to his father. His dad was dead, though, killed in a construction accident while helping to build a corn silo. He adjusted the focus.

"The driver's hurt," he said.

"How can you tell?" asked Hooper.

"He's bleeding," said the young man.

The older men stared and then grunted. "You got good eyes, Morgie," said Tully.

Morgie Mitchell did not acknowledge the compliment. His eyesight had qualified him as a tower guard, but he wanted to work down here on the ground. In another year they'd let him join the town watch as a cadet. And after that . . . well, when Morgie looked into the future, he saw himself sitting on a tall horse, a shotgun across his lap and a real steel *katana* slung over his shoulder in the rear fast-draw style Tom always used. That future Morgie wore a Freedom Riders sash and worked the roads from New Eden to Haven and every town in between.

For now he was only an apprentice fence guard. A job of no distinction and long hours.

Morgie was fine with that.

Now was now, and the future was something he'd get to.

The longer the shift, the less time he would have to be alone. And he didn't believe that he deserved any distinction of any kind. Not yet. He didn't want the borrowed celebrity that came from having studied with Tom Imura. That was Tom's fame.

And Tom was dead. Buried out in the Ruin near the charred bones of the evil place Tom had destroyed. Gameland.

Morgie wished he'd been there. He should have been there.

Even if it meant that he would have died there. Even an unmarked grave on that field would mean something.

Tom had changed the world that day. Everyone knew it.

Until Morgie had the age, the strength, the power to change even a splinter of the world, he'd work the jobs he could get.

He continued to study the scene that was unfolding beyond the fence.

The field between Mountainside and the forest was more than half a mile wide. It was thick with weeds except for a few select paths that laborers dressed in heavy carpet coats and football helmets kept clear. The trade roads had to be in good order or the flow of supplies into town would dry up.

The field, however, was not empty. There were zoms. There were always zoms. Sometimes only a few dozen scattered along this part of the fence, sometimes as many as two hundred. Some of them had been there since the town was created. Those were the ones whose relatives lived behind the fence; relatives who could not bring themselves to authorize a bounty hunter to quiet their beloved dead. The others were wandering zoms who had come this way following prey. Often they came in a slow, ragged line behind a trade wagon or a bounty hunter returning from the great Rot and Ruin.

Today was one of the in-between days. Morgie counted about seventy zoms out there.

The road from the forest to the gate was straight as an arrow, but the wagon wandered on and off it. At least a dozen zoms followed, and more were staggering toward the wagon, arms outstretched. It kept ahead of them only because a zombie could not lead its target or plan a path of interception. The zom always went directly for where something was at the moment, adjusting only as it moved away.

"What's that driver doing?" breathed Hooper as the wagon rolled out of the well-worn ruts and into the thick weeds.

They all stared at the wagon as it came closer. The horses were heavily protected with light carpet coats covered by a net of steel washers linked with metal wire. Their legs were wrapped in padded canvas, and their tails were bobbed. Unless the horse stopped and stood in place, a zom would never manage a bite. They kept moving forward, trail wise enough to know the route home and frightened enough of the dead to keep moving despite the erratic control from the driver.

Tully cupped his hands around his mouth. "At the gate!" he bellowed, and the team there turned toward him. "Wagon's coming in. Driver's hurt. Get the quarantine pen ready and call the field medics. C'mon, hop to it!"

The gate crew fetched their rifles, and a half-dozen apprentices snatched metal pots and spoons from where they hung on the fence. They ran fifty yards up the fence line and began banging and clanging. Most of the zoms turned toward this new and louder sound.

"Let's go bring him in," said Tully.

Hooper dropped his binoculars to let them hang and unslung the pump shotgun he carried. He jacked a round into the breach.

The wagon was a quarter mile out now and the horses were picking up speed, determined to get inside the safety of the fence line.

Tully tapped Hooper on the arm. "Let's go."

The three of them jogged over to the gate, and as soon as the crowd of zoms outside had thinned, Tully nodded for the big gates to be swung open. They started to head outside when Tully suddenly slapped a stiff forearm across Morgie's chest.

"Whoa! Not you, son."

"But I'm a—"

"You're a trainee, Morgan Mitchell," said Tully. "And all you have is a wooden sword. You stay here and let the professionals handle it."

"But—"

"Pay attention and learn something," said Hooper with a grin.

They headed out, first at a light trot. Then, as their path cleared, they ran at full speed toward the wagon.

Morgie adjusted the focus on his glasses. As the wagon drew closer, he could see the blood splashes on the man's arms and chest. He could see the pale face and dark eyes. The reins were wrapped around his hands, but those hands jerked and swung with no apparent sense.

Hooper reached the wagon first. He held his shotgun in one hand and waved toward the driver, calling to him to slow down so he could climb aboard.

The driver turned to him, and the reins slipped from his hands.

Morgie watched all this through his binoculars, and he saw the expression on the driver's face. One moment it was slack with fatigue from his serious injuries, and then as Hooper reached up toward him, the lips suddenly peeled back from bloody teeth.

"Wait!" cried Morgie. "No!"

But it was too late.

The driver flung himself from the wagon and slammed into Hooper, driving the man down to the ground in an ugly way. The impact caused Hooper to jerk the trigger, and the buckshot blasted the front of the wagon. Some of the pellets struck the flank of one of the horses. It screamed and reared and then bolted forward, spooking the other horse into instant flight. Tully tried to get out of the way, but he never had a chance as steel-shod hooves ground him into the dirt. His screams were as shrill as a heron's until the wheels crushed him to silence.

The horses raced toward the gate in full panicked flight with the wagon bouncing and jouncing behind them. The three gate guards gawped in surprise and horror, and they were two seconds too late in trying to close the gates. The horses smashed into them, flinging all three men into the air like rag dolls.

Morgie threw himself to one side. He rolled, as Tom had taught him, and rose to the balls of his feet, knees bent, sword in his hands. As Tom had taught him.

The back of the wagon was splashed with blood, and the door hung open on a single twisted hinge. Shapes moved inside the wagon. As Morgie watched, they moved with dreadful slowness into the dying light. Pale white and bright red and the utter black of empty eyes. Traders, four of them. Big men who spent their lives working the Ruin to bring goods and supplies from the Rat Pack scavengers to the Nine Towns. They were covered with bites and the marks of violence.

Maybe one of them had been bitten out in the Ruin and the others had taken him into the wagon to try and treat him. Or maybe they'd all been walking beside the wagon to lighten the burden for the horses when zoms had attacked. Perhaps one had been bitten but hadn't told his fellows because a bite was a death sentence and he wanted to keep every last bit of life he had left.

There was no way to know.

There was no time left to care.

They boiled out of the back of the wagon and threw themselves at Morgie.

Part 2

The Storm Lands

"A ship is safe in harbor, but that's not what ships are for."

WILLIAM G. T. SHEDD

One of the infected wild boars got inside the gates today. Two of the soldiers from the bridge chased it on quads and shot it. I saw them dragging the carcass into one of the hangars on the other side of the trench.

What do they want with a dead zombie boar?

I asked a couple of the monks, but they always say the same thing: "We do not speak of that, sister."

ONE MONTH AGO . . .

Sister Sun followed the Red Brother out of the hot Nevada sun and into the cloying darkness of an old convenience store. The wire racks had long since been picked clean, and the floor was littered with animal droppings, bones, and trash. There were splashes of blood on the floor and walls, and Sister Sun imagined she could almost hear the screams of heretics who had been brought in here to be interrogated by the saint. The desert outside was filled with blind and skinless dead who wandered without purpose.

Behind the counter, Saint John sat on a stool, carefully cleaning his many knives. His fingers were long and deft, and if she watched them too closely, Sister Sun knew she could be hypnotized by them.

The saint did not look up. "How pleasant of you to join me, my sister."

She bowed. "Honored One."

"Mother Rose is back, did you know?"

"Yes, Honored One."

"I am told that she visited the Shrine of the Fallen yesterday."

"Yes."

He glanced up finally, and there was amusement in his eyes. An almost prankish merriment.

"I am told that she was satisfied that the seals of the Shrine were intact," he said, "exactly as she left them."

Sister Sun nodded.

The saint glanced past her to the killers of the Red Brotherhood who stood silent and vigilant by the door. "Leave us," he said. "No one enters until I say otherwise."

They nodded and, quiet as ghosts, left the store.

Saint John let silence settle over things for a moment. His clever hands worked steadily with cloth and oil and a small pick to dig out even the slightest flake of drying blood from the skinning knife he held.

"You have had one month with the materials from the heretic Dr. McReady," he said.

"Yes, Honored One."

"Tell me."

Sister Sun took a breath to steady her nerves. It was not fear that made her tremble. It was a terrible excitement.

"As I have said many times, Honored One," she began, "science is like a knife. Used by a heretic, it is a thing of great evil. Used in the cause of righteousness, it is a holy weapon of great power."

"And do you believe that you have discovered a way to turn these evil things to holy purpose?"

"Yes," she said. "I have."

He set down his knife. "Explain it to me."

She did. It did not take very long. Saint John had a first-class intellect. And it was a cold mind, capable of separating rational assessment from emotions and religious passion. Sister Sun told him what she'd discovered in those notes, and how it coincided with theories she had been working on prior to kneeling to kiss the knife and join the Night Church. She explained what she'd learned from those notes, and she outlined what she did not yet know.

"You say that the notes include a formula to cure the Reaper Plague?" asked Saint John.

"A treatment," she corrected. "But it amounts to the same thing. McReady was poised to eradicate the plague and all the gray people. But she apparently went elsewhere to complete her research."

"Could you create a countermeasure to this 'treatment'?" asked the saint.

Sister Sun chewed her lip, then gave a slow shake of her head. "No. Not as such," she said. "But I could take her research and turn it to serve us."

"How?"

Sister Sun told him.

"What would be required for you to do this?"

She said, "I need a lab. Or at least basic equipment."

"We're in a desert."

She shook her head. "There's a biological testing facility less than two hundred miles from here. I can use that. It would have a portable generator, which could be repaired and refueled. With ten reapers as assistants, I can have the lab running inside two weeks."

He considered this, his lips pursed.

"And if you had fifty reapers as assistants—how quickly could you get it running?"

She stared at him. At his dark and glittering eyes. At his smile.

Then she smiled too.

BENNY LOOKED FOR NIX THE REST OF THE DAY BUT DIDN'T FIND HER.

While he was walking back to try the mess hall again, he caught movement out of the corner of his eye and turned to see a blue balloon floating on the hot air. It was on the far side of the trench, though, and the zoms all raised their dead eyes to stare at it. The balloon had barely any lift and bounced from one to another of the zoms, touching the tops of heads, rebounding from clumsy fingers.

It must have escaped from Eve, he thought.

Then it occurred to him—how was it able to float at all?

Benny knew about helium from Peppertoes, the clown at the harvest fair in Mountainside. He had a big tank of helium—an item that must have cost him a fair percentage of the ration dollars he was paid by the town to perform for the kids. Every year Peppertoes would give a helium-filled balloon to the kid who grew the biggest sweet pepper. Morgie's cousin Bethy won twice.

But who around here had a tank of helium?

He watched the balloon bounce and bounce, and then he saw a zom make a successful grab at it. The blue orb vanished into the crowd of the dead, and a second later there was a loud *pop!*

Benny frowned at the zoms, then scanned the sky for more balloons. There were none. And when he looked over at the playground, the children were gone. Siesta time?

Benny shrugged and forgot the balloon as he resumed his search for Nix.

Finally he asked Sister Hannahlily if she knew anything, and the nun confirmed that Nix and Lilah had been attacked by the living dead. From the disapproving look on the nun's face, Benny knew that the attacking zoms had been quieted. The way-station monks and nuns opposed violence in all forms, especially against the "Children of Lazarus." They considered it sinful to harm the mindless dead. She did not say as much, but her feelings were written on her pinched features.

"Is she okay?" asked Benny urgently. "Nix. And Lilah, too. Are they okay?"

The nun hesitated. "They were not physically injured."

"But—?"

"But they were both very upset. Perhaps the weight of their actions was too much for them."

And maybe bright blue monkeys will fly out of my butt, thought Benny, but he left it unsaid. "Where are they?"

"In the women's dormitory," said Sister Hannahlily.

"Can you—"

"They've had a hard day, young brother," said the nun. "If you care for them, allow each of the girls adequate time to reflect on her actions, and to look inward for forgiveness from God."

Benny tried fifteen different ways to convince Sister Hannahlily that he needed to get a message to the girls. He might as well have been trying to convince a zom to juggle and tell jokes.

"Perhaps an evening of quiet reflection and prayer would do you some good as well," said the nun. With that she turned and headed toward the chapel tent for evening prayers.

Benny went to the women's dormitory doorway, but the nun on guard there was a gargoyle-faced bruiser named, of all things, Sister Daisy. She listened to Benny without a flicker of expression, then told him to go away. She did not actually threaten physical harm—she was after all, a nun—but there was such palpable menace in her voice that Benny felt himself dwindle. He crept away.

He ate alone and went outside for a walk along the trench. There were so many things to consider and process. As the sun fell behind the mountains, the desert transformed from hot tan and burning red to a soft, cool purple. Benny came upon a huddled shape seated alone on the edge of the trench. He was ten feet away when he heard the sound of muffled sobs.

"Riot—?"

The figure straightened, and Riot turned a puffed and tear-streaked face toward him. She sniffed. "Hey, Benny."

Benny came and sat down next to her. "You okay?"

She sniffed again. "'Bout as good as I look, I suppose."

"Can I help?"

"Not unless y'all got a time machine or a magic wand."

"I wish."

They watched the sky darken from purple to bottom-less black. Stars ignited one after the other, and soon the ceiling of the universe burned with a million points of light.

"Your mom . . . ?" Benny ventured.

But Riot shook her head. "That's part of it."

"Eve?"

"That poor little girl," Riot said in a tiny voice that was too fragile to hold back the tide of sobs.

"Shhh," soothed Benny, "she's safe now. She'll be okay."

"No, she won't," said Riot. "No . . . oh, Benny, I can't stand it. She's so lost. She's all alone in the dark and I can't reach her. No one can. They killed her. Damn them to hell, but they killed that sweet little girl."

The sobs overwhelmed Riot, and the sound of her weeping came close to breaking Benny's heart. He wrapped an arm around her and pulled her against his chest. He wanted to say something—anything—that might pull Riot back from her pain, but really . . . what was there to say? Her mother had been a monster and was now a zombie. Eve's mother and father had been murdered, and Eve was so badly broken that there might not be a way to mend her.

She's all alone in the dark and I can't reach her.

Those words were all the uglier for being true.

Sometimes there aren't words, Benny knew. Sometimes there are hurts so deep that they exist in a country that has no spoken language, a place where all landscapes are blighted and no sun ever shines. Benny had left his footprints in the dust of that place. It was on the day Tom brought him to

Sunset Hollow, to the house Benny had lived in as a baby, to the place where his parents waited, year after interminable year, tied to kitchen chairs. Tom could have quieted their parents years ago, but he'd waited because he knew that one day his little brother would need to have a hand in the closure of their shared pain. That day—that terrible, terrible day—Tom had taken his knife and quieted Benny's dad, Tom's stepfather. Then he'd given the knife to Benny. It was an act of kindness and of respect that felt like the worst betrayal, the worst punishment.

Holding Riot, he closed his eyes and was right back at that moment with everything as clear and precise as a razor cut.

Benny stood behind the zombie, and it took six or seven tries before he could bring himself to touch her. Eventually he managed it. Tom guided him, touching the spot where the knife had to go. Benny put the tip of the knife in place.

"When you do it," said Tom, "do it quick."

"Can they feel pain?"

"I don't know. But you can. I can. Do it quick."

Benny closed his eyes. He took a ragged breath and said, "I love you, Mom."

He did it quick.

And it was over.

He dropped the knife and Tom gathered him up and they sank down to their knees together on the kitchen floor, crying so loud that the sound threatened to break the world.

The way Riot wept now was her passport to that country. Nix had been there too. And Lilah. Each of them had wandered alone through that land, refugees among the war-torn devastation of their innocence.

Benny did not tell Riot that it was okay, because it wasn't.

He didn't tell her that this would pass. The moment would, but the scars would always be there. It was the thing that would always identify them as travelers through the storm lands of the soul.

On a hot afternoon Sister Sun staggered out into the sunlight. Saint John and the army had been gone now for weeks, marching to California to find nine towns filled with heretics. By the time Sister Sun had returned from the remote lab two hundred miles away, the saint had already left. She felt empty without him; he was a great source of strength for her.

Her Red Brotherhood guardsmen snapped to attention. The nearest of them saw how unsteady she was on her feet and rushed to catch her as Sister Sun's knees buckled.

"Sister—" he began, but she cut him off.

"No, I'm fine . . . I just need to sit down. Send a runner to find Brother Peter. At once. Good. And some water. Thanks. . . ."

She sat in the shade under a Joshua tree and sipped water from an aluminum canteen. Her hands shook so badly that the water sloshed against her lips and splashed onto the front of her shirt, darkening the black cloth and soaking the angel wings.

"Brother Peter is coming up the hill," said the reaper who'd helped her sit.

Sister Sun looked up to see the unsmiling young man walking toward her at a brisk pace, his own guards fanned out behind him.

"Are you unwell, my sister?" he called as he jogged the last few yards. Sister Sun grabbed his wrist and pulled him close.

"Send them away," she whispered.

Peter snapped his fingers and the Red Brothers immediately retreated out of earshot but within visual range.

"What is it, sister?" asked Peter, his tone gentle and filled with concern. "Is it the cancer . . . ?"

"No," she said, a smile forming on her lips, "it's not me. It's nothing wrong."

"Then—?"

She clutched two handfuls of his shirt with desperate excitement. "I figured it out, Peter," she cried.

"You . . ."

"I know how to kill them."

"Kill who?"

Sister Sun could feel the glorious madness blossom in her eyes. And from Peter's reaction, she knew he could see it too.

"Everyone," she said. "I figured out how to kill . . . *everyone*."

The day we found Sanctuary we also saw the jet. It landed on the airfield, but by the time we reached the base, the plane had been shut down, the lights and engine turned off. We never saw the pilot or crew.

Every time they bring me over to the blockhouse for an interview, I ask where the jet's crew is, and they never tell me. All they'll say is that they're being debriefed—whatever that means.

Joe won't tell us either.

What are they hiding?

36

"HOW DO YOU FEEL TODAY?" ASKED THE VOICE.

"I've developed an irresistible hunger for human flesh," said Benny.

There was a long, long silence. The interview cubicle was so dark that Benny could barely see the wall-mounted speaker. He bent close to listen. He could hear the interviewer breathing.

"Hello?"

The voice said, "When you say that you've developed a—"

"Oh, for God's sake, it was a joke."

After a moment the voice said, "A 'joke'?"

"Yes. I'm sure even you lug nuts have heard that word before."

"Mr. Imura . . . why would you make a joke about something like that?"

"Why not?"

There was no answer.

Benny knocked on the speaker. "Hey—you still there?"

"How do you feel today?" asked the voice, as if the conversation was just starting.

Benny sighed. "With my hands."

"Mr. Imura . . ."

"Why don't you tell me what you're doing to help my friend Chong."

"We're doing everything we can."

"Is he getting better?"

"He's stabilized."

"Is he getting better?" Benny asked again, more slowly, over-enunciating each word.

"We . . . are not sure we can expect an improvement at this time."

"Then let me out of here."

"What?"

"Let me out. We're done."

"Mr. Imura," said the voice, "you are being immature about this."

"Immature?" Benny laughed. "I went out to that plane yesterday to look for those stupid research notes. I didn't see you out there."

"We have to stay inside the quarantine of the lab."

"I didn't see your soldiers out there either. In fact, you know who I did see out there? A freaking reaper. And you know what I did? I freaking killed him. That's what I did. You want to hide behind your stupid wall inside this freaking bunker and call me immature?" Benny kicked the speaker as hard as he could. The little grille buckled. "You're not doing anything for me or Chong or anyone else, so tell me why I should help you? Tell me what we're accomplishing with these little chats of ours. All you're doing is wasting my time and pissing me off."

He gave the speaker another kick.

Almost three full minutes passed before the door opened.

In that time the voice did not return, did not ask another question.

Benny got up and stepped out into the hot sunlight. A monk was there to guide him across the bridge.

No way I'm going back in there, he told himself. *I'd rather be stuck in a zombie pit at Gameland with my hands tied behind my back.*

Suddenly that fragment of broken memory from yesterday skittered across his mind again.

He froze.

"Brother—?" inquired the monk, but Benny held up his hand.

"Gimme a sec . . ."

He closed his eyes and repeated what he'd just thought. There was something there.

Zombie pit.

Yes.

Sergeant Ortega. A big soldier.

In a zombie pit?

Yes.

No. Not exactly. Not a zombie pit.

Not at Gameland. Benny was sure of that much. Sergeant Ortega.

He could see the face.

Not a living face. Dead.

Definitely zommed out.

But also definitely Sergeant Ortega. No doubt about it.

In a pit.

Zombie.

Pit.

What other pits were there with zombies in them?

And suddenly he had it.

His eyes snapped open.

He remembered exactly where he had seen Sergeant Luis Ortega. And if he was right, then the man—the zom that had been that man—would still be there.

Benny bolted from beside the monk and ran as fast as he could across the bridge.

37

BENNY FOUND NIX IN THE MESS HALL. SHE WAS SITTING WITH RIOT, THEIR heads bent together as they spoke.

"Nix!" he called from halfway across the room.

Her head jerked up and she looked around. Then she immediately got up and started to turn away, to leave. Benny ran to her and caught her wrist.

"Nix—I heard about yesterday. Are you all right?"

"Yes. We're both okay."

"Thank God!" he said breathlessly. "Listen, I need to talk to you."

"Benny—no, I can't . . . I . . ."

He gently pulled her around to face him. Her eyes were red, as if she'd been crying a long time, and her whole face was pink and puffy. Her scar and her freckles always grew darker when she was upset, and now they were very dark.

"Listen, Nix—"

She looked up at him with such pain in her green eyes that it stalled him. "I *saw* him."

"You saw . . . Chong?"

"Riot and I went over yesterday. They let us see him."

Benny half turned to see the look on Riot's face. She hadn't told him that last night. There were other storms raging through her life, and Benny held no grudge.

Before he could say anything, Nix flung herself into his arms and clung to him with all her strength.

"Oh, Benny . . . he looked so bad," she wailed. "He looked so sick. So lost."

Her words disintegrated into sobs that were so deep, so shattered, that it silenced the entire mess hall. Those sobs were every bit as terrible as Riot's had been.

Benny enfolded her in his arms and held her close. Her body was furnace hot against his; her tears burned like acid. She trembled with the kind of deep grief and pain that went all the way down to the core. Benny understood that kind of anguish. He held her and kissed her hair.

The monks at the tables turned away. A few of them gave him small smiles and encouraging nods, but they said nothing and did not interfere.

Benny led Nix back to her table and they sat down together, awkwardly, still clinging to each other. Riot got up and came around behind them, wrapped her arms around them both, and laid her cheek down on the tops of their heads.

Eventually the storm passed, as all storms pass.

Nix gradually straightened and pulled away. Riot sat down on her side of the table. Everyone used the napkins to wipe their streaming noses and eyes.

"Nix, I—," Benny began, but she touched her fingers to his chest.

"Please, Benny, let me say something first."

"Okay."

She dabbed at her eyes. "What I said yesterday about Chong . . ."

Benny nodded but said nothing.

"Please, don't ever think—"

"No," he cut her off. "Listen to me, Nix, you don't need to say this, and I don't need to hear it. We . . . kind of just said it all anyway."

Riot said, "See, I was right about you, Benny. You *are* smarter than you look."

It was a lame joke, but it broke the bubble of tension that had been expanding to crowd the moment.

"I'm sorry," Nix said. "I needed to say that much. I really am."

Benny kissed her.

Nix kissed him back.

Riot made gagging sounds. "Y'all better get a room or name the baby after me."

Benny made a covert and very rude gesture.

Then he leaned back to catch his breath. "Listen," he said, "I need to tell you a bunch of things, but first I want to hear everything about yesterday. All I really heard, Nix, was that you and Lilah got jumped by some zoms. . . ."

Nix told him the full story. Benny's heart sank.

"Fast zoms? Four of them?"

"Three fast ones and one that might not have been," corrected Nix.

"Even so," said Riot, "that's crooked math. Y'all were lucky to walk out of there with skin still on your bones."

"Tell me about it," Nix said, rolling her eyes.

"What was that bit with the red powder?" asked Benny.

"I don't know," Nix admitted. "I showed Joe and he kind of freaked. I haven't seen him since."

"Wonder what it is," said Riot.

"Listen," Benny said, changing the subject. "I had a crazy day too. I need to tell you guys, and then I need your help with something. I'd ask Joe, but nobody knows where he is and we're running out of time. So . . . I need both of you to help me do something incredibly dangerous and incredibly stupid."

"Dangerous and stupid?" asked Nix, and her pretty face wore its first smile in over a day. "Sounds like one of your plans."

"I'm on the hook already," said Riot. "I haven't done anything dangerous or stupid in weeks. I'm about due."

He explained everything that had happened yesterday. The story of the fight with the reaper wiped the smiles away. The account of the Teambook raised their eyebrows. The tally of the reaper forces stole the color from their faces. But the thing that filled their eyes with fear was when Benny explained where he had seen Sergeant Ortega.

"You want us to go *where*?" demanded Riot. "You're touched in the head, boy."

"You're absolutely out of your mind," said Nix. "I mean seriously, Benny, you're deranged."

"I know, I know," he said. "But are you in?"

Nix and Riot stared at him and then at each other, and then at him again.

"We're in," said Nix.

38

MILES AND MILES AWAY . . .

Captain Strunk sat on an overturned bucket, resting heavily with his forearms on his knees. The trade wagon stood ten feet away. On the ground, covered with pieces of canvas, lay four bodies. Fifty feet away, just inside the fence line, lay three more. All of them had been quieted.

Two figures stood in front of him. A short man and a tall boy.

The man was Deputy Gorman, Strunk's second in command.

The boy was Morgie Mitchell.

On the ground between Morgie and Captain Strunk was a length of wood. A bokken. Smeared with blood, broken in two.

"I checked him, Cap," said Gorman. "No bites, no scratches."

Strunk nodded.

"I told you that I wasn't hurt," said Morgie. "You could have taken my word for it."

"You fought four zoms with a stick, kid," said Strunk. "I wouldn't take anyone's word that they did that without a scratch."

Morgie said nothing.

"Tom taught you all those moves?"

Morgie nodded.

"You ever fight a zom before?"

"No."

"You ever fight anyone before?"

Morgie shrugged. "Nothing serious."

In his mind, though, he remembered his last act of violence. No one had been physically hurt, but it had been a terrible moment. Shoving Benny and knocking him down, right there in Morgie's yard. The day Benny left town. The day Morgie had killed his friendship with Benny. And Nix. Chong, too. The day he lost all his friends.

Nothing serious. Except that it ended everything.

Strunk said, "The tower guard tells me you kept your head when those zoms came rushing out of that wagon."

Morgie shrugged.

"He says that after you took down the zoms from the wagon, you went out to help Tully and Hooper."

"I wasn't fast enough. By the time I got out there they were already dead."

"'Wasn't fast enough,'" echoed Gorman. "Jeez."

"The tower guard says that you quieted Tully and got Hooper inside the gate while he was still alive."

"I didn't quiet him, though," said Morgie. "The other guards—"

"I know," interrupted Strunk. "I'm not criticizing you. Just laying out the facts."

Morgie said nothing.

"Your supervisor tells me that you only took the fence job because you were too young for the town watch."

"Yes, sir."

"How young?"

"I'll be sixteen in eight months."

Strunk glanced at Gorman, who smiled faintly and shook his head.

A shadow fell across Morgie, and he turned to see someone standing just behind him, a person he had only ever seen on the painted fronts of Zombie Cards. The man wasn't tall, but he was powerfully built, with a shaved head and a gray goatee. He had dark-brown skin and he wore a red Freedom Riders sash across his chest. He wore a pair of matched machetes in low-slung scabbards that hung from crossed leather belts.

Morgie's mouth went absolutely dry.

The man nodded to Strunk. "This is the boy, Cap?"

"This is him. Morgan Mitchell."

The newcomer studied Morgie. "You trained with Tom."

"Yes, sir," Morgie said.

"You friends with Tom's brother? You one of Benny's friends?"

The question was worse than a knife in Morgie's guts. It took him a long time before he trusted his voice enough to answer the man.

"Benny was my best friend." His voice almost—*almost*—broke. "I wish I'd gone with him and Tom."

The man nodded. "From what I heard just now, Morgie, Tom would be proud of you. Benny, too."

Morgie turned away to hide his eyes.

The man put his hand on Morgie's shoulder. "I don't think you have a future in the town watch."

Morgie snapped his head around and stared in hurt and horror at the man. But he was smiling. So were Strunk and Gorman.

"I think you need to come and train with me," said the man.

"W-what . . . ?"

"Do you know who I am?"

"Yes, sir. You're Solomon Jones."

"I'm building something important. Something Tom would approve of," said Solomon. "And I'm looking for some real warriors."

Morgie stared at him.

Solomon held out a muscular hand.

"Want to join me?"

THERE WAS ONE THING THEY HAD TO DO FIRST, AND IT WAS NIX WHO SAID it. They stood in the shade behind the mess hall.

"We have to tell Lilah," Nix said, and Benny winced.

"Good luck with that," murmured Riot.

Any conversation with Lilah was difficult. The Lost Girl had spent many years living alone and wild in the Ruin, killing zoms and preying on the bounty hunters working for Charlie Pink-eye and the Motor City Hammer. During those long years she had had no personal contact at all. No conversations, no interactions. Not even a hug, a handshake, or a kind word; and in that social vacuum she'd grown strange. Even now, after months of living with the Chong family in Mountainside, training with Tom, and traveling with Nix, Benny, and Chong on their search for the jet, Lilah was still strange. It was impossible to predict exactly how she would react to anything, though any bet laid a little heavier on the possibility of a violent reaction had a better chance of a return. For a while she'd started coming out of her shell when, against all logic and probability, she and Chong had fallen in love—but with Chong's injury and infection, Lilah had gotten stranger still. She rarely spoke, and when she did, it was brief and terse. Benny doubted that he'd exchanged as many as two hundred words with Lilah in the last three weeks.

"She won't want to leave here," said Nix. "I think she believes that the only reason they haven't quieted Chong is because they're afraid of how she'll react."

"That ain't altogether a stupid fear," said Riot. "When grown men with guns are afraid of a girl with a spear, then there's something to take a close look at."

Benny nodded, though he had a separate concern about Lilah. He was afraid of what she would do to herself if Chong died. Lilah was emotionally damaged and was caught in a prolonged anger phase of the grief process. Her little sister had been killed, her guardian had been murdered, Tom had been murdered, and now Chong lingered in a twilight between life and death. Benny didn't know how much more life could push Lilah before she snapped. He'd said as much to Nix, and when he glanced at her, he could see it in her eyes. Neither of them said it aloud—Riot was a friend, but she wasn't yet part of their family.

"I'll tell her," said Nix.

Benny shook his head. "If she gets even a whiff of—"

"Of what? Of me saying that Chong should be quieted? That was before, Benny. I said that before I went down and looked at him."

"I'm just saying . . ."

"I got your back, Red," said Riot. "Question is . . . where is she? She's usually walking the trench line, but I don't—"

There was a soft sound above them, and they suddenly turned and looked up to see Lilah perched like a hunting hawk on the raised corrugated metal shutter over the mess hall window. She peered down at them from between her bent knees, and only the tip of her spear rose above the shadows into the sunlight. Lilah's eyes looked as black and bottomless as those of a skull.

"Lilah . . . ," gasped Nix.

Benny instinctively shifted to stand between Nix and Lilah. "Listen, Lilah, I can explain."

The Lost Girl hopped forward and straightened her lithe body as she dropped to the ground. It was a ten-foot drop, but she landed easily, though there was a twitch of a grimace on her tight mouth—the only concession to the wound she'd suffered less than a month ago. She'd badly gashed her cheek and jaw while escaping from a white rhinoceros and a field of crippled zoms. Injury or not, the expression in her eyes was fierce. Deadly.

"God," breathed Nix. Riot pulled her slingshot. Benny's hand darted toward the handle of his sword.

Lilah walked forward a few paces, ignoring Riot. She got to within inches of Benny.

"Move," she said.

"Lilah," Benny said, holding his ground, "you don't understand—"

But it was Nix who moved. She stepped out from behind Benny, pushing him gently out of the way. She was much shorter than Lilah and more than a year younger. Her weapons were holstered and sheathed, and her hands were empty.

"What did you hear?" she asked.

"Everything." Without the shadows to mask her face, Lilah's eyes were the color of molten honey. Hot, but without any trace of sweetness. "You wanted to quiet Chong."

Nix took a breath. Benny could see that her hands were shaking.

"Yes," she said.

"Is that why you went to see him?"

"No."

"Then why?"

"Because he's my friend. Because I love him. Because I wanted to see for myself."

Lilah drew a slender knife from a thigh sheath. "This is Chong's knife."

"I know."

"They won't let me see him," said Lilah.

"I know."

"I *can* see him. I can get in there. You know that?"

"Yes."

Benny and Riot nodded too. None of them doubted that Lilah could find a way into that building. People might die in the process, but she could get in.

"No one quiets Chong but me." Lilah's voice was a deadly whisper. "You understand?"

"Yes," said Nix, her voice small.

Lilah looked at the others. "You all understand? No one but me?"

Benny nodded. So did Riot.

Lilah raised the knife so that sunlight glanced from it and painted Nix's face in bright light.

"You tell me," said Lilah, "do I need to use this today? Is Chong lost? Is he gone?"

Nix slowly shook her head.

"Say it," growled Lilah. "Do I need to kill my town boy?"

"No," said Nix. "God . . . no."

Lilah's eyes roved over her face for a long time. Then she slipped the knife back into its leather sheath. Then she nodded. A single nod, small and curt.

"If he has to die . . . you tell me."

Nix was unable to speak, so she gave her own single nod.

Lilah looked at Benny. "You too. Tell me if I have to go in there."

"I will," said Benny. "But . . . maybe we don't have to."

And he told her about his plan.

She was in too.

Once upon a time the woman had been a scientist, part of the Relativistic Astrophysics Group at the Jet Propulsion Lab in Pasadena, California. Now she spent day after day blowing up balloons.

This was her ninth straight day of it, and the strain of taking in huge breaths and forcing the air into the balloons was really getting to her. She was light-headed all the time now, and planets and galaxies seemed to swirl around her head.

She sat in the shadowy mouth of a cave. At least they gave her plenty of water and a stool. And runners came to her three times a day to bring food for her and the two other people working with her, a former Los Angeles Realtor and an actor who had won two Emmys for a show that was on HBO before the dead rose and ate his audience. The Realtor blew up balloons too. His face was red from effort, his eyes dark with disillusionment.

Like the woman, the other two were useless people. Neither of them could fight. They were lousy hunters. Their survival had been the result of no qualities they possessed. Each of them had been helped through the apocalypse. All three of them were refugees. The scientist even believed—deep down in the secret place in her heart—that none of them knelt to kiss the knife because they believed in anything but a sure way to live through the moment. None of them had ever killed anyone. At least the scientist knew she had not. After testing her in combat training, the reaper-trainer had dismissed her in disgust and assigned her to the "support legion."

That was a kind label for the growing mass of reapers who had no useful skills beyond cooking, sanitation, scavenging, and, apparently, blowing up balloons.

She finished the balloon and handed it off to the actor, who perched on a taller stool beside a rusted metal tank. He took a hose, fitted the mouth of the balloon around it, and squeezed a plastic trigger. There was a tiny burst of sound—the sharp hiss of gas under pressure—and the balloon lifted a bit. There was not enough helium in it to make it float; merely enough to let it bounce as if weightless. He tied it off, half turned on his stool, and gave the balloon a light tap, which sent it bouncing deeper into the cave where it bumped up against the thousands of others.

When the scientist reached for another balloon, her stubby fingernails scraped the bare bottom of the box that was positioned beside her.

"I'm out," she said.

Another reaper, a child with a burn-withered leg and melted face, stood up from the shadows at the far side of the cave mouth. She pulled a black plastic trash bag with her and held it open for the scientist, who reached in and took a handful of small plastic bags. Fifty colored balloons in each bag. The scientist and the burned girl worked together to tear open the bags and dump the contents into the box. When it was filled, the girl limped back to her spot.

The scientist took a long drink of water and squinted out at the sun-bleached landscape. Such a terrible place. From where she sat, hidden in the shadows, she could see the tall metal spires of the siren towers of Sanctuary.

She picked up another balloon, stretched it, took a deep breath, and blew her air into the bright red rubber.

THE MONK GUARDING THE QUADS SAW THE FOUR OF THEM COMING AND immediately began shaking his head as he walked to meet them.

"Captain Ledger left express orders that no one is to take a quad without his permission."

Benny glanced at Nix. "Do you see Captain Ledger anywhere?"

"No."

"You see him, Riot?"

"I don't see hide nor hair of that big ol' boy anywhere."

"Lilah?"

Her answer was a sour grunt.

"The captain was very specific about it," insisted the monk. "He mentioned Brother Benjamin in particular. Under no circumstances were you to take a quad."

Benny patted the monk on the arm. "I believe you'll find that was more of a suggestion than a rule."

The monk sputtered at them, but there was nothing he could do. Nix gave him a smile as bright as all the flowers in the world. Riot winked at him. They unslung their gear and began looking through the compartments of their quads.

They had food, carpet coats, their entire remaining supply of cadaverine, every weapon they possessed, and a first-aid kit. Benny wore his sword slung over his shoulder the same way Tom used to wear it. Nix had *Dojigiri*, the Monster Cutter—the ancient sword given her by Joe—in her belt, and Tom's old Smith & Wesson .38 revolver snugged into a shoulder holster. Riot wore her bandoliers of firecrackers, a Raven Arms .25 automatic in a belt holster, various knives, and her favorite weapon—a sturdy pre–First Night slingshot and a full pouch of sharp stones and metal ball bearings. Lilah had weapons everywhere, including a nine-millimeter pistol. They each wore vests with many small pockets crammed with other survival gear.

The monk gave up trying to physically stand between them and the bikes and began fretting over them. He double-checked their food and water and admonished them about using violence against any of God's creatures, living or dead.

Nix slid into the saddle of her quad, a fiery red Kawasaki. "Brother," she said, "we don't ever want to hurt anyone. We're actually trying to *save* lives."

The monk studied her. "Seriously?"

Riot held up a hand. "Swear to God."

That put a puzzled look on the monk's face, and it was still there when they fired up their quads and drove away.

They passed through the chain-link gate, and Riot took the lead. Even though Benny, Nix, and Lilah knew the way, Riot was the expert; she knew every inch of this country. As soon as they cleared the twisted maze that was the hidden path leading from the open desert to Sanctuary, Riot raised her hand over her head and swung it in a circle. They immediately revved their engines, and the four of them burned their way back toward the dying forest.

They drove fast, and except for the roar of their engines, they traveled in silence. Benny kept reviewing everything that had happened since yesterday morning: Chong, the strange interviews with the scientists, the fight with Nix, the ugly truth about the missing D-series files, the fight with the reaper who used to be a soldier, the discovery of the Teambook, the conversation with Joe, and the realization that he knew where Sergeant Ortega might be. No . . . where Sergeant Ortega *was*.

They paused once on a rocky hill overlooking a big swath of the forest. The plateau with the crashed transport plane was off to the east. The densest part of the forest was north and west of them. A thin man-made stream that was part of the golf course's original landscape design cut through the terrain, and from this distance they could catch glimpses of it as a blue ribbon winding haphazardly through the trees. Farther west was a big field that had once been a fairway. A ruptured irrigation pipe had carved a channel through the field, undercutting the foliage to create a long, crooked ravine that was surprisingly deep. The ravine was in a natural depression in the landscape, so Benny figured that what little rain runoff there was had helped to cut the channel through the loose and sandy soil.

Benny pointed.

"There," he said, though they all knew it. It was the place where Benny and Nix had first met Riot. That first meeting had been strange. Riot had used the sharp bangs from her firecrackers to scare off a pride of hungry lions that had trapped

Benny and the others. The rescue hadn't been a kindness—Riot's true goal had been to save Eve, who Benny had found in that very ravine. Eve was part of the group of refugees fleeing a reaper massacre; Riot was taking them to Sanctuary when Eve went missing. Oddly, it was an attack by reapers that had allowed Benny and Nix to escape Riot and her companions. That had been another very strange day.

Nix took her binoculars out of their holder and surveyed the landscape, shook her head, and handed them to Lilah.

"See anything?" asked Benny.

"No," said Lilah.

Benny wasn't much relieved. Zoms were surprisingly hard to spot in a landscape like this. Unless they were actively pursuing prey, they tended to stand still. Absolutely still, with none of the small, reflexive, or habitual gestures all humans make after a while.

Riot took a long pull on her canteen, then cocked an eye at Benny. "Are y'all sure about this?"

"Pretty much."

Riot grinned. "'Pretty much' ain't as comforting as y'all might think."

"It's what I have," confessed Benny.

"Fair enough."

"Stop talking," said Lilah. She gunned her engine, crested the rise, and went roaring down the slope.

"Fair enough," Riot said again. She winked at Benny and plunged after Lilah.

Benny cast a meaningful look at Nix.

"He'll be there," said Nix, but her words were pitched in exactly the tone people use when they're trying to help you brace for a disappointment. She aimed her quad toward the ravine.

The voice inside Benny's head said, *On the plus side, if this works, people might stop thinking you're a half-wit.*

"Oh . . . shut up."

Benny gave the Honda some gas and raced downhill to catch up.

If I was in charge, I'd do things differently.

Ever since I was ten I've been collecting every bit of information I could about zombies. How they move, how they attack. I've talked to every single member of the fence guards and all of the members of the town watch. I talked to everyone whose job it is to protect the town against the living dead. And the thing is . . . they're doing it wrong.

They think that the fence and the watch-towers are the right way to go because we've never been hit with a big wave of zoms. Tom said that it's because zombies won't go uphill unless they're actively following prey. Mountainside is way up in the Sierra Nevadas. That's why there are so many more zoms in the valleys and lowlands. So . . . it's not that our defenses are all that great, it's just that we're lucky because of where we are.

What if that changes? There are faster zoms now, we've seen them. We fought some of them. And since leaving town we've seen zoms moving in flocks. The reapers can even make the zoms move in flocks or herds.

If a big wave of zoms attacked, the chain-link fence wouldn't stop them.

I've read so many books about fortifications and defenses. From ancient Rome to medieval sieges, to the Napoleonic wars to the tunnel wars in Vietnam. There are a lot of ways to make better defenses. The people in town are too lazy to be smart.

If I was in charge I'd do things differently.

I'd do them better.

THEY PARKED THEIR QUADS AT THE FAR SIDE OF THE FIELD, TURNED OFF the engines, dismounted, and then ran quickly and lightly through the shadows under the trees. They found a good spot several hundred yards away from the edge of the clearing, and there they stopped to observe the place where they'd parked. Lilah touched a finger to her lips, but they were all cautious enough to make no sound. Benny remembered one of Tom's lessons about stealth and observation. *When in doubt, observe, listen, wait, and evaluate.*

The roar of their quads had been an unavoidable noise, which meant that they had announced their arrival to everyone and everything. The spot where they'd parked the quads was in deep shadow, though. It was impossible to tell from any distance where the riders of those vehicles were. If there were predators out here—zoms, reapers, the pride of lions, or anything else—then they would be observing that spot, waiting for movement.

Riot gestured to the others to indicate that she was going to go deeper into the woods and circle around to check the vicinity. Lilah nodded and took off in yet a different direction, leaving Nix and Benny where they were. With the two best hunters abroad in the woods, they'd be able to establish a very good idea of how safe they were.

Long minutes passed, and gradually the natural sounds of the forest returned. There were plenty of birds in this part of the forest, and some chattering monkeys. Insects buzzed through the air. A deer stepped tentatively out from under the trees on the far side of the field and began grazing among the juniper bushes. After ten minutes, Lilah walked out of the woods near where the quads were parked. Her pistol was holstered, and she held her spear loosely in her hands. Seconds later, Riot came trotting out from between a rock and a big bristlecone tree. She waved all clear.

"Let's go," said Benny, and he and Nix left the shadows and walked out into the sunlight. The field was covered in tall, dry grass that sighed with every breath of wind.

They walked through the tall grass and approached the edge of the ravine with caution, testing the ground with their feet in case it was undercut. A month ago Benny had stood on the edge of this ravine and thought he was safe from a group of pursuing zoms, but the edge had collapsed under him, tumbling him down to the bottom along with dozens of the dead.

They found one very solid spot and stood shoulder to shoulder looking down.

A sea of white faces looked back up at them.

Zoms.

"God," said Benny, "they're still here."

Riot looked at him. "I thought that's exactly what you expected."

"Sure," he admitted, "but think about it. These zoms are going to be down there forever. Just standing there. Year after year."

"That's horrible," said Nix.

"That's hell as far as I see it," said Riot.

"That's the Ruin," said Lilah coldly.

They all glanced at her, then they looked down again. The faces of the dead were as pale as worms, their skin streaked with dirt, their eyes dusty, their hands reaching upward.

"How many you reckon are down there?" asked Riot.

"More than before," said Nix. "A lot more. After the first bunch fell in while chasing Benny, others must have been drawn to the sounds."

Lilah walked along the edge of the trench. Benny marveled that she could walk without a limp. It was only a few weeks after her injury, and every step had to hurt. The fact that she did not limp at all meant that she was eating her pain with each step. That was nearly as impressive as it was creepy.

We all eat our pain, observed his inner voice. *All four of us, and Chong, and Joe and everyone else. Eating our pain gives us the fuel to keep fighting.*

For once Benny could find no fault with what that inner voice said. He nodded to himself.

"I'll take the other side," he said. "Nix, Riot . . . you guys go down to the other end and start up from there." He gave them as good a description of Ortega as he could remember.

Riot started to go, but Nix lingered a moment.

"What?" asked Benny.

She stepped closer and kept her voice low enough so that only he could hear her.

"Benny, yesterday was a mess."

He shrugged.

"No," she insisted, "it was. I freaked out about Chong, and I reacted the wrong way."

"It's—"

"I know we already talked about it, and I know we're supposed to be over it," she said. "But I'm not over it. I don't know who that was yesterday, but that wasn't me."

"Yeah," he said with a gentle smile, "I get that."

"Do you?"

"I really do."

Nix touched Benny's cheek, but the action was tentative, almost fearful. "Can—can I ask you one question, Benny?"

"You can ask me anything."

She took a breath and seemed to be steeling herself for what she was about to say. "Do you . . . do you still love me?"

He almost laughed.

Luckily, his inner voice and whatever common sense he possessed grappled with his automatic reaction and wrestled it to the floor. So instead of a laugh, he gave her a smile. Even so, Nix's face instantly clouded.

"I'm serious," she said sharply.

Benny nodded. "I know."

He kissed her.

"That's the silliest question I've ever been asked."

Her frown deepened. "It's not silly."

"It is to me. Of *course* I still love you. I'm always going to love you," he said.

Nix looked at him, troubled and puzzled. "Why?"

"What?"

She shook her head. "Why on earth do you still love me? Why on earth do you want to?"

"I—"

"I'm vicious and moody and nasty, I'm cold to you too much of the time, and sometimes I bite your head off when you're just trying to be nice. I'm a monster."

"Yeah, and I'm always a yummy box of chocolates. C'mon, Nix, how shallow do you think I am?"

Before she could answer, Benny turned away and began walking along the ravine, peering down through shadows at the pale faces below. He could feel Nix's eyes on him, and he thought he could imagine at least some of what was going on in her head. Some. However, he wondered if she was trying to guess what was going on in *his* head. Benny remembered something Captain Strunk of the town watch once said on a hot summer afternoon on the porch of Lafferty's General Store. Benny, Chong, and Morgie were sitting on the porch steps, opening packs of Zombie Cards; Captain Strunk was sitting in an old kitchen chair, and a bunch of other town men were with him. Mayor Kirsch; Wriggly Sputters, the town's mailman; big one-armed Leroy Williams; Morgie Mitchell's dad; and four or five others. The men had been talking about relationships, before and after First Night. When one of the men had, in exasperation, pronounced that all women were crazy and that all men were crazier for falling in love with them, everyone laughed. They agreed that there was just no understanding the mysteries of love. No sir, no how. Chong, who was twelve at the time, said, "What's not to understand? People fall in love."

The men goggled at him for a few moments, and Captain Strunk said, in a dry, amused voice, "Kid, if it turns out that you well and truly understand love, I will personally nominate you for King of the World, and I can guarantee that every man here will vote for you."

Everyone burst out laughing. Chong had turned as red as a radish.

As he walked, Benny could almost hear the echoes of that laughter. He'd been confused by the exchange back then, but he wasn't anymore.

Three minutes later Lilah called, "Here!"

They came running to where she stood on the edge of the ravine, using her spear to point down into the darkness. A zom, taller than the others, big-armed and big-chested, stood in a middle of a pack. They could see only his shoulders and head, but it was enough to recognize the pattern of the camouflage of the American Nation. And to see a strap across his chest—a strap Benny vaguely remembered was attached to a satchel. He had taken only peripheral note of it before, ascribing no more importance to it than to the man's shoes or belt or other items. At the time his entire focus had been on fighting this man. He'd tried a big lateral sword slash of the kind he'd seen Tom use to cut through the legs of a zom. Only the angle of Benny's cut had been bad, and the blade had stuck fast in the zom's heavy thigh bone. The sword handle had been torn from Benny's hands, and the blade might have been lost had Lilah not somehow managed to recover it. Until today, Benny had assumed she'd quieted the zom in order to take back the sword, but that wasn't so. The zom looked as powerful and deadly as ever.

Benny crouched on the lip of the ravine. "Hello, Sergeant Ortega," he said.

"HOW DO WE GET HIM OUT OF THERE?" ASKED NIX.

"Good question, Red," murmured Riot. "There's more dead down there than wood ticks on a coon."

"How many do you figure?" asked Benny.

"Rough guess," said Riot, squinting into the gloom, "near on about—"

"It's 261," said Lilah.

"Oh, crap." Benny sighed. "On the bright side, that's only sixty-five each."

No one laughed at the joke. Not even Benny.

Riot fingered the silver dog whistle she wore around her throat. Each of them had one. "I had a crazy idea about two of us calling the gray people from different ends of the ravine, to thin the herd, but that plain won't work. Too darn many of 'em."

"So what's plan B?" asked Nix. "Do we go down at one end and try some kind of systematic quieting thing? I mean, the ravine's narrow enough that only three or four of them could come at us at a time."

"Stupid," said Lilah dismissively.

Nix colored. "I know, I was thinking out loud."

Lilah eyed her. "Don't. Unless you have a smart plan."

"Thank you, queen of tact," said Benny under his breath.

They began hashing out an idea that involved using the quads to pull big branches, small fallen trees, and other bulky debris, then pushing that stuff down on either side of Sergeant Ortega. Push enough stuff down and they could create temporary walls that would lock in Ortega—and probably a few other zoms standing close to him. The end result would be a much smaller number of zoms they'd have to deal with in order to gain access to Sergeant Ortega's pockets and that satchel.

Then they began picking holes in the plan.

"The more we use the quads, the more chance other zoms will hear us," said Nix.

"Reapers, too," added Riot. "It ain't all that far from where Benny got jumped yesterday."

"Besides," said Benny, pointing down into the ravine, "if we block off the tunnel, that'll still leave Ortega and a bunch of zoms in a tight little space. If one person went down, the zoms would have a feast. If all four of us went down, we'd be so crowded we'd get in each other's way. And we can't shoot the zoms because of the noise."

"We can come back tomorrow with Chong's bow and arrows," suggested Nix.

"No," said Lilah. "Too much time. I can lean down with my spear, try and stab them in the head . . ."

"And probably fall in," said Riot. "Ground's too iffy, and you wouldn't have squat for leverage."

They stood there and stared.

Benny sucked thoughtfully at the inside of his cheek. An

idea occurred to him, and he looked at the coil of rope looped slantways across Lilah's body. "Huh," he grunted softly.

"What?" asked Nix.

"Riot—you said something a couple of minutes ago," he said slowly. "About herding the zoms?"

"Sure, but the whistles won't do the trick," she said.

"No, but I read enough Western novels to know a little bit about how cowboys herded strays." He removed the coil of rope. "Anyone here know how to throw a lasso?"

As it turned out, they all did.

Nix knew a little bit about it from the Scouts back in Mountainside. Lilah had handled rope while struggling to survive—lassoing trees to climb and roping wounded animals she was hunting. But Riot was the real expert.

"After I skedaddled from the Night Church," she said as she began fashioning a lariat, "I fell in with a group of scavengers. Called themselves the Rat Pack. They were a crazy bunch of kids who raided towns and tagged buildings that had good supplies. The kids were all into extreme sports—or I guess what *had* been extreme sports before the Fall. Skateboarders, BMX bikers, in-line skaters, and free runners."

"What's that?" asked Nix.

"It's a kind of sport where you do all sorts of acrobatics over obstacles and up walls and suchlike. Looks like a bunch of crazy monkeys, but it's amazing. Fun, too."

"You did that?"

She shrugged. "I learned me a few tricks. There was a boy named Jolt who taught me a lot of things."

A dreamy and distant look floated through Riot's eyes, and Benny glanced at Nix, who clearly saw it too.

"Was Jolt your boyfriend?" Nix asked carefully.

"We had a little thing going," Riot said coyly, but didn't elaborate.

"What happened to him?" asked Benny, though he was afraid of what the answer would be.

"I don't rightly know. 'Bout a year ago, while I was running some people out to Sanctuary, the Rat Pack's camp was overrun by reapers. I got there maybe two days after it happened and found half the people I knew slaughtered and the rest gone. They lit out in every possible direction, and from the tracks it looked like there were reapers in hot pursuit of every single person." She sighed heavily. "I quieted the dead. Near on twenty of them. Some little ones, too. Only a few reapers, though. The scavengers ain't much into killing, even in self-defense."

"Stupid," said Lilah, and Riot shot her a hard look.

"You're welcome to keep your opinions to your damn self, missy," snapped Riot, throwing down the rope and getting nose to nose with Lilah. "That Rat Pack was the closest thing I had to a real family, and I won't hear a word against them."

Lilah looked genuinely surprised by Riot's reaction.

"But they let themselves die," insisted Lilah.

"So do the way-station monks," interjected Nix. "Not everyone believes in killing."

Lilah pushed Riot back, but not with anger. Just to create distance. "You were with them? A scavenger?"

"Yes," said Riot.

"And you kill."

Riot looked down at the ground. After a moment, she sighed and picked up the rope.

"Jolt and the others? They were better than me. All they wanted to do was find food and supplies, and have some fun while the rest of the clock ticked down." She glanced again at Lilah. "You want to tell me that's wrong?"

This time Lilah held her tongue. She looked confused, unable to frame a reply.

Benny said, "Did you look for Jolt?"

"Oh yeah," said Riot. "I looked all over this desert for him. Haven't found so much as a footprint."

"Well," said Benny, "when this is over, when things settle down . . . maybe we can help you look."

Riot smiled and shook her head. "Don't you know nothing, boy? This ain't never going to be over."

She looked at the rope she held in her hands. Then, without another word, she finished tying the loose knot.

Below them, the big soldier stood in a throng of maybe a dozen smaller zoms: some women, a few teenagers, and two men of average height. Ortega looked to be about six-four or -five.

"They're pretty thick down there," said Riot. "Best place to lasso someone is around the chest, 'bout midway down the upper arm. But our boy's reaching up. Might have to hook an arm and try to drag him out that way."

Riot crept as close to the edge as she dared. The undercut ground creaked a little even under her negligible weight. Benny picked up the rope and stood behind her to anchor her in place.

"Do it!" he said.

Riot swung the lasso over her head a few times and then hurled it down.

She snagged three different arms, two of which belonged to other dead.

She eased the slack and tried again.

And again.

And again.

After eight tries she was cursing a blue streak and using language so intensely and descriptively foul that Benny was extremely impressed.

Finally Riot stepped back from the ravine and threw the lasso onto the grass.

"So much for your brilliant plan," she groused. "I might as well hang myself with that damn thing."

She started to stomp off, got about ten paces, and stopped. She turned with a quizzical look on her face. The same expression was blossoming on Lilah's and Nix's faces; and Benny was sure he wore an identical look.

Riot had said it.

Hang myself.

They looked at the lasso. Everyone smiled.

Ten seconds later they were kneeling together at the edge of the ravine, dangling a much smaller loop down into the shadows.

"A little to the left," suggested Benny. "No, too much. Back . . . back . . ."

Lilah crouched next to Riot, her spear extended all the way down, using the blade to bat aside reaching hands and to tap the loop toward Ortega.

"Little more . . . ," breathed Benny. "Little more . . ."

The edge of the loop brushed against the big zom's face. Everyone held their breath as, with infinite care, Riot eased it over the crown of the man's head and then slowly, slowly down until it hung pendulously below his chin.

"Now!" cried Nix, and Riot jerked back on the rope. The slack loop snapped tight, constricting like a noose around Sergeant Ortega's throat.

They had him.

Kind of.

He was still down in the pit.

They grabbed the rope and began to pull.

Benny, though slim, was the heaviest of them; but, like the girls, the hardships of warfare, frequent injuries, small meals, and stress had leaned him down.

Sergeant Ortega, before death and desiccation had wasted him, probably weighed 260 pounds. Now he was probably 220. They had a two-to-one weight advantage over him, but they were lifting from the top, with the majority of his weight below the noose, and they were trying to pull him up a twenty-foot wall. While he fought and writhed and struggled.

It went from a brilliant plan to a brutal struggle. The sun hammered down on them and sweat burst from their pores as they pulled. They set their feet into the sandy soil, using tufts of the tall grass for traction. They groaned and growled and yelled and cursed.

The sergeant was an improbably heavy weight. He felt like he weighed a thousand pounds. They moved another foot back.

And that was as far as they got.

Benny strained and strained until his blood sang in his ears and black poppies seemed to burst in his eyes.

Finally they collapsed. Their hands ached; their lungs

burned with oxygen starvation. They lay sprawled where they'd fallen, except for Nix, who crawled like a battlefield victim to the edge of the ravine and peered down.

Nix, who was never one for cursing, repeated a few of the phrases Riot had used a few minutes ago.

"What?" asked Benny listlessly.

"It's the other zoms," she said.

Benny lifted his head. "What?"

"They grabbed at Ortega as soon as we started pulling him up. Some of them are still holding on to him."

Benny let his head drop back with a thump. He felt Nix crawl up beside him and collapse. They lay there, defeated.

Finally, Lilah gasped out a single word. A statement and a question.

"Quad?"

Benny thought it was Riot who started laughing first. He had his eyes closed and couldn't tell. First her, then Lilah's creaking ghost of a laugh, then Nix. Then him. They burst out laughing as they lay on the withered brown grass.

When they could walk, they fetched Benny's quad, tied the end of the rope onto the back of the Honda, gunned the engine, and pulled Sergeant Ortega out of the ravine as easy as pulling a carrot out of soft soil. Four other zoms came up with him. Lilah and Riot were waiting for them, and blades flashed in the sunlight. Withered hands clutched at the big sergeant, but they were no longer attached to anything.

As Benny dragged Sergeant Ortega away from the ravine, Nix trotted beside the zom, her Monster Cutter sword raised to deliver a quieting blow.

But she didn't have to.

The soldier lay still and silent on the grass.

Benny killed the engine and ran back to stand beside Nix. Riot and Lilah trotted up. The sergeant lay in a loose-jointed tangle of arms and legs. His face was placid in that slack rest of final death. At a glance, he looked like any other zom. Less comprehensively withered than the people who'd died on First Night, but still leathery from the Nevada sun. The only thing that was noticeably wrong with him was his neck.

It was too long.

Inches too long.

Between the pull of the quad and the drag of the other zoms clinging to him, the bones of the dead man's neck had separated, and the spinal cord had stretched too far and snapped. Had the strain been a little heavier, or the process of pulling him up taken a few seconds longer, the envelope of skin and muscle that comprised his neck would have torn and all they would have pulled out of the ravine was a head.

They stood around him, their shadows falling over the zom like a shroud.

"I'm glad we don't have to quiet him," said Nix. The others, even Lilah, nodded.

Benny knelt down and lifted the satchel strap. He had to raise the total slack weight of the sergeant's head in order to pull the satchel off. He winced but did it anyway. As soon as he had it off, Nix and Riot knelt down and began going through the sergeant's pockets and laying the items out on a clear patch of dirt. Lilah sorted the items.

They found a rusted multipurpose tool, a Las Vegas poker chip that Ortega was probably carrying as a good-luck charm, a plastic pocket comb, a pencil with a tip that looked like it had been sharpened with a knife, and several folded pieces of paper money of a kind none of them had ever seen. Instead of a picture of a president, the central image was a star, and Benny saw a phrase in Latin: *POPULUS INVICTUS.*

Nix, reading over his shoulder, translated it. "A Nation Unconquerable."

Unlike Benny, she had paid attention in language arts.

"I think that's the motto of the American Nation," suggested Benny.

Lilah nodded her agreement, but Riot snorted.

"What?" asked Benny, shooting her a look. "You don't think so?"

"Close to three hundred million Americans have died, son, during the Fall and in the years after," said Riot. "How many have to croak before y'all consider it game over?"

"All," said Lilah.

"Absolutely," agreed Nix. "We're still fighting."

"Yeah," said Benny, nodding. "Besides, it wasn't *our* generation who was defeated when the dead rose. I still believe there's a future, and I intend to be there to see it."

Riot considered him, and a slow smile spread over her face. "Well look at you, Captain Hero."

"Oh, shut up," said Benny, but he was grinning.

The last thing they found was a folded slip of paper with a series of numbers written on it:

+36° 30' 19.64", -117° 4' 45.81"

"What are those?" asked Riot.

"Map coordinates," said Benny and Nix at the same time. They'd both taken orienteering in the Scouts.

"Coordinates of what?"

Benny shrugged. "Probably Hope One, but I'd need a map to figure it out."

He crammed the useless stuff back into the dead sergeant's pocket. Then they turned their attention to the satchel, which was crammed with papers. In another climate, rain and humidity might have turned the papers to mush or made the ink run and fade. But between the good leather of the satchel and the dry desert heat, most of the papers were legible, though they were all dried to a fragile brittleness. Joe said that Sergeant Ortega had been a logistics coordinator, and the papers bore that out. There were copies of loading manifests, supply lists, personnel lists, written orders, and a lot of stuff that was so heavy with military acronyms that it looked like totally random collections of letters and numbers.

"Well, that's as helpful as toenails on a snake," observed Riot.

"What are we looking for?" asked Nix.

"A small leather notebook," said Benny. "Joe said that if McReady wasn't onboard the plane when it crashed, then the logistics guy would know where she might be, and that the details would be in a leather notebook he usually carried in his shirt pocket."

"I checked the pockets," said Nix. "Nothing."

They rifled through the satchel again, digging through every pocket and pouch, and came up empty.

Lilah became frustrated with it all and stalked off to scout the vicinity. She soon vanished into the woods.

Depression punched Benny hard in the chest. He sat down heavily and tossed the empty satchel away. Riot and Nix were still huddled together as they went through the crackling papers. They read each page in mounting disappointment and stuffed everything back into the satchel. All that remained were a handful of small scraps of paper, and Nix sat cross-legged going through them.

"Benny!" Nix suddenly cried aloud, and held up one piece of paper. "Look at this. I think I found something."

Benny hurried over, dropping to his knees between the girls. The slip of paper read:

URGENT: REPT OF R3 ACTIVITY VCNTY OF DVNP—REL.
WIT. *** FTF?

"Don't make a lick of sense to me," said Riot.

But Benny said, "Oh crap . . ."

"I know," agreed Nix, and despite the heat she shivered. "God . . . R3's."

"What's an R3?" asked Riot. "Y'all look like you both swallowed bugs."

Benny said, "When we first found the plane, we also found one of Dr. McReady's field reports. She wasn't just looking for a cure; she was studying several weird new mutations of the zombie plague. She divided the zoms into different groups. R1's are the normal zoms, the slow shufflers."

For most of his life those were the only kinds of zoms Benny had known, and his first encounters with them had been absolutely terrifying. He still dreamed of the erosion artist, Mr. Sacchetto, recently risen from the dead, attacking him in Benny's own living room. Benny nearly lost that fight. Times had changed, though, and Benny knew that he was becoming a skilled fighter. In a pitched fight, he was sure that he and his sword were a match for any six or even eight of them. Unarmed, he figured he could do pretty well against two or three at a time. They were slow, uncoordinated, stupid, and weak.

"The R2 zoms," continued Benny, "are known as 'fast walkers' by McReady's people—quicker and a lot more coordinated. Nix and I ran into some of them near Yosemite Park and again during the battle of Gameland."

Benny had fought a couple of the R2's so far, and it was a whole different matter taking one of them down. He wouldn't want to try it without a sword.

"So what are R3's?" asked Riot.

"The fast ones," said Nix. "Like the ones that attacked me and Lilah yesterday. According to Dr. McReady's report, the R3's can problem-solve, evade some attacks, use simple weapons, and even set rudimentary traps."

"Ah. Like the ones that some genius let out of a crashed airplane."

Benny shook his head. "Don't remind me."

In order to create a diversion that would save Nix from a pack of reapers, Benny had climbed aboard the crashed plane and released all the zoms Dr. McReady's team had collected: R1's, R2's, and a few R3's. The zoms had created the diversion, and that saved Nix's life; however, it was one of those same R3 zoms who picked up a stick and nearly bashed Benny's brains out.

"So, according to this message," said Benny, "someone spotted R3's somewhere. I guess 'activity vcnty of' means 'activity in the vicinity of,' right?"

Nix nodded. "And the 'Rel. Wit.'? What's that? 'Reliable witness'?"

"Sounds right."

"Then what's DVNP?" asked Riot. "And FTF?"

"FTF sounds familiar," said Benny. "I'm pretty sure I saw that in the Teambook I gave to Joe. Wait, it's right on the tip of my brain. . . ." He snapped his fingers a couple of times, then brightened. "Got it. There was a note. Something about Field Team Five."

"Field Team?" murmured Nix. "If they were going to investigate something like R3 activity, then a 'field team' would sound about right."

"It listed the names, but all I can remember was Dr. McReady. She was at the top of the list."

They looked at one another for a long time without saying anything, though their eyes said it all.

"Well, skin me and hang me out to dry," breathed Riot at last. "Doc McReady was never on that plane. At least not when it crashed. Either of you think any different?"

Nix shook her head.

Benny said, "I've been thinking that all along. Ever since Joe told me that the D-series notes were missing."

"If it was a field investigation," began Nix, "why would she take her research? Why not just send it on to Sanctuary?"

"I don't know."

Riot tapped the note that Nix still held. "What's this part here? 'DVNP'? Y'all have any clue what that is?"

"I don't know," said Benny. "More military initials, maybe? Department of something-something-something."

"Useful," said Nix. "No, I think it's a place. R3 reported in the vicinity of . . ."

"Vicinity of where?" complained Riot. "They flew from Washington State to Nevada. That's a lot of gol-durn places to be in the vicinity of."

Benny took the note and held it firmly between thumb and forefinger. He wanted to shout at it, to make it speak in a human voice and unlock its mysteries.

And then it spoke to him.

Not in words, but in implication.

His head snapped up and whipped around toward the fallen body of Sergeant Ortega.

"No," he said as he leaped to his feet and ran. "*No*. No freaking way."

Nix and Riot stared at each other for a split second, and then they were running after him.

The loose papers were in the satchel. Benny whipped back the flap and began furiously digging through the pages.

"No freaking way," he said again. "No." Then he snatched up a small, folded piece of paper, opened it, and yelled, "Yes!"

"What is it?" demanded the girls.

"Joe said that Sergeant Ortega was a real detail-oriented person," said Benny. "He kept track of everything. Every detail. Even the minor stuff."

"So what?" asked Riot.

"Well, someone who takes the time to keep track of minor stuff is definitely going to keep track of the important stuff. Like where Dr. McReady and Field Team Five went while investigating mutant zombies. No way that bit of information *wasn't* going into his report."

"Sure. DVNP," said Nix. "So what? We don't know what it is or where it is."

"You're wrong, Nix. We don't know what it is or where it is right now, but I think we might have our first real clue."

He showed them the folded slip of paper.

+36° 30' 19.64", -117° 4' 45.81"

The map coordinates.

"So what?" asked Riot. "For all y'all know that's the coordinates for that Hope One place."

"Maybe," said Benny, "but Sergeant Ortega had it in his pocket, right? If this was something that was part of the original mission, wouldn't the coordinates be printed out like all the other mission stuff? No, he wrote this down and it was on him when he died. That means he probably did it while aboard the plane or shortly before. If Dr. McReady went somewhere else, then I don't think it's any kind of stretch that *these* might tell us where she went. This might be the key to ending the plague."

The three of them stared at him for a long moment and finally burst out laughing. They hugged one another and shouted, and they were only interrupted by the sudden roar of quads as a dozen reapers came tearing out of the forest.

"RUN!" SCREAMED NIX AS SHE SCRAMBLED TO HER FEET.

But the reapers were already between them and three of their own quads. Only Benny's machine, the one they'd used to haul Sergeant Ortega out of the ravine, was close at hand.

The reapers closed on them at top speed, dragging behind them tall plumes of tan dust. Sunlight glittered on the sharp steel of their knives and swords.

"God," cried Benny. He stuffed the papers into his vest pocket, snatched up the satchel and slung it over his shoulder, then quickly drew his sword. "Nix . . . take the quad and get out of here."

Nix drew her pistol and raised it in a two-handed grip, setting her feet wide, her body angled the way Tom had taught her.

Riot looked desperately around. "Where's Lilah? I can't see her anywhere. Did they get her?"

"No," breathed Nix, but it was only a denial of that as a possibility. In truth there was no sign of the Lost Girl. Nix swung the barrel toward the closest of the reapers. The sound of their engines was becoming deafening.

Benny raised his sword into the high two-handed grip the samurai used when facing a cavalry charge. It was a lesson Tom had taught them once that none of them ever expected to use. He widened his stance and shifted his weight to the balls of his feet, knees bent, ready to cut and evade and run and kill. He could feel his pulse racing faster than the quads.

There was no real chance of escape. They had the zombie-filled ravine behind them and a converging half circle of reapers everywhere else. Even if they managed to cut through the reaper line, those machines could turn and give chase no matter where Benny and the girls ran. And their quad could never get to top speed if all three of them managed to climb aboard. It was a good trap. Smart and well-planned. Benny figured that the reapers had pushed their quads to the edge of the forest, engines off for silence; and then when the trap was set, they fired up the motors and attacked.

Very smart, and Benny approved of the tactical intelligence it showed.

It would be no comfort at all, though, to be slaughtered by intelligent killers.

Dead was dead.

Nix shifted to stand on Benny's left flank, and Riot moved to his right, a steel ball bearing socketed into the pouch of her powerful slingshot.

Twelve to three. Nix had a gun with five bullets in the cylinder. She was a good shot, so Benny figured she'd get at least three. The ball bearings in Riot's slingshot were slower than bullets but just as deadly, and she could fire and reload with lightning speed. Benny had his sword. Unless the reapers intended to grind them under the wheels, the killers would have to dismount.

How many could they take?

Six? Eight?

Defeating all twelve was a heroic dream, but not a probability.

If Lilah was here . . . maybe.

The quads were not slowing.

"They're going to run us down," Riot yelled, reading the situation the same way he was.

"Back up," snapped Benny. "All the way to the edge. They can't run us down if we're right on the edge."

The edge, though, might not hold their combined weight, and Benny knew it. Pulling Sergeant Ortega out of the ravine had weakened an already fragile structure. But that was a different problem. Or maybe it was another problem that would overlap this one, forcing their odds from weak to impossible.

Benny scanned the faces of the reapers as they closed in. All but one of them had red hands tattooed on their faces. They looked wild and fierce, like barbarians out of an old storybook.

As the reapers closed in, they realized that they couldn't use the machines as weapons. A stern-faced young man—the only reaper not marked with the red hand tattoo—raised his fist, and the reapers revved their engines, the combined drone pulsing like the breath of a gigantic dragon.

He's the one, thought Benny. *He's their leader.*

The young man looked like a warrior. Lean and muscular, with big hands and eyes as hard and dead as desert rocks.

Even through the din, Benny heard Riot say, "Brother Peter . . . oh my God."

It was a name that struck a big bell of terror in Benny's heart. He hadn't met this man, but he knew about him. He knew him from a thousand terrifying tales Riot had told them. From firsthand descriptions by survivors of reaper massacres. From accounts by monks who had witnessed acts of savagery so grotesque that their minds were scarred by the memories. From surveillance photos Joe had shown them.

Brother Peter, the right hand of Saint John.

Even Joe said that Peter was one of the most dangerous men alive. Deadly with any kind of weapon, and equally deadly in unarmed combat. A man totally without mercy or remorse.

Like an echo from out of the shadowed past, Benny thought he heard Tom's voice. *Don't give in to fear. Be warrior smart and survive.*

Benny nodded as if Tom could see his agreement.

Hot wind blew dust plumes past them, momentarily obscuring them, turning them to wraiths. Then the dust blew past Benny and his friends and on across the ravine. The waist-high grass swayed drunkenly in the breeze.

The reapers were in a tight arc around them. They kept revving their engines, and the sound seemed to beat on Benny's chest.

"Nix," he said, speaking just loud enough so she could hear him beneath the pulsing roar of the quads. "If you have to shoot, go for Brother Peter."

Nix swung the pistol around toward the man.

Brother Peter saw this and smiled. Then he slashed down

with his clenched fist, and suddenly all the reapers cut their engines at once.

The silence was crushing. It collapsed the world into a surreal bubble that enclosed the ravine, the killers on the quads, and the three of them.

Where the hell is Lilah? wondered Benny. *Did they already get her? Is she dead somewhere out in the forest?*

Brother Peter sat in silence, studying them. When his gaze drifted over to Riot, his eyes widened for a moment.

"Sister Margaret," he said, and the other reapers recoiled at his words. Some of them actually hissed and spat onto the dirt.

"Don't call me that," warned Riot.

"Why not? You are the daughter of Mother Rose, that traitorous witch."

"My mama died a long time ago," said Riot. "She was just another victim of Saint John and his sickness."

At this, three of the reapers suddenly made as if to leap off their quads, but Brother Peter held up a hand. "No," he said. "Words can't harm the honored saint, and this child can't tarnish her soul any more than it already is."

"You can kiss my fanny," suggested Riot.

"You pile sin upon sin," said the reaper. "Have you no fear for your soul?"

"My soul's just fine, thank you." Her words were flippant, but Benny could hear the fear in her voice. Riot was a tough and brutal fighter, but she was clearly terrified of Brother Peter.

For his part, the reaper seemed not to care that Nix's pistol was pointed at his head.

Brother Peter looked at Benny. "Do you know who I am?"

"I know," said Benny. "But I don't care."

"You should care."

"Look, all I care about is you and your goons getting back on your quads and leaving us alone. We didn't do anything to you, and we don't want any trouble."

"Do you know how frightened you sound?"

"Do you know how you'd feel with a bullet in your brain-pan?" asked Nix.

"At this range, little sister, you wouldn't get more than two shots off, and then we'd open red mouths in your pretty skin."

"Maybe," conceded Nix. "First shot will still be through your ugly face."

The reaper shook his head. "So what? Am I supposed to faint from fear? We're reapers, child. We pray for the darkness to take us. Every morning, every night, we pray that Lord Thanatos takes us."

"All praise his darkness," intoned the reapers.

"You say that," Nix said, "but I've seen some of your people run away, too."

"I was the very first of the reapers," said Brother Peter. "My companions are members of the Red Brotherhood. Ask Sister Margaret if she thinks we will run away. From you or from anything."

Riot said nothing, which was not all that encouraging. Benny swallowed a lump of dry dust.

"If you want to test my faith, little sister," said Brother Peter, "then pull the trigger."

The gun was steady in Nix's hand, but when Benny cut a

look at her, he could see lines of fear sweat running down her freckled face.

When Nix didn't answer or fire, Brother Peter nodded. He pointed at Benny. "Yesterday you took something from one of my reapers. Something that was not yours to take."

"Yeah? Says who?" asked Benny, trying to make his voice sound tough. It didn't.

"I watched you do it through my binoculars. I saw you arrive, saw your fight with Brother Marcus, and saw you rob him after he'd gone into the darkness."

Benny said nothing. It made him feel immensely disturbed to know that that had all been witnessed yesterday. He thought of the fight, of his tears, of how vulnerable he must have looked.

Brother Peter nodded to the satchel slung on Benny's shoulder. "Today you came out here to defile and rob one of the gray people. That bag was not yours to take."

Nix said, "This gun's heavy. If you have a point, get to it."

Benny almost smiled. It was the kind of line he read in novels, and she said it with the kind of bravado he'd tried for a moment ago. Nix was better at it than he was. Benny wasn't sure if Nix had cribbed it from a book or if she was simply that incredibly cool. Probably both. Despite everything that was happening, he wanted to kiss her.

Brother Peter looked faintly amused, though the expression on his face in no way qualified as a smile. Benny remembered Riot saying that this freak never smiled.

"If you give me what you took," said Brother Peter, "the bag on your shoulder and whatever you took from my reaper, we will let you go."

"Oh, really?" said Riot with so much acid that it could have burned the paint off a tank.

"Really," said Brother Peter.

"Last time I checked," continued Riot, "you reapers only left people alive when they got down on their knees and kissed your knives. Isn't that how it works? We get to live if we become reapers too?"

"Oh, fallen sister," said Brother Peter in a sorrowful tone, "there is no place for you in the Night Church. You are an outcast, forgotten of god, unworthy of the darkness. You are an excommunicate and a blasphemer and you will be punished by a long life of suffering."

"Suits me," said Riot.

"Yeah, works for me, too," agreed Nix.

Benny nodded.

"Really," repeated Brother Peter. "That appeals to you? A life spent wandering blind and disfigured, screaming for mercy without a tongue, shunned by everyone because your face will bear the mark of damnation upon it."

Riot proved that her earlier demonstration of foul language had only been a warm-up. She described an act so physically appalling and improbable that even Benny winced—and he appreciated this kind of thing. Several of the reapers blanched and fingered their knives.

"You prove your worthlessness with every breath." Brother Peter dismissed Riot with a casual wave of his hand and turned his focus back to Benny. "Make your choice, little brother. You can walk away, unharmed, untouched, alive if you give me what does not belong to you. Return what you took from my reaper, and hand over the bag you stole from the dead."

Benny looked at him, at the other reapers, and at the vast, unforgiving world around them as if it was able to offer answers to the madness of the moment. He held his sword with one hand and touched the strap of the satchel.

"Give me the bag," said Brother Peter in a voice that was eerily calm. He could have been commenting on the weather. "Give it to me and live."

"It's a trick," said Riot. "Don't do it."

"Benny, you can't," said Nix.

Benny smiled.

"Sure," he said.

"WHAT?"

Nix, Riot, and Brother Peter all said it at the same time.

Benny shrugged and lowered his sword. He slid the bag off his shoulder and held it out. "I said, sure. Take it."

Brother Peter studied him with suspicious eyes. "It would be unwise to try a fast one, little brother, I'll—"

"I know. Red mouths, tongues cut out. What is it with you guys and threats? You need to work on your people skills."

Everyone was staring at Benny. He smiled and swung the bag back and forth. His heart thumped like a crazy monkey, but he was sure he was managing a pretty good reckless smile. It hurt his face to keep it in place.

Brother Peter snapped his fingers, and one of the Red Brothers dismounted and stepped forward to take the bag. Nix shifted the pistol toward him, and the reaper stopped.

"If he takes another step," said Benny, "she'll blow his head off and then she'll shoot you."

The reaper threw a questioning glance at Brother Peter, who gestured for him to remain where he was. Instead he dismounted and held his hand out to Benny.

"The bag," he said.

Benny wondered if there was even the slightest chance that Brother Peter was not going to kill him the moment he handed over the bag. Riot said that the reaper had a dozen knives hidden in special pockets and that he could draw and cut faster than lightning. She'd seen him do it too many times.

So Benny slung the satchel at him instead of handing it over. He slung it hard, hoping to catch Peter in the mouth, but the man simply snatched it out of the air. He opened the flap, and the dry wind rifled the pages. Brother Peter nodded approval.

"Now give me what you stole from my reaper yesterday," he said.

"Ah," said Benny. "That's going to be a problem."

Brother Peter lifted an eyebrow.

"I don't actually *have* that stuff," said Benny. "I gave it to Captain Ledger. Maybe you know him? Big guy, real grumpy, has this huge dog?"

"Joe Ledger." Brother Peter pronounced the name slowly, tasting it, hating it but enjoying it too. Benny could see all that flicker through Peter's dark eyes, and he also enjoyed the look of profound discomfort that rippled across the faces of the other reapers.

Joe scares the pee of out them, he thought. It elevated the ranger another notch in his book.

"That's the guy," Benny said. "So . . . you're going to have to ask *him* for it."

"No," said Brother Peter, "I think you'll go and get it from him and bring it back to me here."

"You think I'd really do something that stupid just because you ask?"

"I'm not asking you, little brother. I'm telling you."

Benny shook his head. "No. I played fair. I gave you what we took from the zom. Not going to argue jurisdiction over that stuff. But the stuff I took off the reaper yesterday belongs to me. Your reaper attacked me. That means that anything I took from him is mine by rights. Spoils of war."

"This isn't a war, boy."

"Well, what the hell do you call it?"

"You are defying god's will."

"I'm pretty sure I'm not."

Brother Peter sighed. "Then let me simplify things for you. I'll send you back to Sanctuary. You'll get whatever you gave to Joe Ledger and bring it back here to me."

"Why on earth would I do something stupid like that?"

Brother Peter did not answer. Not in words.

He stood a yard away from Nix, apparently ignoring the gun pointed at his head. And then he moved. So hideously fast that there was no time to react or cry out. Brother Peter snatched the pistol from Nix's hand, spun her, and wrapped an arm around her throat. He let the pistol fall and suddenly there was a knife in his hand, the edge of the blade pressed against the soft flesh beneath Nix's jaw.

Benny's sword flashed from its scabbard, but Brother Peter froze him in place with seven horrible words.

"I will paint you with her blood."

The pistol lay on the ground by Brother Peter's foot. He kicked it into the ravine.

"And now," he said calmly, "tell me again that you refuse to get what belongs to me. Tell me, boy, and watch this girl's life flow out of her."

"No!" cried Benny.

Nix stared at Benny with wide eyes filled with total terror.

The reapers began climbing off their quads, grins forming on their tattooed faces.

Riot pivoted and aimed her slingshot at the nearest one, but Benny knew that it was no good. She could bring the man down, Benny could take the next few with his sword, but that knife was already at Nix's throat.

Then suddenly there was a sharp metallic sound behind the reapers. A sound so specific that everyone knew what it was before they turned and looked.

A slide being racked on an automatic pistol.

The Lost Girl rose up out of the tall grass behind the half circle of reapers, her big automatic pistol held in a two-handed grip.

"Let Nix go," she said in her graveyard whisper of a voice, "or I'll blow your head off."

The reapers froze in place, some with weapons half-drawn. Brother Peter turned to face Lilah.

"Kill me and she dies too."

"You're threatening to kill her anyway. Might as well kill you first."

"My reapers of the Red Brotherhood will slaughter you."

Lilah said, "Look into my eyes. Tell me if you think I care."

Brother Peter did look into her eyes, and Benny thought he could see something shift in the man's expression. It was not fear—Benny didn't think this man was capable of that emotion—but perhaps it was a kind of understanding, of acceptance.

He lowered his knife and gave Nix a small push. She

staggered forward, and Benny caught her with one arm. Nix immediately wheeled and tried to kick Brother Peter in the groin. He parried the kick as effortlessly as if he was swatting a fly.

"Nix," cautioned Benny as he pulled her away from the reaper. She jerked free of his grip and drew her sword. *Dojigiri* glittered in the bright sunlight, but for all its deadly promise, Brother Peter seemed not to care in the slightest.

Lilah's pistol was rock-steady in her grip. "Get out of here."

Without an iota of haste, Brother Peter slid his knife back into its sheath. "Listen to me," he said softly. "We all walk away from this moment. But understand me—I want what you gave to Captain Ledger. You *will* bring it to me."

"Why do you think we'd even consider it?" snapped Nix.

Brother Peter held out his arm, pointing across the miles toward Sanctuary. "Because I think you care about those people at Sanctuary. The sick, the helpless." He paused. "The children."

Benny heard Riot's sharp intake of breath.

"You think that Sanctuary is a fortress," said the reaper, "that you're safe there."

"We *are*," said Nix firmly.

Brother Peter picked up the satchel and stowed it in the rear compartment of his quad. "Fail to bring me what you stole and you'll learn exactly how safe Sanctuary is."

"She's right," said Benny. "Try anything and the army will stop you."

Brother Peter snorted. The reapers laughed. Harsh, brutal laughs that seemed to be fueled by some certain knowledge of what Brother Peter was suggesting. They winked at one another and traded high fives.

"You're a strange boy," said Brother Peter. "Do you really think the 'army' will rise to your defense?"

"Me personally? Probably not," admitted Benny. "I'm no one. But if you try to take it from Captain Ledger, then, sure, they'll have his back. But it's stupid. You have knives, they've got guns."

Brother Peter shook his head. "There aren't enough bullets in the world to stop the will of Thanatos—all praise to his darkness."

The reapers echoed his words.

"I'll give you until sunset tomorrow," said Brother Peter as he climbed onto his quad. "That should be more than enough time to find a way to trick Joe Ledger into returning what you stole. Bring it here and leave it on the edge of the ravine weighted down with a rock. We won't interfere with you delivering it."

"Hey, man, I gave you the satchel," said Benny. "Like I said, I get to keep whatever I found yesterday. Call it a draw."

"No," said Brother Peter, "let's not."

Lilah edged around to stand with Benny and the others. "Get out of here," she said.

Brother Peter's eyes were filled with dark mystery. "There is a storm coming," he said. "It is the breath of my god, and it will be more powerful than any hurricane you've ever seen. The clouds will open and a rain of blood will pour down upon you. The coming storm will blow down the structures of your old world; it will seek out the blasphemers no matter where they hide. It will cleanse the earth, and when it has passed there will be no proof that you—that any of you—ever even lived."

Benny wanted to hit him with a snappy comeback, but there was something in Brother Peter's voice, some look in his eye that made the words die on his tongue.

"You have until tomorrow evening," said Brother Peter. He signaled the reapers to start their engines. They turned and drove away, crossed the clearing, and passed single file into the forest.

THE LOST GIRL LOWERED HER GUN AND PICKED UP HER SPEAR.

Nix let out a long, ragged breath, sheathed her sword, turned, and punched Benny in the chest as hard as she could.

"Wait—OWW! What was that for?" he bellowed.

"You just *gave* him the satchel?" seethed Nix. "You just up and handed over the only clues we have to where Dr. McReady might be?"

"No, I—"

"What in tarnation is going on in your head, boy?" asked Riot. "Or is there anything at all happening in there?"

"No," said Lilah, "he's not very bright."

"Look, I—"

Nix shook her head in complete disgust. "And are you planning on asking Joe for that stuff?"

"Good luck with that," said Riot, and added under her breath, "moron."

"Hey, wait, I—"

"What were you *thinking*, Benny?" asked Nix.

"You guys are great," he said sarcastically. "Thanks for the vote of confidence . . . but I'm not *actually* stupid."

He reached into his vest pocket for something and held it out an inch from Nix's face. The girls studied the papers. Nix took one; Riot took the other. Lilah came and peered over their shoulders.

Nix's read: URGENT: REPT OF R3 ACTIVITY VCNTY OF DVNP—REL. WIT. *** FTF?

Riot's read: +36° 30' 19.64", -117° 4' 45.81"

Lilah said, "Wait . . . what?"

"I don't know what Brother Peter was looking for," said Benny, "but I'm guessing this is it."

A slow smile formed on Nix's face and even her freckles seemed to glow.

"I shoved those in my pocket when I saw the quads. Nothing else in the satchel looked to be important."

Riot grinned and shook her head. "By golly, boy, you are as slick as a greased weasel."

"Thanks, I think."

Lilah gave him an appraising stare as if surprised that he wasn't mentally deficient after all.

Nix's smile faltered. "What happens when Brother Peter realizes he doesn't have these?"

"How do we even know that *he* knows what he's looking for?" asked Benny. "They must have been watching us and saw us take the satchel. Then they saw us put stuff back into the satchel, and now they have it. What we need is to get our butts back to Sanctuary." He paused. "Yesterday Joe told me that when they couldn't find the D-series records, we lost our last chance to beat this thing. I don't think that's true."

Nix said, "What do you think Brother Peter meant about a storm coming?"

"He was bluffing," said Benny. "Lilah had a gun on him and he was talking trash."

Lilah gave a slow shake of her head. "No, he wasn't."

"You don't think so?" asked Benny.

"Snow White's right," said Riot. "Brother Peter wasn't bluffing at all, no sir. You could tell it from his voice. He thinks he's going to win."

"Against Sanctuary?" Nix laughed. "Against Captain Ledger and the soldiers? *How?*"

No one had an answer to that.

"Then it's some kind of weapon," said Lilah. "Something we haven't seen yet."

"Reapers only use knives," said Nix.

Riot shrugged. "Before I left them, they would never have used a quad. It was old-world science, totally taboo. Now look. So who knows what else they might try?" Riot shook her head. "No . . . we have to be ready for them to do anything at all to win."

Without another word they got their quads and raced back to Sanctuary.

BROTHER PETER PULLED HIS QUAD INTO THE CLEFT OF A TUMBLE OF HUGE rocks and killed the engine. Sister Sun sat on a stool under the shade of an awning erected for her by her reaper body-guards. She sipped water from a plastic cup. She looked older than her years and as frail as an icicle on a warm morning.

"How did it go?" she asked as Brother Peter came over and sat down across from her.

He poured himself some water, sipped it, and set his cup aside.

"It went exactly as planned," he said.

She reached out and patted his hand.

"Good."

Benny isn't the same boy I grew up with.

It's been less than nine months since all our troubles started. Nine months ago Benny was really young. Cute and smart, but immature for his age. Everyone thought so, but nobody was mean enough to say it to his face.

After the first time Tom took him to the Ruin, Benny started to change. He smiles a lot less, and sometimes he still says dumb things and acts immature. But . . . sometimes I wonder if the way he acts during those times is a defense mechanism. I wonder if he's still trying to be a kid when everything else in the world is trying to make him old.

Is he aware of it?

Since we came to Sanctuary, he's changed even more. I'm not sure how to describe it. It's like he's leveled out. He's even. Does that make sense?

This new Benny is a lot more like Tom. Independent and strong, but also not like Tom. Maybe Benny's becoming someone else.

I hope Benny likes the person he's becoming.

I do. Maybe more than I ever have.

MILES AND MILES AWAY . . .

The sign read SLAUGHTERHOUSE ROAD.

It made Saint John smile, as much for the visceral imagery that it conjured in his mind as for the poetry that he always found written into the mundane events of each day.

He stood in the shade of a billboard on which a smugly smiling figure once promised that everyone could, without question, hear him now. Saint John had never owned a cell phone. Even before the Fall he had believed that they whispered suggestions of temptation in the ear and sucked away both common sense and faith the way a tick sucks blood. Besides, before the dead rose, whenever Saint John felt the need to say something of importance to someone, he took them to some remote place and shared his secrets in the pauses between screams.

The weeds and grasses grew tall all around the billboard, and a haphazard forest of young trees had grown up along the road. The road surface was cracked by roots and weather, but it was relatively clear of vegetation. When Saint John's scouts saw this, they alerted him, and a platoon of the Red Brotherhood had come this way, following what was clearly a well-traveled route. Dried mud from recent rains showed the marks of horses' hooves, wagon wheels, and booted footprints. A trade route or something else had been the guess, and now here was the proof.

Four trade wagons made their slow way along the road. All of them had been converted from farm carts. The frames were a mix of truck chassis and wooden cart wheels, with big boxes bolted to the frame. Each box was covered in sheet metal, and the teams of horses were protected by carpet coats covered in nets made of steel washers connected by heavy-gauge wire. The horses of the men riding alongside the carts were similarly armored, and all the men and women in the party wore ankle-length carpet coats, thick leather gloves, and helmets of all kinds, including fencing masks, football helmets, old Norman steel caps looted from museums, and even a plastic fishbowl with holes cut for ventilation. There were four mounted riders and ten guards on foot. Everyone was armed, and apart from knives and swords, many of them had guns.

It was a considerable defensive force, and old bleached bones lying along the road spoke to the effectiveness of their many preparations.

Saint John approved of the weapons, the clever design of the carpet coats and metal armor. All of it was more than sufficient to stop an attack by the living dead.

"Take them," said Saint John.

The reapers of the Red Brotherhood, who had been poised like a fist, struck.

Arrows, carefully aimed, darkened the sky for a moment,

and then bodies were falling and horses were screaming. Suddenly all those careful preparations disintegrated as predators far more dangerous than the walking dead proved what all wise killers already knew: that nothing was more dangerous than living men.

ONCE BENNY AND THE GIRLS WERE BACK AT SANCTUARY, THEY PARKED their quads and hurried over to the bridge.

"We need to see Captain Ledger," said Nix urgently.

The guards said nothing. They didn't even look at her.

"Hey," said Benny loudly, "we're speaking to you."

Nothing.

Riot pointed. "Look, y'all, the Lost Girl is breaking her fifty-foot restriction. She's right here at the edge of the trench. I think y'all ought to report that to Captain Ledger."

One of the guards looked at Lilah, smiled, then shrugged. It was the most extensive response any of the bridge guards had ever given them.

"Screw this," muttered Benny as he tried to push past the soldiers and reach for the cotter pin that held the bridge.

The closest soldier shoved him. Very fast and very hard.

There was a rasp of steel and Nix's sword, *Dojigiri*, flashed in the sunlight.

A hundredth of a second later there were guns pointed at them. One each at Benny, Nix, Lilah, and Riot. M16s, fully automatic rifles.

"I'm going to tell you this once," said the guard who'd

pushed Benny. "Walk away. Do it right now or we will fire. Don't make the mistake of thinking this is a discussion. Walk away."

"We need to see Captain Ledger," insisted Benny.

"First bullet goes through your kneecap, boy," said the guard. "You call it."

They walked away, but within ten paces Benny broke into a run.

51

ONE MILE AWAY . . .

"What did they find, my sister?" asked Brother Peter. He crouched like a pale ape on an outcropping of red rock.

The engine of Sister Sun's quad was off, but she still sat in the saddle, resting her weight on the handlebars. She sighed and sat back, resting a hand on the satchel that lay on her thighs.

"This," she said.

Brother Peter jumped down from the rock and took the satchel. He quickly and thoroughly searched the papers.

"The coordinates?"

"Gone," said Sister Sun.

They looked at each other.

And smiled.

It was an unlooked-for piece of luck.

Not blind luck, though. It was, to them, proof of the power of their god.

BENNY HUNCHED OVER THE HANDLEBARS OF HIS QUAD AND GUNNED THE engine.

"What are you doing?" yelled Nix over the roar.

"Remember in the Scouts Mr. Feeney said that survival requires a proactive attitude?"

"Yes, but—"

"I'm being proactive."

Any comment Nix might have made was lost beneath the roar as he shot past her, engine bellowing, wheels kicking sand behind him. He thought he heard her screaming his name, but he didn't look back.

Benny shot past the playground and the orchard. The monks and the children all stared at him, but no one said anything. Or maybe he heard one of the older monks yelling even louder than Nix had. Something about slowing down, probably. Benny chose not to hear that admonition. This wasn't a convenient time for obeying rules.

This was a time for taking action.

The trench was forty yards ahead. Once he cleared the last of the orchards, he angled left, heading toward the point where the steel bridge was lowered twice a day. There was a yard-long lip of metal that stuck out over the drop, and it was wider than the bridge. Good enough on either side for the wheel width of the quad.

Benny hoped.

On the other side of the trench there was only a metal plate. No bridge or other obstructions.

He had never done this before, of course. Not even in his head.

It was all a matter of speed and angle.

And luck.

"Come on, Tom," he growled as he gave the quad more gas. "Little help from beyond would be cool."

He gave the engine all the gas it would take, and the motor roared like a living thing. Feral and alive and powerful.

"Come on . . . *come on!*" Benny yelled.

The raised bridge was there, right there, the four soldiers flanking it. They gaped at him as if he was absolutely out of his mind. Benny could see their point.

Two of them brought up their rifles, and Benny flattened out over the steering column, making himself the smallest possible target.

Of course, if a bullet did hit him, it would nail him on the top of the head. That gave him a moment's pause. The quad, undeterred by thoughts of mortality, kept racing onward.

"HALT!" roared the guards.

There was the hollow *krak-krak-krak* of gunfire.

Benny braced against the impact.

Felt nothing.

Kept going.

Benny hurtled toward the bridge, gathering every ounce

of speed, and then at the last possible second he turned the wheels and the quad shot past the guards and past the upraised steel and flew out over empty space.

There was a single *bump* as one rear wheel brushed the edge of the gate. Just that one tap; Benny had done it right.

He screamed—loud and raw and free—as the sense of speed seemed to vanish and the quad hung in the air, untethered by gravity, a beautiful soaring thing. Below him the twenty-foot span of the trench seemed to move with a strange slowness, as if time itself had wound down. He looked down and saw, with a flash of panic, that the front wheels were already starting to dip toward the bottom of the trench, and the far side looked a million miles away. Benny pulled on the handlebars as if he could lift the whole machine through sheer force of muscle and will.

Then the lip of the trench was there, and the soft tires chunked down onto the ground inches past it. There was a second thump as the rear wheels hit, and the jolt rattled Benny's bones and snapped his teeth shut. His hands were still rolled forward, still feeding gas to the engine, so there was a moment when inertia and impact and gravity collided into a grinding nothing as wheels turned and great plumes of tan sand kicked up behind him and the quad shivered like it was coming apart. Then the tire treads bit deep and the thrust of the engine overcame the downward pull of gravity, and Benny's quad shot forward like a bullet from a gun.

Benny let rip a yell of rough joy and sheer excitement.
Krak! Krak!
He could hear the shots, but nothing hit him. Or he

prayed not. There was no pain, no heavy thud of impact, no burn of ruined nerves and tissues.

He cut a quick look over his shoulder and saw that two of the soldiers were sprawled on the ground. Benny slewed to a sideways stop that built a wall of dust between him and the zoms. The dust seemed to freeze there—a brown stain painted on the moment. A third soldier—the one who had refused to pass along the message to Captain Ledger—leaned against the bridge, clutching what looked like a badly broken nose. The fourth was standing, unarmed, with his hands raised.

Nix, Lilah, and Riot had apparently come up on the soldiers' blind side while they were shooting at Benny.

Well, thought Benny, *I guess it sucks to be them.*

Even so, he hoped the girls hadn't injured anyone too badly. It was just too bad the guards lacked the sense, permission, or manners to pass along a simple message.

Benny saw Nix turn to him and shake her head in exasperation. He knew that had she been aware of his plan, Nix would have done anything she could to stop him. And yet . . . a big, bright smile blossomed on her face.

Lilah glanced at Benny and gave him a brief nod.

Benny was sure he'd get an earful about his rashness, but for the moment some *other* guys were taking the brunt of the collective female outrage. He was very cool with that.

Movement made him turn, and he saw that the dead, all four hundred thousand of them, were facing him. And shuffling his way. Here and there Benny could see zoms dressed in black clothes adorned with red cloth streamers tied to wrists and ankles. These were reapers who had died in the big fight three weeks ago. Benny recognized a few of their faces. The reapers looked like ordinary people—well, zommed-out versions of ordinary people—but they had been so vicious in life, so determined to end all life. That concept was more alien to Benny than the fact that these people were now undying corpses.

Life is truly weird, he thought. *And it's not getting any less weird the farther I get from home.*

Then, with a collective moan of boundless hunger that shook the world, and the tramp of eight hundred thousand withered feet, they surged toward him. When he'd first met Joe Ledger, the ranger had estimated two hundred thousand zoms. The monks counted twice that many.

And he laughed.

"Bite me!" he yelled at the top of his voice.

He fed fuel into the quad and kicked it forward, first racing toward the advancing wall of death, and then at the last second cutting to the left, zooming away from the hangar and the concrete blockhouse, past the silent blood-splashed jet, shooting down the line of reaching hands, driving at full speed toward the far end of the runway.

The zombies all turned to follow.

He soon outpaced them. The farther Benny went, the fewer the zoms. Soon he was in open country, where only a solitary zombie wandered in a slow and pointless circle, its sad pattern created by a missing foot. Benny cut right, heading toward the squat building at the foot of the row of siren towers.

He cast a quick look over his shoulder and saw that he was at least half a mile ahead of the leading edge of the zombie wave.

Perfect.

He drove over to the small building. A soldier stepped out, rifle in hand.

"Stop right there," he commanded. "Who are you and what are you doing over here? This is a restricted area."

"No kidding," said Benny. "I need you to turn the sirens on."

The soldier began raising the rifle.

Benny immediately spun the quad to kick up a thick cloud of choking dust. Then he shot south along the line of siren towers. He cursed aloud, repeating every foul phrase he'd learned from Riot. That girl had a truly poisonous mouth, and Benny felt a little embarrassed grumbling those descriptions, even though no one could hear him.

The zoms kept coming, drawn as much by the dust plume as by the roar of the quad. The dust plume was hundreds of feet high now, and the breeze, though slight, was steady—it continued to push the plume, reshaping it, shoving it away toward the mountains. The dead followed as if mesmerized.

Once Benny was sure he was well beyond the range of any rifle shot, he roared up and down at the base of the mountains, luring the zoms.

"Come on," Benny said through gritted teeth. "Come on . . ."

It took the zoms nearly twenty minutes to reach him.

When the closest zoms were fifteen feet away, Benny fed gas to the quad and shot away, running even farther to the south. They turned like an inhuman tidal surge, but he was moving too far and too fast. Then Benny cut right and right again to head north, but he angled away from where the mass of zoms were, keeping the engine speed low so that it purred rather than growled. The zoms would eventually hear him, but not right away.

By the time he got back to the blockhouse, Nix and the others had finished tying the soldiers up. Lilah stood over them, her Sig Sauer pistol held loosely at her side. Riot and Nix were trying to figure out how the locking assembly on the bridge worked. Dozens of monks had come out of the other buildings on that side of the trench. Some harangued the girls for their violence, but most watched in a kind of mute fascination.

Benny pulled to a stop by the blockhouse air lock. He killed the engine, dismounted, and did a very quick, very quiet circuit of the entire building to make sure that he hadn't missed any zoms.

There wasn't a single dead person around.

Benny grinned.

He ran to the edge of the trench and called Nix's name.

The first thing she said was, "You're an idiot."

"Yeah, not a news flash."

"But I love you."

He nodded past her to the soldiers. "They okay?"

She gave a single, cold, dismissive shrug.

What amazed Benny was the difference between his lingering male-centric perception of girls as weaker, shy, and incapable of violence or cruelty and the way they actually were. And it wasn't like he had seen any proof to the contrary. Lilah was a walking statement about girl power. So was Riot. And Nix, who was every bit as good with a sword as Benny was. Even with all that, the splinter of gender prejudice still festered in his mind. He wondered if he would ever stop being surprised when his preconceptions were trounced by the truth.

Riot sauntered to the edge. "Y'all got an actual plan, boy, or are you hoping for divine intervention?"

"Little of both," Benny admitted.

"Do we get to know the plan?"

"It's simple," he said. "I'm going to knock on the door until they let me in."

The girls gave him long, flat stares.

"Hey," Benny said, "I'm open to better suggestions."

Lilah, who had been listening, called, "Knock loud."

He knocked loud.

Every time I think about Mountainside and the other towns, I worry. Risking everything on a chain-link fence is just dumb. Even that psycho Preacher Jack was smarter about things. At Gameland they had all sorts of defenses. Smart stuff. They had a heavy chain-link fence too, but it was only the outer barrier. And it was hidden between two rows of thick evergreen hedge that acted as screens. Zoms couldn't see through the hedge and had fewer things to visually attract them.

After the fence, the road led through this complicated network of trenches. There were rows of trip wires, and deadfall pits covered by camouflage screens. Directions for how to make it through the defenses safely were written on large wooden signs. That's smart because humans can read but zoms can't.

The Gameland defenses weren't based on the way people used to protect towns and forts against attacks; these were specifically designed against an enemy that couldn't think but also would not stop.

The trench at Sanctuary is smart too.

Tom said that to stay safe you have to understand the nature of the threat, not react to your assumption of it. I didn't understand that at first.

I do now.

"OPEN THE DAMN DOOR!" BENNY YELLED, AND HE YELLED IT SO LOUDLY that echoes banged off the distant red rock mountain and ricocheted back to him over the heads of the hundreds of zombies who now shambled slowly back toward him. His fist ached and his throat was getting raw, but he stood there and kept at it. Hammering, yelling.

"Kid . . . yo, *kid!*" a voice said. "They can't hear you."

Benny whirled to see the big ranger, Joe, standing behind him. He hadn't heard him approach.

"Where'd you come from?"

"Originally? Baltimore. Just now—the hangar."

"It took you long enough." Benny massaged his hand. "Where have you been?"

"Busy. Want to tell me why you and your crew of girl-thugs just beat the crap out of four soldiers? And while you're at it, how about explaining the stunt with the quad? I've seen stupid and I've seen stupid but that was—"

"Stupid, yeah, I saw where you were going with that."

That put a half smile on Joe's face. "So—what's the deal? Is this about seeing your friend Chong? Roughing up soldiers and breaking rules isn't going to—"

"I'm trying to get inside," said Benny. He gave the door another hit.

"I figured that much, which is why I came out here. I'm trying to keep you from wasting your time." Joe pointed at the tall steel doors set into the concrete facade of the building. "Read my lips here, kid, try to follow. *They. Can't. Hear. You.*"

"Why not?"

"It's an ultra-secure soundproof hardened facility. It's designed to withstand anything except a direct hit from a nuclear weapon. You could march up and down all day long with a brass band and they won't hear a peep. Nothing. Nada. Am I getting through to you in any way?"

Benny ignored him.

"It's also designed to keep out a gazillion zombies like the ones who are—oh yeah, coming this way."

"They won't be here for at least ten minutes."

Joe grunted. "Fair enough. Door's still going to be locked when they get here . . . and the geeks inside won't even know that the zoms are chowing down on a pigheaded teenager."

"Why?" he demanded. "They have to know we're out here."

"They do. Once in a while one of them even looks at us on a video monitor."

"On a what?"

"A kind of electronic window."

"Then if they're looking at us, why don't they open the door?"

"Why would they?"

Benny pointed backward, jabbing a finger at the building. "Because I'm knocking."

"No offense, kid, but who the hell are you?"

Benny punched him.

He didn't even know he was going to do it. His hand was already moving when it clenched into a knot and slammed into the side of Joe's jaw.

The blow had all of Benny's anger and frustration in it.

It rocked Joe. It knocked him back half a step.

And that was all it did.

Benny threw a second punch, but Joe caught that one in his open palm like a shortstop catching a grounder. Joe's fingers closed around Benny's fist like iron bars. Then his hand darted out and clutched a fistful of Benny's shirtfront, and suddenly Benny was up on his toes, nose to nose with the ranger. Joe's blue eyes bored into him like drills, and the man's mouth twitched as if he fought to bite down on the words he wanted to say.

Finally he smiled and pushed Benny back.

He rubbed his jaw. "Nice punch. I honestly can't tell you the last time anyone caught me with a sucker punch."

"I hope it hurts."

"It does," Joe admitted. "Though . . . probably not as much as your hand."

Benny was trying to ignore his hand. It was a white-hot ball of pain at the end of his wrist.

"Let me tell you something, kid," said Joe. "Because you're Tom Imura's brother, and because you're probably not recovered from that head wound you got, I'm going to let this slide. I can understand you being upset—your best friend is in there and maybe he's dying or maybe he's already zommed out—but you need to learn how to pick your fights.

I'm not your enemy, and I'm not much in favor of being a punching bag for someone who wants to vent."

"I can't let Chong die without doing everything I can," said Benny. "I can't."

"Fine, I admire that. Bravo for you," said Joe. "How is all this crap going to help him?"

Benny dug his hand into his pocket and removed the two slips of paper.

"We went out to the Ruin today," he said. "To a ravine near where the plane went down."

"Why?"

"Because that's where Sergeant Ortega is. Or was. He's dead. Really dead, I mean."

Joe narrowed his eyes and nodded to the pieces of paper. "You took those from him?"

"Yes." Benny handed one of the slips to Joe. "I think we found out where Dr. McReady is."

Joe studied the paper. It was the message that read: URGENT: REPT OF R3 ACTIVITY VCNTY OF DVNP— REL. WIT. *** FTF?

Benny watched the big man's reaction. Joe went dead pale. Then his eyes widened and widened until Benny thought they'd bug out of his head.

"Where . . . ?"

Benny explained about the visit to the ravine, how they pulled Sergeant Ortega out, what they found, and the subsequent confrontation with Brother Peter and the Red Brotherhood.

"He said he wanted what I gave you."

"Fat chance," said Joe.

"He said that if I didn't give it to him by sundown tomorrow, the reapers were going to attack Sanctuary."

Benny expected Joe to laugh that off, but he didn't

"Joe?" asked Benny. "The reapers can't actually take Sanctuary . . . can they?"

But Joe didn't answer. "Where's the satchel you took from Sergeant Ortega?"

"I . . . um . . . gave it to Brother Peter."

Joe's face went from bloodless to a livid and dangerous red.

"Are you *deranged*?" thundered the ranger. For the second time he grabbed a fistful of Benny's shirt. "You stupid, bone-headed little—"

And Benny held up the second slip of paper.

The one with the coordinates.

"You soldiers have been at war too long," said Benny. "Try having some faith in other people."

Joe stared at the paper. It had been neatly torn in half. "This is only half of it. . . ."

"I know. We'll give you the other half as soon as you give me your word on two things."

"You're on thin ice, boy," said Joe in a low and dangerous voice.

Benny leaned toward him. "I've been on thin ice since zombies ate the world. I want your word on two things. Two conditions."

Joe studied him with steely eyes. "What conditions?"

"First, you tell me what's going on inside the lab and the hangar."

"Believe me, kid, you don't want to know."

"Don't tell me what I want to know. And don't assume that I can't handle it."

"What's the other condition?"

"You take me with you," said Benny. "Me, Nix, Riot, and Lilah."

Benny waited, his whole body tensing for the argument, the outrage, the refusal that he knew was coming. The ranger looked past him at the three fierce girls on the other side of the trench. Then he turned and looked at the zoms, who were less than a quarter mile away. Finally he looked down at the torn piece of paper in his hand.

"You're doing all of this because of your friend? Because of that Chong kid?"

"I'm doing this because this is our world too. You don't have a right to shut us out of the process of saving it."

Joe drew in a deep breath and exhaled slowly through his nose.

"Let me tell you something, kid," he said. "Because I liked your brother, I'm going to forget that you're trying to extort me here."

"Thanks, but it's not extortion," snapped Benny. "And even if it was, I can't let Chong die without doing everything I can."

Joe looked up to judge the angle of the sun. "You have one hour to pack. One change of clothes, water and food for a week, every weapon you have. You meet me at the bridge and have the rest of those coordinates."

Benny dug a hand into his pocket and removed the other half of the paper and held it out for Joe. The ranger smiled and took it.

Benny smiled back. "Like I said—you should have more faith in people."

Blowflies swarmed around Saint John as he stood with his hands clasped behind his back, eyes and mouth composed and thoughtful, his dark clothes glistening with blood. The cooks and their assistants were busy butchering the slaughtered horses. The quartermasters of the reaper army were searching through the trade goods in the four wagons for anything of value. Much of what the traders had brought with them was sinful—paperback books, holy books from a dozen false religions, jewelry, antibiotics, toys, luxuries. Things that made people want to enjoy being alive, and how grave an insult that was to Thanatos—praise to his darkness—who had decreed that human life should end, that anyone who stayed alive did so as an affront to god. Except for the reapers, and they all knew that when the great cleansing was done, they would open red mouths in one another and go into the darkness, where a vast and eternal nothingness awaited them.

The saint's orders to his reapers had been precise: Kill no one.

The flight of arrows that had stopped this convoy had been precisely aimed. To kill the horses, to wound every other guard. The effect was a predictable one. As the uninjured guards saw their fellows to the left and right of them fall, saw the arrows and the blood, heard the shrill screams of pain and fear, their hearts fled them. They threw down their weapons and begged for quarter. For mercy.

Only two guards possessed courage greater than their own sense of self-preservation. Or perhaps they believed themselves to be powerful enough to fight through this attack. One man, a Latino with a barrel chest, leaped from his dying Tennessee walking horse. He wore a necklace of wedding bands and carried a pump shotgun, which he emptied into the first wave of Red Brothers. When the gun was empty, he dropped it and drew a Glock nine-millimeter pistol and killed eight more reapers before the next wave crashed into him. The man went down hard. He killed and maimed with a knife he took away from one of the Red Brothers, and when that became lodged in the chest of a reaper, the Latino used his bare hands.

Saint John shouted to his reapers to take this man alive.

They did, but the figure they dragged before the saint had a dozen red mouths in his flesh and one foot already in the darkness. It saddened Saint John. This was the kind of fighter who, had he been encouraged to kneel and kiss the blade, would have made a superb Red Brother.

Saint John stood over him now, hands clasped, lips pursed. The other survivors were being tied up. Some were being taught the manners necessary to survive an interview with the saint. Their screams filled the air.

"What is your name, brother?"

The Latino glared up at him. "Hector Mexico," he snarled.

Then he punctuated that with a string of obscenities in English and Spanish that made the reapers around Saint John blanch.

The saint ignored the words and their suggestions of improbable physical acts.

"You are dying," he said. "The darkness hungers for you."

Hector Mexico spat blood onto Saint John's shoes. "Maybe so, *pendejo*, but I put twenty of your boys in the dirt, so kiss my—"

Even the reapers who watched did not see Saint John draw his knife. All they saw was a blur of movement, and then the Latino man screamed as the tip of the knife drew a line across his forehead.

"No," said Saint John, showing him the knife. "Bravado and insults will not ease your journey. You have insulted my god. There will be no heroic end to your tale."

Hector had to grit his teeth to keep another scream locked in his throat.

"Unless," said Saint John mildly, "you do a simple service for the Night Church."

Hector said nothing.

"Tell me the best and quickest route to the town of Mountainside."

Hector shook his head.

"Or any of the Nine Towns."

Silence.

Saint John sighed, then signaled to his reapers. "Bring another one."

They dragged a wounded and terrified young man over. He had blond hair and freckles and could not have been older than eighteen. They forced him to his knees in front of Hector.

The saint stood over the boy, his blade in his hand.

"I need to know the way to the Nine Towns," he said. "I only need one of you to tell me. That person will not need to spend his last hours screaming for death as the things that define him as a human being are removed one piece at a time. That person will be welcomed into the Night Church and will become one of us."

He held the knife out and let blood drip onto the dirt between Hector and the young man.

"Who will it be?"

Hector said, "Don't do it, Lonnie. Be a man . . . it won't hurt for long. . . ."

But Saint John said, "Oh yes, my brothers, it will. It will hurt for such a long and delicious time."

One voice spoke out, begging to tell.

The other screamed out, cursing and damning the reapers.

Through it all, Saint John smiled and smiled.

JOE ARRANGED FOR THE SIRENS TO CALL OFF THE ZOMS SO BENNY COULD cross the trench and go pack. When Benny and the girls returned to the bridge with their gear, there were four new soldiers guarding it. The soldiers were pale-faced strangers Benny had never seen before.

As Benny approached, one of them, a hatchet-faced man with startlingly blue eyes, put his hand on the butt of his holstered .45. He had the faintest echoes of facial bruising that was almost gone, and a purple scar through his eyebrow that looked like it had required at least eight stitches. His name tag read PERUZZI. He ignored Benny and locked a lethal stare on Lilah.

"I remember you," Peruzzi said with a malicious grin.

"You should," said Lilah, unperturbed by the implied menace in that smile. Benny realized that Peruzzi had to be one of the soldiers Lilah had roughed up after Chong nearly died. Several of the soldiers had been hospitalized. When he glanced at the others, he could see similar traces of recent trauma.

Oops, he thought.

"What's your problem?" demanded Nix, standing firm beside Lilah. "Who are you?"

"Nobody's talking to you, pint-size," said Peruzzi.

"Well, *I'm* talking to *you*," said Nix.

Peruzzi laughed and gave her a slow, invasive up-and-down stare. "Big boobs don't make you a grown-up, little girl," he said in an ugly voice. "Mind your manners and shut your mouth."

Benny's hand flashed toward his sword, but the solder had his pistol out so fast the blade was only a quarter drawn. The barrel dug hard into Benny's cheek, right beside his nose.

"Give me a reason," said Peruzzi.

The other soldiers chuckled, and they swung their rifles up toward the girls.

Peruzzi sneered. "You suckered those idiots who were working this detail earlier. You ever touch any of my men again and I'll hurt you in ways you ain't ever heard of."

The gun barrel was cold, but it felt hot against Benny's skin. He was absolutely terrified, but at the same time a vicious rage was boiling in his gut.

"Y'all better put that gun down," advised Riot.

"And *y'all* better shut your ugly mouth," said Peruzzi, mocking her Appalachian accent.

"Just trying to give you fair warning is all," she said, seemingly unflustered by the guns.

"Yeah, well how about you kiss my—"

And there was a low growl.

A deep-chested growl that sounded like it came from a bear.

Riot smiled. Everyone else turned to see Grimm standing inches behind the rearmost soldier, dressed in his full battle armor except for the spiked helmet. The dog was more massive than even the largest of the men, and anger made muscles bunch and flex under his hide. The motion clanked the chain mail he wore, and yet everyone had been so absorbed in the confrontation that they hadn't noticed the mastiff's approach.

The big ranger, Joe, walked slowly toward the group. He was dressed in camouflage, with boots, gun belt, sidearm, sword, and rifle. He carried a heavy duffel bag easily in one hand.

Nobody said a word as the ranger drew near. However, Peruzzi lowered his pistol.

"Grimm," said Joe, "down."

The dog immediately stopped growling and sat. But his eyes burned with a clear desire to bite something that would scream.

Joe walked up to Peruzzi and then kept walking so that the soldier had to give ground and back away. He backed the man all the way to the upraised bridge. Peruzzi's shoulders, heels, and the back of his head thumped against the steel. Without taking his eyes off Peruzzi, Joe reached down and took his pistol away from him. He dropped the magazine into the sand, ejected the round, and tossed the pistol into the trench.

Peruzzi opened his mouth with the beginning of a sharp protest, but Joe leaned in so close that their foreheads touched.

"Go ahead, sergeant," murmured Joe quietly, "say it. Say something. Tell me exactly what's on your mind, because as you know I've always been fascinated by the particular species of thoughts that evolve in your brain. It's like science fiction sometimes. Hard to believe a human brain is at work here."

Peruzzi was able to hold eye contact with Joe for three seconds, and then he looked down. But Joe wasn't interested. He leaned back far enough to bring his hand up between them and tap Peruzzi sharply on the forehead.

"I didn't catch that," he said. "I missed the part where you apologized to these young women and to my friend Benjamin here."

"S-sorry," mumbled Peruzzi.

Joe patted his cheek. "Yeah, I know you are." His back was still turned to the other three soldiers. "It would suck for all parties involved if I turned around and saw that you three stooges were still pointing your weapons rather than standing at attention with rifles slung."

Grimm growled again, softly but meaningfully.

The soldiers snapped to attention.

Joe gave Peruzzi a last penetrating stare. "We're not going to have this discussion again, are we, Sergeant Peruzzi?"

"No, sir."

"And I can sleep soundly at night—every night—in the sure knowledge that nothing untoward will happen to these four young people here . . . or their friend in the blockhouse. I mean, we can agree on that, right?"

"Yes, sir."

Joe smiled. It was a big, toothy, happy smile. What Mayor Kirsch would have called an "aw shucks" smile. Benny knew that the humor in that smile went less than a millimeter deep.

"Good," said the ranger. "Now how about signaling the siren house and then getting this bridge down?"

The soldiers turned quickly away and set to work.

Joe glanced briefly at Nix, Lilah, Riot, and Benny. "Can't stand around trading Zombie Cards all day, kids. We're burning daylight."

SAINT JOHN RAISED HIS FACE TO LET THE BLOODRED HEAT OF THE DYING sun bathe his face.

He could hear the rustle of the reapers behind him. The Red Brotherhood formed the first ranks—five hundred strong. Beyond them was the main body of the reaper army.

Teams of quartermasters ran along the ranks with buckets brimming with the chemical created by Sister Sun. Every reaper dipped his red tassels in the buckets and retied them to ankles and wrists, threaded them through belt loops, and pinned them to their shirts between the outspread angel wings. This was the most noxious and powerful version of the chemical, the formula revised by Sister Sun to accommodate the spike in aggression from the gray people. Sometimes a reaper would be dragged down and consumed regardless of the chemicals, but that was okay. If it happened, then god willed it to be so, and the surviving reapers celebrated as one of their own went on into the darkness.

Besides, Saint John could afford to lose a few reapers. He could afford to lose hundreds. The army had grown as riders on quads contacted units scattered all over California, Utah, Idaho, and Nevada. Some of those riders had been sent out on the night Saint John walked away from Mother Rose's defeat at the gates of Sanctuary. He had over three hundred working quads and many thousands of reapers. Some of those reapers had kissed the knife as recently as this afternoon. Among the new acolytes were former trade guards and bounty hunters who lived in the Nine Towns. They had been so eager, so willing to share every secret of each of those towns.

What amazed Saint John, even after everything he had seen and learned about the foolishness of people, was that most of the towns had only chain-link fences for protection against the gray people.

As if the dead were the only threat.

As if the dead were even a serious threat.

As if the will of god were so easily ignored.

It angered Saint John. He felt that it showed no respect at all for the importance of his mission. It felt like a challenge, a boast. Or an invitation to prove to each and every sinner behind those frail walls that the will of Thanatos—all praise to his darkness—could not be deterred.

He opened his eyes and looked once more at the sign that had caused him to stop and savor the moment. It was not one of the machine-printed road signs from before the Fall. This was hand-painted on the side of an empty hardware store that squatted by the side of the four-lane highway.

WELCOME TO HAVEN

POP. 5,219

COME IN PEACE, LEAVE IN PROSPERITY

GOD AND ALL HIS ANGELS PROTECT YOU ON THE ROAD

The road sloped downward for a thousand yards and stopped at the gates of a chain fence. He touched the silver dog whistle that hung around his neck.

"'Welcome to Haven,'" Saint John read aloud, enjoying each separate syllable.

He lifted the whistle to his lips.

It was not the reaper army that he called.

The answer to his call was a moan of hunger so loud that the thunder of it rolled down the hill toward those metal gates.

57

WHEN THE ZOMS WERE ALL AT THE FAR END OF THE AIRFIELD, JOE motioned for Benny and the girls to follow him, and he led them past the blockhouse and the first two hangars. Grimm trotted beside him, his armor clanking with each step; and he kept throwing angry glances at the sirens and the zoms. A sturdy chain-link fence was in place to create a safe corridor between the zoms and the hangars. The frame of the fence was mounted on wheels so the whole thing could be swung wide for aircraft and other vehicles. The main doors of the hangars were closed, but Benny saw that smaller doors stood ajar, and he went over to peer inside.

The first hangar was filled with parts of dead machines: helicopters, small planes, tanks, armored personnel carriers, Jeeps, Humvees, and motorcycles; all of them stripped and scavenged for parts. Nothing looked whole, and all of it looked old.

"What is it?" asked Nix, leaning past him to look.

"Junk," he said.

"Where's all the other stuff?" she asked. "I thought they were rebuilding."

"More like dismantling."

They hurried to catch up to the others, but paused again at the second hangar. This one had a row of quads painted in military camouflage. There were big worktables, chain hoists from which unidentifiable engine parts hung, tool chests on rollers, and machine schematics taped to the walls. But again there was a flavor of disuse about it all. Like the work of repairing the machines had been abandoned. Weeks or even months ago.

"Where are all the soldiers?" asked Nix. "And the technicians? The monks said that there are more than two hundred people over here. We've seen maybe ten different soldiers and Captain Ledger. And three or four different voices in the interview air lock."

"I don't know, but it's creeping me out," Benny admitted. Nix nodded, but she looked more than creeped out. She looked deeply hurt by it.

"Let's go," he said, and they hurried off.

Joe and Grimm stopped at the entrance to the third hangar. The smaller door was open, but he stood in front of it.

"I know you kids have about a million questions about what's going on over here," he began.

"Maybe two million," said Riot, "and that's just me. Red over yonder's been writing questions in that journal of hers, and she's got every page filled, front and back."

Nix nodded.

"I have a few hundred thousand just off the top of my head," said Benny. "Any chance we're actually going to get some answers?"

"There's a lot going on that you don't know about," said Joe, "and a lot of it is classified."

"Why?" asked Lilah sharply.

"Because the military likes to keep its business to itself."

"Why?"

Joe smiled. "Because secrecy can become an addiction. That's been a problem as long as people have tried to covet power for themselves. Sure, governments need to keep some secrets, but too often the people inside the government create for themselves the illusion that because they know things nobody else does, it makes them more powerful. That kind of thinking creates a kind of contempt for anyone on the outside. It's born from a belief that their own power will diminish in direct proportion to the transparency of their actions. So secrets become the currency that buys them membership into a club so exclusive that their agendas are never shared, and the value of what they hold is measured only from a first-person perspective." He paused. "Are you following me on this?"

"Yes," said Benny.

"There's more, though," said Joe. "Greed and a feeling of inadequacy aren't the only reasons people keep secrets. Sometimes they hide things—information, the truth, themselves—behind layers of secrecy simply because they're afraid."

"Afraid of what?" asked Lilah.

"You," said Joe. "Everyone who held any kind of power, everyone who kept any secrets, everyone who was part of running the world before First Night is terrified of you kids."

"Why us?" asked Nix.

"Not just you four—but your whole generation. You scare them to death."

"But . . . *why*?" asked Benny.

"Three reasons," said Joe, ticking them off on his fingers. "Because you want to know the truth. Because you'll eventually learn the truth. And because you deserve to know the truth."

Benny looked past him at the open door. "What truth, Joe?"

The ranger said nothing.

"The Reaper Plague," Benny said softly. "There are all kinds of theories about how it started. A new virus . . ."

"Radiation from a returning space probe," said Nix.

"The wrath of God," added Riot.

"Something that was accidentally released from a lab," said Lilah.

Benny closed his eyes. "None of that's true, is it?"

When he opened his eyes, he saw a look of such deep sadness on Joe's face that it made his heart hurt.

"Before First Night," said the ranger, "I spent my entire adult life working for a government organization that did only one thing: We hunted down the kinds of people who wanted to see the world burn. Terrorists, religious extremists, actual mad scientists, governments that had gone off the rails. Time and time again I led good men and women into battle to stop the release of a doomsday weapon. I won every single time. I lost a lot of friends along the way. I even lost the first woman I truly loved. My body's covered with scars from injuries taken in the line of duty. Me and my guys, we were sometimes all that stood between the world and the end of everything. Sounds grandiose, right? But that's how it was." He sighed.

"You failed," said Lilah. She made a statement of it, harsh and naked.

He raised his hands as if indicating the whole world. "Some people kept their secrets a little too long and a little too well, and by the time my team knew about it, the devil was already off the leash." He shook his head. "That's not an apology, and it's not an excuse. I want us to understand each other. I'm a ranger. I do not work for the American Nation. I work *with* them. There are some good people helping to build a new government. But there are some people who still hold on to the old ways. Their religion is the cult of secrecy, and they are every bit as dangerous as Saint John and the psychopaths running the Night Church."

"Why tell us all this now?" asked Benny. "What aren't you telling us?"

"Benny," cautioned Nix, but Joe shook his head.

"He's dead right, honey. When we go into that hangar, you're stepping outside of the world you knew and into a bad slice of the old world. They're going to want to push you around. They're going to try and close you out of their vault of secrets. You're civilians and you're kids and they believe that you don't matter."

Joe removed the slips of paper they'd gotten from Sergeant Ortega. "This is a different kind of currency, and down on the level of reality and sense, it's worth a lot more than the secrets the people on this base are holding."

He handed them to Benny.

"I told them that you had information about where Dr. McReady might be. They want that information very badly. They think that it's your obligation to simply hand it over. If you do, they'll kick you right back onto the other side of the trench. Don't let them. This is your world. It was always yours.

277

We didn't have the right to break it, and we shouldn't be allowed to keep any more secrets."

The four of them stood there in front of Joe Ledger, weighing his words, reading the implications. Grimm licked his jowls and watched them.

Finally Benny said, "The Reaper Plague was no accident, was it?"

"No," said Joe in a ghost of a voice. "We made the monster and we let it out of its cage."

"Deliberately?" asked Nix, aghast.

His eyes were filled with great sorrow. "You ever heard of Friedrich Nietzsche?"

Nix nodded and in a small voice said, "I was just thinking about that earlier. 'Battle not with monsters, lest ye become a monster, and if you gaze into the abyss, the abyss gazes also into you.'"

"Exactly," said Joe. "We stared into the abyss so long we liked what we saw. God forgive us all."

JOE TURNED AND WALKED INTO THE HANGAR. GRIMM WAS RIGHT AT HIS heels. Riot and Lilah exchanged a glance, then followed. Benny paused, touching Nix's arm. He didn't like the wild look in her eyes.

"You okay?"

"Oh, sure," she said tightly. "I'm just fine. I shouldn't even be surprised. After everything that's gone on with Charlie and the Hammer, Preacher Jack, Mother Rose, Saint John . . . I don't know why I don't just give up on believing in people."

"I know why," said Benny.

She gave him a long, cold look. "Oh really? Why?"

"Because *we're* people. Your mom was a good person who never hurt anyone. Tom died trying to help people. That guy George who spent all those years taking care of Lilah and her sister. The Greenman. Guys like Solomon Jones and Sally Two-Knives and everyone who helped destroy Gameland . . . they're people. Eve is a person. So is Riot, and she was raised to be a monster. She left all that behind, and for the last few years she's done nothing but risk her life to help people. They're good people, and that's what I believe in, Nix. That goodness exists and that it's powerful. And I think that's what you believe in too."

She closed her eyes and leaned her forehead against his chest. "But there are so many of *them*. Look at what they've done. They destroyed the whole world. . . ."

"No," Benny said softly. He hooked a finger under her chin and gently raised her face. "Not the whole world. And not the best of it."

Nix's mouth trembled and she hung there at the edge of tears, pinned to the moment by the enormity of Joe's words.

"I can't live in a world like this," she said. "I can't live if everything's broken and there's only pain."

"No," agreed Benny, "neither can I. So let's live in a better world than that."

She suddenly wrapped her arms around him, and they clung to each other.

"Promise me," she begged.

"I promise," he said.

As he held her, Benny looked into that promise. It was a simple enough thing to say in the heat of heartbreak and tears. But he knew as he said it that this was going to mean more to him than anything else. Something shifted inside his head and his heart, like a switch being thrown on some machinery that had been carefully built but never turned on. He wasn't sure, then or ever, what powered that machinery. Maybe love, maybe hate, maybe a moral outrage so hot that it caused gears to turn and motors to combust.

There are such moments in a life. Solitary seconds on which the reality of what life means pivots and turns from a dead end toward a road of untrodden grass that stretches on forever. It was a moment in which the words he said aloud and the whispers of his inner voice spoke in perfect harmony. And Benny knew thereafter that he would never hear that inner voice as a thing separate from himself. It was as if he had caught up to the idealized version of himself that had always walked a pace or two ahead.

I promise, was what he said.

I will, was what he meant.

THEY ENTERED THE HANGAR, WHICH WAS VAST BUT MOSTLY EMPTY. TWO big, black helicopters squatted on the concrete pad. Unlike the ones in the first hangar, these hadn't been stripped of parts. They looked fierce and sinister and ready to growl their way into the air. Benny had read about helicopters and thought they might be Black Hawks, though this one had stubby wings as well as rotors, and he was pretty sure that some of the stuff mounted on those wings were chain guns and missiles. Part of him thought that they were pretty cool; but the other aspect of him—the facet of his personality that had just shifted into the forefront of his mind—viewed them merely as a tool. Potentially useful, but in no way designed for anything but destruction. Even if that destruction was necessary.

He thought about the phrase "necessary evil" and believed he understood it better at that moment than ever before. It was like the sword he carried. And that sparked a memory of something Tom once told him, an old samurai maxim that describes the apparent contradiction of those who prepare for war but do not crave it.

"We train ten thousand hours to prepare for a single moment we pray never happens."

Benny nodded to himself.

Most of the hangar was in shadows. One corner was well lit, though, and it was occupied by a big metal folding table. A woman in a military uniform sat at the table, and she rose as Joe led them over.

"Kids, meet Colonel Reid," said Joe. "She's the base commander here at Sanctuary."

Colonel Reid was a stern, unattractive woman roughly the size and density of a packing crate. She had iron-gray hair cut short, a lipless slash of a mouth that was compressed into a line of stern disapproval, and eyes that had all the warmth of frozen blueberries.

Despite his immediate reaction to her, Benny wanted to get this started on the right foot. He smiled and extended his hand.

"Pleased to meet you, ma'am. My name's—"

"I know who you are, Mr. Imura," she said, cutting him off sharply. She eyed the four of them with the disapproval of a disgruntled diner looking at side dishes she hadn't ordered. "I know who all of you are."

Joe sighed.

Benny's hand hung for a moment in the air.

"Okay, taking it back," he said, lowering his arm.

Reid eyed Joe. "What's your new mission status? Child-care professional?"

Joe sliced off a wafer of a smile. "They earned their spot."

Reid shook her head. "It's on you, then. I don't have troops to waste minding them."

"We didn't ask to be minded," said Benny.

"Right," said Nix, "I heard that four of your guys were in the infirmary."

Reid's icy expression dropped to absolute zero. "You have a smart mouth, girl."

"And you have a—"

"Okay, *enough!*" roared Benny. "Everyone cut the crap."

They all looked at him, momentarily shocked to silence.

"What the hell is it with everyone?" Benny continued, his volume lower but his voice still hard as fists. "If you're mad at us for roughing up some of your soldiers, then too bad. Get over it. They could have acted like human beings instead of robots."

"They were following my orders."

"Then maybe you should start giving better orders," Benny said coldly. "I mean, who do you think you are? Who do you think we are? We're not on opposite sides in this thing. Unless I'm mistaken, it's us against them, and the 'them' are the reapers and the zoms. *We* are supposed to be working together to save the world."

"*We* are," Reid fired back. "The American Nation is using its full resources to combat the Reaper Plague."

Benny leaned on the edge of the table. "And me and my friends? We're what to you? A nuisance?"

"I believe you already tried to play the card of importance due to finding the plane."

Benny smiled. "Yeah, I thought I recognized your voice. That was you I talked to yesterday. You said that our finding the plane was only self-interest. Are you actually that dense? Are all you people that close-minded? We shared that information because that's what people do. That's how everyone survives. Maybe you haven't been outside lately, colonel, but zombies ate the world. People have been scratching and clawing to survive for fifteen years. My own town is in California. Your jet passed right over us. Are you going to tell me that you didn't see it? Are you going to tell me that you don't know about the Nine Towns we have up in those mountains? Captain Ledger knows about them, so I'll bet a brand-new ration dollar that *you* know about them."

"We are aware of those towns," conceded Colonel Reid. "What of it?"

"What of it?" Benny slapped the flat of his palm on the table so hard it sounded like a gunshot. Echoes banged off the hangar walls. "Why the hell didn't you *tell* us? We thought we were alone all those years. We thought that the rest of the world was dead. Don't you think it would have helped us to know that there were other people out there? That there was a new government? That scientists were working on a cure? That people were trying to put the world back together into some shape that made sense? Are you so removed from human emotions that you can't realize how much that would have helped people? Helped *us*? It would have given us *hope*."

Colonel Reid started to reply, but Benny wasn't finished with her. "I read enough about the way things were before First Night to know that people were always fighting. Not just wars, but political fights, social fights, all sorts of things. I swear, sometimes reading those history books I wondered if people wanted to fight more than they wanted to survive." He straightened and fixed her with a cold stare. "When we saw that jet, we thought that things were going to be okay. We thought that it represented a chance for a better future than the one we were handed. I can't even put into words how sorry I am—how cheated I feel—to find out that things are just the same."

The silence in the hangar was absolute.

Finally, Riot murmured, "The boy's right . . . we're up to our eyeballs in the alligator swamp and y'all won't let us in the boat."

Colonel Reid brushed nonexistent lint from her lapel. Nix balled her hands into little fists that she squeezed hard enough to make the knuckles creak.

In a calmer voice, Benny said, "Right now you *need* us."

He produced the sheets with the coordinates.

Reid's face went scarlet, and she wheeled on Ledger. "You said that you had the coordinates."

"I did," admitted Ledger. "And I gave them back to Benny. After all, he found them."

"That's treason. I could have you shot for this."

Joe smiled. "You could try, Jane. But I don't think that would work out for you as well as you'd like." He shook his head. "Besides, those papers belong to Benny."

"They are the property of the American Nation."

"Excuse me," cut in Nix, "but exactly where are the borders of the American Nation?"

"Is that a joke?" demanded Reid.

"No, it's a straight question. We found those papers out here in the Ruin. Benny took some off a reaper and the coordinates from a walker. Are you saying that that happened inside your legal boundaries?"

"The whole continent is the American Nation."

"From the Atlantic to the Pacific?"

"Of course."

"So—central California is part of that, right?"

Reid snapped her mouth shut, but it was too late. Her foot was in Nix's bear trap.

"You're saying that our town, Mountainside, and all the other towns in the Sierra Nevadas are part of the American Nation?"

Reid kept her mouth clamped shut, but her face darkened by at least two shades. Benny wanted to laugh, but he kept his own mouth shut.

"You admit that our towns are part of your new nation, and yet never once did you send anyone to us. What were we? Inconvenient? Too much trouble? Did you just write us off?"

When Reid didn't answer, Lilah gave a derisive snort. So far it was her only contribution to the conversation, but it was eloquent.

Finally Reid couldn't hold it back anymore. "You arrogant little snots. Who the hell do you think you're talking to? I've dedicated my entire life to protecting this country."

"Really?" asked Benny. "How much of that time was spent protecting the *people*?"

Reid shook her head. "You're not capable of understanding what it takes to protect a nation."

"I am," said Joe quietly. "And the kid asks a good question. My rangers put together maps of all the populated settlements. I was in Asheville three times over the last two years to request permission to establish connections and resources to provide technology recovery services, medicines, and communication equipment. People like you argued against it every time. It wasn't the best use of resources. The distances were too great. The indigenous populations of those settlements did not include a high enough percentage of scientists and research-ers. Lots of excuses, none of them worth a drop of moose spit."

"It's not in your pay grade to question policy, Captain."

"It's not in anyone's pay grade to devalue tens of thou-sands of human lives because protecting them is inconve-nient. I can't begin to tell you how deeply ashamed I am for not taking matters into my own hands. I should have told this boy's brother about the American Nation. I should have told everyone. I should never have followed orders about leaving it to my superiors. Never. They deserve to know."

"They would have been contacted at the appropriate time. There's a timetable for this."

"Contacted when?" asked Nix. "After we were all dead? After the reapers or the zoms slaughtered us? When exactly would the 'appropriate' time be?"

"This conversation is ridiculous," Reid said with a dismis-sive shake of her head. "You'll hand over those coordinates so I can assign a team to—"

"No," said Benny.

"Don't test me, boy."

"The answer's no. You don't get them."

Reid laid her hand on the pistol holstered at her hip. "You want to play games, boy? Do you want me to *take* them from you?"

Nix and Lilah drew their pistols as fast as lightning. Riot, however, very casually took her slingshot from her belt and socketed a ball bearing into the pouch. Joe Ledger folded his arms and leaned a hip against the table.

Benny did nothing except give Reid a small, cold smile. "Like Captain Ledger said—you can try."

But Reid was not easily flustered. "Captain Ledger, I order you to—"

"Colonel Reid, I hereby resign my commission in the army of the American Nation, yielding all rank, pay, benefits, and privileges effective as of right now."

"You can't do that."

"Just did. In fact, a long time ago Tom Imura offered to let me sleep on his couch and help set me up as a bounty hunter in Mountainside. So I'm retroactively taking his offer, which means that I am declaring myself a citizen of Mountainside, one of the Nine Towns of the Sierra Nevadas. You can't tell by hearing it, but I'm capitalizing Nine Towns. If no one else has declared them a sovereign nation, then I am."

"You—"

"Unless," Joe said, "you would like to formally accept those towns into the American Nation, extending to the citizens the full support and resources of the American Nation."

Before Reid could answer, Joe stepped forward. His smile was strange, Benny thought. Feral, like a wolf's. It was almost as if a different person—more savage and more intense—glowered out through his blue eyes.

"Listen to me, Jane, and you'll do yourself a lot of good by keeping your ears open and your mouth shut," he said, his voice as soft as a whisper. "I've fought for my country and I've fought for my world. You sat behind a desk. You haven't logged an hour of field time in thirty years. You don't understand what it was that built this country in the first place. You take a lot of pride in being an officer in the 'American' Nation. So do I, but that rank and uniform comes with a price—no, an obligation—to protect the people as well as the real estate. Some of our colleagues didn't always grasp that before the Fall. Some did, a lot didn't. Those were the boneheads who thought it was a smart idea to nuke the cities rather than try to protect the survivors and retake the land. Those were the ones who used 'assets' and 'collateral damage' to describe people and loss of life. Well, guess what . . . that ends right here and right now. America was born in the fires of a revolution, with people who wanted to push back against oppression. It was made tougher in the furnace of a civil war to make everyone free. In every single decade there were people who stood up and spoke out, people who made a stand. I look at you and what you represent, and I look at these four kids here and all their integrity and potential, and sister, you don't measure up too well."

"You're a hypocrite," said Reid.

"I know it. But that was five minutes ago. Miracle of miracles, I have officially come to my senses. Now how about that? And from now on I'll do whatever I can, whatever I need to do, to atone for being a pigheaded jackass and a company man for way too long." He took a small step closer. "Oh yeah, and theft. I'm going to steal one of those helicopters so I can try and find Dr. McReady."

Benny nodded to Nix and the others, and they lowered their weapons.

"You don't want to do this, Captain," said Reid.

He stepped back and shrugged. "I'm not a captain anymore."

Joe walked over to the helicopter, entered it, and did something that caused the big motor to whine to life. Then he climbed out, crossed to the wall near the door they'd entered, and pressed a big red button. Immediately the massive hangar doors began rolling sideways, letting the hot afternoon air spill in, bringing with it the stink of zombie flesh.

While Joe did all this, Colonel Reid stood exactly where she was. She said nothing and did nothing.

The ranger came back to the table. "Once we're airborne," he said, "we'll radio you with the coordinates. Just in case. Maybe once you see where we're going, you'll understand."

Reid's face was wooden.

Joe paused. "I know what you're dealing with, Jane. And you know that I'm doing the right thing."

Her lips curled slowly back to reveal small, hard teeth. "I hope you die out there," she snarled.

Joe sighed and walked away. Benny felt sad. That was exactly what Morgie Mitchell had said to him before they'd left him behind in Mountainside. Even now Benny didn't think the colonel meant those words, any more than Morgie had. Sometimes you can be so hurt, so sad, and so confused that the only words you can force out are hateful ones.

Benny started to turn, but paused as Lilah pointed a finger at Reid. "Take care of Chong."

"Louis Chong is a patient in this facility," said Reid. "Don't insult me."

Lilah shook her head. "It's not an insult. It's a threat. I thought that was clear."

She turned and walked toward the helicopter.

It occurred to Benny that this had all been going on a long time without any of Reid's soldiers interfering. That didn't seem right.

"Colonel?" he asked, keeping his voice neutral. "Where are the soldiers? Where's everyone else?"

He expected a sharp answer or at least some sarcastic remark. Instead he saw sadness flood into her eyes. Her shoulders sagged for a moment, as if some tremendous weight pressed down on them.

But she did not answer Benny's question.

THEY CLIMBED INTO THE HELICOPTER, AND JOE BUCKLED EVERYONE INTO A seat. Grimm threw himself onto the deck with a loud clank of armor. Only Riot remained standing.

"You need to buckle up, girl," said Joe.

But she shook her head. "I ain't going. I don't like to leave Eve here alone. Little bird's been hurting something bad, and I want to keep an eye on her."

No one could argue with that. Lilah did something that surprised Benny. The stern, detached Lost Girl reached over and took Riot's hand, giving it a reassuring squeeze. For a fierce moment Riot clutched that hand like it was a lifeline. Lilah bent and kissed Riot's hand. There was no romance in it, just a connection on a wordless, human level. A conversation through action rather than words.

It stirred Benny's heart. Since Chong got sick, Lilah had become almost a nonperson. Cold, incredibly remote, and harsh. Could she be thawing? Or was Eve too powerful a reminder of Annie?

Benny said, "Give Evie a kiss from me."

Riot gave him a sad little smile. "She liked those balloons."

"It was nice to see her smile."

That changed Riot's expression, but she turned away to hide whatever was in her eyes. At the door she paused.

"Y'all come back safe and sound, hear?"

Then she stepped outside, and they could hear her crunching steps as she ran back to the bridge.

"Balloons?" asked Joe.

Benny explained about the pack of brightly colored balloons he'd found in the reaper's quad. "Can't figure why he'd have them, though."

"Everyone's a scavenger these days," observed Joe. "Maybe he knew some kids and thought they might like them."

That thought didn't make Benny feel any better. Kids waiting for the reaper to return with a present for them.

He sighed and busied himself with trying to adjust the straps. Seats requiring buckles were as far outside Benny's experience as helicopters were. However, he couldn't tell if the hammering of his heart was because of the thought of actually *flying*—particularly in a machine that was as extinct to his experience as the dinosaurs—or because of the confrontation he'd just had with Colonel Reid. He suspected that it was both in roughly equal measures.

Nix sat next to him, her small hand in his, fingers entwined, skin icy cold. Lilah sat across from him, and her thoughts were clearly directed inward. Shutters had dropped behind her eyes.

Joe slid the door shut, squatted down, and shouted over the whine of the engine. "We used to have an expression: 'This just got real.' Well, that's where we are. We're stealing government equipment, and we have no friends here at Sanctuary except a bunch of monks."

"Is that meant as a pep talk?" asked Benny.

"Just stating the facts."

"Thanks," said Nix, "but I'm pretty sure we're already scared enough as it is."

Joe grinned.

"Do we even know where we're going?"

"We do." Joe removed a big map from his pocket and spread it out on the floor and tapped a spot with a forefinger. "Right here."

Nix leaned in and read the words printed on the map. "Death Valley National Park. Oh, isn't that wonderful."

"'Death' Valley?" asked Benny. "Seriously? Death Valley?"

"That's the DVNP on the note we found," observed Nix. "It fits."

"I get that, but really . . . *Death* Valley?"

"I think we all appreciate the irony," said Nix.

"Not sure you do," said Benny. He reached out with the toe of his shoe and tapped another spot. "Does that actually say the 'Funeral Mountains'?"

"Don't let it spook you, kid," said Joe. "Those names were given long before the dead rose."

"That's actually not a comfort," said Benny, and Nix nodded agreement.

"We're heading to a spot called Zabriskie Point on the eastern side of Death Valley, south of Furnace Creek. It's in the badlands. . . ."

"Oh, 'badlands.' Also very comforting."

Joe said, "Look, if we pool all of what we know, we come up with a picture that's a little grim and a little hopeful. I think we can safely deduce that Dr. McReady was not on the

C-130 when it crashed. It seems clear that the plane stopped at the Umatilla Chemical Depot in Oregon, where I believe Doc McReady and Field Team Five deplaned and took alternate transport to Death Valley."

"Why did Dr. McReady stop at the base in Oregon?" asked Lilah. "What's there?"

"Ah, well," said Joe diffidently. "One of our dirty little secrets. Even though that base had been officially decommissioned, it was actually still in operation at the time of the outbreak."

"You mean there were still chemical weapons there?" Benny asked.

"Were," agreed Joe, "and are. Chemical and biological weapons, agents, compounds, and ingredients. It was all stockpiled there. The decommissioning process was a smoke screen. The government was making a show of complying with the Chemical Weapons Convention, an arms control agreement that outlawed the production, stockpiling, and use of all chemical weapons. The international agreement was administered by the Organisation for the Prohibition of Chemical Weapons based in the Netherlands."

"But we kept the weapons?"

Joe looked pained. "There are a lot of skeletons in the closet, kids."

"Okay, so why would Dr. McReady stop there?" insisted Nix.

"Because there is a lot of crucial equipment there," said Joe. "Stuff the American Nation can't manufacture yet. Stuff like hazmat suits, biohazard containment gear, pretty much everything McReady might need if she was going to collect field samples of a mutating pathogen. And there were planes there too. It's possible that one of them—a prop job, not a jet—could have been repaired. Or maybe that had already been done and McReady got wind of it. Doesn't matter. What's important is that she stopped there, got some alternate transport, and as far as we know she's still alive somewhere."

"In Death Valley," said Benny.

"Possibly."

Nix said, "Death Valley isn't that far, is it?"

"Hundred miles and change," said Joe.

"And the doc went missing a year ago?"

Joe nodded. "Closer to eighteen months. We've been looking, but the country's too big. And we don't have enough resources."

"If she's still alive," said Nix, "she can't be trying all that hard to get home. She could have walked it half a dozen times by now."

Joe winced, but gave another nod. "Don't think I haven't thought of that. But we still have to try and find her. Now sit back and enjoy the ride. None of you have flown before, right? Well—you're going to love this, I guarantee it."

They did not.

Lilah was the only one who didn't throw up.

THE MOTION OF THE HELICOPTER CHANGED, AND JOE CALLED THEM ALL to join him. Green-faced, sweating, nauseous beyond imagining, Benny and the others unbuckled and staggered forward to crowd through into the tiny cockpit. Joe chased Grimm out of the copilot seat so Nix could sit there, and the mastiff sulked his way back into the main cabin. Benny and Lilah jammed the doorway.

"Welcome to the badlands of Death Valley," said Joe as if he was happy about it. "Zabriskie Point is dead ahead."

Below them was a landscape that Benny thought looked like the surface of some alien world. Stretches of barren ridges, wind-sculpted badlands, deep hollows cut into the terrain by millions of years of erosion, and the black mouths of caves carved by wind into the sides of grim mountains. Here and there were desperate splashes of color from hardy trees and shrubs that even this hostile wasteland could not kill.

"This makes Nevada look like a rain forest," observed Nix. "Guess the name isn't ironic."

"And there's not much out here. California State Route 190 cuts through this area, but that was mostly used by people who wanted to get through this territory as quickly as possible," said Joe. "No towns, almost no animals, no—"

"Whoa," said Benny suddenly, "what's that?"

Joe looked where he was pointing, and his eyebrows rose in surprise. "Well, well, well . . . Isn't that interesting as all hell?"

Half a mile ahead there was an unnaturally flat shelf of rock set among the higher reaches of the rippled sedimentary rock. As Joe steered the helicopter toward it, they could see that it was paved with concrete. The surface was cracked and overgrown by some determined but leafless creeper vines. A symbol was painted on the shelf. A big circle with a capital letter *H* had long ago been painted in the center.

"That's a helipad," said Joe. "A landing pad for helicopters."

"I thought you said there was nothing out here," said Nix.

"I did."

Benny nodded to the helipad. "So . . . what on earth is that doing out here?"

"Guess we're going to find out."

They rounded the end of a wall of eroded rock and hovered a hundred feet above the shelf. There were foot trails running down into the badlands, but no visible road and no buildings or structures.

"Weird," said Benny.

Joe consulted his instruments. "That helipad is dead center of the coordinates. This is definitely where McReady's team was headed."

"You said they probably took a small plane here," said Nix. "Could a plane have landed on that?"

"No. Only another helicopter . . ." Joe's words trailed off.

As they continued to swing around, they could see down the slope on the far side. It was a sharp drop of hundreds of feet. Halfway down, smashed in among spikes of jagged rock, was the wreckage of another helicopter. Most of the wreckage was twisted into meaningless shapes, but as if to mock them, a flat section of the hull lay on a smaller shelf in plain view. And painted on the side, faded by a year and a half of harsh sun and wind, was the flag of the American Nation.

"Oh God," gasped Nix.

Benny said, "No one could have lived through that."

"It's a wreck," said Joe, "but let's not read too much into it yet. We don't know if it crashed when they got here or sometime later. Those crags are inaccessible. If anyone died in that thing, their zoms would probably still be trapped there."

Nothing moved, however.

Joe brought the helicopter back up to the level of the helipad. The rear wall of the shelf was flat, but there was a ring of cracked boulders around the shelf, some as big as two-story houses.

"What's that?" asked Lilah, pointing to the rear corner of the shelf.

A smile appeared slowly on Joe's face. As he drifted closer, they could all see it. The object was eight feet high and five feet wide, and though it was caked with dust and clots of dirt, it was clearly made from solid steel.

"An air lock," breathed Benny.

"An air lock," agreed Joe.

Nix turned a suspicious eye on him. "That's just like the one at Sanctuary. Is there another lab hidden in there? Did you know about this?"

He shook his head. "If so, then it's news to me."

"More secrets?" asked Benny.

"Too many secrets," Joe said with a slow nod. "Too damn many secrets."

"Is Dr. McReady in there?" asked Lilah.

No one answered. The door looked like it hadn't been opened in years.

"Well . . . on the upside," said Benny, "at least there aren't any zoms."

But once again the day seemed to want to mock them. A figure stepped from the shadows of a tall, rocky cliff and glowered up at the helicopter. Another joined it. And another. They moved out of the cave mouths and crawled from under the branches of large shrubs until at least a dozen of them stood in a cluster, hands reaching upward to the noise of the rotors.

"That," said Joe, "is not good."

Some of the zoms were dressed in the rags of what had once been military uniforms. One wore a bloodstained lab coat. A few wore black clothes with red tassels and white wings painted on their chests. Only three of the zoms were dressed in ordinary clothes.

"This is really not good," Joe muttered.

Nix pointed to the zom in the white lab coat. The distance was too great to see the creature's face, but the thing was clearly a woman.

"Oh no . . . is that Dr. McReady?"

Joe worked the joystick to bring the helicopter down, which made the engine whine increase. The zoms clawed at the sky as if they could tear the machine down and crack it open to get at the sweet meat inside. The ranger leveled off and hovered, then took a pair of binoculars from a holster beside his chair and peered through them. They all watched him, seeing the muscles locked in tension beneath his clothes. After a full minute, that tension eased by a few strained degrees.

"No . . . that's Dr. Jones. Merry, I think her name was."

Merry, thought Benny. What a sad name for a creature that would spend eternity down there, perpetually hungry, lingering in dried flesh long past the point where life had any meaning.

Joe handed the glasses to Nix and nodded toward where the Teambook was tucked under the dashboard. At his direction she found the page for Dr. Merry Jones and confirmed the identity of the zom in the lab coat. Then she flipped through the other pages and identified three of the soldiers—Engebreth, Hollingsworth, and Carr. The others were reapers. She began to close the book when Lilah stopped her.

"Go back," she said urgently, and as Nix fanned back through the pages, Lilah thrust a hand out and stabbed one photo with her finger. "There."

It was the page for Sergeant Louisa Crisp.

"What about her?" asked Joe.

"There, she's down by that tall rock," said Lilah. "See her?"

"That girl's a reaper," began Nix, but Benny cut her off.

"No . . . look at her."

They did, their eyes flicking back and forth between the reaper who stood at the edge of the pack and the face of the staff sergeant in the Teambook. The thick black hair was gone, but the woman had a very distinct Native American face. She looked a lot like Deputy Gorman from the town watch, who was full-blooded Navajo.

"That's her," Lilah said with certainty.

"Damn," breathed Joe. "Louisa Crisp was the squad leader for Field Team Five. It was her job to protect the science team."

Nix shook her head. "But she became a reaper. Why?"

Joe didn't answer that. His finger rested lightly on a plastic trigger mounted on the control joystick. "Listen to me," he said. "We have to set down and try to get through that air lock. That's going to take time, and it's going to leave us exposed. We have two choices. We trust to cadaverine and hope that it works on them. Smells don't travel as well in air this dry."

"Or . . . ?" asked Benny with a sinking heart. He knew where this was going.

"Or we eliminate the threat here and now."

"God," breathed Nix. "We can't just kill them. They're victims. . . ."

"We all know what they are, Nix," said Lilah. "But I don't see any real choice."

But something else was bothering Benny, something beyond the ethical dilemma. "Wait a sec," he said. "Joe, can this thing get closer to the ground? I mean, can you like . . . skim just above the ground from one side of the clearing to the other? Maybe get almost to the ground near them and then sort of—I don't know what to call it—*drift* away from them. Not up, but across the ground. Can you do that?"

The ranger started to ask why, then smiled and nodded, getting Benny's meaning. "Let's give that a try."

Joe lowered the helicopter so that the wheels bumped against the rocky ground ten yards from the cluster of zoms. The zoms instantly broke into a flat-out run, screaming like demons, hands tearing the air as they swarmed forward. Joe didn't bother to drift backward and instead rose to fifty feet and hovered.

The truth was obvious.

They were all R3's. Every last one.

Joe slowly turned the Black Hawk to face the zoms, who had now stopped below the machine. Some of them tried jumping up to catch the helicopter, even though it was too far above them. The ranger curled his finger around the trigger.

"You kids go back," he suggested. "You don't want to see this."

"No," said Benny, "we don't."

"Who would?" asked Lilah.

Nix spoke some words very softly. It was a prayer they'd heard twice the day before they'd left town. First in one cemetery as the Houser family was buried, then in another cemetery as Zak Matthias, Charlie Pink-eye's nephew, was put into the cold ground.

A prayer for the dead.

In the cabin behind them, Grimm tilted his big head and bayed like a hound from some old-time horror novel.

As Joe opened fire with the thirty-millimeter chain guns, Benny thought he heard the big ranger murmur a single word.

"Amen."

THE BIG BLACK HAWK HOVERED ABOVE THE SCENE OF CARNAGE. WHERE A minute ago there had been a cluster of R3 zoms, the fastest and most dangerous kind, now there was torn meat and broken bones. The chain guns had literally torn the dead apart.

"God almighty," breathed Nix.

Joe's face was set and grim as he put the machine down on the center of the helipad. The whirling blades threshed the gun smoke and scattered it to the dry desert wind, and blew most of the body parts over the edge. He cut the engine.

"Okay," Joe said, "gear up."

Lockers in the back of the helicopter were filled with protective clothing. Thin leather jackets covered with wire mesh and metal washers, arm and leg pads, and gauntlets for their hands. Helmets, too, with wire grilles. All the joints were flexible and the stuff was surprisingly lightweight. Joe showed them a special feature.

"Will this take long?" Benny asked. "Brother Peter said we had until tomorrow night to—"

"Let's worry about Brother Peter tomorrow," said the ranger. "We've enough to do today."

But Nix said, "Will he really attack Sanctuary?"

"He can try," said Joe. He tapped the minigun that was mounted on tracks inside the door. "Knives and axes don't stack up well against a rate of fire of six thousand rounds per minute."

"Rockets, too," said Lilah enthusiastically.

"Rockets, too." Joe shook his head. "If Brother Peter shows up tomorrow, we'll explain the facts of life to him."

The ranger knelt down and buckled on the rest of Grimm's armor. The dog's helmet was set with daggerlike blades, and spikes sprouted all up and down the mastiff's powerful body.

"Note to self," murmured Benny, "don't hug the puppy."

Grimm agreed with a big wet *glupp*.

Lilah dropped the magazine of her Sig Sauer, checked the rounds, and slapped it in place. Joe did the same. Nix, too.

"Benny," called Joe, "you want a handgun?"

"No thanks. I'm not a very good shot."

In truth Benny didn't like guns. Tom had been shot to death. Benny had no moral objection to Nix and the others having them; no, his decision was entirely personal. He was afraid that if he carried one, then he would be tempted to use it too often, to use it to solve problems rather than finding other solutions. That view was entirely his own, and he never shared it with Nix or tried to convince anyone that it was the only viewpoint or even the best. It was his decision.

His sword? That was different. Perhaps it was the old belief that a samurai's soul lives inside the steel of the sword that cast that weapon into a different aspect in his mind. This sword had once been Tom's; now it was his. The sword was a close-range weapon; it required great skill. And despite the grim purpose for which it was created, there was an elegance and beauty about it.

They clustered by the door.

"This is how we're going to do it," said Joe. "I lead, you follow. Everybody keeps their eyes open. Keep chatter to a minimum. If anything happens or if we get separated, head back here to the chopper. There are enough supplies and weapons here for a couple of weeks. But let's not need those supplies, okay? We stick together. We all go in, we all come out, no surprises, no drama. Got it?"

"Warrior smart," said Lilah.

"Warrior smart," they echoed. Even Joe.

He pulled the door open, and a blast of hot air blew into the cabin. Grimm leaped out first, his spiked armor clanking as he landed and immediately began sniffing the ground. Joe was next, and everyone else followed him out into blistering heat that made the desert around Sanctuary feel cool by comparison. Only Joe seemed unaffected by it.

"Not bad for May," he said. "Probably no more than 110. I was here in July once and it was 134."

Nix plucked at the fittings of her combat suit as she stepped down. "Couple of hours in this suit under that sun and we'll be baked hams."

"Baked hams are juicy," observed Benny, dropping down next to her. "We'll be more like beef jerky."

The helipad was pocked with hundreds of bullet holes. Shell casings had rained down and gleamed amid the pieces of things that had once been zombies. There was no blood, but black muck was splashed everywhere. There was more of it than Benny had ever seen around a dead zom, and it seemed to ooze out of the torn tissue. When he bent to examine it, he saw tiny white specks, like pieces of thread, wriggling in the mess.

Grimm suddenly barked at Benny, and Joe wheeled around sharply. "Don't touch that!"

"Not a chance," said Benny, "but what is it? Looks like worms, but I've never seem worms in zoms before."

They all clustered around. "They've always been there," said the ranger. "At least the eggs have. In most zoms the larvae die off after laying eggs. They go dormant right around the time the zoms stop decaying. Some hatch, but they burrow deep into the nerve and brain tissue. They keep the zoms alive—or alive-ish—but don't ask me how. Something about proteins they excrete."

"Okay, eww," said Benny.

"These aren't eggs," said Nix. "These are worms, just like in the zoms Lilah and I fought."

"Exactly," said Joe. "The R3's, the fast zoms. The larvae are active in the fast zoms. In the wild boars, too. It's part of the mutation the science team was studying."

"Are they contagious?" asked Nix, shying back from them.

"Very," said Joe. "Not too bad if you get some on your skin and wipe it off fast, but if you get it in a mucous membrane . . . eyes, nose, mouth, an open wound . . ."

He didn't need to finish.

Benny had a horrible thought. If Chong was infected, then those eggs—or larvae—were in his body too. He wanted to scream. That was why the scientist had asked him if Chong had gotten any fluids on him. He kept his thoughts to himself. It would be abominably cruel to share this with Lilah, and he hoped she wasn't already thinking those thoughts.

He even avoided looking at her, for fear she'd read his mind.

They backed well clear of the black goo and followed Joe to the air lock. It was almost exactly like the one at Sanctuary, with a small glass-fronted box set into a recess beside the door. The hand-scan device—the geometry scanner—was dark, the glass cracked and filled with sand. Joe punched two buttons and placed his hand on the glass, but nothing happened. He used the butt of his pistol to knock out the glass in order to access the wires, but after fifteen minutes of connecting one wire to another he flipped them back into the recess with a disgusted grunt. Then he pounded on the door with the side of his fist.

Nothing happened.

"I thought you said that beating on the door doesn't do any good," observed Benny casually. "They can't hear it inside."

Joe shot him a venomous look. "Ever fall off the side of a helipad into a bunch of jagged rocks?"

"Point taken," said Benny.

"Now what?" asked Nix. "Do we go looking for a back door?"

"No," said Joe, turning to walk back to the Black Hawk, "now we try plan B."

Once they were all inside the bird, Joe fired up the engine and lifted the helicopter into the air. It drifted backward from the air lock, past the edge of the drop-off.

"There's an old military saying," mused the ranger. "If at first you don't succeed, call in an air strike."

"What's that mean?" asked Benny.

"It means, 'Fire in the hole!'"

Joe flicked a switch on the cyclic grip and depressed a trigger. There was sound like steam escaping from a boiler, and then something shot away from under the stubby wing of the helicopter. Benny had only a hundredth of a second's glimpse of something sleek and black, and then the entire front of the cliff seemed to bloom into a massive ball of orange fire. Chunks of stone and metal flew everywhere, but Joe was already rising into a fast climbing turn, and nothing hit the Black Hawk. The helicopter swung all the way around until it faced the cliff again. The fireball crawled up the side of the cliff, chased by smoke and hot wind. Then it thinned and fell apart into sparks. Joe angled the helicopter to use the rotor wash to whip away the smoke that clung to the helipad.

The six-ton air lock looked as if the fist of a giant had struck it. It lay on its back, driven nine feet inside the mountain. The spot where it had stood was a gaping maw almost big enough to drive a trade wagon through.

"Holy . . . ," began Benny, but had nowhere to go with that, so he repeated it. "Holy . . ."

Lilah smiled with a lupine delight.

"What *was* that?" gasped Nix.

"Hellfire missile," said Joe.

Grimm gave a deep-chested *whoof* as if he approved.

Benny shook his head. When Joe had used the rocket launchers to defeat Mother Rose's reapers, Benny had been unconscious, the victim of a blow to the head. He'd never witnessed anything like this. But from the expression on Nix's face, he could tell that this "Hellfire" missile was far more devastating than the shoulder-mounted rockets. They'd read about weapons of war in school, but Benny had never really

310

put much thought into their true destructive power. It was deeply disturbing.

Chunks of rock littered the helipad, but there was more than enough room to land.

Joe cut the engine.

"Okay, let's try this again."

63

M<small>ILES AND MILES AWAY</small> . . .

Morgie Mitchell sat on the top porch step of the empty Imura house. He'd already been inside. The floors were swept, fresh curtains were hung on the rods, and the creaking sixth step had been repaired. His sword lay near his left hip, a bottle of pop was slowly going warm next to his right.

Tomorrow was his first full day of training with Solomon Jones and the Freedom Riders. He had no idea what to expect. The people who rode with Jones were all famous; all of them were on the Zombie Cards. Morgie had gone through his stack and pulled the cards of the active Freedom Riders. He went through them over and over again, looking at their faces, trying to imagine what they'd be like in person.

Sally Two-Knives with her wild Mohawk hair and glittering bowie knives.

J-Dog and Dr. Skillz, who spoke in an old surfer slang that no one really understood.

Fluffy McTeague with his lipstick, diamond earrings, and pink carpet coat.

Sam "Basher" Bashman with his baseball bats.

Quick-Draw Carl, who still wore the broad-brimmed brown hat of his legendary dad, Sheriff Rick.

Bobby Tall Horse, an Apache who wore a Roman breastplate and horsehair helmet into battle.

The crazy woman, Dez Fox, who they said traveled with the mummified hand of her dead husband in her backpack.

And so many others.

Each of them was a hero; each of them was surrounded by mystery and tall tales.

He shook his head. Who was he to even think that he was worthy of training with them, let alone riding out with them?

Who did he think he was?

He turned and looked at the house.

Morgie collected all his cards and put them neatly into his pack. Then he picked up his sword and walked out into the yard to practice the drills Tom had taught him.

GRIMM RAN AHEAD AS THEY APPROACHED THE SHATTERED FACE OF THE cliff. The air lock was a twisted ruin. Beyond it was a wide chamber with metal walls and concrete floors. Soot streaked those walls now. Shattered light fixtures swung from the ceilings on webs of torn wiring.

They stepped carefully and silently inside. The entrance chamber split into two corridors.

"Should we split up?" asked Lilah. "I can—"

"Not a chance," said Joe. "This isn't a bad horror movie. We stay together and we watch each other's backs. No one goes into the basement in a negligee to investigate a strange noise."

Lilah looked at him as if he was deranged. "What?"

"Nothing. Old pop-culture reference whose expiration date has apparently passed. Sad."

Benny thought he heard the Lost Girl mutter the word "idiot."

They took the left-hand corridor first, for no other reason than because it was closer to where they stood. There were closed doors on one side of the corridor. Joe stopped in front of the first one and gently tried the knob. It turned easily.

He glanced at Lilah, who took up a defensive position beside him, then turned the handle the rest of the way and kicked the door open.

It was a closet. Metal shelves filled with boxes of office supplies. No zoms, no people.

They moved to the second door and repeated the process.

And froze.

There was a person in the room.

Seated behind a big desk. A laptop computer was open on the desk. The office was decorated with big framed photographs of running brooks, snowy mountainsides, lush autumn forests. The man in the chair sat with his head—what there was of it—thrown back. A shotgun stood on its stock between his thighs. Even from the doorway Benny could read the scene. A person—either desperate or perhaps infected—sits down, props the shotgun on the edge of the chair, thumb on the trigger, barrel under the chin, and says good-bye to everything in the most final way possible.

The wall behind the desk, and part of the ceiling, was painted with chocolate brown that had once been bright red and moldy green that had once been gray brain matter.

All very disgusting, all very final. And a long time ago. Months, at the very least.

No reanimation.

What made it worse was what the man had written in black ink on his desk blotter:

MAY GOD FORGIVE US FOR WHAT WE HAVE DONE

WE ARE THE HORSEMEN

WE DESERVE TO BURN

There was no signature. There was no need for one.

They stood around the desk.

Nix looked from the writing to the body sprawled in the chair. "That poor man."

Benny nodded. "What does it mean, though?"

"Watch the hall," Joe said as he began quickly going through each drawer. He rummaged through the contents, tossing some things onto the floor, ignoring others. Then he found a sheaf of papers that made him stiffen and stare. He cursed softly.

"What is it?" asked Benny.

"I think I found out why Dr. McReady came to this facility." He showed the top page to Benny and the girls.

ZABRISKIE POINT BIOLOGICAL EVALUATION AND PRODUCTION STATION

UNITED STATES ARMY

"What's that mean?" asked Benny. "'Biological Evaluation and Production'? Is this some kind of lab?"

Joe took the papers back and crumpled them up, his face a mask of disgust.

"This is a monster factory," he said.

BROTHER PETER WATCHED AS TWO OF THE RED BROTHERS CARRIED SISTER Sun up the slope. Every day the woman seemed to have aged ten years. The cancer that consumed her was a merciless and ravenous thing. It would take her soon. A few days, a week at the most.

In a way, Brother Peter envied her. She would be going into the darkness soon, and he was doomed to live until the work of the Night Church was completed.

The reapers set her down, and one of them produced a small folding stool and supported her as she sat down on it. Peter ordered one of them to fetch water and directed another to erect the portable awning.

They were in a cleft of rock that provided an excellent view of the chain-link fence, the airfield, the row of siren towers, and the hangars on both sides of the miles-long trench. However, from a reverse position, the reapers were invisible inside a bank of deep shadows.

A reaper came trotting into the cleft.

"Beloved of god," he said to Sister Sun and Brother Peter, "we are ready."

Brother Peter nodded. "Good. Has there been any sign of the helicopter?"

"No, my brother. I have ten scouts watching for it."

"Very well."

"The wind continues to veer," said the reaper. "Sister Alice thinks it will shift two or three more points, but I ran the math a couple of times. We're good to go now."

Brother Peter nodded again. "Go down to the fence and wait for the net crews. Sister Sun will be giving the signal."

The man bowed and left.

Sister Sun smiled at Brother Peter and reached for his hand and squeezed it with what little strength she had. "You'll let me do that? That's so kind of you, Peter."

"This is your victory, sister."

"I know that Saint John is so proud of you," she said, "and you will be gathered in with loving arms when it is your time to go into the darkness."

He bent and kissed the skeletal hand and pressed it to his cheek. On the other side of the desert, beyond the red rock mountains, the sun was beginning its long fall toward a fiery twilight. To both of them, the vital young man and the dying older woman, it looked like the whole world was about to burn.

There was a rustling sound behind them, and they turned to see a dozen reapers walking in pairs along the shaded path by the rock wall heading down to the fence. Each pair held a bundle of rope ends that were connected to huge nets. The nets looked impossibly huge, but they were wrapped around clusters of brightly colored balloons. Thousands of them in each net.

The men in each net crew nodded their respect as they

passed. Down below, closer to the fence, the reaper known as Sister Alice was tossing handfuls of sand into the air to watch the direction of its fall.

"It's time," said Brother Peter.

But before she could give the signal, a terrible coughing fit struck Sister Sun. She bent over as sharply as if she'd been punched in the stomach, and drops of blood splattered her lap and knees and the dust at her feet. Brother Peter watched helplessly as the fit tore the dying woman apart. Other reapers stood by, their faces mournful. Even though each of them wished only the soothing darkness for Sister Sun, they ached for her to first witness the triumph of her plan.

By slow, torturous degrees the coughs eased in intensity and then slowly, slowly passed.

Sister Sun perched on the edge of her stool like a frail puppet held in place by a single frayed string. The reapers—and the world around them—held their breath, and even the wind slackened for a moment as if unwilling to blow without her permission.

Her right hand trembled in her lap, and it was clear that she could barely lift it. Finally it rose. First barely an inch, then another, and another.

Brother Peter let out a burning ball of air that was searing the walls of his lungs, and in a ringing voice he called, "Sister Sun has given the word. May the darkness bless us all."

The reapers at the fence made final cuts in work they had already begun with tin snips and bolt cutters. A quarter-mile length of the fence collapsed to the ground. Immediately the net teams rushed onto the airfield, running between the two southernmost of the siren towers. They formed a long line, and other reapers ran up to help them slash the lines that formed the nets. Immediately the captured balloons tumbled out and were shoved away by the wind that blew out of the southeast.

Darkness was closing around Sister Sun's thoughts, but as the red and yellow and blue and green balloons bobbed and danced across the hot sands, she thought a single word and her lips formed it silently.

"Beautiful."

Then the darkness wrapped her in its arms and she fell forward.

"WHAT'S THAT SUPPOSED TO MEAN?" ASKED BENNY. "WHAT KIND OF monsters did they make here? Or is that a naive question?"

The ranger didn't answer.

Benny snorted in disgust. "More and more often I get the feeling that growing up *after* civilization ended is a better deal."

"More and more often I agree with you, kid." Joe nodded toward the dead man. "That's why I resigned today. I reached my limit of shame and guilt for being a part of the old system."

"Did you know about the Reaper Plague?" asked Nix.

"Nah, that's not what I mean. Like I told you, I was the guy who tried to stop this sort of thing. I loved my country, and I guess I still do, though I kind of feel the way a kid might feel when they discover that not only are their parents not perfect heroes, but they're deeply flawed."

"Was the whole country like that?" asked Benny.

"No—not even close. For the most part it was pretty great. But there never was a country, no matter how noble or well-intentioned, that wasn't infected by a greedy and power-hungry few. It's no different from those parasites infecting the zoms. We can't really blame the afflicted person any more than we can blame the entire country, but we can sure as hell despise those parasites."

Lilah stood closest to the dead man. "Who was he?"

"According to the paperwork we found, he was the deputy director of this facility in charge of operations. He kept this place running, before, during, and after First Night. He's been keeping those old secrets all this time This place is way off the grid. . . . I'll bet there are all sorts of things here that shouldn't be anywhere."

"Well, isn't that comforting?" said Nix sourly.

They went back to the hallway. The corridor they'd been following ended at a blank wall, but on the far side of the blasted entrance was a much longer hallway that stretched off into shadows. Some residual smoke hung in the air, shifting like ghosts in the breeze. It obscured the hallway like fog in an alley on a humid night.

"I lead," said Joe, "you follow. Lilah, you watch our backs."

A month ago—or perhaps a few hours ago—Benny knew that he might resent Lilah being picked out for the more important job; but his mind was running in a different gear now and he knew it. Lilah was the better fighter, and she was far more experienced with being alert and moving with caution. Of course she was the better choice. He also knew that if Riot were here, she would have made a good alternate choice.

There was a certain comfort in accepting these things. It touched on an old lesson Tom had given him, about seeing things as they are without being filtered through anticipation, expectation, or assumption. There was something liberating in seeing things with that clarity.

I'm not who I was, thought Benny as he fell into step behind Nix. *This is who I am. I'm not Tom and I'm not little Benny anymore. I'm me.*

Despite everything Benny smiled to himself.

He wanted to tell Nix about this. He knew she would understand, and thinking that made something else click into place in his mind. He and Nix had fought a lot since leaving Mountainside; their relationship had eroded to more of a friendship than romantic love. He thought he understood why. The two people who'd fallen in love were naive and innocent kids back in a secluded town hidden behind a fence. Those kids didn't exist anymore. For Benny the separation from naive child to aware teen had started the first time Tom took him out into the Ruin and he saw the realities and brutality of the world outside. The real world in no way resembled the version he'd constructed in his head. Even the things like combat and adventure were different beyond the gates. They weren't fun, they weren't part of a game. People got hurt and they died and there wasn't always a happy ending and you couldn't just clear the pieces off the game board and start again. For Benny, it began with that, but the process of change included fighting for his life, killing to save his life and the lives of others, seeing people die, seeing Tom die, and then leaving the place where Tom was buried and traveling farther out into the Ruin, past all known places and all chance of safety. Out here, where every day was a hardship and every choice was a hard one, something had happened to the old Benny. It wasn't that he died, but the child in him stepped back and something else emerged. Not an adult—but an older teenager who was in charge of his own life.

A similar process must have been going on in Nix. She wasn't the funny, happy, easygoing girl Benny had first fallen in love with. Life since then hadn't given her many reasons to laugh, and happiness was hard to maintain under the brutal sun of a wasteland. And who was easygoing out here in the Ruin? Joe pretended to be, but Benny knew now that the old ranger was playing a role. In truth, he was a heartbroken man who'd spent his entire life trying to save the world while constantly being disappointed in some of the people he should have been able to trust. His banter and jokes were probably the only props that kept him on his feet.

Nix must have felt his thoughts, as she so often did. She turned and looked at him. Benny gave her a small nod and a brief but genuine smile. Nix's brow furrowed for just a moment, and then he could see the exact moment when she understood that *he* understood. She was already there.

That was when Benny saw something in Nix's eyes that he hadn't seen since before her mother died.

Joy.

Only a spark of it. But proof that her fire hadn't gone out any more than his had.

It made him want to laugh out loud, to shout, to hug her.

But Nix turned around and followed the ranger and his dog. He followed her through smoke and shadows in a place of mystery and death, but Benny Imura was truly happy and content for the first time in his life.

Yeah, he thought, *this is who I am.*

THEY MOVED THROUGH THE BUILDING. THERE WERE STOREROOMS FILLED
with scientific equipment, offices whose only occupants were
spiders in dusty old webs, and some rooms in which they
found dead bodies. A few had been left to rot, but most were
wrapped neatly in plastic. Once they were past the damaged
entrance, they found that the electricity was still working. They
passed through a generator room where a big unit encased in
metal hummed with patient diligence.

They entered a room marked MESS HALL. It was big, with two
other doors leading out; one that bore the sign STAFF QUARTERS,
and the other that led to the kitchens. The kitchen doors were
propped open, but the room beyond was in total darkness. The
whole mess hall was lit by only two functioning overhead lights.
All the tables had been pushed back to make room for stacks
upon stacks of plastic boxes. Five boxes to a stack, five stacks to
a row. They stretched from just inside the door almost to the
far wall. Beside the containers were waist-high heaps of large
clear-plastic bags. Each bag was in turn filled with smaller bags
crammed with clear capsules filled with a bright red powder.
Benny guessed that there were at least a thousand of these big
bags, and countless hundreds of thousands of the capsules.

When Joe Ledger saw those bags, he stopped dead in his tracks.

"That powder," said Nix in a hushed voice. "Is it the same stuff that was on the fast zoms?"

"I think so," said the ranger. "Color's a little different, though. The stuff I took off the zoms was paler."

Benny reached out to pick up one of the bags, but Joe caught his wrist. "No. Not without gloves."

"Why? What is this stuff?"

"I think it's Archangel."

"Is that a poison?" asked Lilah.

"No . . . not poison," said Joe, but before he could finish, Grimm suddenly turned toward the open kitchen doorway at the far side of the room, uttering a low and very menacing growl.

All four of them spun around and brought their weapons up. Joe moved quickly to the front, his right index finger stretched along the outside curve of his pistol's trigger guard, barrel aimed at the center of the doors.

"What is it?" asked Nix.

But Benny only shook his head. He shuffled sideways to give himself and Nix enough room to swing their swords.

"Look . . . ," said Lilah in an urgent whisper.

There was a suggestion of movement beyond the doors, inside the darkened kitchen. It was formless and indistinct, like a piece of shadow shifting, and Benny couldn't even be sure it was anything at all.

There was a sound. A scuff. Soft and passive, like a foot being dragged.

"Get ready," whispered Joe. "If this goes south on us, I want you to haul your asses back to the chopper."

Something was emerging from the darkness. It did not look human. It was big and monstrous, with a misshapen head and limbs as thick as tree trunks.

Grimm's whole body trembled, either with the urge to attack or flee, Benny could not tell. For his own part, Benny wanted to run.

The lumbering creature kept moving forward, and now Benny could see that it had some weird, wrinkled skin. Pale and unnatural.

"Shoot it," urged Lilah. "Joe . . . *shoot it!*"

When Joe didn't pull the trigger, Lilah raised her spear and tensed to spring, ready for the kill.

"No," Nix said slowly, "don't . . ."

Benny glanced at her. She wore a puzzled expression, and she slowly lowered her sword.

They froze in place, watching in mingled horror and anticipation as the thing shambled toward the open doorway. It paused, still within the bank of shadows inside the kitchen. Joe slipped his finger inside the trigger guard.

Benny felt sweat run down his cheeks.

Then the thing in the shadows stepped into the light.

"Oh my God," said Nix.

It was not a monster.

It was not a zom.

It was a person, covered head to toe in a wrinkled, many-times-patched, white hazmat suit.

The figure took a trembling step forward and then dragged its leg. Benny could see now that the leg of the suit was stretched around something—a cast or brace.

But what truly caught his eye, what stopped his breath

and jolted his mind, was the name stenciled on the front of the hazmat suit. His lips formed the three syllables, though it was Lilah who actually spoke the name aloud.

"*McReady.*"

She flinched at the sound of Lilah's voice, or perhaps at her own name. Then she looked at Joe Ledger—at his gun and his murderous armored hound.

"Have you come to kill me?" asked Dr. Monica McReady, her voice muffled by the suit.

The ranger's mouth hung open.

Dr. McReady nodded as if in answer to her own question. "It's about time."

"WHAT'S THAT?" ASKED BROTHER ALBERT.

His teacup was halfway to his lips when he froze, head raised to listen. Across the table from him, Sister Hannahlily was buttering a piece of bread.

"What's what?" she said absently.

"There!" said Albert. "Did you hear it?"

"I didn't hear . . . " Hannahlily's voice trailed off as she suddenly *did* hear something.

A faint *pop*. Then a few seconds later, another.

"What is that?"

"It's coming from outside," said the nun. She rose and crossed to the doorway. Other monks and nuns were rising too.

Pop!

Pop-pop!

Albert joined her as she stepped out into the lurid redness of the sunset.

Pop!

"I don't see anything," he said. But then he did, and in his total surprise he forgot his manners, his vows, and his decorum. "What the *hell*?"

He stared, goggle-eyed, at a sight that made absolutely no sense. It was weird, impossible. Surreal in a way that teetered on the thin edge between comedy and unpleasantness.

The sky was filled with balloons.

They bounced along the ground, skittering between the legs of the dead, riding puffs of air above them. The Children of Lazarus were drawn to the color and movement. Dead-white hands reached for them. Grabbed them. Jagged fingernails tore through the thin rubber. Broken teeth bit into the glistening toys.

Pop-pop-pop-pop . . .

JOE SHOVED HIS GUN INTO ITS HOLSTER AND STEPPED TOWARD DR. McReady, but the scientist recoiled from him.

"Monica!" he cried. "Good God, Monica . . . it's me—it's Joe."

"I know who you are," she snapped in a voice that sounded rusty from disuse. "Of course it's you. Who else would they send but their number one killer?"

That stopped Joe in his tracks.

Ouch, thought Benny.

All they could see of McReady was her eyes. They were filled with suspicion and more than a little wild.

Joe held his hands up in a no-threat gesture. "Monica . . . nobody sent me to hurt you. We've been looking for you for months."

"Eighteen months, one week, six days," corrected McReady. "And I've been here all that time, haven't I? How hard have you been looking?" The bitterness in her voice was filled with jagged edges.

"We didn't know where you were," insisted Joe.

McReady's laugh was short and harsh. "Oh, I'm quite sure. There was a planeload of people who knew where I was.

I hand-wrote the coordinates and put them into Luis Ortega's hand myself. Are you say he didn't—"

"Dr. McReady," said Benny, taking a half step forward, "you don't understand."

McReady's head swiveled toward him. "And who are you? Is Jane Reid recruiting kids now?"

"Dr. McReady," Benny said calmly, "my name is Benjamin Imura. These girls—Phoenix Riley and Lilah—are my friends. We found your plane."

Her eyes narrowed with instant suspicion. "What do you mean, 'found'?"

"It crashed. We found it."

It took McReady a three-count to respond to that. "W-what?"

"He's telling the truth, Monica," said Joe. "It crashed in the desert ten miles short of Sanctuary. Luis Ortega's dead and so's the flight crew. These kids found the wreckage and told me. I got your research to Sanctuary, but there was nothing on the plane to indicate where you'd gone. Then Benny and his friends found Sergeant Ortega. He was infected, but they managed to search him and get the coordinates for this place. All that happened today, and we came out here right away."

"The plane . . . .crashed?" McReady was clearly having a hard time processing this news. She slumped and sat down heavily on the edge of the destroyed air lock. "It never reached Sanctuary?"

"No."

"My God . . ." McReady began absently to undo the Velcro seals of her hazmat suit. Her hands shook visibly. She pulled off the hood to reveal a face that looked considerably thinner and older than the picture Benny had seen in the Teambook. Monica McReady's chocolate-colored skin had faded to a dusty gray. Her eyes still retained their intelligence, but there was a deep and comprehensive weariness in them, tinged by sadness as she thought about the plane. Her hair was clipped very short and it was a bad job, as if she'd done it herself.

Then she stiffened and demanded, "Did they get it all done? The mass production and distribution? Has the mutation worked its way through the population . . . ?"

Her voice trailed off. She looked from face to face, and when no one answered, McReady began to visibly shake.

"Tell me Jane Reid's team got this out to the whole damn world!"

Joe knelt in front of McReady. "She couldn't, Monica. Reid's people weren't able to pick up where you left off. They need those last notes."

She stared blankly at him. "Which *last* notes?"

"The last stuff. The D-series material. Without that—"

McReady suddenly shoved Joe, knocking him right onto his butt. Grimm barked in alarm. "What are you *talking* about?" she screamed. "*Everything* was on that transport. Every scrap of research. All the field notes, our clinical studies, the mutation projections. The complete formula for Archangel. All of it."

Benny helped Joe to his feet.

"The D-series notes weren't there," said Nix. "We thought you took them with you."

"Why would I take them with *me*? I sent it all back to Sanctuary so Reid could start production."

"Production of what?" asked Lilah.

McReady looked puzzled. "Of the cure. What do you think I mean?"

"Wait, wait, hold on," said Benny. "You're saying that you *cured* this thing? Is that what Archangel is?"

"Of course," snapped McReady. "Why do you think we left Hope One?"

Lilah shook her head. "Joe told us that you wanted to evacuate because the dead were becoming too active."

"Exactly," said McReady flatly. "That was the whole point. We developed a metabolic stabilizer first, and then we figured out the cure. Archangel. It was radical, sure, but it worked."

"But—but—" Lilah looked around in confusion.

"Monica . . . this isn't making sense," said Joe. "We're talking in circles. We thought that Hope One was being overrun. That's what Colonel Reid told me. The walkers were getting too frisky, and you wanted to get your team back to Sanctuary."

Before he even finished, McReady was shaking her head. "We knew exactly how active the walkers were. We'd already rounded up the random ones to send back to Sanctuary, so Jane Reid's team could study the range of mutations. The rest were our own test subjects. We released them into the wild near Hope One to see if they'd contaminate others with the mutagen. They did. Very, very quickly, too. Once we saw how that worked, I told Jane I wanted to bring my team back to Sanctuary to get the real ball rolling."

"Wait," said Benny, "you're still not making sense. Start at the beginning."

"Listen, Monica," insisted Joe, "the D-series records either weren't on the transport or someone took them off the wreck."

"They were on the damn plane," growled McReady.

"Then they've been taken. We can't find them, and the records we could find suggest that you took them with you."

Benny asked, "Do you think someone messed with them? Left a deliberately false trail?"

"Beginning to look that way, doesn't it?"

"Why?"

"To be determined." To McReady he said, "Is there any way to duplicate Archangel without those notes?"

She considered. "Without the D-series notes? No. *With* those notes, sure. All you need is some basic chemicals, some minerals, a pig, and a walker. Anyone can make Archangel. The only trick is reducing it to a powdered form, but there was a paper on how to do that, too. I prepared that so Reid could transmit it to every lab in the Nation." She stopped and sagged a bit as the full weight of it hit her. "God, we lost eighteen months. This thing should have been *over* by now. All the walkers should have been dead by now."

"LOOK AT ALL THE BALLOONS!" SAID EVE, AND HER FACE WAS SUN-BRIGHT with joy.

Riot rose from where she'd been sitting on the sand with the little girl. People were coming out of all the hangars and the dormitory and mess hall to stare at the weird spectacle. Thousands of colored balloons bobbed among the dead, and the crowd of zombies was quickly becoming agitated as they lunged and grabbed and bit at the things.

This was something totally outside of Riot's experience. It was so absurd, so bizarre, that she found herself smiling.

Had the monks done this?

No, that was ridiculous.

The soldiers at the hangar?

As if in answer to that thought, the sirens abruptly began their banshee wail. The dead paused, and many of them turned toward the sound. A few even lumbered that way, drawn by sound or some rudimentary habit of the limbs and nerves. But the others did not follow.

The sirens were far away. The balloons were right there.

"Stay here," Riot said to Eve, and she slipped out of the

play area and ran to the edge of the trench. Her pulse was already fluttering in her chest.

One by one the dead turned away from the sirens. They grabbed the nearest balloons, growling when they popped. Riot saw a flash of color. Not the bright yellows and blues and greens of the rubber, but a bright red that puffed into the air as each balloon burst. Was it dust?

Or . . . powder?

It clung to the skin of the zoms. It fell on their eyes and into their open mouths, propelled by the explosion of the balloons.

"What in tarnation?" she said aloud.

Some of the dead stopped where they were, their bodies shuddering and trembling as if they stood on ground troubled by an earthquake. However, the cause of their agitation came from no external force that Riot could see. It had to be something *inside* them. Something that rippled under the surface of their withered skin.

Then the world was rocked by a series of explosions. Not close—they were to the east, beyond the distant fence. Riot squinted through heat haze as fireballs leaped up from the fields.

There was a rumor among the monks and nuns that the army had laid mines out in those fields. Until now Riot hadn't believed it.

There was movement out there, and Riot, long practiced at telling the difference between the living and the dead, saw masses of zoms running across the minefield. Running and then flying apart as the mines exploded. More came behind.

And more. The mines detonated, and the zoms kept coming, running as if they had a purpose.

Running as if driven.

Behind them, Riot saw a wave of reapers on quads.

As they drew closer, she could see that they wore scarves wrapped around their heads and old-fashioned swimmers' goggles over their eyes. Each of them had a silver dog whistle clamped between his teeth. They drove a flock of zoms across the minefield, clearing it by exploding it. Opening the way for the mass of reapers who followed.

And here, closer, the balloons bounced along. The dead caught them, bit them, exploded them, and were doused by red powder.

Riot had been trained as a warrior and a leader of warriors. She understood what was happening. She turned and looked at the blank and unresponsive wall of the blockhouse, at the closed doors of the hangar. At the helpless masses of monks and the dying people they tended.

She turned slowly back to watch the oncoming tide of death.

"God," she breathed.

71

THIS THING SHOULD HAVE BEEN OVER BY NOW.

All the walkers should have been dead by now.

Benny actually felt as if Dr. McReady's words were physical blows that pounded him in the heart and over the head.

"Are you . . . serious?" asked Nix.

"Of course I'm serious," barked McReady. "You think I'd joke about something like that?" She nodded to the plastic containers of Archangel. "Why do you think I came here? This base is the best biomaterials production facility west of the Rockies. Ten times better than the setup at Sanctuary, but even a lunkhead like Jane Reid should have managed *something*."

Joe sighed. "Without the D-series notes, all she managed to do was make the metabolic stabilizer and a very, very weak version of Archangel. She tried it on a few walkers and got mixed results."

McReady closed her eyes. "Save me from idiots."

"Listen, Monica," said Joe. "How'd you even know about this place? I sure as heck never heard of it."

McReady snorted. "There are half a dozen bases like this you never heard of. Places *nobody* ever heard of unless they were on the right lists."

"I was supposed to be on *every* list."

"Oh, cry me a river," said McReady. "There's always another level of secrecy, don't you know that? I know about this place because I wrote the protocols so they could build it. Just like I wrote the protocols for the redesign and repurposing of the Umatilla Chemical Depot in Oregon."

"Why?"

"Because the United States of America needed to stay safe, and we couldn't afford to let naive international chemical weapons treaties hamstring us. Every third-rate country who couldn't afford a nuclear weapons program but got a Junior Chemistry Wizard set for Christmas was cooking up bioweapons and nerve agents. What were we supposed to do? Wait until someone launched something and then complain to Congress that we had no response because our funding was cut and our charters revoked? Grow up, Joe."

"I guess that worked out really well for you," observed Nix.

Dr. McReady gave her such a lethal and venomous look that Benny thought Nix would drop right there; but Nix narrowed her green eyes and gave it back full blast.

Before the two could explode into an argument, Benny asked, "Where's the rest of the staff? We saw some bodies. One guy in his office . . . ?"

"Shotgun?"

"Yes."

"Dick Price. He was the last. No great loss." The scientist gave another derisive snort. "The rest are dead. Most of them killed themselves. Cowards."

Benny felt sorry for the scientist, but it was getting harder and harder to like her.

"By the time my team got here," said McReady without a trace of remorse, "more than two-thirds of the staff were already gone. Before and after we got locked in. The staff who'd been here were torn up by speculation as to whether some of the biological terrors they'd helped to create had been used to destroy the world. Might be true, too. There were suicides . . . murder-suicide pacts. Heart attacks from stress. A couple just wandered off into the badlands to let the desert or the dead have them." She shook her head in disgust. "We're struggling to save the world, to preserve life, and these idiots can't wait to catch the bus out of here."

"That guy, Mr. Price, left a message," said Benny. "He wrote, 'May God forgive us for what we have done . . .'"

"'We are the horsemen. We deserve to burn,'" finished McReady. "All very dramatic."

"If he killed himself out of guilt," she said, "what were you all guilty of?"

McReady's eyes didn't blink or waver. "If you're asking me if I participated in the development of the Reaper Plague, then no."

"I'm sorry—"

McReady pointed down the hall toward Price's office. "*He* did. The people here did."

"They started the plague?" asked Benny, aghast.

"Don't be an idiot. Why would we release a doomsday plague? We're scientists. We research, we develop—we don't implement. Other people—politicians and generals—take science and turn it into a weapon. I expect Captain Ledger here's been filling your head with his left-of-liberal antimilitary propaganda."

"First off," said Joe, "I was a moderate back when elections mattered. Second, I'm *in* the military. Now, stop evading their questions, Monica. We come here to rescue you and we find a base that I should have been told about, a staff that's killed themselves in remorse, and suicide messages that talk about guilt. Stop being such a hard-ass and *tell us what happened*."

Benny thought that the scientist was going to argue, but instead she seemed to deflate. "Okay, okay . . . I'm sorry. I guess I've been alone too long. Months. Here's the short version. I took my team to Hope One to investigate reports of mutations among the population of walkers in Washington State. I was very interested in this because mutation was deemed unlikely, since Reaper was designed to be ultra-stable. As you may or may not know, Reaper is a combination of several designer bioweapons, including nine separate viruses, fourteen bacteria, and five genetically altered parasites including the big daddy—the jewel wasp. The core is something called Lucifer 113, which was developed by the Soviets during the Cold War. That one got out of the bag a couple of times and almost lived up to its promise of being an ultimate weapon. It was stopped, though, and all known samples of it were either destroyed or sent to secure facilities like this one. But someone obtained a sample of Lucifer 113, and that sample wound up in the hands of some off-the-radar design lab, which married it to an old terrorist bioweapon called *seif al din*—wasn't that one you stopped from being released, Joe?"

"Twice," he said sadly, and then cursed.

"Our bioweapons teams were given that super-plague and tasked with creating the ultimate version, and then using that as a staring point to create a defensive protocol in case it—or anything like it—ever got out. But somehow the superstrain of it was released, *our* version. No one knows quite how, and we all have proof that there has never been a more aggressive or deliberately destructive disease.

"Because Reaper is driven by parasites, there's no such thing as natural immunity, though there is a range of reaction time in terms of symptom onset, necrosis, and other factors. Bottom line: Everyone who's exposed is infected, and everybody worldwide is exposed. Whoever released this spent years laying the groundwork. They must have introduced eggs and bacteria into water sources all over the world. We started getting wind of it almost two years before the actual outbreak. Labs were reporting the presence of the components in soil throughout the agricultural regions, in water tables and reservoirs, even in processed foods. Best guess is that these components were introduced into the biosphere beginning no later than ten years before the global outbreak. It would have needed at least that much time for the bacteria and parasites to spread. The World Health Organization, the Centers for Disease Control, the Environmental Protection Agency, the National Institutes of Health, the Food and Drug Administration—all the power players were involved in researching the spread of the components, but no one really understood what kind of a threat it was."

She shook her head. "In a strange way you have to admire the *scope* of that. A coordinated worldwide release of components of a doomsday plague. For that to happen there had to be huge money—hundreds of millions of dollars—and a large number of persons involved. Just the administration of something like that is staggering."

"Could have been a cult," suggested Joe as he knelt and removed Grimm's helmet. The mastiff's tongue lolled from between rubbery lips. "There were some big cults and pseudo-religions gaining followings around the world. My team ran into a few of them over the years. Some were well funded, highly organized, and extremely militant."

"I thought about that too," said McReady. "But really—who cares? The damage is done. They accomplished what they set out to do. They released a doomsday plague, and for most of the population of planet Earth, that's what it was. Seven billion people died. If some groups hadn't been able to find defensible positions and learn to work together instead of panicking like mice, we'd be as extinct as the dinosaurs. We're lucky as many people survived as they did." She shrugged. "Anyway, we heard about mutations in Washington, and we had to go check it out. The possibility of a mutation was exciting, because it meant that there was a chance of identifying the mutagen taking control of the mutation process."

"What good would that do?" asked Lilah.

McReady nodded as if she approved of the question. "The pathogen is in a perfect form. You couldn't make it more deadly than it is. Any change to its nature or structure would actually result in a reduction of its overall threat, because it would mean that it had shifted away from immutability. Follow me?"

"I . . . think so. If it's changing, then it isn't perfect anymore."

"Smart girl," said McReady.

Nix said, "We've seen some of the mutations. The R3's. They're so much faster and scarier."

"Smarter, too," said Lilah.

"How's that a good thing?" asked Benny.

McReady shook her head. "Those are short-term effects. What's happened is the dormant parasite eggs have been made to hatch. There are active threadworms in the newly infected, but they die off after they've laid eggs. As they die off, the process of host decomposition goes into a protracted stasis. We still don't know how long a walker will last once they've reached the stasis point—clearly many years—and we still haven't cracked all the science on that. Maybe someone will one of these days. Not my concern. When we set up Hope One, we found all sorts of mutations up there. Smarter walkers, faster walkers, with abilities all up and down the Seldon Scale, the evaluation method we developed after the plague started. It was exciting stuff. Dangerous, too . . . we learned the hard way about how smart and fast these mutations were. Lost a third of our staff in the first few weeks, and we lost more when we started actively looking for the most extreme mutations."

"That must have been terrifying," said Nix.

McReady shrugged. "It was worth it. This was real science again. We were doing ten, fifteen autopsies a day, every day. Running tissue samples and other cultures around the clock. What we found was that there was a new bacteria in the mix. This is one of nature's little jokes, because after we'd looked at every kind of organism or causal agent that might trigger the parasites to hatch, the one we found shouldn't even have an impact on the jewel wasp, which is the parasite at the heart of the Reaper disease cluster. It is in itself a mutation; in this case it's a mutated form of the bacteria *Brucella suis*, a zoonosis that primarily affects pigs. My guess is that the walkers in northern California attacked some wild pigs and wild boars, biting and infecting them but not killing them. The Reaper interacted with the bacteria *Brucella suis* and caused a mutation there. This probably happened early on, ten, twelve years ago. The rate and form of the mutation is consistent with exposure to radiation, so these walkers may have been survivors of the nukes dropped on San Francisco or even Seattle. In any case, you have radiation causing mutation in the walkers who bit the pigs, and then the presence of the bacteria, which allowed for further mutation. . . ."

Her voice ran down as she looked around.

"Are you following any of this?"

Benny held his thumb and index finger a half-inch apart. "About this much."

"We met some of those infected pigs," said Joe. "One of them nearly cut Lilah here in half."

McReady sighed. "Live ones or dead ones?"

"Dead," said Joe, "but spry."

"That's something we were afraid of. The bacteria *Brucella suis* allowed the Reaper pathogen to adapt to the pig's biology. They started turning up about four years ago. We brought two from Hope One, and I radioed ahead to Dick Price to have his people get more of them for when my team arrived. He did, but in the process of bringing the infected boars to Death Valley, he may accidentally have spread the bacterial infection to the walkers in this area. In any case, he managed to get us the boars we needed. We had a pen of about forty of them for a while."

"You *kept* them?" gasped Lilah.

"Of course we kept them," said McReady. "Live boars and reanimated boars were a perfect place to grow the bacteria."

"What happened to the boars?" asked Benny.

"When we got to the point where we'd devised a way to grow the bacteria synthetically, I ordered the boars terminated. Dick Price sent all ten of his soldiers out there. Not one of them came back."

"The boars got them?"

"The boars got what was left of them. Reapers laid an ambush. We didn't even know they were in the area. They trapped our team outside, forced them to give them the access codes to enter this complex. They killed a lot of our people and even let some of the boars loose in here. We had to fight them using brooms and folding chairs and whatever we could grab. The soldiers were all outside being slaughtered. Price's science team panicked and overreacted. They used grenades and makeshift explosives to fight back, and one of the blasts did something to the air lock so we couldn't get out. The reapers trashed our communications center. We cut them down, but it was too late. They also pushed our helicopter over the edge of the cliff. That was about a month after we got here. We killed the last of the reapers and slaughtered the pigs they let loose, but so what? We were stuck in here with no communication and no way out of this facility until you blew the door in. Between those who died in the ambush and the rest who killed themselves here, I've seen forty-one people die since coming here."

72

BENNY UNDERSTOOD THE DESPAIR NOW.

The suicides and hopelessness.

McReady and her people had been trapped in this locked tomb of concrete and steel for almost a year and a half—a place that was so secret even Joe Ledger and his rangers didn't know about it. The scientists and staff must have thought that they were doomed to die in here, forgotten by a dying world. Until McReady and then the reapers showed up.

Benny said, "Not everyone from the transport plane died in the crash. A few survived, and they joined the Night Church. I . . . um . . . killed one of them." He cleared his throat. "One of them must have had a copy of the coordinates and gave them up when he joined the reapers. That's probably how they found this place."

McReady considered, sighed, and nodded. "That might also explain what happened to the missing notes and the samples of mutagen and Archangel I sent to Sanctuary."

"We recovered some stuff," said Joe. "Enough for Reid to make some weak versions of the mutagen, but she couldn't work out how to process the mutagen into the cure. Without your notes Reid said that all they'll ever hit are dead ends."

"Damn." McReady rubbed her eyes. They were paler in color than Benny had expected, less of the intense dark brown of the face in the Teambook photo and more of a dusty burned-gold hue. "The one upside to working in total isolation is that it focuses your concentration." She nodded at the stacks of containers and heaps of bags. "See those boxes? Eleven tons of a powdered version of the mutagen, boxed to make it easier to transport and store. But you do not want to get any of it in a mucous membrane. Any moisture will activate the bacteria, and that starts the worms hatching." She laughed. "Those worms are something else. Industrious and clever little buggers. Once they become active in a walker, all the walker's tissues become softer, more pliant. This is why the R3's are able to move so much more quickly."

"What's in the bags?" asked Nix. "Is that the cure? Is that Archangel?"

"Yes. We have 968,000 capsules as of yesterday's count. They have enough supplies back at Sanctuary to make a million doses a month."

"We can save the world," whispered Nix.

McReady rubbed her eyes. "Yes," she said hoarsely. "Yes, we can."

They stared at the bags. Benny felt like the floor was tilting under him.

Lilah cut into the silence. "The mutagen doesn't just make the zoms faster. They got smarter, too."

Benny nodded. "One of them picked up a stick and hit me with it."

"Mm," McReady said diffidently. "The appearance of increased intelligence is nothing magical. From the initial infection, the parasites feed tiny amounts of oxygen to the brain as well as other key proteins and chemicals to the nervous system. That means the brains never die a complete death as they do in ordinary mortality. The parasites have to preserve some of the cranial nerves in order for the host body to walk, grab, eat, chew."

"But they don't need to eat," said Benny. "Everyone knows that."

"Sure they do. When they don't or can't, they go into a deeper stasis. They stop moving, stop expending energy. It's like a super-amplified version of the hibernation state, similar to that of a ground squirrel. The squirrel's metabolic rate drops to one percent, but with the walkers it's down to one thousandth of one percent. They are dead by any standard clinical model, but not in point of fact. The parasites can't let the host body completely decay, otherwise it's of no value as a vector for spreading the disease. So the process of necrosis is slowed to an almost negligible level. However, when they do eat, the food they consume is broken down by enzymes at an incredibly slow rate. It might take them months or even years to fully digest whatever protein they've consumed. All the while the parasites are being fed."

"Why don't people *know* this?" asked Nix.

"People do," said McReady. "Everyone in the American Nation knows this. It's taught in school. I'm surprised you *don't* know it."

"That's not the kind of thing they teach us at home," said Nix.

"Pity," sniffed McReady. "Knowledge is power. Lack of knowledge is suicide."

Benny did not reply to that. He asked, "I'm confused about a few things. Like, why did that man, Mr. Price, write what he wrote?"

"Price spent his life designing bioweapons. Airborne Ebola and a form of tuberculosis used for assassinations, that sort of stuff. He was Dr. Death for thirty years before the Fall. I guess he thought he had a lot to answer for. He probably *did* have a lot to answer for. Maybe not Reaper, but enough other monsters."

"Why did you think Joe was here to kill you?"

She almost smiled. "When I saw Joe, I thought that Jane Reid or one of her masters figured I'd gone off the reservation, maybe gone crazy and joined the reapers. Whatever. Generally, if you see Joe Ledger show up pointing a gun at you, I guess you start reexamining your conscience."

"I'm not an assassin," said Joe mildly.

"I'm sure that was never on your business card," was McReady's cold reply.

"There's something else," interrupted Benny. "You said that there were R3's in Washington and then some around here . . . but Nix and I saw some fast zoms near where we live, up by Yosemite National Park, in Mariposa County."

"Drifters," said McReady. "Probably wild boars spreading the mutation."

"But what about the boars that attacked Lilah in Nevada, and the R3's Nix and Lilah fought? Wild boars don't live in deserts."

McReady grunted. "I . . . don't know." She looked at Joe. "Could Reid have been—?"

"Reid doesn't have the D-series notes. I gave her some

samples of the mutagen, but she didn't know what to do with it. And even if she did, she wouldn't try it on walkers in the wild. She's not a genius, but she's not suicidally stupid."

"Reapers," said Lilah.

Everyone looked at her. McReady said, "Only if they had the missing notes and a good scientist. A chemist, a molecular biologist, an epidemiologist. Someone who understands the kind of science we're talking about."

"Could the reapers have someone like that?" asked Nix. "I mean . . . they're religious nuts."

"They're religious nuts now," said Benny. "Who and what were they before they joined the Night Church?"

It was an ugly question, and the answers seemed to scream at them.

"I have a question," said Nix into the silence. She nodded to the wall of plastic containers. "You made all this. Why? I mean . . . if you were trapped, if you thought you'd never get out, why did you—?"

McReady's eyes softened for the first time. "Because there's always hope, isn't there?"

"Is there?" asked Lilah, her voice strained. "Hope for whom?"

"For everyone. Even if we died in here, there was always the chance someone would find us and find the stores of Archangel. And—I thought that my notes, my research, was in the hands of Jane Reid's people at Sanctuary. I thought by now they'd have mass-produced a million tons of it. They *should* have. Once the parasites are active again, the process of decay kicks in, and the swine bacteria accelerates it. The walkers will become more dangerous, that's a given, but only for a week or so. Then the decay will have weakened their connective tissues. They'll start falling apart."

"The zoms outside looked pretty spry," said Joe. "I had to gun 'em down."

"No, that's the natural mutation from the pigs. They're faster, but the decomposition is still slow. We figure it will take forty-eight to sixty months for those walkers to fall. Our synthetic version of the natural mutagen—the one we developed before we evacuated Hope One—is different. You get a very fast walker for two or three days, and then you get one that's slow and awkward, and then you have a pile of meat and bones."

"What about someone who's infected but not dead?" asked Lilah. "Would Archangel save them . . . or kill them?"

"You have to give them Archangel before they're exposed to the mutagen. At least a full dose. Two capsules. Luckily, it kicks in fast, but without Archangel in their system, the mutagen will only kill them faster."

"And *with* Archangel?" demanded Lilah.

"Depends on what you're asking. If someone takes Archangel and dies, they don't reanimate."

"My brother died and he didn't reanimate," said Benny.

McReady nodded. "Same thing happened to a few people here. We think that's a side effect of the mutation. As the new version of the pathogen spreads, some people are developing immunity to the reanimative aspects of the plague. Our computer models indicate that in time—maybe ten or fifteen years—as many as one percent of the population will develop immunity. While that sounds hopeful, it isn't an answer. You say your brother didn't reanimate? Then count yourself lucky."

"No, said Nix, "that's not how it is. We saw maybe fifty

or sixty people killed in that fight, and at least six or seven of them didn't reanimate. That's more like ten percent."

"Then there must be a higher concentration of the *Brucella suis* bacteria in certain places. Again, count yourselves lucky. In most places the concentration is very low, and the bacteria won't even grow in certain climates. Just be happy that your brother caught a break."

"He still died."

"Everybody dies," said the scientist.

"What about someone who's infected but not dead?" asked Lilah again. "Would Archangel save them or kill them?"

McReady straightened. "Why do you ask?"

The grief and fear in Lilah's face was almost too much for Benny to look at.

Lilah said, "My . . . I mean, Chong . . . the . . . boy I . . . love is infected."

"How did it happen?"

"Kid was shot with an arrow dipped in walker flesh," said Joe.

"How long ago?"

"Little over a month."

"But—he should be dead." Then McReady nodded. "He's at Sanctuary, isn't he? Joe, you said they have everything except the D-series?"

"Yes."

"Then they definitely have the metabolic stabilizer."

"Yes. They used it on him."

"On Chong," said Lilah. "His name is Chong. They gave him injections."

"Is he conscious?" she asked. "Do you know what his

vitals are? What's his core temperature? Has it gone below ninety-six? Does he have a—?"

"We don't know," barked Lilah as tears boiled from the corners of her eyes. "He's sick. He's lost and he doesn't know me. My town boy doesn't know me."

Nix hurried over to her and put her arm around the Lost Girl's shoulder.

"Is there any hope for him?" asked Benny. "Any at all?"

Dr. McReady looked at him for a long time before she answered. The only sounds were Grimm's panting breaths and Lilah's sobs.

"Yes," said McReady, "there's definitely hope."

Everyone stiffened; every eye was on her.

Dr. McReady undid the fastenings on the sides of the hazmat suit and let it puddle around her feet. She wore a sweat-stained T-shirt and shorts. Her bare arms and legs were as ashy pale as her face. She turned her leg to show a long, jagged scar. It was curved, top and bottom.

It was the distinctive scar of a bite.

"When the reapers let the infected boars in here," she said slowly, "I was bitten on the calf. Dick Price got the stabilizer into me, and then I dosed myself with Archangel. First human test subject, didn't have a choice."

"God . . . ," breathed Nix.

"Archangel . . . worked?" whispered Lilah. "You're cured."

Dr. Monica McReady smiled. It was a strange smile, made stranger by her unnaturally pale skin.

"I take two pills twice a day, every day, and I probably will for the rest of my life. But . . . at least I have a life." She pointed to the bags. "If you can get me to Sanctuary, I can save Mr. Chong."

73

THEY WASTED NO TIME.

Benny, Nix, and Lilah loaded metal carts with boxes of the mutagen and bags of the Archangel capsules. They were all very careful, but they worked extremely fast. While they worked, Joe accompanied McReady to help her pack her latest research notes, a computer laptop, and other crucial supplies.

They rolled the carts through the hole blasted in the wall and formed a three-link chain to pass the boxes and bags into the Black Hawk. They were only half-finished when Joe and McReady came running out.

"That's enough," yelled Joe. "Get in. We'll come back for the rest. Let's go, go, *go*."

They didn't need any urging. Dr. McReady took the copilot seat, and Joe fired up the Black Hawk's engines. Moments later Zabriskie Point was dwindling behind them. They turned and shot through the darkening skies toward Sanctuary.

Benny and Nix sat on either side of Lilah, each of them holding one of her hands. Her grip was like iron, her face set into a strange, hard smile that was more death mask than anything. The weeks of impenetrable coldness she'd endured had taken a terrible toll on Lilah. During those weeks she'd hardly spoken, barely communicated. Instead of letting Nix and Benny in so they could help her through her pain and grief, she'd closed everything out. Benny knew that she was a practiced hand at eating her pain and pasting on a face of unflappable stoicism, but now a force had come along that was more powerful and dangerous than any enemy Lilah had ever faced. And it was a force over which she had no power.

Hope.

The possibility that Archangel could bring Chong back to her was almost more than Lilah could handle. Tears flowed steadily down her cheeks. They gleamed like hot mercury on her tanned face. Her breathing was ragged and fast, like a sprinter, or like a cornered feral animal whose only option was to destroy everything—even herself.

Hope, Benny knew, was a terrible double-edged thing.

"Lilah," he said softly, "it's going to be—"

"Shut up or I'll kill you," she said through gritted teeth.

Benny had no doubt at all that she meant it.

He shut up.

But he never let go of her hand.

The Black Hawk slashed through the last pale streamers of sunlight, heading at full speed to the darkness in the east.

Toward Sanctuary.

Toward Chong.

74

JOE LEDGER'S VOICE BOOMED AT THEM THROUGH THE LOUDSPEAKERS.

"Get up here right now!"

They tore themselves out of their straps and crowded into the cockpit door.

"What's wrong?" demanded Lilah.

Joe pointed. Deep lines of tension were cut in his skin, and his eyes were filled with horror. The east was a vast black nothing where the land and the sky were indistinguishable from each other. Except at one spot, miles and miles away.

A red-gold glow was painted onto the horizon.

"What is that?" asked Nix.

Joe's voice was a tight whisper. "That's Sanctuary."

They stared at the light. With every moment, with every mile the light grew brighter and brighter. They knew that they were still far away, which meant that a glow like that could never come from a small fire.

"No . . . ," said Nix in a small and hollow voice.

A single, wrenching, shattered sob broke in Lilah's chest.

Benny felt as if he was falling through space, as if a hole

had opened in the bottom of the helicopter. His heart tore loose from its moorings and sank into the darkness.

There, far away across the gulf of a nightmare landscape, Sanctuary was burning.

Part 3
The Truth In Distant Places

"I dislike death, however, there are some things I dislike more than death. Therefore, there are times when I will not avoid danger."

MENCIUS, Chinese Philosopher

THE BLACK HAWK FLEW INTO HELL ITSELF.

The scene below could have belonged in no other place.

The main gates of Sanctuary hung open, the gate patrol cut to pieces. Most of the hangars were ablaze. Fire and smoke curled hundreds of feet into the air. The bridge was down, and steady streams of zoms poured across.

Not walked, not shambled, but *ran*.

Tens of thousands of them were already across. Some of the monks ran from them. Some had formed defensive lines between the hordes of the dead and the entrances to the hospice hangars, but they had no weapons. Some held mattresses and metal-framed cots in front of them in the desperate hope of fending off the dead and protecting the helpless; but as Benny and the others watched in abject horror, the R3 zoms tore these things out of the monks' hands and dragged the screaming Children of God down.

A few monks knelt in the dirt, hands clasped in prayer, heads bowed while they allowed the dead to take them.

"Do something!" screeched Nix.

Joe flew low and opened up with the chain guns. Heavy bullets tore into the zoms, ripping arms and heads off. A few monks shook fists at them and tried to wave the helicopter off.

"What are they doing?" demanded McReady.

"Trying to protect the Children of Lazarus," Joe said dully.

Even as the monks waved and shouted at the Black Hawk, the creatures they tried to protect overwhelmed them and tore them apart. It was sickening.

It was beyond horrible.

"Someone released the mutagen," said McReady. "It has to be deliberate, but who would—?"

"Reapers," said Benny. It was more than an answer; he pointed down into the melee to where reapers on quads chased a group of nuns, herding them into the arms of the dead.

McReady grabbed Joe's arm. "Joe—"

"On it," he said and he turned the guns on them. The quads exploded one after the other. However, the zoms swept past the burning quads and crashed like a wave onto the nuns. Joe kept firing, but there was no real point. There were tens of thousands of fast zoms swarming into the hangars, and hundreds of reapers ferreting out the monks and nuns. And it was clear this battle had been going on for too long already. Many of the zoms down there were the reanimated dead who had risen from their own murders.

Dr. McReady punched the dashboard. "No! This isn't how it's supposed to be. The mutagen was intended for careful release after human populations were evacuated from an area. It's only viable until after the host dies off. In a week even any residual powder exposed to the air will be inert. Damn it, this isn't how it's supposed to *be*." She caved forward and put her face into her hands.

"Brother Peter said they wouldn't attack until tomorrow," said Benny.

Lilah grabbed his shirt. "And you *believed* him?"

But Nix shoved her back. "Stop it. We all believed him. This isn't helping and this won't get us to Chong."

Joe steered the Black Hawk away from the hangars. Benny saw tears cutting jagged tracks down his grizzled face.

"Can you see Riot?" begged Nix. "I can't see her anywhere."

No one answered.

One figure staggered past the row of swings, but when Joe shone a spotlight on it, the face that looked up at them was not Riot's or Eve's. It was Sister Hannahlily. Her mouth was smeared with red, and she held a human arm in her hands. She hissed at the helicopter.

Sickened, Joe swung the light away.

They hovered for a moment over the bridge. There were now more of the dead on the monks' side of the trench than on the other. Many more. A group of twenty reapers manned the bridge, herding the zoms over.

"Screw you," growled Joe as he armed a Hellfire missile. "Go to hell."

The missile blasted away from under the Black Hawk's stubby wing and struck the rocky ground near the bridge. The blast was immense, and when the rotor wash blew the smoke away, there was a crater in the trench wall. The bridge was still there, but all around it were charred ashes that were unrecognizable as ever having been human.

Then they saw a ripple of flashes by one of the hangars. At first Benny thought it was a string of firecrackers set off by the flames.

"Those are guns," yelled Nix. "The soldiers are fighting back."

Joe swung the Black Hawk toward the gunfire. Zoms chased the machine, and reapers on quads and on foot raced across the tarmac in the same direction. He fired one more missile at a crowd of mixed zoms and reapers and then flew straight through the fire and smoke.

The gunfire was coming from inside the hangar where they'd met Colonel Reid. There were bodies on the ground surrounded by the hunched figures of zoms who feasted on their victims. Benny could not tell if any of those bodies belonged to Riot or Eve. The dead poured into the hangar, and there were living reapers among them, shoving the zoms forward, herding them, driving them from kill to kill.

Joe dropped almost to the ground and flew the helicopter slowly and carefully in through the open hangar doors. The gunfire was concentrated in one corner, and Benny could see a knot of soldiers moving in a tight cluster, toward a door set in the back wall. Some of them fired at the advancing horde of zoms; others fired toward the door to clear it. But there was no doubt that some zoms and reapers had already passed through that doorway.

"They're inside the complex," said Joe. "That door leads to a tunnel that connects all of these buildings."

McReady looked up, her face going paler still. "The equipment . . . the lab."

"Chong!" cried Lilah.

The look on Joe's face was as feral and cruel as any monster as he opened up with the chain guns. He turned the helicopter in a slow circle and maintained continuous fire,

366

creating a kind of hell Benny had never seen before. One man and one machine turned the entire hangar into a slaughterhouse. Reapers and zombies flew apart. Others were punched backward into each other or against walls. Shell casings fell like rain. But then the guns clicked on empty, the rounds exhausted.

Joe landed the Black Hawk in a swirl of blood-tinged smoke.

The group of soldiers were at the door now. They gunned down the last of the reapers in their way and vanished inside the entrance to the tunnel.

And they slammed the door shut behind them.

76

"Everybody out," bellowed Joe as he erupted from the pilot's seat. "Now—*now!*"

They grabbed their weapons, but Lilah also scooped up two bags of the capsules. Benny saw this and grabbed a couple as well, shoving them into his backpack.

"You never know," he said.

Joe snatched a machine gun from a rack and began stuffing extra magazines into his pockets. "Lilah, you're with McReady. If you want your boyfriend back, kill anyone who even looks at her."

Lilah bared her teeth.

"Nix, Benny, you two hold the line and watch my back. I have to get through that door, and it's going to take a minute. If I don't and things get weird, go back into the chopper and close the door. There are enough guns and ammo in there to stop an army."

Then Joe clicked his tongue for Grimm, and as soon as the dog turned its massive armored head toward him, Joe quickly reached out and touched Nix on the shoulder.

"Family," said Joe, and Grimm barked once in acknowledgment.

Joe touched Benny. "Family," he said again.

Another bark.

"Protect," said the ranger, and the dog gave a third deep-chested bark.

Joe rolled back the door of the Black Hawk and was firing before he even jumped out. That corner of the hangar was littered with the dead, but more were pouring into the hangar through the massive open doorway. There was a narrow slot, almost a cattle chute, formed by the wall and the helicopter, and this allowed only a couple of the dead to rush forward at a time.

Nix gave Benny a single brave smile. "Warrior smart," she said.

"Warrior smart."

And for no reason at all other than that the world was insane, they laughed.

The dead rushed forward, and Benny and Nix—last of the samurai—went to meet them.

Benny edged forward and left and his *kami katana* felt alive in his hands, like it wanted this, craved it. Or maybe it was that now that Benny's own spirit had come fully alive in him, the part of his spirit that resided in the steel of the sword had come alive too. In either case, as the first zombies rushed at him, Benny met the attack with cut after cut after cut. Dead limbs flew, zoms that were suddenly legless crashed down in front of the creatures behind them. The dead collided and fell over one another, and Benny was there, holding his ground, the blade flashing and flashing. Nix positioned herself ten feet away and swung *Dojigiri* with equal ferocity.

Grimm leapt into the gap between them, spikes and blades

bristling from head and shoulders and flanks. As the dead flung themselves forward, the monstrous mastiff cut them to pieces. Not with teeth, but with all that razor-sharp metal.

While all this happened, Benny felt another change occurring deep within him. His mind felt like it was detaching from the moment and from the normal flow of time. It drifted back to watch from a distance that offered a different perspective, more of a spherical view of the situation. One that allowed him to see his position, that position's relevance to where Nix fought, the distance to where Joe knelt in front of the locked door, the opening of the chute, the numbers of the dead, the presence of the living reapers among the crowd. The big ranger worked feverishly to pick the lock.

All this was delicately separated from any emotional involvement, as if a surgeon's deft cut with a scalpel had removed it so that it would not be impeded or influenced by any normal human involvement. It was how Benny imagined great chess players viewed a game. Clearly and from a distance.

He saw his own body, its posture, the spacing of his hands on the handle, the angle of his cuts. He saw small imperfections in the movements, and as he observed them his body made the corrections that increased the speed and efficiency of each cut.

The dead began to pile up in front of him, his enemies becoming his bulwark against the main body of the horde. Benny knew, with perfect clarity, that had he been in a fight with so many of the fast zoms even a month ago—even a week ago—he would have already died. Even a week ago. The change he'd felt earlier tonight had somehow snapped together all the disparate parts of him. All the aspects of himself that had been growing like weeds—fast, but wild and in different directions—suddenly came together within his soul. They were all there inside him. His experiences in the Ruin. The lessons from Tom and the lessons learned from both victories and defeats. The love he felt for Nix—and his new understanding of the forces at work in this red-haired warrior girl that he loved. The fierce anger at the injustices committed by the Night Church in the name of religion. The determination to have a future despite all the adult voices that kept crying out that there was no future to have. The faith in himself—in this person he had become. All of that coalesced inside a quiet space in Benny Imura's mind.

There were sharp *cracks* as Lilah, standing guard over Dr. McReady, fired carefully aimed shots through the open gap between Nix and Benny. Every shot hit a target, but not every bullet struck the head. Unlimited and perfect head shots every time were an impossibility with a handgun, and Benny understood that now. It was a logical thing, and therefore it was open to his new perception.

This is how a samurai thinks, he mused. *This is what it was like for Tom when he was in a battle. That's why he always looked calm.*

Even that thought was cataloged without emotional involvement. It was a truth, and it became part of his experience.

"Let's go!"

The shout drew him back to his body, and Benny turned to see Lilah and Dr. McReady vanish through the opened door. Joe brought his rifle up as he stepped into the space between Benny and Nix.

"Grimm! Back!"

The dog spun around, retreated, and raced to Joe's side, leaving the gap unguarded.

"I got this," Joe yelled. "Get inside."

Benny and Nix wasted no time. They spun too, and ran for the door as Joe hosed the opening of the chute with automatic gunfire. Then he jacked a round into the grenade launcher mounted below the rifle barrel and fired. Jacked and fired, jacked and fired. He angled the blasts toward the wall, well away from the Black Hawk, but the blast radius destroyed anything that stepped into the chute.

Then Joe spun and dashed for the door.

As he leaped through, Nix slammed it shut and Benny shot the bolt on the inside. Grimm howled in rage and triumph, and the echoes banged off the walls.

Outside, dead hands began pounding on the door.

77

"WILL THE DOOR HOLD?" ASKED NIX, HER FACE FLUSHED WITH FEAR AND excitement.

"It'll stop the dead," said Joe, "but those reapers will figure a way in. No time to waste."

They were in a stone hallway that led to a flight of stairs that plunged down into shadows. Joe tried the light switch and a few lights flickered on, but most of the bulbs had been smashed. Shell casings littered the floor, and the walls were smeared with blood along with some of the black mucus.

"Don't get any of it on you," warned McReady.

"Wasn't planning to," said Benny.

From below, they could hear a confusion of sounds. Gunfire, moans, shouts, and screams.

Lilah dropped the empty magazine from her pistol and slapped in a new one. "Chong's down there."

Joe touched her arm. "Listen to me, Chong is in the basement below the blockhouse. That's three hundred yards from here, and there are a lot of doors between here and there. There's also ten ways to get to those cells, or at least to the central corridor that leads down to the cells. We have to get down these steps and find the maintenance access door. We can use that and maybe slip past the zoms, maybe get ahead of them. You understand?"

She nodded.

Joe touched her cheek. "We'll get to him."

But there was a deadness in Lilah's eyes, and Benny feared that the Lost Girl was already losing hope.

Nix said, "Wait, what about the soldiers? Where are they? Why aren't they fighting back? All I saw were the guards who usually take care of the bridge . . . where are the rest of them? Where are the soldiers we just saw run in here?"

"That's right," said McReady. "There are two hundred men here. . . ."

"There are forty-eight soldiers here," Joe said. "And thirteen members of the medical staff."

"Did the others ship out?"

Joe's eyes were bleak. "I wish."

Distant gunfire and screams seemed to answer for him. He put his rifle stock to his shoulder and went quickly and quietly down the stairs. Benny looked at the others, saw the varying expressions in their eyes. Joe's last two words had punched everyone in the gut.

One by one they followed him down the bloodstained stairs. They found two dead soldiers who were just starting to reanimate. Joe put them down with precise single shots to their heads.

Benny went last, and as he ghosted along behind the others, he thought about all the bad things Joe's words could mean. And he wondered if, in all this madness, they would ever find Riot and Eve. Were they alive? Were they dead? Had the wild former reaper somehow managed to battle her way through the sea of killers to defend the little girl she treasured?

If anyone could, Benny knew that she would.

The steps went down, turned a corner, went down again, and then ended in a round chamber from which four corridors spiked off in different directions. Joe paused and they all stopped to listen. The most intense sounds of battle came from the left-hand corridor. There were indistinct sounds from the middle two, and only silence from the one on the right. But the lights were out in that tunnel, and the edge of the wall leading into it was smeared with black goo.

"Let me guess," said Benny sourly, "that one's the one we have to take, right?"

Joe gave him a tight grin. "What's wrong, you want to live forever?"

"Not forever. Maybe another seventy years, though."

"Let me know how that turns out for you."

"Flashlight?" asked Nix.

Joe clicked on the small light that was mounted on his gun and dialed it up to its widest beam; but the light was small and the illumination didn't reach very far into the gloom. No one else had a flashlight.

"Don't bunch up," said Joe. "I don't want a sword up my backside."

They entered the hallway, following the blue-white splash of Joe's flashlight. Once more Benny took up the rear position. No need to cede that responsibility to Lilah anymore. He felt capable of defending them.

But as they went deeper and deeper, the light from the

staircase landing faded and then vanished, leaving everything behind Benny as black as the pit.

Don't be cocky, he told himself. *And don't be scared. Sight isn't your only sense. Listen to what the darkness has to tell you.*

It was one of Tom's lessons filtered through his own personal understanding.

He let the others move ahead so the sounds of their footsteps and the rattle of their equipment faded. He listened to the darkness.

Everything behind was silent.

Silent.

Until it wasn't.

He heard a sound.

Soft. Quick.

In darkness the sound of running is often defined by the panting breath of the runner as much as by the slap of feet on the ground.

Unless . . .

Unless the runner did not need to pant, did not need to breathe.

Benny suddenly realized that the others were too far ahead, which meant that the meager spill of light from Joe's flashlight was sending almost no reflected illumination this far back.

And something was coming.

Something was running toward him.

Silent.

Fast.

And he couldn't see it.

78

Benny had two seconds to decide.

Stand and fight in almost total darkness or . . .

He turned and ran.

He ran as fast as he had ever run before. He ran so fast that all he could hear was the harsh grating of his own breath in his ears. That sound blocked out the noise of whatever pursued him, which meant that almost at once he lost any sense of how close it was.

He ran and ran.

Up ahead Joe Ledger turned a corner and took his light with him.

The corridor became completely black.

Benny thought he could hear a sound behind him.

Not the rhythmic panting of another runner, but the low, continuous moan of something so hungry that it would run and run forever until it caught its prey and dragged it down.

"*Joe!*" Benny yelled.

He wanted to yell more, he wanted to yell for light, but he saved his breath for running.

And then there it was.

A splash of light so bright that it blinded him. He recoiled from it, throwing up an arm to block it.

Suddenly something slammed into him from behind.

The impact sent him crashing painfully into the wall. The sword fell from his hands and clattered to the ground. The air left Benny's chest with a whoosh, and cold fingers clawed at his shirt and neck and tried to hook into the corners of his mouth.

The image of the tiny white worms in the black muck filled his brain as immediately and intensely as a grenade exploding. It galvanized Benny into action.

He spun along the wall until the zombie that clung to him was caught between him and the unyielding stone, then he planted a foot and kicked himself forward halfway to the opposite wall, then kicked out again, braced his foot on that wall, and thrust backward with all his strength. The ping-pong action sent Benny and his attacker crunching backward once more, but this time the impact was many times harder. The creature lost its grip and collapsed to the floor.

Joe's light was getting closer, and everyone was yelling and running toward him.

The zom—a man dressed as an American Nation soldier— came off the ground at him, snarling and biting the air.

Benny kicked him in the chest and knocked him once more into the wall.

And then with a snarl of fury Grimm crashed into the zom. They fell sideways, and Benny ducked backward away from the wet pieces of things that flew and splatted against the wall.

"Off!" cried Joe, and the hulking monster froze. Red blood dripped from its spikes. The zom still had blood in its veins and tissues, proof that it had turned only minutes ago.

As Joe came running up and shone his light on the zom, Benny realized that he knew this man.

Sergeant Peruzzi.

Dead now, torn to pieces.

Benny heard Nix make a small, sad sound.

He'd been rude and threatening to Nix, but he didn't deserve this.

No one did.

Benny glanced at Joe and expected to see the hard, dismissive face of a killer, but there was sadness in the big man's eyes.

"Let's go," he said.

Lilah picked up Benny's sword and handed it to him.

"Thanks," he said. "I—"

But the Lost Girl got up in his face. "Chong is waiting for me. Don't slow us down again."

There wasn't the slightest trace of compromise or mercy in her face.

All Benny could do was nod.

They turned and ran.

They passed two side corridors, but both were empty. Joe quickly explained that one led to the maintenance hangar and the other went to the generator room.

They went up a flight of stairs and along a corridor that was better lighted. There were two sets of heavy doors set fifty yards apart, and at each one they found blood and shell casings.

"Someone's making a fight of this," observed Joe. "Using doors and corridor bends as opposition points."

There were no bodies, though. Nix pointed this out.

"Does that mean that they're already inside?" she asked.

"With the mutagen, reanimation is very fast," said McReady. "More of a transition from one state to another instead of death and a return to life. Anyone who died here could have been up in seconds."

"Is anyone left?" asked Nix.

A new rattle of gunfire answered that question. It came from deeper inside the complex, along the path they were following. McReady and Joe listened, each of them judging distance. Their eyes snapped wide at the same time.

"God," said Joe.

"The infirmary," said McReady.

Everyone broke into a dead run as the gunfire continued, interspersed with moans and screams. To Benny every hallway and staircase looked the same, and he had the irrational feeling that they were running in circles.

Then one corridor ended with an air lock similar to the one they'd destroyed in the badlands. The door was ajar, held open by a slumped figure with a bullet hole in its forehead. A zom, Benny saw. There was red powder on its hair and face and black muck smeared on its mouth.

Beyond the air lock was a small chamber and then a second air lock, also blocked by the legs of a dead woman, whose head hung on an absurdly crooked neck. The woman was not one of the zoms from outside, nor was she was a reaper. She wore a soiled white lab coat over a military uniform.

"God—that's Karen Lansky," cried McReady. "She's a nurse here."

The sounds of battle were much closer now, but the intensity was less.

Fewer shots. Fewer screams.

Benny did not think this was a good sign.

As they gathered themselves to pass through the air lock, Benny bent and kissed Nix quickly on the lips.

"For luck," he said.

"I know," she replied, smiling. "But we won't need it. We're going to get Chong, find Riot and Eve, and get out of here."

It was a strangely positive thing for her to say, but Benny saw no doubt in her eyes. She believed it.

It made him want to kiss her again.

Joe looked over his shoulder at them. "Benny—you've been bugging me for a month to tell you why the soldiers and scientists here haven't done much to help you. Why they haven't let you in here." He looked grim. "Sometimes you have to be careful what you wish for."

With that he stepped through the air lock, took a brief look, and immediately opened fire.

Lilah was right behind him, her pistol bucking in her hands as she fired and fired.

Benny and Nix adjusted their grips on their swords.

"C'mon, Doc," said Benny, "we won't let anything happen to you."

The doctor's eyes were skeptical. "Too late for that, kids. But . . . thanks."

They heard two more shots, and then a sudden silence fell over the whole complex.

Joe Ledger called to them. "It's clear," he said, his voice rough. "It's all over in here."

They passed through the air lock and saw four reapers and five zoms lying in a tangle beyond where Joe stood.

Gun smoke from the ranger's rifle hung in a blue pall around him.

Benny and Nix stepped into another scene of horror and madness.

There was a bed right inside the door. A man lay in it, his eyes wide with fury and pain, his pajamas soiled with blood and muck, his limbs thrashing as he fought to rise. Not to escape—but to attack. Ropes held him to the bed, lashing his arms and legs and torso to the metal frame. Black spit flew from the man's screaming mouth.

Benny stared past him at the occupant of the next bed. And the next.

And all the others.

Hundreds of beds. Each one filled. Each person thrashing and moaning and biting the air. Each one trapped there by ropes.

Their uniforms hung over the backs of chairs, or were draped over the ends of the beds. The uniforms of soldiers of the American Nation. The lab coats of scientists. The special jackets of pilots.

Nix's sword drooped in her grasp until the tip of the blade made a hollow *tink* against the concrete.

This was why there had been no real resistance to the reaper invasion.

This was why the jet sat idle on the tarmac.

This was why the soldiers and the scientists were so bitter.

"They're all infected," Benny murmured. "All of them . . ."

He heard a sob and turned to see Dr. McReady trembling. "No," she said. "No . . ."

Joe swapped out his magazines, his face wooden. "The

infection started three months ago," he said. "A few guards on patrol by the siren towers got swarmed by a pack of R3's. One fatality, but a couple of the others got the black blood on them. I don't know if it got in someone's eyes or mouth, or if it was on one of the soldiers' hands and he touched his face. We'll never know. But he brought the mutagen into Sanctuary with him. We sent word to the American Nation to quarantine this place. To write it off."

He shook his head sadly.

"Sanctuary is dead."

They all gaped at him.

Benny got up in Joe's face. "*You* brought us here, damn it. Why bring us to a graveyard?"

Joe shook his head. "When I brought you here it was to save you from Saint John and Mother Rose. But we never let you inside. We kept you away from the plague until we could make sure you were uninfected. If it wasn't for your friend Chong, I'd have taken you kids south to North Carolina. Now you're inside the quarantine zone. You're as trapped as everyone else at Sanctuary."

SIX CORRIDORS AWAY, A TEAM OF RED BROTHERS MOVED SILENTLY THROUGH the shadows, knives ready, eyes alert, killing anyone they met. Brother Peter ran with them, his face flushed with exertion, his clothes soaked with blood.

Two soldiers tried to hold a doorway, but Brother Peter ordered a pair of reapers to rush them. The men smiled at the chance to serve their brother, serve their god, and leaped like heroes into the darkness. They let out earsplitting roars as they charged straight into a hail of bullets. The rounds chopped into them, splattering the walls with blood, turning the killers into dancing puppets and finally into inhuman rag dolls.

But as they collapsed, Brother Peter, who had run up behind them at full speed, leaped over their corpses, a knife in each hand.

The soldiers did not have time to scream.

The rest of the Red Brothers swept through the doorway and into the lab complex. Gleaming machines, racks of sanitized instruments, cabinets of medicines, and banks of computers filled the room.

One scientist was there.

A woman, with gray hair tied in a bun and reading glasses that hung on a delicate chain around her neck.

She dropped to her knees as Peter and the reapers fanned out around her.

"Please," she begged. "Don't."

Brother Peter knelt in front of her. "Why not, my sister? Tell me."

Her eyes glittered with tears. "We're so close," she said. "We can *cure* this. We're *going* to cure it. Please . . . just give us time. We can save everyone . . . please believe me."

"Believe you?" mused the reaper. "My sister, I *do* believe you. I believe with all my heart that you can cure the plague that has come so close to destroying all human life."

Her expression softened from abject horror to one of surprised hope. "Then you'll leave us alone? You won't hurt us? You won't wreck everything?"

He set one of his knives down and used that hand to caress her face. It was an act of such gentleness, such tenderness, that the woman actually closed her eyes and pressed her cheek against his rough palm.

"I said that I believed you, my sister," said Brother Peter as he leaned close and rested his cheek on the top of her head. "And may god have mercy on you for the sins you have committed here in this place of blasphemy."

Her eyes snapped wide.

Not because of his words.

They opened with shock because of the pain. She sagged back from him and looked down at the knife that Peter had buried in her chest.

"May you find forgiveness in the formless eternity of the darkness."

"All praise to his darkness," said the others.

Peter looked around at the reapers and then at the machines that filled the room.

"Destroy everything," he said.

THE HORROR AND SADNESS OF WHAT SURROUNDED THEM WAS AWFUL. On some level Benny had feared that the answer to the mystery of Sanctuary might be something like this, but he'd never allowed that thought to fully form. Now it was incontrovertible.

"Can you do anything for them?" asked Nix as she shrugged out of her pack.

"We can try," said McReady, "but some of them . . . I think some of them have already gone too far over the line."

However, she stood frozen, as if shocked by her own words and all that they implied.

Benny understood what she meant; he could see it. Some of the infected looked different from the majority of the poor people in the beds. The different ones had paler, grayer skin, and there was a quality missing from their eyes. All the infected had rage and hunger burning in their eyes, but for some that was all there was. Beyond those two things there was a blackness, like the empty shadows at the bottom of a ditch. Whatever indefinable quality that separated infected person from infected zom was gone, consumed by the insatiable appetites of the Reaper Plague.

For the rest, though . . .

The spark of humanity was still there. Flickering in a dark wind, but there nonetheless.

McReady still stood unmoving.

Then Lilah crossed to her in two quick strides, spun the woman, and slapped her across the face with shocking force. "*Do something.* Test the drug. Show me that it works before I give it to my town boy. Show me now or I'll *feed* you to them."

It was a vicious threat, and Benny had no doubts at all that Lilah meant it. Joe took a step toward the doctor, and Benny and Nix moved in the same instant and put the tips of their swords against his chest.

"Don't," warned Benny.

Joe gently pushed the sword blades aside. "And don't you forget who your friends are." To McReady he said, "Lilah gave you an order, Monica—not a request."

McReady glared hot death at him, but then she snatched the backpack from Nix and hurried over to the bed of a woman who still had the spark of humanity.

"Help me," said McReady, and Lilah was right there. "Hold her head steady, yes, just like that. I need her mouth open. Good . . ."

As Lilah followed the directions, McReady took two capsules from the bag and unscrewed them.

"Normally we'd let her swallow the capsules and wait for digestion and absorption through the stomach mucosa . . . but we don't have that time. Hold her—she'll buck. The first dose is painful. The parasites in the body will fight it."

Lilah's muscles bunched and flexed, and the woman's head did not budge at all. McReady poured the powder into the gaping mouth.

"Water," she called, and Nix was there with a canteen. She dribbled some of the water into the woman's mouth and then directed Lilah to force the jaws shut.

Immediately the woman began thrashing ten times more frantically than before. Her muscles went rigid as iron, and her body arched and bucked with such force that Lilah had to lie across her to keep her from breaking her own bones. The screams were terrible, the worst Benny had ever heard. High, plaintive, piercing.

"It's not working," said Nix. "God, it's not . . . ."

Suddenly the woman went limp.

It was as quick as a heartbeat. Her body flopped back against the bed and she lay there, staring blindly at the ceiling, her chest rising and falling with alarming rapidity as air puffed in and out between gritted teeth.

They gathered around her bed, fists balled in tension, held breath burning in their chests.

"Come on," McReady muttered. "Come on . . . come on . . ."

Then someone said, "God . . ."

They all stared.

The voice spoke again.

"God . . . help me . . ."

It was the woman.

Wasted, drenched with sweat, covered with her own filth, ragged, and worn to a skeletal thinness.

But it was a person who spoke.

Not a monster.

Joe snapped, "Everyone—two teams. Go."

It was impossible. It was a task assigned in hell. It was the hardest thing Benny had ever done. But as Joe went through the room and quieted those whose life spark had burned out, the rest of them worked in pairs—Lilah holding patients for McReady, Benny holding for Nix.

It took forever.

Forever . . . And with every second Benny thought about Chong.

But they got two capsules into the mouths of every remaining person in the room.

Soldiers.

Scientists.

Support staff.

Flight crew.

One hundred and sixty-two people.

It took forever.

But they did it. Lilah kept saying to herself, *It works. We can save my town boy.* Over and over.

By the time they were finished, Benny could hardly stand. Nix was weeping openly. So were many of the patients.

Archangel was a miracle drug, they all knew that; but Benny had read too many science fiction novels where miraculous cures are instantaneous. He willed the infected to all suddenly snap out of it, for their eyes to clear, and for the *thing* that dwelled inside them to flee. Not all of them did. For some it was fast, for others amazingly slow. Reality is often harsher than fiction. Slower, and far less satisfying.

For most of the infected the Archangel pills triggered shrieks and convulsions, and it filled their eyes with screaming madness.

"You're killing them!" Benny yelled.

"Shut up," said McReady. "It's the parasites—they are programmed to defend themselves."

A few of the patients sagged back into panting semiconsciousness. Some turned aside and wept into their pillows, as if ashamed of the dark thoughts that had set up court in their heads. Some stared fixedly at the ceiling as if frozen in time.

Some died.

Benny began to untie one of the treated patients, but McReady stopped him, warning that a relapse, though unlikely, was possible. Observation for several hours would be needed.

They gathered around the bed of one of the worst cases. A soldier who screamed and thrashed and finally collapsed back, his eyes and mouth open, his chest suddenly silent. McReady snatched up a medical chart that hung on a hook at the end of his bed. "This soldier was bitten on patrol. Looks like he was already pretty far gone when they gave him the metabolic stabilizer."

"Is he dead?" asked Lilah in a frightened voice.

"Yes."

"We killed him," breathed Nix.

McReady looked sad. "He had almost transitioned to a reanimate. All the parasitic eggs in his system must have hatched. The strain . . . it was simply too much for him, and his heart gave out."

She examined the other fatalities.

"This one had a preexisting heart condition," she said, reading another chart. "And this one looks like she had a stroke."

Lilah said, "What about Chong? Will this . . . I mean will Archangel . . . ?"

The doctor shook her head. "There's no way to tell. It's going to be different for every infected person. There will always be a risk."

She sighed and rubbed her tired eyes.

"I'm exhausted," she said. "I need to sit down and—"

"No!" growled Lilah as she grabbed a bag of capsules and glared at McReady. "We have to find my town boy. *Right now.*"

BROTHER PETER ENTERED A LONG, DISMAL CHAMBER LINED ON BOTH SIDES with iron-barred cells. All the cells were empty save one. The thing in the cage glared out at him from behind strings of matted black hair. His eyes were dark and bottomless. Pale lips curled back to reveal wet teeth.

"Hello, little brother," he said. "Why do they have you in here? What sin have you committed that they've locked you away like an animal?"

The thing in the cage growled. It was an animal sound with no trace of humanity. There were gnawed bones on the floor, and its metal water dish was battered and twisted.

"Looks like he's about to cross over," observed one of the Red Brothers. "You want to leave him or let him go?"

The creature in the cage murmured a single word. "Hungry . . ."

"Still alive," said the Red Brother.

"Then he's still a sinner," said Brother Peter as he turned to leave. "Send him into the darkness. Do it quickly, then bring the rest of the Red Brothers. I want to make sure that the sinners in the medical center have been dealt with."

The reaper nodded and bowed as Brother Peter left.

There was a ring of keys on the wall, and the reaper fetched them and tried several before finding the one that unlocked the right cell. He drew a long knife and opened the cell door.

"Best to just let it happen, little brother," said the reaper. "All your pain will be over soon."

Screams filled the whole cell block.

"The holding cells are right through here," said Joe as he led the way.

"Why'd they put the boy in the cells?" asked McReady. "There were three or four beds left upstairs."

"They didn't want us to see that the whole staff was infected," said Nix.

Joe nodded. "You know Jane Reid, Monica. She's addicted to secrets."

He turned the last corner and suddenly stopped dead as if he'd struck a wall. Then he took two clumsy steps backward.

Benny and Nix stared in abject horror. They all stared at Joe.

At his stomach.

"No . . . ," whispered McReady.

A knife was buried nearly to the hilt in Joe Ledger's stomach. Blood pumped out of the wound and poured down the front of the ranger's body.

A figure stepped out of the side passage.

Grimm barked in fear and surprise.

Nix screamed.

It was Brother Peter.

The right hand of Saint John.

Except for the saint himself, he was the most dangerous of the Night Church's army of killers. An unsmiling monster with the face of an angel. A master killer.

The hallway behind him was crowded with reapers, who each had red handprints tattooed on their faces.

"R-run . . . ," cried Joe in a voice that was little more than a whisper. He dropped to his knees and his rifle clattered to the ground. "For God's sake . . . run. . . ."

GRIMM TENSED TO LUNGE, BUT JOE SNAKED OUT A RESTRAINING HAND AND clung to the dog. There were too many of the reapers. They would butcher the mastiff. But Grimm snarled and thrashed, incensed by the smell of fresh blood, craving carnage and revenge.

Brother Peter looked at them all and nodded to himself.

"I saw you little birds fly away in that big black machine," he said softly. "Then I heard you come back. I thought my trick hadn't worked."

"What trick?" demanded Benny. Then he got it. "Your ultimatum . . . that was fake?"

"A necessary lie. I wanted you to take this sinner away from here." He spat on Ledger, who huddled groaning and bleeding on the floor. "We didn't want him here when we moved on Sanctuary. We knew what he was searching for and how desperately he wanted to find it. So we gave him a few useful little clues." He pointed a finger at McReady. "But we *did* want her. We wanted you and this sinner to go find her and bring her back. You've been so resourceful that I had no doubt at all that you'd rescue the doctor and bring her—and her blasphemous cures—to me. And you have."

He did not smile, but cruel lights danced in his eyes. He was enjoying this.

Benny looked past him. The men with him were huge, and they were all armed. Lilah and Nix's guns were still in their holsters. The only way they'd have time and a chance to draw those guns was if he used himself as a shield to buy them two seconds. Would he last that long?

Benny was sure that Brother Peter would cut him down. He had no illusions about being able to beat this man. Would dying to slow Peter down be worth the sacrifice?

If Nix and Lilah couldn't kill Peter and at least half the big reapers with bullets, then they would have no chance at all with their blades. It was a terrible moment, and Benny racked his mind to find some way out of it. What would a samurai do in this situation? What was the warrior-smart thing to do?

Joe coughed and rolled away from them, curling his body into a ball, face to the wall. Blood pooled under him.

"Odd," said Brother Peter to the fallen ranger, "but we were all so frightened of you. You are the closest thing to a boogeyman that we reapers have."

Joe said nothing. His body twitched and shuddered.

"Turn him over," said Brother Peter to his men. "It's fitting that he see how futile are the sins he has committed."

Grimm lowered his head and kept uttering a menacing growl.

"Why can't you leave us alone?" asked Nix. "Why is it that people like you always think they can force everyone to do what they want?"

Brother Peter placed one hand on his chest, fingers

splayed. "I am a servant of god," he said. "I do his will. I don't *want* you to do anything."

"Then let us go."

A few of the reapers chuckled, but Brother Peter snapped at them. "No, my brothers. Don't mock her—she's young and doesn't understand. None of them do—except for this fallen sinner and that great blasphemer there." He pointed to Dr. McReady. "*She* understands."

"How do you even know who she is?" asked Benny.

"I met her in the same way you did, little brother," said Peter. "As a picture in a book. A book you stole from one of my reapers."

"The Teambook . . ."

"My reaper was on the way to the wreck to plant it near the plane, where Ledger could find it, but instead he met you. That was a very fortunate encounter, and my reaper had been given several contingencies. Either plant the evidence for Ledger to find; or kill anyone from Sanctuary who comes near the shrine and plant the book among their possessions. You provided another alternative—killing the reaper, and that only made the story more plausible. *You* took the book back to Sanctuary. How perfect. It couldn't have worked better if you'd rehearsed it. Then that bit of staged drama by the ravine. If you hadn't gone after Sergeant Ortega, you would eventually have found another set of those coordinates. There are four sets, all carefully planted. It was inevitable that you find one, so we watched and waited and adapted our plan to what you sinners did."

Benny felt sick, but at the same time none of this truly surprised him. Tom had always warned against coincidences, and now he understood why.

McReady said, "Look, mister, I don't really know who you are, but I know enough about the Night Church. You think that we're acting against your god's will by trying to preserve life. But everything I learned as a doctor, every oath I took, was to preserve life, to hold all life as sacred. How is that a sin? How is acting according to my beliefs a sin, even if they're different from yours?"

"Because your oaths were made to a false god," said Brother Peter.

It was a pointless argument and everyone knew it. The reapers would not be swayed from their beliefs—if they could, they never would have invaded this facility. They were too deeply entrenched in their hatred of life.

"You're going to kill them all, aren't you?" said McReady flatly. "The people in the infirmary . . . you're really going to slaughter them."

"We are going to release them from their torment," corrected Brother Peter.

"No—*I've* released them. I've given them the cure. They're going to get well. Most of them, anyway. They don't have to die now. You can't just kill a bunch of sick people while they're tied to their beds. It's inhuman. . . ."

"It's the mercy of Thanatos. . . ."

"All praise to his darkness," echoed the reapers.

"But if their bonds are what's troubling you, don't worry," continued Peter. "We'll cut them loose so they can freely accept the kiss of the knives and the forgiveness of the darkness. Just as we released the thousands imprisoned on this side of the trench above us. We set all captives free." He pointed back the way the reapers had come. "We even found a lonely wretch in a solitary cage back there and set him free—in both body and spirit."

"You *what* . . . ?" said Benny, looking past Brother Peter.

"In a cage?" echoed Lilah, her face going pale. "Chong—?"

"I'm afraid he was unable to tell me his name. I left one of my reapers to unlock his chains so he could go unfettered into the darkness that waits for us all."

The scream that filled the hallway was terrifying. It was torn from such a deep place, such a shattered and broken place, that it lacked any trace of personality or language or humanity. It did not—could not—have come from a human throat.

And yet it did.

Lilah shoved Nix aside and leaped at Brother Peter, driving the spear through the air toward his heart. It was such a murderous blow that it would have torn a red hole straight through his body.

But Brother Peter was not there.

He moved so quickly that his body seemed to melt out of the way of the spear. Instead Lilah's spear killed the reaper behind him, punching through stomach and spine and driving the man down to the floor.

Brother Peter lashed out with his empty hand; it caught Lilah on the side of the face and drove her to her knees. The impact was terrible, and anyone else would have collapsed there and then, but the rage in Lilah was too hot, the grief too awful. She dove at Peter's legs, wrapping her arms around them and bowling him over. He fell, a cry of genuine surprise bursting from his mouth.

Benny snapped out of his shock at the same moment the

reapers did. Two of them darted in to help Brother Peter, but Benny's *kami katana* flashed and slashed, and the hands slapped against Lilah's back but they were no longer attached to the reaching arms. Jets of red splashed the struggling figures.

In an instant the hallway was a circus of murder and mayhem.

"Grimm," croaked Joe weakly, "*hit, hit, hit!*"

Reapers with axes and swords ran forward to try and kill Joe—the man they all feared—but Grimm met their charge. Benny had a split second's view of heavy weapons chopping down and heard the heavy clang of knife edges against armor, the yelp of a dog, the scream of a man. Then he had no more time to do anything but fight.

Benny whirled and kicked one of the screaming reapers so that he fell backward into the knot of others; and Benny lunged again, thrusting his blade in and in again, first on one side of the man and then the other. Two reapers shrieked as red mouths opened in their chests.

Then the others surged forward, shoving the dying men at Benny, using them to block as they advanced. Suddenly Nix was there with *Dojigiri*, and the ancient blade cut low and high and low again, savagely slashing across knees and thighs.

In a wider hallway the reapers would have already won, but the confines of the narrow hallway made it impossible for the killers to surround them. Nix and Benny fought side by side, slashing the way a samurai does—not chopping with muscle but stroking the long length of their *katanas*, using the smooth draw of the edge to make the steel bite deep. Somewhere—a million miles away—Dr. McReady was screaming.

Benny was vaguely aware of Lilah and Peter rolling over and over on the bloody ground. The reapers of the Red Brotherhood surged forward, and suddenly it seemed as if the world was full of knives. He and Nix blocked and parried and retreated, fighting with all their skill simply to stay alive. These killers had rebounded from their immediate shock, and now Benny could understand why they were the elite of the Night Church. Each one of them was a superb fighter; any one of them might be enough to beat the two teenagers with swords and end things right here and now.

He caught a glimpse of Grimm. The dog was still on his feet, still fighting, his armor splashed with blood. Men, none of them whole, lay on the ground around him. A reaper had picked up Lilah's spear and was trying to kill the mastiff with it. Grimm ran and jumped at him, propelling his two hundred and fifty pounds and forty pounds of spiked armor into the air. The reaper fell backward—and his body seemed to fly apart.

McReady's screams took a sharper, higher note as something slammed into the back of the last reaper in the hallway. Something that bore him to the ground with such ferocity that the man's head smashed against the stone floor. Something that leaped like a mad ape at the next man in line and tore at his throat with broken fingernails and strong teeth. Something that roared and howled and growled out a single terrifying word.

"HUNGRY!"

The Red Brothers turned.

Benny and Nix stared.

Grimm barked in fear.

The creature bared bloody teeth at them.

Nix was the only one who could find her voice.

"Chong!"

BROTHER PETER WAS LOCKED IN A DEATH STRUGGLE WITH LILAH, BUT HE managed to shout an order to his startled men.

"Kill it!"

It was the wrong thing to say.

Yes, it snapped everyone out of their shocked tableau; but it switched the focus of the fight to the wrong place for a fraction of a second too long.

As the reapers lunged forward to subdue the savage monster that was Chong, they momentarily forgot Benny and Nix.

Tom Imura's young samurai made them pay for that inattention.

Without a word, without even a shared look of agreement, Benny and Nix attacked. Their blades whipped and slashed with all the speed they could muster, all the skill they possessed, all the rage that burned in their hearts. They did not try for killing blows. That required more time than this fragile moment of opportunity offered. Instead they cut at tendons and muscle, across the backs of knees and the backs of arms. Men and weapons crumpled. Screams filled the corridor, the echoes punching the struggling figures from every direction.

Benny heard a meaty *thud*, and out of the corner of his

eye he saw Lilah pitch sideways, reeling away from Brother Peter's vicious punch. It was the second blow he'd delivered, and tough as she was, Lilah was still a teenage girl, while Brother Peter was an adult man in the full prime of his physical strength. She rolled against the wall, dazed and bleeding from nose and left ear.

Grimm attacked the knot of reapers from the side, slamming sideways against them to use his shoulder spikes. The Red Brothers stabbed at him and broke their blades on his armor.

A few yards away Brother Peter staggered to his feet. He was bloody and panting. One eye was puffed nearly shut, and there was a ragged bite mark on his cheek from when Lilah had savagely bitten him. He had a long, shallow cut across his chest that caused the whole front of his shirt to hang down, exposing muscles that were sharply defined beneath bloody skin. For all those injuries, however, the young reaper seemed unconcerned. He still held one short knife, and as he rose he drew another from a concealed pocket inside his clothes.

Reapers screamed as they were caught between the savagery of Chong's feral attack and the whistling blades of *Dojigiri* and the *kami katana*. The surviving reapers were fighting back to back, trying to use their blades to stop the longer steel, but now they were on the defensive.

Grimm raced along the wall toward Brother Peter, but the reaper deftly sidestepped and kicked the dog in the side. Even with the armor, the kick was powerful enough to knock the mastiff into the wall, where he lay winded and whining.

With a snarl of annoyance, Brother Peter waded into the fight, blocking Nix's blade with one knife and slashing at her with the other. Blood erupted from amid the freckles on Nix's cheek, the slash bisecting the scar that ran from her hairline to her jaw.

Nix cried out in pain and retreated, cutting with redoubled speed, but everywhere her sword went, Brother Peter's knives were there to deflect it. He moved so fast that it looked like he had eight arms. Metal rang on metal as he drove Nix back.

Benny wanted to jump in to help her, but the other reapers renewed their attack, forcing him back. Other killers surrounded Chong.

Suddenly a shot rang out and one of the reapers went spinning away, blood erupting from a hole in his throat.

For an irrational moment Benny thought it was Joe Ledger, but the ranger had only managed to get to his hands and knees and was leaning against the wall, gasping like a fish on a riverbank.

The shock of the gunfire temporarily stopped the fight in the hallway. The reapers backed away from Chong, uncertain of what was happening; and Chong scuttled away from them, bleeding, glaring, and confused.

A figure raced up from behind Dr. McReady, grabbed the scientist, shoved her away from all the fighting, and fired two more shots. Reapers dodged and yelled, and one of them fell with a wound in his shoulder. The newcomer wore a military uniform that was torn and bloodstained, and she had a wild look in her eyes.

Colonel Jane Reid.

She fired another shot and a reaper clutched his chest and fell, but then the slide locked back on Colonel Reid's pistol.

Brother Peter saw this and dodged Nix's cuts and ran at Reid, eyes blazing.

In a freakish way Benny could understand the reaper's rage. Colonel Reid was the commander of Sanctuary, and this whole place stood as a symbol of everything the Night Church wanted to destroy. Killing her must be to Brother Peter what killing one of the archdukes of hell would have been for a crusading knight of old.

Benny stepped into the reaper's path, his sword raised. "Stop!"

If Brother Peter was impressed in any way by Benny and his sword, he did not show it. He merely looked impatient. Benny shuffled backward to keep his body between the reaper and the colonel.

"No," he said.

All the fighting in the hallway stopped. Even Chong hung back, his body hunched like an ape's, his eyes feral and watchful, bloody teeth bared.

Brother Peter stopped.

"If it is your wish to die a hero, boy," he said, "then I will oblige you."

"That's not how it's going to be."

"Ah," said the reaper, "is this the point where you make a lovely speech about how we can all walk away with our lives intact? Will you offer me and mine safe passage out of here if we leave you and these other sinners alive? Is that what this is?"

"No," said Benny. Despite the shadows the hallway seemed bright. All sounds were so clear and distinct. If his body trembled with fear, at that moment Benny couldn't feel it.

"Or," said Brother Peter, looking coldly amused, "are you going to play the hero and challenge me to a winner-take-all duel? Two champions fighting for our separate causes. It's very grand, but—"

"Not really."

The reaper's eyes darkened. "Then what is it? Did you simply want everyone to watch your great death scene?"

Grimm, who had finally struggled to his feet, uttered a long, low growl.

"No," Benny said again. He licked his lips. "This isn't a grandstand play, and it's not a scene from a storybook. This is me, Benny Imura, just a kid from a small town, telling you that I'm going to kill you. Right here, right now."

Brother Peter shook his head. "Why is it that you people can't understand that we *crave* death—all death, including our own. Why do you persist in trying to unnerve us with threats?"

"That's not what I'm trying to do," said Benny. "I don't really care if you want to die or not. I don't care if killing you is like giving you a puppy on your birthday. I don't really care about anything, you big freak. I'm just telling you that I'm going to kill you."

Brother Peter raised his arms out to his sides, as Saint John so often did in the moment before he taught another blasphemer the error of his presumptions. "Then go ahead, little sinner. If you think you can kill me . . . then kill me."

Benny Imura looked into the dead eyes of this master killer.

"Sure," he said.

And he attacked.

Tom once told Benny this about fighting: "Pit two amateurs against each other and the fight will go on all day. They'll break a lot of furniture and they'll bloody each other up a bit, but at the end of it, no one's likely to get badly hurt. However, in a fight between two experts—two people with some skill and a real determination to kill each other—then it's all over in a second or two. Sportsmen duel, killers kill."

It was all over in two fractured halves of one second.

In the first half of that second . . .

Brother Peter parried Benny's sword with one knife, spun off the point of impact, and drove the other knife into Benny's back. The blade tore through the tough body armor and skittered along the back of his rib cage, exploding a fireball of alien heat in Benny's body.

But Benny was not shocked by the pain. Or the damage.

He was not surprised by being stabbed.

He expected it.

He'd planned for it.

Brother Peter was too good to be defeated in such a duel. Maybe Tom, at the top of his game, might have done it. Maybe a younger and faster Joe Ledger might have. But no one in that hallway—not Nix or Lilah, not Grimm, not Chong, or Colonel Reid even if she had more bullets—none of them could ever beat Brother Peter.

Benny knew that Brother Peter would parry his attack because Peter was expecting the attack. Benny knew the reaper would stab him, because Peter was too good not to. So Benny attacked and was parried, and he was stabbed. And he was ready for all that. His first move was a big, fast *kirioroshi*, a downward cut. His raised arms gave Brother Peter something to block but also kept the killer's knives away from his own throat.

In the last half of that one second . . .

As the blade chunked into his back, Benny pivoted in place. A sloppy move filled with agony, but perfect in its selection. It used the force of the stabbing knife to power the turn as Benny swung his sword between himself and Brother Peter. A *yoko-giri*, a tight lateral cut that cleaved the air between them.

Except that there was not enough distance for the sword to pass unhindered.

Brother Peter was too close.

Too close to avoid that blade.

Too close to escape the moment and all its red truths.

The sword drew a line through both of the reaper's biceps, and through the flat plates of the man's pectoral muscles, and grated along the bones in his chest, grooving the sternum so deeply that it collapsed inward. Brother Peter coughed as those jagged bones did awful work inside his body.

The *kami katana* flew from Benny's hands as he staggered past the point of impact. He managed a single reflexive step before the pain drove him down to his knees. He fell against

Colonel Reid, who—like everyone else—stared in abject horror at what had just happened.

The second came and went, and in its wake there was wreckage that would last forever.

Brother Peter stood for a moment longer. The stern, unlined face of the man who had never smiled now wore its first smile. A bemused smile, as he looked down at his chest and saw the red mouth that stretched all the way across his body. He dropped to his knees with such force that the sound of bone on concrete was like gunshots.

Benny turned and looked at him. They were only three feet apart, both of them on their knees.

"You—you haven't won," said Brother Peter in a voice that was wet and trembling.

There was a sound—the sharp, harsh, metallic sound of someone working the bolt of a machine gun—and Benny saw Joe Ledger, still bleeding, his face gray with pain, leaning against the far wall. His weapon was in his hands, barrel pointed at the remaining reapers.

"Yes, we have," said Benny, and his voice was firmer than he thought it would be. He expected to speak in a dying whisper, but the lights in his head were not going out. Not yet. "We have a cure now. _We_ win."

The reaper sneered at him, blood dribbling from between his lips. "Take your . . . cure . . . see if it will save . . . anyone . . ."

His words were torn apart by a fit of coughing that sent him crashing to the stones. He fell over and stared at Benny with glazing eyes, but his lips still moved. Despite the agony in his own body, Benny crawled to him and bent to listen.

"Your sins . . . are already . . . paid for . . . ," wheezed Brother Peter. "Even now . . . Saint John and our . . . army . . . are closing in on your . . . *home.*"

"Home? What are you talking about?"

Brother Peter was fading quickly, the lights burning out in his eyes. "Mountainside will burn."

With that smile still on his lips, the reaper sagged back and seemed to settle against the cold stone. Benny wanted to grab him, to shake life back into him, to force him to live another moment longer so he could make sense of what he'd just said.

Mountainside will burn.

It was insane, impossible. How could the reapers know about Mountainside? Then he thought of the slip of paper he'd found that showed how many reapers were already in California. Two armies . . . one of forty-five hundred and another with over nineteen thousand of the killers. *Already* in California.

And they knew the name of Benny's hometown.

They knew about Mountainside.

God . . .

How could his town defend itself? And with what? A tiny town watch and some fence guards? A frail chain-link fence?

Against an army of twenty-four thousand killers?

Suddenly Benny felt himself falling over.

He felt hands catching him. Women hovered over him.

Dr. McReady.

Colonel Reid.

They were both speaking at once, shouting, calling his name, yelling at each other.

Then the sound of gunfire drowned it all out.

Benny saw reapers trying to fight their way to Brother Peter; saw them suddenly jerk to a stop and dance like marionettes on the strings of a madman, their twitches and jumps purposeless. As they fell, their bodies riddled with bullet holes, Benny saw Lilah and Chong facing each other, both of them crouching like animals.

He bared his teeth at her.

She bared hers at him.

Chong attacked, pouncing like a panther; but the Lost Girl moved into the attack, slapping his head to one side, wrapping a muscular brown arm around his throat, bearing him to the ground, wrestling him, pinning him, screaming and screaming a single word that Benny fought to understand.

"Pills! PILLS!"

Nix stood there, torn between rushing to her and rushing to Benny.

Benny managed to raise one arm and made a pushing gesture toward Lilah.

She needs you, he wanted to say. *Chong needs you. Help them.*

Grimm stood by Joe Ledger, who had collapsed into a limp sprawl.

Benny tried to say something that would make sense of this moment.

He needed to tell Joe and Nix and Lilah about what Brother Peter had whispered to him.

Mountainside will burn.

But when he opened his mouth, all he could do was scream.

Then a hand of darkness wrapped its cold fingers around him and closed them into a fist.

Part 4

Invictus

"Out of the night that covers me,
Black as the Pit from pole to pole,
I thank whatever gods may be
For my unconquerable soul.

In the fell clutch of circumstance
I have not winced nor cried aloud.
Under the bludgeonings of chance
My head is bloody, but unbowed. "

**WILLIAM ERNEST
HENLEY, "Invictus"**

A VOICE SAID, "YO, MONKEY-BANGER . . . YOU GOING TO SLEEP FOREVER?"

Benny's first reaction was surprise. In his dreams he was dead, killed by Brother Peter or eaten by zoms. Or gored by a white rhino. Or shot by Preacher Jack.

But dead in any case.

His second reaction was confusion. Not at being alive, but at who was talking to him.

That wasn't the right voice. It wasn't Joe, and it wasn't any of the girls. It wasn't even Brother Albert.

Whose voice was that? It sounded like . . .

He carefully, tentatively opened one eye.

He was in a hospital bed. Metal tubing for the frame, stiff white sheets, the pervasive smell of antiseptic with other, nastier smells buried beneath it. Electric lights in the ceiling.

There was a chair beside his bed and a figure sitting in it. Thin, angular, and impossible.

"Ch-Chong?" stammered Benny.

"What's left of him," said his friend. Louis Chong looked like a stick-figure version of himself. He was wrapped in a blanket, cradling a cup of steaming tea between his palms. His skin was a dreadful shade of gray-green. His hair was freshly washed and combed back from his face. "Welcome back from the land of the dead."

"How?" pleaded Benny. "How are you—I mean—"

"You guys saved me," said Chong.

Benny had to reach deep into the shadows that clung to his memories. He had only a vague idea where he was—the infirmary at Sanctuary—and an even vaguer idea of how he got there. The most recent memories that were sharp and clear involved the hidden bioweapons lab built into the baked rocks of Zabriskie Point. He remembered Dr. McReady, the mutagen . . . and Archangel.

"The . . . pills?" he asked tentatively.

"The pills," Chong said, nodding. "Nix and Lilah told me how you found Dr. McReady and brought her back here."

Benny lay on his side, and his body did not seem to want to move. He raised his head and looked around. Most of the staff were sleeping in their beds, but a few ragged-looking nurses were working to clean them up. One was helping a newly recovered soldier to his feet. No one screamed or thrashed.

"Archangel really works," said Benny. "God . . ."

"It was weird," said Chong slowly. "I could feel the stuff in the pills working right away, but it was like someone was throwing buckets of water on a brush fire in my head. Every second was another bucket. How long before I stopped wanting to do crazy things to people—like fricking *eat* them? Hours, man. And even longer before I could actually *say* that to Lilah so she'd untie me. But that was all last night."

"Last *night*? What time is it—?"

"Past six in the morning now. Best I can tell, you've been out of it since around ten last night. So about eight hours." He sighed. "Been a long night, man."

"Do you . . . do you remember what happened after Riot brought you here?" Benny paused. "Do you remember being . . . um . . . sick?"

A shadow passed across Chong's face. "I remember all of it. Every last minute. Getting shot with an arrow . . . the ride here on Riot's quad. The changes. God . . . the *hunger*. I even remember you coming to visit me in my cell." He touched his temple. "It's all up here for me any time I want to look at it."

He spoke in the ironic, amused tone he always used, but it was clear that demons had taken up residence in the house of his memories, and Benny wondered if they could ever be exorcised.

"Hey, man," he said, "we found the cure, right? Let's focus on that. . . . " His voice trailed off as pain flickered behind Chong's eyes. "What is it?"

"Benny . . . about that. Those pills . . . they're not really a cure. They're a treatment. I'm *still* sick. If I take the pills I'll still be me, more or less. But if I stop, I go back to being that thing you saw in the cage. That's how it's going to be. Unless they come up with a real cure, something that gets this out of my system forever, I'll always have to take medicine. And . . . I'll always have to be really careful. This is contagious, y'know?"

Benny swallowed a lump the size of a fist. "And . . . Lilah?"

"She knows. We have to be really, really careful. We can touch and all, and we can kiss. But for anything else . . . Jeez,

Benny, this is crazy. I love her, man," said Chong, wiping at his eyes. "I love her more than anything, but I don't want to make her sick."

"I know . . ."

"No," said Chong, "you don't. I told her that she should stay away from me. She shouldn't ever touch me; she shouldn't ever get close to me. Dr. McReady told her the same thing. . . ."

"What did Lilah say?"

Chong gave a short, rueful laugh. "She threatened to punch Dr. McReady's teeth down her throat and told me to stop being a stupid town boy. She said that if I ever tried to go away from her again, she'd break my legs. She's very romantic, that girl. Sweet as a kitten . . . if a kitten was a Siberian tiger with mood issues."

Benny grinned. "Yeah, but for some inexplicable reason she loves you."

"That only proves how crazy she is."

Benny looked around. "Hey—where's Nix?"

"Nix was here until like a minute before you woke up. I think she went to the bathroom. They have actual bathrooms here. No squatting behind bushes and wiping your butt with poison ivy."

"That's not exactly what we did."

"Felt like it."

"And where's Lilah?"

"Ah," he said, his smile fading. "The doctors wanted to give her something called an MRI. No idea what that is, but they said that she might have a skull fracture." He shook his head. "I can't have anything happen to her, Benny. Nothing."

Benny reached out to try and give him a reassuring pat on the arm, but then winced as pain shot through his back.

"*Owwww!* What the hell?"

Chong nodded. "Yeah, they said the painkillers would be wearing off pretty soon."

"Painkillers . . . ? For what?"

"Aww, it's so cute that you thought of me first before remembering that you had a big ol' sword fight with a psycho killer. That little twinge you're feeling is a knife wound, genius. They said that the anesthetic might make you a little slow. Not that this is a new mental state for you."

"Bite me," said Benny through gritted teeth.

"No thanks," said Chong. "From now on I'm going to explore that whole vegan thing."

"This . . . hurts. How bad is it? What happened?"

"Basically you got stabbed in the wrong place," Chong said, and he told Benny enough so that the door of memories opened up. The fight with Brother Peter replayed in Benny's mind with painful clarity.

"How am I not dead?"

"Because fortune favors the stupid," said Chong. "The knife hit your ribs at the wrong angle. Didn't puncture anything important enough to kill you. More like a scratch."

"Could have freaking fooled me. If I'm only scratched, why did I pass out?"

"Because you're a girlie-man?"

"Really, seriously, bite me."

"They said it was blood loss, shock, and something about nerve compression. They put in a crapload of stitches. They said that you'll be able to get out of bed today, though only for a couple of minutes at a time. The armor you were wearing kept the knife from going in too deep. And they examined Brother Peter's knife. There was no infectious matter on it. Not like on the arrow I got shot with."

"That's something."

"I can't believe you agreed to a duel with a guy who makes Charlie Pink-eye look like a punk."

"It wasn't a duel. I had a plan."

"A plan to get stabbed?"

"Yes," Benny said, and he explained what he'd done. "It was like sacrificing a queen to get a checkmate."

Chong stared at him. "That hovers somewhere between the bravest thing I ever heard of and the stupidest. It's probably both."

"Probably," agreed Benny.

Chong shook his head. "As for the rest, I got bits and pieces of everything else. That guy Joe is here somewhere too. Is he the same Joe Ledger from the Zombie Cards?"

"Yes. Is he all right?"

"He caught a break too. They operated on him and were able to save his life. Lots of damage, though. Dr. McReady said it'll be months before he can fight again."

"Oh, man . . ."

"Point is, Benny, we're both alive, and so are Nix and Lilah." Chong paused. "After what happened, after things started to go bad in the forest out there . . . I thought this was it, you know? I thought we were all dead. It seemed like the logical end to all of this. I mean, who were we? Four kids who had no business leaving home. Okay, so maybe Lilah's

424

different, but after Tom died, we should have gone back to Mountainside."

And that fast the cobwebs in Benny's head blew away.

"Mountainside!" he cried. "Oh my God!"

THEY FORMED A CIRCLE AROUND JOE LEDGER'S BED. BENNY IN A WHEEL-chair, Chong and Lilah holding hands, Nix standing next to Benny. Dr. McReady and Colonel Reid were there too.

The ranger was awake and in great pain. His color was bad, and sweat beaded his forehead. Dr. McReady was angry with him because he refused to take any pain meds.

"I need to think," he growled, "and I can't do that pumped full of morphine."

"Pain increases stress and—"

"Oh, stick a sock in it, Monica," he fired back. "I've had a lot worse than—"

"I know, I know, Joe, I've heard all the stories. You've been shot, stabbed, run over, and mauled by wild animals. I'm very impressed with your level of testosterone, but the simple fact remains that those injuries happened to a much younger man and—"

"Like I said, stick a sock in it."

Grimm—no longer wearing his armor—lay beside the bed and gave a hearty *whuff*.

Joe turned his red-rimmed, bleary eyes to Benny. "Go on, kid . . . what did you want to tell us?"

Benny repeated what Brother Peter had said with his dying breath.

Mountainside will burn.

"We have to get home," finished Benny.

"We can't," said Colonel Reid. "We've secured this facility, but topside it's still a war zone. All my soldiers are either dead or in the infirmary, and there are half a million infected out there. More, now that they've probably killed all the people in the hangars. God knows how many reapers."

"And all the monks," said Nix. She wore a fresh bandage over the cut from Brother Peter.

Chong said, "What about Riot and that little girl, Eve?"

No one wanted to meet his eyes.

"They were up there," said Benny. "We . . . didn't see them when we landed."

The implications of that hung in the air.

"You're saying they're dead?" asked Chong.

"There are places to hide," said Joe weakly. "And Riot knows every one of them."

"Maybe," said Reid, "but that doesn't change any-thing. We don't have the manpower to take the compound back from the dead, and we can't call for help. The reap-ers trashed the communications center. And we're running on the backup generator because they destroyed the main power plant."

"We can't be stuck down here," said Benny, banging his fist on the metal tubing of Joe's bed. "Our town—"

"Your town might as well be on the far side of the moon," said Colonel Reid. "Those balloons were filled with the muta-gen. It's a red powder, sticks to everything. Until the mutagen

427

weakens the infected through decomposition, we're trapped. I just hope the generator lasts long enough for that to happen."

"We have to get out of here," said Nix sternly. "We have to try and find Riot and Eve, and then we have to get back to our town."

"To do what? Four kids can't save a town," said Reid. "And from what Joe told me about Mountainside, it's indefensible. A flat field and a chain-link fence is no defense at all."

"Yeah," said Nix bitterly, "I guess you found that out here. The minefield beyond the fence didn't stop the balloons, and sensors inside the fence couldn't alert anyone because everyone was sick. The reapers just waltzed in here."

Reid's face darkened.

Nix dug her journal out of her pack. "See this? I've been collecting everything there is to know about zoms, and about the way people fight zoms. I've also asked Joe about a million questions about tactics and strategies. If I can get home to Mountainside, I can help them get ready. Earthworks, deadfalls, spiked walls, fire pits . . . I *understand* this stuff. It's all I've been thinking about."

"She's not joking," said Chong. "If we can get out of here, we might actually be able to do something to help our town. We need to find a way out of this compound."

Reid started to shake her head, but Chong cut her off.

"My *family* is in Mountainside," he said, and his voice held an edge Benny had never before heard there. "I've been through too much hell over the last month to want to debate this."

"He's right," said Benny. "Look, Colonel, your soldiers are either dead or recovering from the plague, so right now I

428

think there are more of *us* than there are of you. We're going to get out of here. The question is whether you help us, in which case you get to lock the door behind us, or you *don't* help us, and you take your chances with whoever or whatever walks through that door."

The moment stretched as Reid looked from Benny to Chong to Lilah to Nix.

In the silence, Joe Ledger spoke. Benny knew that he had to be in terrible pain, and yet the ranger imposed a degree of control over his voice that spoke to an incredible strength of will. Like Tom's. Unique in its own way, but also like Tom's. Brothers of a kind.

"Jane," he said evenly, "I know what you're thinking. These are four teenagers. Kids. Benny's stitched up and looks like he was thrown down an elevator shaft. Chong— hell, a few hours ago Chong was willing to eat people. Lilah's been punched twice in the face by a powerful adult male. And little Phoenix—she's not even five feet tall and looks like she's ninety pounds of red hair and freckles. Kids, sure. And who are kids compared to what's out there? Kids aren't able to do this kind of thing."

"That's just it . . . they don't stand a chance out there."

"If I thought that, I'd crawl out of this bed and tackle them myself. Or I'd sic Grimm on them."

Grimm said, *Whuff.*

"So, yeah, they're teenagers, but let's face it . . . they're not kids anymore. There was a line in the sand somewhere, and they each crossed it. Look at them, Jane. Look in their eyes. Every one of them is a seasoned fighter. They've been in battle. They've killed. Humans and zoms. I couldn't have found or saved Monica without them. And if it wasn't for these four young samurai, we'd all be dead in the hall downstairs, or we'd be shambling around looking for a hot meal of human flesh. Because of them we still have Archangel, which means, like it or not, these kids may actually have helped save the world. The actual world, including the part you're standing on with such self-righteous indignity."

The room tumbled into a big well of silence.

Monica McReady shook her head, but it was more in exasperation and helplessness than in protest. Reid stood foursquare at the foot of the bed and said nothing.

Finally she said, "How? Tell me that, Joe. How do we help them get out?"

"I'm working on that. Jane, can you get the hangar doors closed?"

"They are closed," she said. "We sealed the place while you were in surgery. The, um, girls helped."

Benny already knew about that. Nix had told him while they were waiting for Reid and McReady to join them. Once the exterior doors, including the big hangar doors, were closed, then it was a matter of going room to room, hall by hall, tracking down the dead and any stray reapers and cutting them down. Grimm was with Reid and the girls, and even though he was bruised from Brother Peter's kick, the monstrous mastiff had been as useful as a pet tank. He smashed into zoms and cut them down, leaving the wounded wrecks for Nix, Lilah, and Reid to finish. The whole process took five grueling hours.

The worst part was clearing out the hangar. There were more than a hundred zoms in there. Colonel Reid had to do most of the work with a machine gun, and the girls offered backup and protection while she reloaded.

Joe said, "Okay, so all we need now is a plan."

Benny cleared his throat. "Actually," he said, "I think I have one. But I'm pretty sure no one's going to like it."

He told them.

As usual . . . no one liked it.

But they did it anyway.

NIX PUSHED BENNY'S CHAIR, LILAH PUSHED CHONG'S, AND MONICA McReady pushed Joe's. The elevator was turned off because of the limited power available from the backup generator, but Reid temporarily shut down the lighting and air-conditioning long enough to use the lift. Joe had a pistol on his lap—completely against doctor's orders. Reid had a .45 in her hands. Benny sat with his *kami katana* resting between his knees, and Chong had the bow that had been used to fire the arrow into him. Riot had kept it, and it was among Chong's possessions in the infirmary. The arrows in the quiver had all been steam sterilized, though. Benny approved of the choice of weapons. In the Scouts and in gym class, Chong had always excelled in archery.

Once they were back at ground level, they moved through a few dogleg turns until they rolled out into the hangar. The state of the vast room gave everyone pause, even Nix and Lilah, who'd helped cause this. There were bodies everywhere, and splashes of blood and black muck on virtually every surface.

Benny reached up and took Nix's hand and gave it a squeeze.

Words really couldn't cover this sort of thing. However,

as Joe had said, they'd stood on too many battlefields by now to need words. Sometimes all that really matters is the knowledge that someone else understands.

She bent and kissed his fingers and then the top of his head.

They made their way to the helicopter. It wasn't easy. Bodies and parts of bodies had to be dragged out of the way to make room for the chairs.

No one said anything until they were at the door of the Black Hawk. Colonel Reid grasped the handle and rolled the door back while Lilah covered her with a pistol. Just in case there were any surprises in there.

There weren't.

It was a small, meager slice of relief that they all dined on.

Then Joe had to talk Reid, Lilah, and Nix through the process of reloading the thirty-millimeter chain guns that were mounted below the Black Hawk's stubby wings. Reid, despite being an officer, was really a bureaucrat. She'd never done this kind of work. Joe knew every bit of it, and he talked them through it. He didn't bother getting them to replace the missiles he'd fired.

He said, "This bird is configured to carry sixteen of them on those ESSS wings. I used six, so we have ten left. If ten Hellfires won't git 'er done, then we're using them the wrong way."

The one real problem was gas.

"We have enough fuel for thirty minutes of flight time," he said. "And that will be cutting it awful damn close. These things won't fly on good wishes or prayers."

Refueling was out of the question. The fuel truck had been blown to scrap metal during the raid.

"We have to try," said Benny.

Joe nodded. "Yes, we do."

The toughest part was getting Joe Ledger out of the wheelchair, into the cockpit, and buckled into the pilot's chair without bursting any of the stitches, outside or in. Benny and Chong sat next to each other and watched, wincing and tensing with each painful, careful, dreadful step. By the time he was settled in, everyone looked ten years older. Benny and Chong had also added several new words and phrases to their vocabulary of astounding vulgarities.

"Wow," said Chong after one of Joe's outbursts. He nodded appreciatively. "Livestock, too."

"I like the one with the iguanas and the jalapeño peppers. That's wrong on so many levels."

"So true."

They cut looks at each other and grinned.

"Really missed you, man," said Benny.

"I really missed me too," said Chong.

Dr. McReady checked Benny's bandage, frowned, and handed him a small bundle with extra dressings, antiseptic, and a bottle of blue pills.

"They're for the pain," she said.

"Will they make me sleepy?"

"Yes."

"Then no thanks."

She shook her head. "Stop being macho and take them. If you don't need them now, once you get started on this goofy plan of yours, you're going to need them. Believe me."

He took the bag.

McReady smiled at him and then offered her hand. "You're fifteen?"

"Almost sixteen."

"When I was fifteen, I was still writing poetry and wondering if I was going to get a date for the soph hop."

"What's that?"

"It doesn't matter." Then she did something Benny would never have expected. She bent and kissed him on the cheek. "Be safe and stay alive."

She turned and walked away to check on Joe. Benny watched her go. The woman, like most people he'd met since leaving town, was a contradiction. Brilliant, thorny, and different from every angle.

Lilah came over and stood in front of Chong, who was trying to get himself out of his wheelchair. "I can carry you."

"No, you can't."

"I'm strong enough," she insisted.

"I'm not," Chong replied. "And Benny would never *ever* let me live it down."

She gave Benny a hard look.

"It's true," he admitted. "Never."

Her lip curled as she fought to think of something biting to say. Instead she growled low in her throat. It sounded a lot like Grimm.

"Then get up and walk, you stupid town boy," she snapped.

Chong stuffed his pockets with bags of Archangel pills, then reached out a hand. "Little help?"

From the look on Chong's face, it was clear that Lilah

nearly tore his arm out of its socket. He stood in front of her, wobbly-kneed and as pale as death. Although Benny would die rather than say it, his friend never looked more like a zom than he did now.

And with that thought came an ugly splinter of speculation. If they did manage to get back to town, and if somehow the reaper army could be stopped—Chong would have to break the news to his parents that he was infected, that he would always *be* infected, that he was only a few tiny steps from crossing the line to being the kind of monster everyone in the world hated and feared.

What would they say? How would they react?

How would the rest of the town react?

He studied the pale face of his best friend and knew that there was no pill that could ease all the pain Chong had yet to face.

He knew one thing, though . . . no matter what happened, no matter what anyone said, Benny was going to be there for Chong. So would Nix. And so, without a doubt, would Lilah.

While Lilah helped Chong, Nix pulled Chong's chair closer to Benny's and sat in it. They held hands and leaned close for a kiss.

"I want to say something," she began.

"Oh God, Nix, if this is going to be some kind of 'in case we die' speech . . ."

She smiled. "Not really. I want to confess something."

Benny tensed, pretty sure that he didn't want to hear anything that followed that kind of an opening. But his mouth said, "Okay."

"After Tom died, after we left Gameland . . . I think I stopped being in love with you."

"Nix, please, I—"

"Let me finish, Benny . . . please." She looked at him with those intelligent green eyes that were always so full of mystery and magic to him. "Out there in the desert I realized that we fell in love too fast. No, don't say it . . . I know it was going in that direction for a long time. Since we were like, I don't know—ten, I think. At least for me. But when we were in the mountains, when we were all alone up in that forest ranger tower, I think I fell in love with who I always imagined you were. Not with *who* you were. Do you understand?"

He wanted to say that he didn't, and he wanted to get up and run away from this conversation. Instead he said, "Yes." Very quietly. Because he *did* understand.

"I think you felt it too, didn't you?"

"Yes," he said. A whisper.

"It was all like being in a fairy tale or an old story of knights and castles. I was the princess; you were the prince. We were supposed to have a happily ever after, but that's not how life is, is it?"

"No."

He wished his mouth would stop agreeing with her. He did not want to agree. He did not want to speak.

"Then, all those months of training, getting ready to go, it was really all about running away. I was running away from my mom's death. So was Tom. And I think he was running away from what he thought was his failure. He wasn't able to save Mom's life. And he was so tired of fighting. He kept trying to get the people in town—in our town and all the towns—to wake up and open their eyes. Tom had a good plan for defending the towns and building a militia so that everyone worked together for defense and to begin taking back the world. He left town because no one was listening to him and it was driving him crazy. And you, Benny . . . you left town for me." She shook her head. "I think you left town because you thought you were supposed to. Because that's what the romantic, heroic prince does for the princess."

Benny said nothing.

"I'm an idiot for making you leave," she said.

"You didn't force anyone to go."

She shrugged. "I could have made you stay. You and Tom. Can you look me in the eye and tell me that's not true?"

He didn't even try.

"After Gameland . . . I thought we fell in love again, but then things got hard and . . . I don't know . . . the *feeling* wasn't there. You felt it too, I could tell."

"It came back," he said.

"Did it? Or did we simply stop trying to force things? Once we got here, we thought we'd lost Lilah and Chong. Even when we got Lilah back, she wasn't the same. She still isn't. She's regressed almost to where she was when we met her. Chong knows it too; you can see it in his eyes and hear it in his voice. He's *managing* her, but she's not really there."

"Where are we going with this, Nix? 'Cause right now I don't—"

"Shh. Just listen, okay? I'm trying not to be a hard-ass bitch for a change. No, don't say anything and don't, for God's sake, defend me to me. I'm not a very nice person, Benny. Even I can't stand myself most of the time. I know I

438

get on your nerves sometimes. And I really don't know how or why you put up with me." She took a breath. "I guess what I'm trying to say is that something's changed. Over the last day, something inside me has changed. I'm not little Nix Riley anymore. I'm not that girl. But at the same time I don't know who I am. I know I'm stronger. Clearing out the compound with Lilah and Colonel Reid? Can you even imagine the Nix of a couple of months ago doing that? Now . . . I just do it. It's part of my life. Swords and fighting and killing. That's part of my life. If we survive this, I think it might still be part of my life. I'm never going to be the kind of girl who sits at home and raises babies, and I'm not going to work in the general store measuring out grain or bagging groceries. I'm an actual warrior, Benny. I *like* being a warrior. When I look at the future, all I can see is how I'm going to take back the land. If I have to clear out zoms, then I'll do that. If I have to go after bounty hunters and outlaws, I'm going to do that, too. That's who I am, Benny. Don't laugh, but I think I've actually become what Tom was trying to make us. I've become a samurai, and I want to go on being a samurai. I want to use everything that I've learned to make things right. And I don't want to put them back the way they were. I want to help make a brand-new world. That's who I am, Benny."

Benny nodded. "I know, Nix. I saw this coming."

She studied his eyes, then nodded.

"So, where does that leave us?" he asked. Then he took in a breath and asked the hardest question in the world. "Do you still love me?"

Tears fell down her cheeks.

"I'll always love you, Benny," she said. "I just don't know if I'm *in* love with you."

She clutched his hand.

"Benny . . . please don't hate me for telling the truth."

Benny Imura pulled her to him, and they clung together in the heat of that awful shared awareness. "I could never hate you, Nix," he said, his words muffled by her hair and by the pain in his heart.

She did not ask if he loved her.

Neither of them wanted to hear the answer to that question. There was no way—no matter how it was answered—that it would not cut like a sword.

Colonel Reid cleared her throat, and Benny let go of Nix. She straightened and stood a few feet away.

"We need to get you on the chopper," she said. Her eyes darted to Nix's face, which was flushed and streaked with tears, and Benny's, which he tried to turn away.

Nix held out her hand and helped Benny out of the chair. Dr. McReady had used a powerful local anesthetic on the knife wound, and it did, by Benny's reckoning, nothing at all. But the pain was a marvelous distraction. It pulled his thoughts away from the even more savage wound in his heart.

They climbed onto the helicopter. Nix wanted to buckle Benny into a seat, but he shook his head, preferring to stay by the door. She reluctantly agreed and started to close the door, but Reid put her hand out to block it.

"You can still change your minds," said the colonel. "You're welcome to stay here. Once the American Nation realizes that our communications are down, they'll send a team. They know we're quarantined, but they'll send helos to observe and report. It might only be a few days."

"The reapers are marching on Mountainside," said Nix.

"For all we know, they could already be there. Saint John left here a month ago."

"All the more reason to stay where it's safe."

Nix shook her head. "Nowhere's safe. Not until we make it safe."

Reid sighed and started to turn away.

"Don't forget us," said Nix. "Just because your people don't see us, just because we're inconvenient, it doesn't mean that we don't matter."

Colonel Reid turned to her, and there was an indescribable look on the woman's face. She didn't say a word, didn't nod or anything. Instead she slid the door shut. Benny and Nix watched through the window as the colonel and the doctor ran for the door back to the compound. It slammed shut and they were gone.

The engine fired up, and the big rotors began to turn. Joe's voice rumbled out of the overhead speakers. "Okay, kids, here we go. If this whole thing goes into the crapper, just remember that it's Benny's idea."

"Great," yelled Benny. "Thanks."

Joe was laughing when he cut off the mike.

A heavy buzzer sounded a warning as the big hangar doors rumbled open, rolling apart on metal tracks.

The dead were right there, right outside. Too many to count. A sea of them.

"God," said Chong, and Benny turned to see his friend standing right next to him. Lilah, too.

"They're coming fast," yelled Benny.

The helicopter trembled as it lifted from the ground. Benny was doing math furiously in his head. From skids to rotor the Black Hawk was sixteen feet high. If the zoms reached up to grab, the tallest of them could reach seven and a half feet. Reid told them that the hangar door was fifty-five feet high. That should give the helicopter thirty feet of clearance. More than enough, Benny told himself. Who cared if the pilot was half-dead and more than a little crazy?

"Come on . . . come *on!*"

They were all saying it, willing the helicopter to rise before the tide of living dead could clear the fifty feet of open concrete.

They weren't shambling.

They were running.

Every last one of them.

"*Come on!*"

It rose.

Even with the whine of the rotors, they could hear the combined voices of the zoms rise in a horrific moan of unsatisfied hunger. There was not enough living flesh in the world to assuage this army of the dead.

They heard hands thump against the skids. They heard fingernails rake along the metal. They felt the machine shudder as it fought against cold fingers that wrapped themselves around the landing assembly.

Joe tilted the Black Hawk forward, cruising inches above the fingers of the dead, dragging three clutching zoms with it. The external drag tilted the helicopter for a moment, and the tip of the rotor struck the field of reaching arms for a split second. Long enough, though, to tear a dozen hands from withered forearms.

Then one of the dangling zoms fell away.

And another.

Then the last one tumbled back down on the seething mass of the dead. The helicopter reached the open doorway.

"You're too high," cried Benny. "Too high!"

But the whirling blades cut only air. The massive doorway passed directly overhead, and suddenly they were out in the golden sunlight of the Mojave Desert.

Benny coughed out the breath he was holding as the chopper rose into the light. Then he heard a soft gagging sound. Nix, Lilah, and Chong were all there with him, staring out of the window at what lay below.

Seen from the air, with the sunshine highlighting every splash of red, every charred body, every gray face, the sight below threatened to take the heart out of Benny.

Nix made a sick sound deep in her chest. "Look . . . look for Riot. She could be anywhere."

"Down *there*?" said Chong hollowly. "How could—"

He didn't finish, and Benny knew that his friend had tried to cut off his own words a few seconds too late.

"She *has* to be down there," said Nix urgently. "She'd have found a place for her and Eve to hide."

But Joe turned the helicopter away, pointing its blunt nose toward the row of siren towers. They were silent now. That part of the airfield was also relatively clear. Except for a few of the old slow, shuffling R1 zoms, the rest of the dead were massed around the hangars on both sides of the trench.

"What do we do if the reapers trashed the sirens, too?" asked Chong.

"That's plan B," said Benny.

"What's plan B?"

"We feed you to the zoms, and while they're eating you—and getting sick to their stomachs—we run away."

Lilah laid her hand on her knife. "No, you won't."

"Lilah," said Chong, "he's joking."

She eyed Benny icily. "It's not a funny joke."

"Apparently not," said Benny.

"Whoa, whoa, guys," said Chong, pointing past him. "Look."

Down below, the siren house was snugged up against the red rock wall of the mountains. The crushed gravel turnaround in front of the bunker was littered with bodies—a few zoms but three times as many reapers—and there was a clear trail of corpses that led in a crooked line back to the burning hangars. A quad sat a few feet from the bunker door, and a knot of eight zoms clustered in front of the door, relentlessly pounding on the metal.

"Someone's in there," said Nix.

"I hope they know how to work the sirens," said Chong.

"Who do you think it is?" asked Lilah.

"I don't know, but those zoms are trying real hard to get in," said Benny. "Joe?"

"Yeah," came the reply. "Got it."

A moment later the chain guns opened up. Lines of impact points ran along the turnaround, kicking up pieces of gravel, until they caught up with the figures at the door. The rounds punched into the dead and flung them in all directions. When they were all down, Joe landed. Lilah had the sliding door open before the wheels were settled.

She and Nix jumped to the ground. Lilah had her spear and Nix drew *Dojigiri*.

"Stay here," ordered Nix. "We got this."

Benny glanced at Chong. "They got it," he said.

"Uh-huh."

Chong helped Benny out of the helicopter, then reached in and removed the bow and arrows. Together they limped painfully after the girls. When Lilah realized they were following, she turned and gave Chong a look that would have peeled paint off of steel plate.

They approached the tangle of dead zoms. Two were still twitching, and Lilah quieted them with quick thrusts.

"Hello!" called Nix. "Is there anyone inside?"

Benny looked down at some of the reapers who lay dead. Not the ones Joe had just killed, but victims of whoever was in the siren house. There were no knife or bullet wounds. Most of them had crushed skulls—or rather skulls that had been dented by precise impacts from small round balls.

He bent very carefully, hissing at the pain, and picked one up. A steel ball bearing.

"Nix," he called, and then held up the ball bearing for her to see. "Riot. Oh my God . . . *Riot!*"

Nix shouted the name.

Then they were all shouting her name.

They pounded on the door, laughing and cheering that Riot had—against all logic and odds—managed to escape to this tiny stronghold.

There was a sound from inside. The scrape of a chair being moved, then the metallic click of a lock. Then the door opened slowly, and Riot was there.

Her clothes were torn. She had gashes on her face, her scalp, and across her stomach. Her arms were bloody to the elbow. Tear tracks were cut through the soot and grime on her pretty face. She held a pistol in one hand and a blade in the other.

"Oh my God," said Nix as she rushed forward to hug Riot. "We were so worried! But I knew you were okay. You and Eve. Where is Eve? We can get you out and . . ."

Her words rambled on and on, filled with joy and relief. Chong grinned and touched Riot's shoulder. Lilah nodded, smiling.

Riot stood there and endured the embrace. She did not return it. Or react to it.

Her eyes looked past Nix's red hair and out into the desert.

"Nix . . . ," said Benny quietly. He touched her shoulder and pulled her gently back.

"Benny, what are you—?"

Nix saw the look on his face. Her smile flickered. She looked at Riot, perhaps finally realizing that the girl had not reacted or responded in any way.

"Riot?"

Riot's eyes shifted slowly toward her. The smiles faded slowly from Chong and Lilah's faces, too.

"Riot . . . ?" asked Nix, uncertainty shading her voice. "Are you okay?"

The former reaper said nothing.

"Riot," said Benny gently. "Where's Eve?"

Riot slowly raised her left hand so they could see what she held. It was a small push-dagger. Like a sliver. The kind of thing that was only ever used for one thing. For one terrible purpose.

The blade was painted with red.

She opened her hand and let the blade fall. It struck the ground at her feet and lay there. The cold and silent steel screamed unspeakable things at them.

Or was it Riot screaming? Benny wondered.

Or Nix?

Or all of them?

BENNY WENT INSIDE.

He found the body. Riot had washed the little girl's face and smoothed out her clothes as best she could. Eve lay on a cot, wrists and ankles tied. There was a bite mark on her arm. It was small, and Benny wondered if it had been another child who'd bitten her.

Riot had gotten her away from the slaughter. At what point had she become aware that Eve was already lost? Before the mad drive out here on a quad? After the door was barred? During the long hours of the night? Had it been quick, or had fate been crueler still and made Riot wait, hour after hour, as the disease consumed the child?

And, oh God, he thought, *how can we ever tell her that the cure for the bite was inside the blockhouse all the time?* Two pills—or maybe one for a little girl—and the night would not have ended with the worst nightmare any of them could imagine.

How could they ever tell Riot that?

How close to the edge did the former reaper already stand? Was she looking into the abyss, or was the abyss already in possession of her mind? Did her soul float in that vast darkness?

Rage trembled inside Benny's body. He could feel the exact moment when it ignited, and as he stood there over Eve's body, that rage spread all through him. His hands curled into fists that were clenched so hard his knuckles hurt. His jaws ground together to hold back—what? A scream? A roar? Whatever it was, if he let it out it would tear his throat raw and bloody. Black poppies seemed to bloom and burst apart in front of his eyes.

It was as if this small death was all the proof of evil that anyone would ever need. Proof that the "holy" mission of Saint John was corrupt to its core—even if that madman believed he had heard the voice of god. No god could ever want this. No god would encourage the kind of harm that had been visited upon this child. The destruction of her town. The slaughter of her parents before her eyes. The disintegration of her sanity. And now the defilement through disease of her body and the ultimate theft of her life. A theft that robbed her of more than the moment, but stole every hour and day and week and year of a life that should have been lived long and to its fullest.

This was the actual cost of war, right here, written with perfect clarity in the blood of the innocent.

He heard a sound in the doorway, and Joe was there. Sweating, worn thin by pain, somehow on his own feet. The ranger shambled over to stand beside Benny. They stood there for a long time looking down at the body, perhaps thinking the same thoughts.

Finally Benny said, "I want to kill them."

Joe sighed.

"I want to kill them all," said Benny. "I want to wipe them from the face of the earth."

"I know," said Joe Ledger. His voice was heavy with sadness.

Outside they could hear Riot, Nix, Lilah, and Chong.

They were weeping. And sometimes they were screaming.

THEY TURNED THE SIRENS ON.

Chong came in before they flicked the switch. He did not look at the body on the bed. "Do you know the legend of the banshee?" he asked.

Benny shook his head. "A ghost of some kind?"

"It's an old Gaelic legend," said Chong. "The *bean sídhe*—woman of the fairy mounds. It's a female spirit who begins to wail when someone is about to die. In Scottish mythology, the *bean síth* is sometimes seen as a woman washing the bloodstained armor of those who are about to die in battle."

Joe did not comment as he flicked the switch and the unnatural wail of the sirens rose like the screams of the damned.

They closed the door as they left. Across the airfield the R3's were already flooding across the bridge from the other side of the trench and running toward the bunker. A million running feet kicked up a dust cloud that blocked out the lingering fires in the hangars and rose to challenge the pillars of smoke for dominance of the morning sky.

Benny wrapped his arm around Riot and kissed her head and walked with her to the helicopter. All this made his back hurt, but he would die rather than complain about that kind of pain. Not now. Not anymore.

They closed the helicopter doors, and when the first of the running zoms reached the turnaround, Joe lifted off and rose high into the air. The Black Hawk hung in the screaming air until the dead were so tightly clustered below that Benny couldn't see the ground.

Joe spoke to them from the radio speakers.

"Last chance to say no."

Nix said it for all of them. "We can't."

The Black Hawk tilted toward the west, and the helicopter tore through dust and smoke back to the hangars.

"Can you blow up the bridge?" asked Chong.

"No. If there are any survivors hiding, that's the only way they'll ever make it to the blockhouse."

"Is there even a chance of that?"

"No matter how bad things are, there's usually some chance left," said Joe. "Wouldn't you say?"

Chong said, "I guess so."

But he saw Riot, who huddled inside a ring of Nix and Lilah's overlapping arms. He knew that Joe was not always right about that.

"Setting down," said Joe. "Some R3's are already coming back this way. You've got about three minutes. Don't stop for coffee."

The Black Hawk touched down between the burning dormitory hangar and the row of parked quads.

This was the second part of Benny's plan. Since the helicopter didn't have enough fuel to take them to Mountainside—and the pilot was pushing his own personal limits in flying at all—they had to find another way to get home. The quads were the only real option. Benny had a road map in one pocket, courtesy of Colonel Reid. Mountainside was 470 miles away. In a straight run, they could be there in twelve hours. Having driven the quads for weeks now, he knew that on flat ground they averaged about forty-five miles to the gallon, and that the tanks held 4.75 gallons of fuel. That meant that they could get a little less than halfway home on a full tank. However, there were equipment racks on the bikes capable of holding a couple of gas cans. Neither Joe nor Reid had been able to decide whether they could carry enough gas to get them all the way. It was a gamble.

If the quads ran out of fuel, then they would have to go on foot or find a traveler with a horse to carry the message the rest of the way to the Nine Towns.

Provided there were any towns left.

Saint John and the reaper army had left a month ago.

A month.

On a forced march, they could already have been there.

They had to march under hot Nevada suns and then climb the long mountain roads in California. If they stuck to the main roads, the path was serpentine, closer to five hundred miles. If they had to forage for food, that would slow the pace. But even so, they could conceivably be at the fence line. That was a stretch, though, and Benny doubted they were already there.

However, Haven was many miles closer. Would Saint John want to take the towns in order?

There was no way to know until they got there.

After a month here at Sanctuary, they were now in a desperate race.

As soon as the Black Hawk settled, Benny and Chong pulled back the door. Roasted air blew in at them, carrying with it the burned-meat stink of so many deaths. Benny gagged and covered his mouth with his palm.

Nix and Lilah jumped down first, and they helped Benny and Chong down. Riot lingered for a moment in the doorway. She hadn't yet spoken a word.

"You can stay here," said Nix.

Riot leaned out and looked around, then turned and stared back the way they'd come. The bunker was invisible behind the mass of running zoms, but the siren towers marked the spot, the metal voices wailing with a grief no human voice could articulate.

"No," said Riot. "I can't."

It was all she said.

Nix helped her down.

"Tick-tock," yelled Joe.

They worked fast. Benny checked the fuel tanks and found five that were topped off. They grabbed a bunch of plastic two-and-a-half-gallon cans and began filling them from a hundred-gallon tank set on trestles. With the fuel truck destroyed, it was the last source of the precious ethanol. The process seemed to take forever. When Benny looked at the zoms, he felt his heart sink. The leading edge was less than a half mile away. They were running at full speed, drawn by the noise of the helicopter and the sight of fresh meat.

Lilah fired up one quad and was yelling at Chong as she explained how it worked. Benny thought it was probably the worst example of a "crash course" that he could imagine. Luckily, Chong was the smartest person Benny knew; his ability to acquire and process information was superb. His reflexes and mechanical skills were less impressive, and he drove the quad straight into a wall.

As he trudged toward another one, Lilah trailed behind, explaining in a very loud voice how useless he was. But on his second try Chong proved her wrong by driving a wide circle around the Black Hawk.

When he passed in front of the bridge, he slowed for a moment as he saw how close the dead were.

"Joe!" Benny yelled.

The Black Hawk shuddered and rose a few feet off the ground and drifted toward the bridge. Benny knew that Joe didn't want to blow the bridge, but time was carving away the question of choice.

Nix and Riot began strapping the filled gas cans onto the backs of the quads. Chong and Lilah pitched in to help.

"Hurry!" yelled Joe, his voice booming from external speakers mounted high on the chopper's hull.

"That's it," shouted Chong. "Let's go."

They hauled the last gas cans over and strapped them on. Each quad could carry two cans, a total of five extra gallons. A bit more than a full refill for each bike. Would it be enough?

"Get moving!" bellowed Joe.

They secured their weapons and climbed onto the quads. Five engines growled to life.

"Go, go, *go!*"

They roared away as, behind them, Joe opened up with the chain guns.

Benny had the route committed to memory. He zoomed ahead and took the lead. The others followed. When he looked back, he saw that the Black Hawk had settled back onto the ground. The dead were pouring over the bridge. They swarmed like cockroaches over the chopper, climbing over each other to get to it. The big propellers turned and as the pile rose and rose, the blades chopped at heads and arms. The guns kept up a continuous fire for almost a minute, and then they fell silent.

Benny slowed and stopped. The vibration of the engine and the posture he needed to maintain in order to ride were setting fires in the knife wound in his back.

Why had Joe landed? Why was he still there?

There were so many zoms around the chopper now that all they could see were the dead.

"No," Benny said.

The others stopped in a line and they all looked back.

There was no more gunfire.

But many of the zoms were running down the access road toward where the five quads idled.

"Benny," said Nix softly, "we have to go."

He hung his head for a moment, sick at heart. But when he caught Riot staring at him and saw the look in her eyes, the rage flared up in his chest again. He bared his teeth and ate his pain as he gunned the engine.

Under the noonday sun, the five quads rocketed along the road toward the gates of Sanctuary.

THEY LEFT SANCTUARY BEHIND AND FOUND THE HIGHWAY MARKED ON Reid's map. They headed north on Route 375, and hours later turned west on US 6—the old Grand Army of the Republic Highway.

They met no reapers on the road.

They wanted to. It would have been satisfying in the worst possible way.

The road was open and empty.

Miles melted away behind them, but the road was so long and straight and the scenery so repetitive that it felt like they were standing in place. Only the movement of the fuel gauge seemed to add perspective to their flight. The endless whine of the motors became a mind-numbing monotony, but beneath it was the rage and the fear. Nobody wanted to quit.

They drove in a ghastly silence, each of them in a different kind of pain.

Except for Lilah. She rode beside Chong, and most of the times Benny looked back at them, she was smiling.

Strange girl, he thought, and he wondered if this meant that she would regain all the developmental ground she'd lost since Chong got sick. Would the joy of having her "town boy" be enough to carry her through the coming years of dealing with the limitations of his illness and the risk of contagion?

For now, though, she was happy. It was the only bright spot in their day.

Riot? She was gone. She rode the bike with competence, and during rest times she did her share of the chores without protest or comment. But she was gone. Benny reckoned that most of her was still inside a stone bunker with a small figure who lay on a makeshift bed. Maybe part of her would always remain in that dreadful place.

The day burned down. They lost time going offroad to avoid clogged highways, washed-out bridges, roving packs of zoms, and collapsed buildings. Each lost minute hurt Benny; each wasted hour was like a knife in his heart. They pushed on until Benny's fuel indicator was nearly buried near the outskirts of Benton, California. According to the map they had to cut through the town, and they didn't want to do that at night. Not as tired as they were. So they took shelter in a house trailer that had been part of a construction site before First Night.

While Lilah changed the dressing on Benny's back, Nix filled Riot and Chong in on the flight to find McReady and the battle under Sanctuary. Benny began cringing when Nix got to the part about Archangel, but Riot said nothing.

Chong said, "Guys, we're busting our butts to get home to warn everyone, but let's face it, this is really bad."

"I've been thinking about that all day," said Benny.

"Me too," said Nix, and even Lilah nodded.

"Well, call me crazy," said Chong, "but don't you think we should be talking about this out loud? I mean . . . let's come up with an actual plan."

They took turns outlining the problem as they each viewed it and then throwing out ideas about how the towns could respond. After a while it became clear that Nix had the best suggestions for tactics of warfare—traps, ruses, physical defenses, weapons. But Benny surprised them all with his grasp of strategic thinking. He saw things from a distance. After Nix—and to a great degree, Lilah—presented a long and gruesome list of battle tactics that could be implemented very quickly, Benny told them how he thought they could win the actual war.

Chong, the logician of the group, played devil's advocate to poke holes in each suggestion. But for once he was unable to tear apart Benny's plan.

"Wow," said Chong when they were done, "I'm very nearly impressed with you."

"Bite me," said Benny.

"Which reminds me," said Chong. "Time for my pills."

Benny went outside to take first watch, and Nix stayed up with him for a bit. They sat close, but they didn't touch.

After a while she said, "Do you hate me now?"

He took his time and thought about what to say before he opened his mouth. "What I am is hurt and angry. Not angry at you, but angry at us. We held hands, closed our eyes, and stepped off a cliff." When she didn't reply, he added, "I can't be angry with you for telling the truth."

Nix got up and shivered in the chill of the desert night.

"I'll tell you one thing, though," said Benny, looking up at her.

"What?"

"I *do* love you. I have for a long time, and I think I always will. When this is over—if we're both still alive and if the world hasn't burned down—I'm going to come looking for you. If the situation and the moment are right, I'm going to ask you out on a date."

"A date?"

"We never had one. We went from being friends to being a couple. The closest thing we had to a first date was getting chased by Charlie Pink-eye, and I'm pretty sure that doesn't count."

He saw her smile etched in starlight.

"So . . . I'll ask and we'll see what happens."

Nix turned and went into the trailer.

Benny sat on a rock and watched the stars wheel in their slow, endless dance above the battered little blue world.

93

THEY WERE REFUELED AND ON THE ROAD BEFORE FIRST LIGHT.

Benton was a terrible place. At the intersection where they turned from Route 6 to California State Route 120, they saw the rusted remains of a major crash involving two school buses and several cars. There were zoms everywhere, and it was likely they had been standing there for fifteen years until they heard the sound of the quads. The whole mass of them—adults and children—began shuffling toward the machines. Benny veered off the main street and cut behind houses and through yards to avoid the zoms. It cost time and fuel, but they managed to escape without a fight.

Benny realized that the one main flaw in his plan was the noise the quads made. Zoms would hear them miles away and be drawn to the sound, so they'd be in the path of the five machines.

But what choice did Benny and his friends have? California was far more densely populated than Nevada, and the deeper they went into greener areas, the more likely there would be zoms. Even so, the whole landscape seemed more brown than green. It had been an early and unusually hot spring, and it was clear that there hadn't been much rainfall. Everything looked brittle and dry. There was none of the lushness of spring, and that depressed Benny. It made him wonder if the whole world was getting ready to die. Or to burn. The fires of hatred ignited by the reapers seemed inescapable.

Then they saw the first billboard advertising Yosemite National Park.

They pulled to a stop in front of it. The faded picture showed a verdant forest and tall, snowcapped mountains. After the starkness of the desert, it looked like it belonged on a different planet, but even then the park in the picture looked withered.

"Mountainside is on the other side of the park," Benny said to Riot as they poured the last of their fuel into the tanks. "If we follow the map, we'll pass Haven first, and then we can cut north to our town."

Riot nodded but said nothing. She replaced the cap, and got back onto the saddle.

Seconds later they were far down the road.

They drove on.

Eighty-four miles later they paused at another billboard.

WAWONA HOTEL

Benny looked at his friends. Lilah, Nix, and Chong all nodded, knowing without being asked what he wanted to do. Benny turned and drove up a side road until he came to the ruins of the hotel. It was nothing but a field of charred debris. The only structure that still stood was a small utility building. Benny turned off his engine and sat looking at it. The others pulled up beside him and killed their engines too.

On the outside of the building, on the wall facing the road, were words Benny had painted a million years ago.

GAMELAND IS CLOSED.
THIS IS THE LAW.
—T. IMURA

Benny got off his quad and walked over to the building, his mouth open with wonder. When he'd painted those words after Tom's death, he'd added his own name, as had Nix, Lilah, Chong, and all the surviving bounty hunters. Solomon Jones, Sally Two-Knives, Fluffy McTeague, J-Dog, and Dr. Skillz. Two dozen names in all.

But now there were other names.

Hundreds of them.

Not copied names, but actual signatures. Each was unique.

Names of people he didn't know. Names of people he did. People who Benny would never have believed would ever step outside the fence line. Captain Strunk. Mayor Kirsch. Leroy Williams. Many others.

And one name, written small, down in a corner, struck Benny over the heart.

MORGAN MITCHELL

Nix saw the name too, and the sound she made was half laugh and half sob.

"Morgie," said Chong. "Damn."

All around the building there were bunches of flowers, handmade corn dolls of a black-haired man with a toy sword, notes pinned to the ground by sharp sticks. A post had been hammered into the ground, and it had a portrait of Tom fixed to it. Benny did not know the artist, but the likeness was excellent. Tom, a faint smile on his face, a look of distant sadness in his eyes. A red sash was draped over the post. Benny raised the cloth to read what was stitched on it: FREEDOM RIDERS.

He had no idea what that was.

Benny felt tears in his eyes, but he was smiling.

He pressed his palm flat against the wall for a full minute. The others did too. Even Riot.

Then they got back on their quads.

They did not stop again until they reached the hill that looked down on Haven, the southernmost of the Nine Towns. They killed their engines, dismounted, and stood there, hidden by the trees.

Below them was a sea of movement and color.

Thousands upon thousands of reapers and R3 zoms flooded through the streets of Haven, while all around them the town of Haven burned.

CHONG EXHALED A LONG, TIRED BREATH OF DEFEAT AND SAT DOWN ON the bare ground.

"I can't deal with this," he said. "That's what they're going to do to Mountainside. That's what they're going to do to my family."

He put his face in his hands. Lilah squatted down beside him and laid her cheek on his head. It was clear she had no idea what to say, and the frustration of that was evident in every taut line of her body.

Riot closed her eyes and did not move. Orange shadows flickered across her face.

Only Benny and Nix stood watching the massacre.

"Maybe if we'd gotten here sooner," said Nix softly. She tugged her journal from her pack. "I have so much information in here. There are things we could have done."

"Against forty thousand reapers?" asked Riot without opening her eyes.

"No army is invincible," said Nix. Then she thought about it and phrased it differently. "Any army can be defeated."

Benny nodded. "Absolutely."

"How?" asked Chong. "The reapers have too many people. They can call as many fast zoms as they want."

"C'mon, man," said Benny, "we had a high-tech army, navy, marine corps, air force, National Guard, and police, and we still lost to the zombies."

"That's because they didn't understand what they were fighting until it was too late."

"Kind of my point," said Benny. "If we could be defeated, then so can they."

Chong just shook his head.

"Maybe we could do a raid," said Nix. "With all those zoms there, they have to keep putting on the chemical—the stuff that's like our cadaverine. If we—I don't know, sabotage it. They couldn't make more of it way out here, could they?"

"Spilling won't do no good," said Riot. "They'd roll around on the ground and get it all over 'em. You'd have to burn it."

"Will it burn?" asked Benny.

"Sure. Burns like all get-out. Saint John lost a mess of reapers that way. Some of 'em get too cocky with torches. Maybe they think fire only burns the heretics." She shook her head. "I saw some of 'em burn last night. You can't tell a reaper's scream from a heretic's, not when they're burning."

"Look, Riot," began Benny, "if we'd known what was going to happen, we'd never have left to—"

Riot shook her head. "Don't," she said, and left it there.

Then she winced as a scream echoed up from the burning town.

"I'd love to see them all burn," she said viciously. "If I thought it would stop them, I'd set myself on fire and go running into their camp. Oh yeah . . . I'd sacrifice myself for that. . . ."

"Don't even think about it," snapped Nix.

Benny walked to the edge of the hill. With the quads running at top speed, they could be in Mountainside in three or four hours. He did some crude math in his head and figured that it was a three- or four-day march for the reaper army. That was no time at all. Even with Nix's book filled with diagrams of earthworks and trenches, even if everyone in town worked together to reinforce the walls, three or four days wasn't enough. The realities of this math conjured images of the reapers invading the town, setting fire to Lafferty's General Store and the school and the town hall. If he closed his eyes, he knew he'd see images of R3's chasing the children from the Sunday school, and climbing in through every door and window of Chong's house. He had witnessed so much carnage since leaving town that it was far too easy to imagine more.

He thought about Morgie Mitchell standing on his front porch, maybe holding the bokken he'd used during those long afternoons with Tom. Morgie, fighting to protect his mother and sisters. Morgie being pulled down and torn to pieces.

There were a few scattered gunshots beyond the veil of smoke. Someone was still alive, still fighting back.

However, Benny's mind was churning on the word Riot had just used.

Sacrifice.

Is that what it would come to? Is that what it would take to stop this?

The gunshots were fewer and farther between. The whole world seemed to be on fire.

Lilah spoke in the silence. "The trees are burning."

It was true. The drought and the heat from the reapers' fires had leeched the last of the moisture from the trees, and the intense heat caused them to burst into flame all around the town. Flaming figures ran among the trees. Zoms, Benny thought, set ablaze but unable to yield to pain until the fires melted their muscles and tendons.

It was horrible.

So horrible.

And yet . . .

It ignited a dreadful idea in Benny's brain.

95

They got back on their quads and drove away.

Twice they had to veer off the roads to avoid running into zoms. They passed through a few small ghost towns that had been cleared of zoms. They rode beside rusted steel tracks on which sat a cargo train that had to be more than a mile long. All the coal hoppers had long since been picked clean by teams of scavengers, as had some of the big chemical tankers. As they passed, Benny saw that each had been marked to indicate content and remaining quantities. There were nine bleach tankers, each one holding thirty thousand gallons. Farther along the road they passed a propane and kerosene company. Benny knew that much of the cooking oil and fuel used in town was brought in from somewhere close. This must be it. There were rows of massive tanks—rusted but still intact. He reckoned there was enough here to supply the eight thousand residents of Mountainside for the next fifty years.

They drove on.

But within a thousand yards Benny slowed, looked over his shoulder, and cut around in a looping U-turn. He saw everyone's puzzled faces as he headed back to the fuel company yard.

The gate was closed but not locked. There was nothing here to attract zoms and more than enough fuel for any of the traders to come and take some. The cost wasn't in finding it but getting it safely back to town. The others pulled up beside him.

Chong looked at the DANGER: FLAMMABLE sign. "While I admire your thinking, dude, I don't think we're going to able to talk the reapers into gathering here for a big psycho-killer cookout."

"Not exactly what I had in mind," said Benny. He told them the idea that had begun forming on the hill above Haven and was taking shape minute by minute.

They stared at him with a mixture of expressions.

"You're freaking nuts," said Chong, appalled.

"It'll never work," insisted Lilah.

"In your dreams," said Riot.

Only Nix remained silent, her eyes narrow and cunning.

"The other day," said Benny, "when I was talking to Joe Ledger, he asked me how far I'd be willing to go to stop Saint John if he was coming after me and mine. He said that if I could look inside my own head and see the line that I won't cross or a limit that's too far, then Saint John will win."

He turned to them.

"So, I guess I'm asking you guys the same thing. How far are we willing to go to stop Saint John?"

Nix pulled her journal from her pack and held it out to Benny. "As far as it takes," she said.

THEY WERE FIVE MILES FROM MOUNTAINSIDE WHEN THEY SAW TWO MEN on horses standing in the middle of the road. Benny slowed his quad and stopped twenty feet from them. Both men wore jeans and carpet coats, and both had red sashes across their chests. The man on the left was the smaller of the two. He had dark skin and a shaved head and machetes slung from each hip. The man on the right was thick in the chest and shoulders, and the handle of a wooden bokken rose above his left shoulder, held in place by a cloth sling. The horses shied at the sound of the engine, so Benny cut the motor off. So did the others.

Everyone—the two men and the five of them—dismounted, and for a few fractured moments they stood in the road and stared at one another.

"Oh my God," Benny heard Nix say.

He walked forward until he stood a foot away from the taller of the two. Close enough to shake hands. Close enough to punch.

He said, "Morgie."

Morgie Mitchell looked at Benny, at the quads, at Chong and Lilah. At Riot.

At Nix.

Benny tensed against what was coming. Rage. Hard words. Fists.

Then Morgie suddenly gave a huge whoop of pure, unfiltered delight and swept Benny off the ground in a fierce bear hug.

"*You ugly monkey-banger!*" he bellowed. He swung Benny around in a circle, scaring the horses. Nix and Chong came running over. They wrapped their arms around Morgie. Nix kissed him. They spun in a crazy circle, ignoring all the stares and gasps and words.

Morgie tugged his arms free and then rewrapped everyone and pulled them close.

"I'm sorry," he said, tears running down his cheeks. "Benny . . . Nix . . . I'm so sorry. I'm a stupid ape and you have every right to kick my ass."

"Ughh . . . sure, okay . . . love to," gasped Benny. "But . . . *ouch.*"

Morgie realized that the look on Benny's face had gone from delight to pain, and he let him go. "Did I hurt you? Ah, jeez, I'm a freaking idiot. I—"

"No," wheezed Benny, backing off and staggering. "I kind of have a knife wound thing going on, and I think I popped my stitches."

"Knife wound?" echoed Morgie.

Benny's knees buckled, and the other man darted forward and caught him.

"I never thought I'd see you again, Benjamin Imura," said Solomon Jones. "I never thought we'd see any of you again."

He helped Benny over to a fallen log and steadied him

as he sat. The others clustered around. Benny could feel wet heat under his clothes.

"How are you *here*?" asked Morgie, his face almost slack with confusion. "And how do you have *cars*?"

"Not cars, Morg," said Chong, clapping him on the back. "Quads."

Morgie looked past him to the girl with the leather vest and scalp tattoos.

"Whoa," he said. "Hello. Where'd you come from?"

"It's a long story," said Nix.

"Plenty of daylight for a good yarn," said Solomon. "We have lots of time."

Benny shook his head. "No," he said. "We don't."

A terse hour later the story was told. The jet and the wrecked airplane. The mutagen and Archangel. Sanctuary and the American Nation. Joe Ledger. Slow zoms and fast. The Night Church and Saint John. Brother Peter. Benny, Nix, and Chong took turns telling different parts of it. Benny tried to read Solomon's face, but the man was too practiced at keeping his emotions and reactions in check. Morgie was a different story—Benny could read everything on his face. Shock, doubt, horror, pity, and fear.

When they got to the part about Haven, Morgie looked like he'd taken a physical blow.

"My cousins are there," he said. "They work in the feed and grain store."

No one felt the need to correct the tense of that word to "worked." It was an unnecessary cruelty.

Solomon straightened and walked a few paces away, his fists on his hips. "Three days, you say?"

"Maybe four," said Chong. "It depends on how long they stay at Haven."

"Forty thousand of them," murmured Solomon. "Holy mother of God."

"And all those zoms," said Morgie. "The fence will never hold."

"No," agreed Nix. "But it might not matter."

Solomon turned sharply. "What's that supposed to mean?"

Nix touched Benny's arm. "Tell him what you have in mind."

Benny outlined his plan.

"No way, man," said Morgie. "That's crazy."

"I know."

"It's impossible. No one would agree to that."

"They could just do nothing and let the reapers kill them," said Benny coldly.

Solomon sat down next to him on the log. He sighed.

"This is your plan?" he asked.

"Nix put a lot of twists in it."

"It's his plan," said Nix, and Chong nodded. Even Lilah agreed.

"You're just a kid, Benny," said Solomon, but even he didn't sound convinced. "How did you get from Mountainside to here?" It was a question about distance traveled that had nothing to do with geography or the length of time they'd been on the road. Everyone knew that. "Tom would never have thought of something like this."

"I'm not Tom," said Benny, and those were very hard words to say. Nix took his hand and squeezed his fingers.

"No," said Solomon, "you're not. And frankly, I don't know

who you are. You're certainly not the kid who left Gameland a couple of months ago."

"No," said Benny. "He died somewhere out in the desert."

His comment wasn't meant as a joke, and no one took it that way.

Solomon ran a hand over his shaved head. "You really want to sell this plan to the people in town?"

"If they can think of another way to stop forty thousand reapers," said Benny, "I'm all ears."

"Even so . . ."

"You think I'm crazy?"

"I think this plan is crazy," said Solomon. "But . . . I also think it's brilliant. Brilliant in a way that hurts my heart, Ben. I can't even guess what it's doing to you."

There was nothing to say to that.

Into the awkward silence, Chong nodded to the red sashes and asked, "What are those?"

Morgie brightened. "It's for the Freedom Riders. We all wear them."

"The what?"

Solomon answered that. "After Tom died, all of us who were out at Gameland—Sally Two-Knives, J-Dog and Dr. Skillz, Fluffy McTeague, the whole bunch of us—rode to Mountainside. We told everyone what happened. We found enough stuff in the rubble to prove that Gameland existed and that people from the towns were routinely going there to get in on the fights in the zombie pits. Easy to prove anyway, since a lot of town folks died out there and there was no other explanation for their absence from town. Mayor Kirsch called a meeting of the councils of all Nine Towns. I told the story again, and I brought a copy of the proposal that Tom had prepared."

"What proposal?" asked Chong.

Benny said, "Tom kept submitting ideas for how to improve the town's defenses and for creating a militia to patrol the Ruin. Like the town watch, but for outside the fence."

Morgie tapped his sash. "This time they listened."

"A militia?"

"We don't like to use that word," said Solomon. "It sends the wrong message. The Freedom Riders are officially a peace-keeping force. Two hundred strong, and almost as many in training, like young Mr. Mitchell here."

"I'm a cadet," said Morgie, and he actually blushed.

"Two hundred," said Benny.

Chong said, "Saint John has forty thousand."

Solomon pursed his lips. "Benny . . . this plan of yours . . . you know it's crazy, right? I mean, you have enough perspective left to grasp that, don't you?"

"Yes," said Benny.

"Then I think you kids better wait here. You roll into town on those bikes, telling stories like this, and all you're going to do is create a fuss or a panic."

"But—"

"Let me talk to Mayor Kirsch. Ever since Tom died, he's had a big change of heart. Him and Captain Strunk. I think I can get them to understand what you want to do and why."

"They won't like it worth a wet fart," observed Morgie.

"Well put," said Chong, clapping his friend on the shoulder.

Solomon smiled, showing a lot of very white teeth. "I guess I'll have to be persuasive."

He swung into the saddle. "You kids take the next turn and go that way two miles. There's a way station there with food and supplies. Wait for me there. But listen up . . . there have been reports of some wandering zoms in the area. Stay alert."

"Fast or slow?" asked Nix.

"We only get one kind around here," said Solomon. "At least so far. Zoms are zoms, though."

Benny shook his head. "Not anymore."

Solomon met his gaze and nodded. Then he wheeled his horse around and spurred it into a fast gallop.

When he was gone, Morgie asked, "What, you're not afraid of zoms anymore?"

"Slow, dumb ones?" mused Chong. "No much. Fast, smart ones? Yup. But you haven't met the reapers yet, Morg. There are scarier things out there, believe me."

Nix helped Benny onto his quad.

"Benny," she asked softly, "maybe I missed it . . . but when did we stop being kids?"

He turned away. He had no answer that felt sane to say out loud.

Part 5

Inferno

"Only the dead have seen the end of war."

PLATO

In three days and three hours Saint John brought the army of the Night Church to the gates of Mountainside.

After the battle of Haven, his army counted out to thirty-eight thousand reapers on foot, two hundred and ten on quads, and one hundred and forty-two members of his elite Red Brotherhood. The forests behind and around them teemed with flocks of the gray people. The handlers worked in teams, using supersonic calls from dog whistles to keep them from scattering. Many of them were well fed now, and their ranks had swelled from the thousands who had gone into the darkness at Haven.

He stood in the shade of the tall trees and looked across a broad field to the town that cowered behind a chain-link fence. There were guard towers, and Saint John could see people in them. There were other people behind the fence. Many of them. Some wore red sashes. Saint John knew that most or all of them would have guns.

That was fine.

Everything was fine.

As he stepped out into the field, the forest erupted with bodies who followed. The reapers of the Night Church, all of them armed with blades—knives, axes, swords, and spears. They moved into the sunlight in their thousands, standing in lines that stretched half a mile on either side of him like impossibly huge wings.

Six of Saint John's chief aides walked with him, three on either side. They all had dabs of jelly smeared on their upper lips. As did Saint John. Pots of the mint gel were being passed among the ranks of reapers.

Saint John stopped thirty yards onto the field.

The place stank.

It was an appalling olio of smells too. Some of it was rotting flesh—but that was everywhere. There was also the stink of ashes from a massive fire pit north of the town where trash and the dead were burned. But the strongest smell was that of bleach. The field had been soaked in it.

"Why did they do that?" asked one of his aides.

"An attempt at chemical warfare, I suppose," said Saint John. "It's caustic. If they can hold us on this side of the fence for any length of time, then the vapors will make us sick."

But he laughed at the worried expressions on the faces of his aides.

"That's a chain-link fence," he said. "Not a castle wall. And see? Their earthworks are not even finished."

There were haphazard mounds of dirt all along the fence line, but they hadn't been molded into barriers. It was a last-minute attempt that they'd been unable to finish. Perhaps they'd abandoned the effort in favor of soaking the ground with bleach instead.

"At least they tried," he mused. "For their own pride, they

have to go down trying. We've seen it in one way or another in every single town."

And they had. One town had tried to stall them with a stampede of beef cattle. Another had used oxen to drag in enough wrecked cars to build a metal wall. And there had been a town that was built high among the trees. There had been moats, and earthworks, and even deadfalls filled with sharpened bamboo spikes. So many kinds of defense, so much effort.

Every one of those towns had burned.

The knives of the reapers had drunk deep on every street and in every house.

Saint John called for a quartermaster and gave instructions that every man and woman tie rags around their noses and mouths. With the mint gel killing the stink of the bleach and the rags protecting the lungs, everything would be addressed except the eyes. And what would happen there? The reapers' eyes would tear. They would weep for the sinners in whose flesh they opened the red mouths.

How poetic that was.

How appropriate. The army of god wept in pity and in joy as they released the sinners from a world of iniquity into the purity of the eternal darkness.

It would create a wonderful legend, and legends are always useful.

He tied a cloth around his own mouth and nose and walked slowly forward. His aides walked a half step behind him. The sunlight made the red-hand tattoos on their faces glow like freshly spilled blood.

The field was a mess, the grass withered and dead from the

bleach, the soil muddy and cut with a thousand crisscrossing wheel ruts. Saint John recognized those signs too. In several towns—if there was enough advance warning—wagons filled with children, the elderly, and the infirm were sent away. To other towns or to some secure building. Sometimes wagons of treasure were carted off as well by people who did not understand the nature of the glory that awaited them. But once the town fell, there would be plenty of time to follow each set of wheel tracks to whatever "safe" place they led to. Knives would be drawn there as well, and the red mouths would cry out in joy at the release offered by the reapers of god.

It was always the same. Even the iterations and variations were becoming commonplace.

Saint John was content in that. With each mystery that became a known quantity, a known tactic, his army became more confident, and the end result of god's total dominion over a silent earth became that much more assured.

With his Red Brothers in tow, Saint John walked half the distance between the trees and the fence line.

And there he stopped. His eyes did not burn as much as he'd expected, and that was good.

He waited for almost five full minutes. He was a patient man, and this was part of the drama. Part of the legend.

He also knew that the longer this part took—the longer the heretics in the town made him wait out here like a tradesman at a side door—the angrier his reapers became. Once, when he was made to wait for two hours, the killing in the town was particularly brutal. Perhaps it would be here as well. His men had marched long and hard through desert and drought-stricken lands to reach these towns. Every moment of privation, every aching muscle, every skipped meal stoked the fires in the hearts of the thousands of reapers who waited in the woods. The people in this town already had a terrible day ahead of them. But if they made him wait too long, they would learn that even a terrible day could get very much worse.

Finally the gate opened.

People began coming out. They did not advance toward him, but instead fanned out along the fence line. And except for one figure in the middle, all the others wore red sashes. Saint John wondered what the sash represented. Was it a variation of a white flag?

The figure without the sash glanced at the people on either side of him, and even from that distance Saint John could see him take a breath to steady himself. His shoulders rose and fell.

Then a small group began walking toward him.

Within a few paces it became apparent that these were not town elders. Not sheriffs or the leaders of a town watch.

They were children.

Teenagers.

One boy walked in front. His hair was clipped very short, and he had a vaguely Japanese cast to his eyes. To his left and slightly behind were two other boys—one Chinese and the other white; to his right were three girls—a tall girl with white hair, a very short girl with wild red curls, and a girl with no hair at all.

"Sister Margaret," breathed one of his aides.

Saint John studied the teenagers. He did not know the Chinese boy or the large white boy, nor did he know the white-haired girl. But the red-haired girl he recognized. His lip curled back in anger. She and the half-Japanese boy had been in the forest near Sanctuary. The boy was nothing to the saint, but the girl had had the cosmic effrontery to call herself Nyx—the name of the mother of Thanatos, all praise to his darkness. At first Saint John had believed her to be an actual physical manifestation of the mother of his god, and thought she might have been clothed in flesh in order to provide some kind of spiritual test for him. But in the end she was nothing more than a sinner whose flesh cried out for the purification of pain.

Saint John caressed the handle of his favorite knife, which was hidden beneath the folds of his shirt. His aides sensed his mood and shifted restlessly.

When the heretics were ten feet away, Saint John pointed to the teen with the Japanese eyes. "I know you, boy."

The teen stopped, and the others stopped a few feet behind him. Except for the large white boy and Sister Margaret—the blasphemer who insisted on being called Riot—the others wore military-style bulletproof vests, with similar pads on their arms and legs. It made them look like black insects. Like cockroaches. However, they all had good knives strapped to their waists or thighs. The girls all wore gun belts. The Chinese boy had a compound bow and a quiver of arrows. The red-haired witch and the lead boy both wore *katanas*, positioned for fast draws. The Chinese boy carried something in his hand, an old-style megaphone, the kind that ran on batteries. Saint John was mildly impressed—working batteries were exceptionally rare.

"Show your manners," said Saint John, pulling the cloth from his mouth. "Name yourselves."

The boy cleared his throat. He gave a formal Asian-style bow, low and deferential.

"My name is Benjamin Imura," he said. "Brother of Tom Imura, samurai of the Nine Towns." He wiped away tears caused by the stinging chemical vapors.

The saint smiled and nodded. It was a very nice title and presentation.

"I am Saint John of the Knife, chief priest of the Night Church and sworn servant of the Lord Thanatos, all praise to his darkness."

The boy bowed again in acknowledgment. The others took his cue and also bowed.

Saint John found that he liked this young man. He had manners, and that was rare in these troubled times.

"Do you know why I am here?" asked the saint.

"Yes, sir," said Benny. He coughed and wiped more tears from his face.

"Have you come to offer terms for surrender?"

"Would it do any good?" asked the boy. "If we open our gate and let you come in, will you show us mercy?"

Saint John smiled. "The day will end more quickly."

"Right . . . meaning we'll be dead before noon and your guys can take a siesta."

The smile faded.

"Look," said Benny, "we both know how this works. You come out here and we talk. What's it called? A parley? Okay, so we're parleying. I know what your terms are. Join you or go into the darkness, right? You have seven more towns to pillage, so you probably want a bunch of us to—what's the expression? Kneel to kiss the knife? Wow . . . creepy and unsanitary. How do I know where that knife's been? Point is, some of us get to live if we agree to help you and your reapers slaughter everyone we know. I mean . . . that *is* the offer, right? That's the plan?"

"You are dangerously close to—"

"To what? Seriously, man . . . what is it you want me to be afraid of? Torture? You're already going to kill me. I don't know if it really matters all that much if I spend the last few hours screaming. I'll still be dead at the end of it. You want to threaten my friends and family? Go ahead . . . you're just going to kill them, too." Benny made a sour face of disapproval. "Maybe nobody's told you, but offering different kinds of murder isn't really a terrific sales pitch. Kill me now, kill me later, torture me . . . in the end all you really want is for us to be afraid of you. You dig the fear. You're like a vampire, only you suck up the terror and pain. You want us to be afraid of you? Sure. You're a serial killer psycho with an army. Pretty scary."

"Are you finished?" asked Saint John.

"Why, what have you got?"

"You had a single chance for a peaceful death. The death of the knife. Handled with care and compassion, a blade is a mercy. Like a scalpel, it cuts away the infection of a life lived in sin. I came to offer you the quickest and cleanest of deaths. A single red mouth and you would feel nothing. The darkness would open its arms to enfold you and give you rest."

"And I blew that with my smart mouth, I know, I get it," said Benny. "It was kind of my intention."

"Do you know what the penalty is for your impudence?"

"I have a pretty good guess. Does it involve lots of very fast dead guys with eating disorders?"

The white boy behind him snorted with laughter. The red-head and the Chinese boy were smiling. Saint John wasn't fooled, though. He could see the fear that turned their eyes glassy and sent lines of cold sweat down their faces.

"The forests behind me are filled with my reapers and with uncounted legions of the dead who—"

"Why do you talk like that?" asked the Chinese boy, speaking for the first time. "Oh, hey, I'm Louis Chong. It's just that I'm listening to this and I'm wondering why you sometimes talk like you're in a fantasy novel. You have kind of a *Lord of the Rings* vibe going on, and it doesn't really work. I mean, sure you have an actual army, and I guess the zoms are good stand-ins for orcs, but really, man, who uses words like 'impudence' and 'uncounted'?"

"Yes," said the white-haired girl, "it makes you sound stupid."

The six teenagers all laughed.

Saint John's Red Brothers growled in anger and drew their knives.

In the same heartbeat three guns and a bow were pointed at them.

"Don't be stupid," said Benny. "We all know that we're mouthing off to you because we're scared, and you're letting us get away with it because you brought knives to a gunfight. Personally, I'd rather go back to the parley. Less flop sweat all around."

Saint John made a small gesture with his left hand, and the reapers reluctantly sheathed their weapons.

"Oh," said the redhead as she lowered her gun and slid it back into its holster, "speaking of knives."

"Right," said Benny in a bad imitation of having just remembered something. "I'm going to pull a knife and toss it to you. It's not an attack, so let's nobody get all weird about it."

Saint John nodded, curious.

Benny reached around behind his back and slid a long knife from a leather sheath clipped to the back of his belt. He weighed it in his hand for a moment and then tossed it onto the ground in front of the saint.

Saint John recoiled from it as if it was a scorpion.

The Red Brothers gasped.

They all knew that knife.

Saint John picked it up and clutched it to his chest. Then he let out a terrible wail as he sank to his knees in pain and grief. Tears burned in his eyes as he recalled the day he gave this knife to a young man, first of the reapers.

"Peter . . ." The saint looked up pleadingly at the teenagers. "*Where did you get this?*"

"Where do you think I got it?" said Benny. "I took it from him after *I* sent *him* into the darkness."

Saint John closed his eyes and bent forward as if the knife had been driven into his stomach.

"Feel that?" asked Riot coldly. "That's what it feels like to lose someone you love."

BENNY IMURA LOOKED AT THE MADMAN KNEELING IN THE DUST.

His nose burned from the chemical vapors that rose from the ground, but he imagined that he could smell Saint John's fear and pain.

Somewhere, deep in the darkness of his fractured heart, he found he liked it.

And with that realization came the screams of all his other parts. The kid that was lost in those shadows. The son who had quieted his parents. The brother to a fallen hero. The young man who had probably lost the love of his life. The traveler and friend, the climber of trees and the catcher of small, fierce fish. The collector of Zombie Cards and the apple-pie eater. Child and boy, teen and young man. All the many aspects of Benny Imura shouted a warning at him as he savored the pleasure of this evil man's pain.

How scary are you willing to be in order to take the heart out of an enemy? Are you willing to be the monster in the dark? Are you willing to be the boogeyman of their nightmares?

The ranger had asked those questions.

He should have asked one more.

Are you willing to become a monster to defeat monsters?

But Benny already knew the answers to all those questions.

BENNY IMURA FELT HIS MOUTH TURN INTO A SNEER OF ABSOLUTE CON-
tempt.

"Get up," he said.

It was not pitched as a request.

It was pitched as an order.

The Red Brothers bristled, their hands flexing on the
handles of their knives and axes and swords. Benny shot
them a look that told them clearly that their chance would
come, but it wasn't this moment. Those men saw something
in Benny's eyes that ignited flickers of fear in them. They
helped Saint John to his feet.

"I will bathe in the blood of everyone you love," said Saint
John, but his voice was hoarse.

"Yeah, sure. Whatever," said Benny. He held out his hand
toward Chong, who handed him the bullhorn. Benny clicked
the button and spoke into it. His voice boomed out, startling
him with the towering volume of it. It echoed off the tree line
and rolled down the field.

"Listen to me," he said, speaking slowly and clearly.
"My name is Benjamin Imura, and I speak for the people of
Mountainside and the other towns. I know who you are and I

know what you've had to do. Most of you were forced to join the reapers. Most of you don't want to do the things you're doing. Murdering innocent people. Killing little kids. I don't believe that most of you ever wanted to do that, and it probably makes you sick to even think about it. I understand. I've done some pretty horrible things myself in order to survive."

"They won't listen to you," said Saint John.

"Sure they will," said Nix.

"I won't let you . . ."

Lilah pointed her pistol at his face.

"Yes you will."

"Kill me and my reapers will tear you to pieces."

Lilah shrugged. "So?"

"You've been told a bunch of lies," continued Benny. "You've been forced to accept those lies as the truth. But they *are* lies. *Here* is the truth. A scientist named Dr. Monica McReady has developed a cure for the Reaper Plague. It's not perfect, but it works. My friend was infected with an arrow shot by one of your reapers. He got the plague and almost turned, but then Dr. McReady gave him medicine and he's right here with me."

Chong raised his bow and waggled it.

"The world hasn't ended," shouted Benny. "There is a new government in Asheville. People are reclaiming the world. The mutagen—the red powder you have—is going to wipe out the dead. It makes them faster, but it will also make them decay. In a week your flocks will fall apart. The plague is ending. We've survived it. Mankind has survived it. *You* and me, we're going to be here when it's over. That's what we've all prayed for. That's the grace of God, and it's the work of good-hearted people. We're being given a chance to make a new world."

"You are wasting your breath," said Saint John. Power was creeping back into his voice, and he still held Brother Peter's knife.

"We need to end this war," pleaded Benny. "*You* need to end this war. Lay down your weapons, tear those angel wings off your clothes, and walk away. On behalf of the Nine Towns I have been authorized to offer a complete and total amnesty. No questions, no punishments. Lay down your weapons and help us rebuild the world instead of helping a psychopath destroy it. Don't be destroyed by his screwed-up view of the world. Open your eyes. Open your hearts. Be alive!"

None of the reapers moved. They stood in endless rows that faded back into the depths of the forest. No knives fell to the ground.

"I am offering you a chance. One chance. Walk away now . . . or burn in hell for what you've done."

Benny lowered the megaphone.

Saint John smiled through his tears. "And you accuse me of being dramatic. 'Burn in hell'?"

"I was in the moment," said Benny, and he smiled too.

Neither smile held any warmth. Neither smile held a flicker of humanity.

"I'll see you bleed," said Saint John.

"I'll see you in hell," said Benny Imura.

Benny and his friends turned and walked away.

As Benny and his friends walked toward the gate, he studied the faces of the Freedom Riders who waited for them. Solomon Jones was there, and beside him was a tall dark-skinned woman with a Mohawk and a matched pair of army bayonets strapped to her thighs—Sally Two-Knives. And dozens of others, some of whom Benny knew from Zombie Cards and the battle of Gameland; some of whom were strangers.

Solomon clapped Benny on the shoulder. "That was some speech."

"It was my first one," said Benny, "and it'll probably be my last. I wanted it to stick."

Solomon grinned. "It was better than the one I gave to the mayors of the Nine Towns the other night. When I told them what was coming and told them about your plan, they wanted to put me in a straitjacket and give me tranquilizers."

"Yeah, well."

"But you should have seen their faces when I told them whose plan this was." Solomon chuckled. "Little Benny Imura. Half of them didn't even know Tom had a brother, let alone one who could come up with a plan like this. If there's anyone left to talk about this, then believe me . . . people will think you're absolutely out of your mind."

"He was born crazy," observed Morgie. "He's been losing ground ever since."

"Nice to know I'm among friends," said Benny. "Shame none of 'em are mine."

"That 'walk away' part of your speech was nice," said Sally. "You cribbed that from what Tom said before we blew Gameland into orbit."

"As I remember," said Chong, "it didn't work then, either."

"You had to say it, though," said Nix, coming to Benny's defense. "You have to give people a chance."

No one replied to that. It was a hopeful statement, but hope seemed to be lying dead somewhere out in the Ruin. For Benny, hope had died with a little girl back at Sanctuary. He looked for some inside his heart, but all he found there was a dark and murderous rage.

They passed through the gates. Benny turned to watch the guards pull it shut.

"God . . . ," he murmured. He looked around. Mountainside looked like it always looked. And after today he knew for sure that he'd never see it again.

"Benny . . . ?"

He turned at the sound of her voice.

"You have to go, Nix," he said. "There's still time."

She shook her head. "I can't go."

Benny felt his heart tearing in half. "Please, Nix . . . I can't do this if you're here. I *can't*."

"You have to," she said. "We have to."

Benny suddenly reached for her and pulled her close and

clung to her. "Nix, please go," he begged, his voice breaking into sobs. "Please don't make me kill you, too."

She started crying too. He could feel the heat of her, even through their body armor, even through the fear. She was so alive, and she deserved to go on living. Someone had to.

"Nix . . . *please* . . ."

She looked up at him with her green eyes. Her freckles were dark, the scars on her face livid.

"Benny," she said softly, thickly, "I'm a samurai too."

"Nix . . ."

"I won't leave you," she said, shaking her head stubbornly. "I won't."

He leaned his forehead against hers and they stood there, weeping, while all around them the town they grew up in prepared to die.

"Benny . . . Nix . . . ," said a voice, and they turned to see Morgie there. "They're coming."

Benny drew a breath and stepped back from Nix. He fisted the tears from his eyes and nodded. Nix sniffed back her tears. She nodded too.

Lilah, Chong, and Riot stood a few feet away.

"This is it," said Benny. "They let me make the big speech out there because this was my crazy plan. But I wanted to say something else to you guys. First . . . I told Nix and I'm telling you, there's still time to leave. You can follow the goat path up the mountain. Or you can go out the north gate on the quads. There's enough fuel to get you at least a couple of miles down—"

"Don't," said Chong. "You know we're not leaving. My family got out, that's all I care about."

Neither of them admitted the reality of that comment. Wagonloads of people had left. Thousands went on foot toward the next town. Only fighters were left here. If everything went wrong, then the reapers would follow the trail north and destroy that town, and the next, and the next. Distance couldn't guarantee safety anymore. Only an end to the reapers could do it, and that would happen here or it wouldn't happen at all.

The odds were that it wouldn't happen, though. The odds were in favor of the Chongs, and everyone else, being hunted down by killers—alive and dead.

Benny turned to Lilah and Riot. "This isn't even your town. . . ."

"It ain't about the town, son," said Riot. "Excuse me for saying it, but I don't give a rat's hairy bee-hind about this town or any other town. I want to see that smug bastard and all his minions burn."

"'Minions,'" echoed Morgie. "Nice."

There were shouts from the wall. "They're coming! God . . . it's the runners! They're coming."

Benny said, "Look, if we do this, then we're not going to be the same people afterward. This is the line that Captain Ledger was talking about. We're about to become monsters."

"No," said Chong, "that's a myth; it's a lie of bad logic. People who don't understand, who haven't seen what we've seen, say that if you use violence in defense, then you're just the same as the people who attacked you, that you're just as bad. But it's not true. If they hadn't started this, we'd never have thought this up. Benny—I grew up with you, I know how that weird little mind of yours works. If Saint John and Brother Peter and Mother Rose and all those maniacs hadn't started a holy war, all you'd be thinking about would be Zombie Cards, fishing for trout, and what Nix looks like in tight jeans. Don't even try to deny it."

Despite everything, Nix blushed and Benny grinned.

"These people want to kill everything that we love." Chong looked at Riot. "You want to talk about a line? They raided Sanctuary and slaughtered monks who never did anything but help everyone they met, and they killed sick people who couldn't even lift a hand to defend themselves. And they murdered all those little children. Like Eve—they murdered *Eve*. There is no line, Benny. We're not like them. If we're risking our souls here, it's to make sure that kind of wholesale slaughter doesn't keep happening. I'm not saying we're heroes . . . but we're not like them."

Morgie clapped him on the back and then held out his hand, palm down in the center of their circle. "Maybe I haven't been with you guys through all that, but I've got your back right here, right now. Tom taught us to be samurai. He taught us to fight . . . so let's fight. Warrior smart."

Chong laid his hand atop Morgie's. "Warrior smart."

Lilah was next, placing her brown hand over Chong's. "Warrior smart."

"I ain't a samurai," said Riot, "but I've got my own dog in this fight. And I guess this was my war before it was yours. So, yeah . . . warrior smart." She placed her hand over Lilah's.

Tears still streamed down Nix's face. "All that time I was writing down how to survive and how to fight in my journal, I thought it was to build and protect something. I didn't think it was to destroy . . . but I guess we don't always get to choose our wars. I love you all. Warrior smart."

Benny was the last to reach out, and he placed his palm over Nix's. Her fingers were icy from terror.

"I know Tom would think we're all crazy," he said. "But when he taught us to be warrior smart, this is what he meant."

They held their hands there for a long moment, and then without another word they turned and headed off to take up their posts.

101

Saint John could not put down the knife. His fist felt welded shut around the handle.

"Honored One," said one of his aides. "Our scouts picked up the trail of a large group of refugees heading north. Thousands of them. The scouts guess they have a two-day lead."

"Send the quads after them."

"How many, Honored One?"

"All of them, and a reserve of five thousand on foot. Hunt them down and send them all into the darkness." He touched the aide's sleeve. "We are no longer recruiting. Everyone goes into the darkness."

The aide bowed and left, and a few moments later the saint heard the sound of hundreds of quad engines roaring to life.

"You cannot escape the will of god," he said to the morning air.

Another aide appeared at his side. He wore a silver dog whistle around his neck. "We've called up the flocks."

"How many answered the call?"

"Eighty thousand of them. At least a third are runners.

However, we've already almost used up Sister Sun's red powder."

Over the last few days, several quads had caught up with Saint John's army, each one laden with plastic trash bags of powder. The last gift of Sister Sun, sent with the fastest quads by Brother Peter.

"Save it for later. We have enough runners for this nonsense."

The aide pointed. "I sent two small flocks ahead to test the defenses."

Saint John watched the dead run in a ragged line toward the fence.

"Send the rest."

"And the reapers, Honored One?"

"Send them all in. I want that town erased from the earth. Tear it down, paint it in blood, and grind it into the mud."

The aide smiled, nodded, and went off to relay the orders. Sending the gray people in along with the reapers was the kind of shock and awe the Red Brothers loved. It made for a quick fight, but a memorable one. He began shouting orders.

Saint John glanced at the reapers behind him. Many of them were ordinary foot soldiers, some of them quite new to the faith. As he looked at them, quite a few dropped their eyes or looked away. They all wept, and he wondered how many of those tears were from the chlorine stench or from their own terror.

Cowards, he thought. *Timid in faith and in heart.*

"Listen to me," he bellowed. "The false one has tried to trick you with lies and promises. He has tried to test your faith and make you question your commitment to god. I say to you now, our god is an unforgiving god. If any man or woman strays from his duty or withholds his blade from the cause of righteousness, then that sinner will be stripped of flesh and left to the gray people. To defy me is to defy god. All hail to Lord Thanatos!"

"All praise to his darkness," thundered the closest reapers, and that cry spread so that soon forty thousand voices shouted it.

Saint John was satisfied. His words might not have removed doubt, but they would make even the doubters crave to dip their knives in the blood of the heretics.

The Red Brothers acted as sergeants and yelled orders.

Saint John pointed with Brother Peter's knife.

"Now," he commanded.

And the army of the reapers surged forth.

They started out walking onto the field, many of them coughing and gagging from the chemical vapors. But soon they were running, shouting, crying out the name of their god. Screaming for blood.

102

BENNY IMURA CLIMBED TO THE OBSERVATION PLATFORM OF THE EAST tower. The field was vanishing, to be replaced by a carpet of bodies. Leading the charge were two packs of R3's. Even from this distance they looked terrifying. They were fresh corpses too, probably victims of the raid on Haven.

Somehow that made it worse. It made it more of a sinful act on Saint John's part. It was a level of disrespect for the dead that offended Benny in ways he couldn't express.

It fed his rage.

He held a pair of binoculars and watched as the zoms ran across the bleach-soaked ground. Reapers with dog whistles ran with them.

No one inside the gate moved. Not a muscle, not a finger. The entire town was absolutely still. Chong stood by the tower rail, an arrow fitted in place, the string pulled back.

Benny said, "Now."

Chong loosed the arrow. The powerful compound bow sent it whipping through the air, fast and silent and true. The arrow struck the stomach of one of the reapers running with the zombie flock. He screamed and pitched backward.

The zoms turned at the scream and the movement and at the spurt of fresh blood. Through the binoculars Benny saw the confusion on the faces of the zoms. He saw how the moment of distraction changed their focus. They had come running out onto the field, driven by whistles, herded forward over the mud. They were not pulled by any smell of meat from behind the chain-link fence. Now that they were on the field, they couldn't smell the human flesh at all. Bleach kills all sense of smell. The reapers, protected by their chemically treated tassels, herded them with sound alone.

But now the moment froze. The reapers still had their whistles, but the zoms' sense of smell was gone.

The chemical protection of the tassels was gone.

The reapers stared into the eyes of the R3 zoms.

The zoms stared back at them.

The reaper with the arrow lay thrashing on the ground. Not dead. Benny did not want the man silent and still. He wanted screams. He wanted movement.

One of the zombies bared its teeth.

Then all of them did.

The reapers tried to blow their whistles.

But that was the wrong thing. They should have tried to run.

With shrieks like a pack of wildcats, the zoms leaped onto the reapers and bore them to the ground and tore them to pieces. All around them the reapers faltered and stared. Then the second flock of zoms, drawn by the screams, came running. They attacked anything that was close. Without a sense of smell to differentiate whole flesh from rotting meat, some of them threw themselves at other zoms.

Benny closed his eyes for a moment, not sure whether to be grateful or beg for forgiveness.

He opened his eyes again to see the forest walls vomit forth a horde of zombies. So many thousands of them that there was no need to count. They swarmed across the field. Some broke away from a straight charge to join the bloody melee. Most of them, though, kept running, drawn by the dog whistles, moving too fast for the effect of the bleach to overcome the call of the dog whistles.

Down at the fence, Sally Two-Knives raised her hand. The line of Freedom Riders held fast, guns ready. They stared in horror at the tide of death that was washing toward them. None of them believed that they'd live through the day. Over the last three days, each in their own way, they'd made peace with their world, their religions, or in the absence of any faith, with themselves. Just knowing that the main population of the town might be safe, and knowing that a cure for the plague existed, put iron in their backs and kept their hearts beating. Some of them wept in fear, but they blinked away tears and took aim.

Sally turned to Captain Strunk, who stood next to her. "Glad I never got to see what I'd look like as an old lady. There's something about an octogenarian with biker tats and a Mohawk that just doesn't work."

"You look beautiful to me," said Strunk. He sighted along the barrel.

Sally slashed down with her hand. "FIRE!"

Far out in the Ruin, many miles to the north, a line of quads raced along the highway. They rode four abreast, and the line of quads stretched back half a mile.

All along the road they saw signs of the passage of people fleeing in a hurry. Dropped dolls, lost shoes, articles of clothing that must have fallen from carts, muddy wagon tracks. It was four days' walk to the next town. The quads would catch up with the heretics in less than an hour.

Up ahead two figures stood in the middle of the road.

The leader of the mobile infantry raised a clenched fist in the universal symbol to stop. The quads slowed and stopped a dozen feet from the two men.

The man on the left grinned at the reapers through the grille of a New Orleans Saints football helmet. He was thin and wiry, with a carpet coat armored with metal squares cut from license plates. He leaned on a spear that had a bayonet blade and a heavy metal ball on the bottom. Under his helmet he wore a pair of cheap black sunglasses.

The man on the right was in similar garb, except that he wore a San Diego Chargers helmet with a plastic shark glued to it. A heavy logging ax rested on one muscular shoulder.

The man on the left gave the reapers a wide, happy grin.

"Wassssabi?" said Dr. Skillz.

"Duuuuude," said J-Dog, nodding to the leader's quad. "Nice ride. Can I have it?"

The reapers laughed. There was the slithery sound of many knives being drawn from leather sheaths.

"No, seriously," said Dr. Skillz. "Let him have the bike. He's got a serious Davy Jones for some vroom-vroom."

The leader looked blank. He leaned toward the reaper on his left. "Did any of that make sense?"

"They're messing with you, brother. Let's gut them and get moving."

"Whoa, bad vibes, brah," said J-Dog. "You need to drink a big chilltini."

"And you need to get right with god," said the leader. He gestured to his men. "Cut their throats and—"

The air was filled with the *clickety-click* of hammers being cocked and slides being racked. In the forest on either side of the road, figures moved. Men and women and teenagers. Hundreds upon hundreds of people; everyone in Mountainside who owned a firearm prepared to shoot. And the narrow country lane was a killing floor. The reapers knew it, and their righteous rage turned to icy sludge in their veins.

"Dudes," said Dr. Skillz, "if you're gonna ride the big one, you better *have* big ones."

J-Dog nodded. "So . . . can I have the bike?"

Saint John tried to see what was happening, but there were simply too many people in the way. He heard the screams, though, and they were too close to be coming from the town.

He grabbed a fistful of an aide's shirt. "Find out what's happening."

The saint thrust the man toward the crowd.

The Freedom Riders fired and fired, and the leading edge of zoms and reapers crumpled a hundred yards out. The next line fell at ninety yards. At eighty.

At least a hundred of the attackers collapsed with each

volley, but the tide was coming in like a tsunami. The mass of attackers rose up and down like sea rollers as they climbed over the dead. Fights broke out as zoms turned on the wounded and dying, their senses confused by the numbing bleach. Some of the reapers had to defend against their own undead shock troops. But even these skirmishes were carried forward like debris on the tide. There was too much forward momentum for anything to stop them.

"Fire!" screamed Sally. She had a bolt-action sniper rifle, and she killed everything she aimed at.

All along the line, fighters yelled out that they were reloading. Then slapped in new magazines or thumbed shells into their shotguns.

They fired and fired.

The tide was fifty yards away now, and Benny knew that nothing could stop it.

It was what he counted on.

It was what he'd planned for.

Down below, he saw Nix, Lilah, Morgie, and Riot dipping torches into buckets of pitch. All along the inside of the fence were unlit bonfires. Hundreds of them, and more of them throughout the town.

The tide was forty yards away. Almost to the first of the mounds of dirt.

How scary are you willing to be in order to take the heart out of the enemy?

"NOW!" Benny yelled.

The four of them slapped their torches against the ground, each at precise points, where slender trenches had been dug. Each trench was a few inches deep and a hand-breadth wide and lined with rags and straw that had been soaked in kerosene. All the tons of it that had been stored at the fuel company Benny and his friends had driven through. It had taken every spare second and every able-bodied man and boy to siphon it out of the tanks and transport it here. Now that kerosene was soaked into the earth, waiting for a single caress of one of the torches.

And now every one of those torches bowed to the ground to kiss the kerosene.

Nix touched her torch to the first of the trenches, and fire leaped up and raced away from her, under the metal rim of the fence and then flashing out along an arrow-straight line to the mound that was farthest from town. The fire reached the mound and then vanished into the mouth of a piece of metal drainpipe.

There was a moment of nothingness.

Then the thirty-pound propane tank buried inside the mound exploded. The dirt flew away from the blast, carrying with it all the broken glass, screws, nails, and other jagged debris that had been packed around it.

The incoming tide turned red.

Saint John heard the first of the explosions.

Then the next, and the next. He saw the fireballs rising above the field and heard the screams of his attacking army turn to screams of pain.

And he heard the moans of the countless dead turn to growls of red delight as they began to feed.

The tower shook with every blast, and Benny had to cling to the ladder to keep from being hurled off by the shock waves. He watched as the explosions opened empty spaces in the storm of attackers, like the eyes of hurricanes, but the storms swept around them.

There was more fighting on the field, though. The zombies were in open revolt now. There was too much blood, too much torn meat, and that sent them into a killing frenzy. The screams and gunfire and explosions washed away any effect of the dog whistles. Now the dead did what they had done for fifteen years. They attacked anything that moved with implacable ferocity and bottomless hunger.

The reapers forgot about the town and turned their weapons on the dead.

Saint John's aides brought up a supply cart, and he climbed onto it to get a better view. The sight nearly took the heart from him. The field in front of the town was a madhouse of battle. Reapers fighting the gray people. Forty thousand of the living against eighty thousand of the dead.

And the town . . .

The town still stood.

He turned to his aides, teeth bared, his face an inhuman mask of fury. "Slaughter the gray people. Pass the word. Do that first, do it now. And then we will pull down that fence and show those heretics the true meaning of holy wrath."

The Red Brothers raced out into the crowds, shouting orders, using curses and kicks and fists to force the reapers into some semblance of order. To get them to fight back. Some of the reapers threw down their weapons and tried to flee, but after the Red Brothers butchered them, the others fell into line, and with the elite warriors leading them, they counterattacked.

The dead, even the running dead, were frightening and incredibly dangerous.

But they were brainless monsters. They had no tactics, no strategy, no skill at arms. The reapers knew how to fight them. Of course they did. Killing was their pathway to paradise, even the killing of the dead.

The Red Brotherhood waded into the fight, swinging two-hand swords and fire axes and farming scythes. They cut swathes through the dead, slaughtering and dismembering with machinelike precision.

Saint John watched this and slowly, slowly, his smile returned.

Any single reaper should be able to defend himself against two or three of the dead. Reapers working together, fighting in military wedges led by the fiercest of their own kind—they were a force like nothing else on earth.

Benny Imura saw the precise moment when this part of his plan failed. The reapers had turned on the monsters that had turned on them. Thousands of blades flashed in the sunlight, and the massive army of the Night Church crushed the legions of the dead.

He leaned his head against the ladder and sighed.

The last of the propane tanks had blown up. The Freedom

Riders at the fence line were still firing, but there were only so many bullets.

Benny knew this would happen.

He had *planned* for this failure.

But he dreaded the next stages, knowing that with each step he was venturing into darker and darker territory. Even in the slim chance that he lived through this . . . could he ever find his way out of the abyss?

He doubted it. Joe's advice about becoming the monster they were afraid of did not come with a suggestion for how to reclaim his humanity.

He already felt lost.

103

BENNY CLIMBED DOWN FROM THE TOWER. THE PAIN IN HIS BACK WAS LIKE a constant scream, but he didn't care. Everything was screaming. The very air seemed to cry out in pain.

Nix and the others ran to meet him. They still held their torches. Chong climbed down and joined them, picking up a torch from the bonfire.

They stood for one moment in a circle.

"Go," said Benny, and everyone turned to run.

All except Nix.

"Benny . . . ," she began, but he gave a fierce shake of his head.

"Not now," he begged.

"I have to tell you in case—"

"No! Don't, for God's sake," he said. "If you say it, I think it'll kill me."

Nix saw something in his eyes, and she took a step backward. Then with a flash of wild red hair, she turned and ran.

Benny hurried over to Solomon.

"They're killing all the zoms," said Benny.

The bounty hunter laughed. "Yeah, shows you what a little cooperation can accomplish."

"We could have used a little more of that cooperation."

Solomon drew the two machetes and gave them a quick twirl. "What's that thing you kids keep saying?"

"Warrior smart."

Solomon nodded. "Warrior smart."

Benny drew his sword and began running along the fence line.

The Red Brothers and the army of reapers tore the gray people apart, but they took heavy losses to do it. Fewer than half of the forty thousand who had followed Saint John from the sack of Haven could still fight. However, half of those were injured. Some had bites from runners, and when their own fellow reapers saw those injuries, knives flashed and bodies fell.

Saint John allowed no infection among his people.

When the field was clear of the dead, Saint John walked out, Brother Peter's knife still clutched in his hand. His cadre of Red Brothers fanned out behind him. The sergeants shoved and growled their men into tight divisions. Sixteen thousand of them stood in ordered lines before the gates of Mountainside. Every eye on both sides of the fence watched Saint John walk across the red-stained field. Now the stench of blood was nearly as strong as the stink of bleach.

Saint John walked to within a thousand yards of the fence. Well within rifle range, but no gun fired. He stopped and pointed his knife at the town.

Behind the gates, the men and women in red sashes suddenly turned and bolted, running in disordered panic from the fence line.

The reapers goggled for a moment, and then laughter

rippled through their ranks. It swelled and swelled until they were all laughing hysterically. It was the sight of the defenders fleeing after all their tactics had failed, and it was the release of fear and tension from each of the reapers.

"They flee!" cried Saint John. "They flee!"

The laughter was like thunder.

Saint John bellowed out two words that floated above the laughter.

"Take them!"

The reapers began marching forward. First in orderly ranks, then faster and faster until they broke into a flat-out run. They hit the fence line, and the sheer weight of their surge tore the fence apart and ripped the poles from the ground—even at the cost of many in the front ranks being crushed at the moment of impact. The reapers flooded into the town, crossing the red zone that separated the fence line from the first rows of shops and homes, smashing through doorways of every building and house they reached. It was like a tidal surge bursting over a levee. The mass of the surge hit the town hard enough to knock walls down and uproot small trees. The thunder of all those feet shattered windows and knocked the frames of doorways out of true. The reaper army flooded into the town, knives ready, spears ready, bloodlust ready.

And they found . . . *nothing.*

The front ranks split apart to follow smaller streets. Knots of reapers burst through doors and ran down the halls of the school and the town hall and the hospital. Every closet door was yanked open, every cellar and attic was invaded.

But there was no one in the town.

As the last of the reapers ran across the fallen fence, the interior mass of them slowed near the center of town. They looked around, confused, frightened by the strangeness. There had been an army here minutes ago. Two or three hundred people in red sashes had fired volley after volley at them.

Where were they? The back of the town was a steep mountain wall. If any of the defenders had climbed the winding goat paths, they'd be as visible as black bugs. There was a massive reservoir near the end of town, but no one was hiding in the silent pump house.

Runners came to report this to Saint John as he walked without haste toward the shattered gates. He frowned at the news.

"There's no one there, Honored One."

"Then they're hiding. Find them."

Saint John stopped at the entrance of town and looked around. The guard towers appeared empty too. Except for . . .

"There," he said, and his aides looked up at the closest tower. A single figure stood by the rail.

The boy with the Japanese eyes.

"Bring him to me," said the saint. "Alive and able to scream. I will tear the answers from him."

Four of the Red Brothers hurried toward the tower, but before they could reach it, the figure far above raised the bullhorn and spoke. His eyes streamed and burned from all the chemicals in the air. The bleach burned his throat and made breathing difficult. But Benny's rage shaved all thoughts of pain and discomfort away.

"Listen to me," he roared. "This is Benjamin Imura, samurai of the Nine Towns."

The reapers laughed and jeered. Some threw rocks at the tower, though no one could reach the observation deck.

"*Listen to me,*" bellowed Benny. "While you still can."

That chilled some of the laughter, though a few rocks still banged off the structure.

"I made you an offer before," said Benny. "It still stands. Lay down your weapons. Do it right now. Lay down your weapons and tear those stupid angel wings off your shirts. The Night Church is a lie, and most of you probably know it."

The rest of the laughter died away.

"Look at what happened already. More than half of you are dead. Whose fault is that? Saint John forced you to fight us. He forced you to die for *him.* I'm giving you a chance to live. To have lives again."

One of the Red Brothers stepped away from the rest of the army and pointed at Benny.

"I think you're about played out, son," he said. He had a leather-throated voice that carried his words to everyone. "Right now you're all alone up there. Your friends at least had the smarts to run off . . . though we'll catch 'em. But you, sonny boy, you're just a little kid playing in a tree house."

"Not exactly," said Benny. "What I am is a kid playing with matches."

He pointed with the bullhorn, and everyone turned to see figures emerging from the ground as if by magic. They rose up from camouflaged spider holes outside the fence that had been hidden by plywood trapdoors covered with mud. A massive and improbable figure in a bright pink carpet coat rose up just outside the fallen gates. He held a smoking torch in his big fist. Fifty yards away another figure—a dark-haired young man with a pair of baseball bats slung over his shoulder—stood up. He, too, held a torch. All around the outside of the town, just beyond the fence line, figures rose up, each of them holding torches.

The man in the pink carpet coat smiled a charming smile. He had thick eyeliner and dangling diamond earrings. He blew a kiss to Saint John, pulled a thick cloth over his face, and tossed the torch over his shoulder. Everyone else flung their torches too.

Not toward the reapers.

But backward into the field.

There was a gassy sound that rose from a hiss to a roar, and the world suddenly caught fire.

THE FIRE ROARED ACROSS THE GROUND WITH INCREDIBLE SPEED. A SPEED possible only if the ground itself was . . .

Suddenly Saint John understood. He now realized that the bleach served a double purpose. Not only had it destroyed the gray people's sense of smell, but it hid other smells. Kerosene or gasoline or whatever flammable liquids these insane people had used to saturate the mud.

The reapers recoiled from the flames, even though the walls of fire were well beyond the town's destroyed fence line. The heat, however, was tremendous. It buffeted them back, smashing them with superheated chlorine. The gas clouds of superheated chlorine bleach rolled against the reapers, making them cough and gag, driving many of them to their knees. Men and women reeled and vomited. The reapers began to scatter, to run into houses, where they grabbed curtains and towels to cover their faces.

But immediately they screamed and dropped the cloths. There was something on them. Some chemical they couldn't smell with their bleach-burned noses.

They staggered back to the streets. Hundreds of them jumped into the reservoir to escape the fumes.

"Here!" cried one of the Red Brothers as he kicked aside one of the small bonfires to reveal a trapdoor. He whipped it up and saw a crudely dug tunnel. Smoke curled upward from the tunnel, and Saint John suddenly understood how the defenders had escaped. They'd gone through the tunnels to the spider holes outside, taking their torches with them.

The Red Brother standing over the trapdoor gagged and staggered backward, blood spraying from a slashed throat. A figure rose up out of the hole, carrying a long spear whose bayonet tip was painted red. She had a wet towel around her nose and mouth, but her white hair danced in the hot wind. She carried a torch in her left hand, and she bent and drove the end into the ground close to where she stood.

Another man screamed a few yards away, and Saint John turned to see the heretic Sister Margaret crawl into the light, a knife in one hand and a torch in the other.

The reapers faded back, clustering into a tight crowd as the bonfires tipped over and defenders emerged. One bonfire spilled right behind Saint John, causing him to dance out of the way, and the false Nyx with the red hair rose up.

The tableau held. Sixteen thousand reapers clustered together in one mass. Three hundred defenders with torches standing in the gap between them and the raging inferno. And the boy on the tower looking down at them.

"Kill them," snarled Saint John. "They are nothing."

The reapers, led by some of the Red Brothers, inched forward.

"Stop!" shouted Benny, his voice amplified by the bullhorn so that it rose even above the roar of the fire.

Everyone froze. Even Saint John and his reapers.

"You can't get out of here without burning," said Benny. He coughed, then pressed a wet rag to his nose and mouth for a moment. When he trusted his voice, he said, "I'm giving you one last chance. Put down your weapons and remove those angel wings."

"Or what?" demanded Saint John from below. "You're running out of tricks, boy. My reapers will tear you down from that tower."

"No, they won't," said Benny.

"My reapers would die to serve our god."

"Maybe," said Benny. "But would they burn for it?"

The reapers milled, confused by this. The fires in the field were still burning, but they weren't getting any closer. They could all see that.

Saint John shook his head and waved an arm toward the tower. "Hollow words from a blasphemous fool. My brothers . . . tear that tower down."

Before they could take five steps, Benny said, "You all know the ranger, Captain Ledger?"

The name sent a buzz of fearful conversation through the crowd; some even looked around to see if the man was somehow here.

"We were talking about this fight. About what might happen if I had to try and stop your whole army. He asked me if I was willing to become a monster in order to stop you. He said that if I could look inside my own head and see a line that I won't cross, then you'd win. Saint John would win. We all know how far he'd go to have his way. You're proof of that. Is there anyone down there who hasn't seen friends or family die because of Saint John? Well . . . today I took that look inside and, no, there isn't a line I won't cross. I'll do anything—any horrible, insane thing—to stop him from killing the whole world. I'll even kill myself, the girl I love, my best friends, and my town."

Benny bent and picked up a torch and held it out over the edge of the tower.

"Everything in this town has been soaked with oil, with kerosene, with cooking oils, with lighter fluid. We used every drop of everything flammable we could find and all that we could transport here. It's in the dirt, it's in every house, it's on the plants and shrubs. If I drop this torch, you'll all burn. We'll all burn. Every single one of us." Benny felt his mouth curl into an ugly smile of raw hate.

"You wouldn't dare," said Saint John, but for a man of great faith there was a terrible doubt in his voice.

Benny looked down at him, and his hate gave way to a strange kind of pity.

"What choice do I have?" he asked. "You forced me into this. What else can I do?"

The moment held and held as the world around the town burned. All of Mountainside could have been an island in hell.

There was a sound behind the saint.

A dull thud.

He turned and saw a sword lying on the ground.

It lay at the feet of one of the Red Brothers. The man said, "I'm sorry." Then he hooked his fingers into the collar of his shirt and tore away the front, ripping through the embroidered angel wings. "I don't want to burn."

Another weapon fell. An ax.

A woman looked down at the bloody knife clutched in her hand. "Oh God," she said, and as the sob broke in her chest, she let the blade tumble to the dirt.

The sound of weapons falling was drowned out by the rending of cloths. And then the sound of brokenhearted tears.

It went on and on until only Saint John stood alone, Brother Peter's knife clutched in his fist. He, too, wept—but his tears were from grief for all the children of his faith who had now lost the grace of god.

Benny doused his torch in a bucket and climbed down from the tower. The others—Nix, Lilah, Chong, Morgie, Riot, Solomon, and everyone else, held their ground, their torches burning. But they stood well back from the dampened mud that marked where the flammable liquids had been poured. It was a narrow safe zone, well within easy toss of a torch.

Benny walked over to where Saint John stood. The saint looked at the knife in his hand and then at the boy who had crushed his world. The boy who had killed Brother Peter and now killed his dream of serving god.

"Let it go," said Benny. "Drop the knife. Let it all go."

Saint John shook his head. "You don't know what you're asking."

"Yeah," said Benny. "I know exactly what I'm asking for. I'm asking for an end to hatred. I'm asking for an end to war. In the whole history of mankind, we've never had the chance before to really *end* all that."

"But . . . that's what I wanted too," said Saint John. Tears carved lines through the soot on his face. "An end to all suffering and misery. It's what god wants. It's all I've ever wanted . . . for the pain to end."

Benny sighed. "I know."

Saint John sank slowly to his knees. But as he did so he looked up at Benny, and for just a moment there was a smile on his face. In that instant something passed between them. Benny felt it, though he could never really define it. It was some message, some shared awareness. And as that message was shared, Benny felt the great boiling hatred in his chest burn down to a cinder and then wink out. And he realized that he no longer even hated this man. All there was left inside him was pity.

"I hope you find peace in the darkness," said Benny.

Saint John nodded.

He closed his eyes.

And drove the knife to the hilt into his own heart.

EPILOGUE

-1-

On a late summer afternoon Benny Imura sat on the back porch of his house. He sipped from a tall glass of iced tea and set it down next to a plate on which was a half-finished slice of apple pie. Dragonflies flitted among the sunflowers, and a mockingbird stood on a branch and told lies in a dozen different voices.

The house was on a green slope and there was a big oak tree in the yard, but the town wasn't Mountainside.

Mountainside was gone.

The oil-soaked houses had been left to rot. There were some sketchy plans to destroy them with controlled burns, but that was someone else's problem. Morgie and Chong were involved, so it would probably go wrong in one way or another.

Benny's new house was a gift from the Nine Towns.

They still called themselves that. Nine Towns. Haven was being rebuilt. And Benny's new town was just being built too. The sound of hammers and saws was constant, and there was a sense of "aliveness" to it, though Benny wasn't sure that was a real word. He'd have to ask Chong.

This new town had the awkward and unpopular name of Reclamation. It was the kind of name thought up by a committee, and it made the town sound like a landfill.

New names were a big thing.

Haven was going to be New Haven.

And the Ruin?

This part of it, the area that stretched from the Nine Towns to the far side of Yosemite, was going to be called Tomsland. That was a name Benny liked a lot.

Movement across the yard nudged Benny out of his reverie, and he saw Nix Riley open the garden gate. She wore a pretty yellow dress with lots of flowers stitched onto it. She did not carry *Dojigiri*. She had no weapons at all with her. Benny's sword was on the porch, laid across the arms of the rocker. He still carried it once in a while.

When he went out into the Ruin.

No. He had to start using its new name.

When he went out into *Tomsland*.

Nix carried a basket that she held out to him. Her red hair was pulled back into a ponytail. She never tried to hide the two scars—the long one that ran from hairline to jaw, and the smaller one that bisected it. He loved that about her.

"What's in the basket?"

"Muffins," she said. "Blueberry."

Benny cocked an eyebrow. "Who made them?"

"I did. First batch ever."

"Really?" He sniffed them. They smelled like old socks.

"You don't have to eat them," she said. "They're nasty."

"Then why—?"

"They're a peace offering."

He took another sniff. "You trying to start a war?"

"No," she said with a shy smile, "I'm trying to ask you out."

It took him a couple of beats to catch up to that. "You . . . wait, I'm sorry . . . what?"

"Should I say it slower?"

"It might help," he admitted.

"I would like to ask you out on a date."

"But . . . I thought the agreement was that when this was all over, *I'd* ask *you* out."

Nix folded her arms. "Um . . . it *is* over, and you haven't asked me out."

"Yet," he said.

"At all," she said.

"I was going to get around to it."

"The world could end before you got around to it."

"Could have," he said. "But it didn't."

"No," she agreed, smiling. "It didn't."

-2-

THE NEXT AFTERNOON BENNY AND HIS FRIENDS SAT AT A PICNIC TABLE whose timbers were so green that pine sap stuck to their plates. It was a party—the first American Nation Day that would be celebrated by the people in the Nine Towns. Most of those citizens were still in some aspect of shock, and Benny could sympathize. The day before Saint John brought his reaper army to California, all those people thought that they were the last people left alive on earth, the last survivors. None of them knew about the American Nation, or the drive to reclaim and rebuild the world. They didn't know that an army was out there fighting back the hordes of zoms—fighting, and winning. They didn't know that science hadn't died with the old world, and that a cure to the zombie plague existed.

There were so many things they didn't know. Or . . . *hadn't* known. Now they had to make as dramatic a readjustment to their lives, their worldview, their expectations of the future as they had when the dead first rose. Now it was the living who were rising to conquer the world.

It was all so strange, even to Benny.

There was a world again, a real world; and that world had a future.

Benny looked around at all the people who'd come to the party. He saw Fluffy McTeague—for once without his pink carpet coat—talking with Captain Strunk and Sally Two-Knives. Solomon Jones was grilling steaks on a fire pit made from an old fifty-gallon drum that had been split down the middle. The two surfer dudes, J-Dog and Dr. Skillz, had started a make-it-up-as-you-go game called "goofball," and they had half the kids in town running around and laughing.

Mayor Kirsch and his wife, Fran, sat at the head table, drinking beers and listening to Captain Joe Ledger explain how he'd survived that day after the fall of Sanctuary. Benny had heard the story. There wasn't a whole lot to it—zoms, even the fast ones, can't eat through a helicopter. The ranger simply waited them out, chowing on military-issue ready-to-eat meals and singing old blues songs until the staff from the blockhouse were sufficiently recovered to rescue him. It was a long five days. He said that the hardest part of it all was the fact that neither he nor Grimm could step outside to relieve themselves. Joe said the helicopter had to be cleaned out with a high-pressure hose.

The zoms at Sanctuary were all gone, collapsed into rotting heaps as the mutagen burned through them.

At the same table, Dr. McReady and Colonel Reid sat and listened and nodded. The doctor had brought enough of the mutagen to give the Freedom Riders a lot of work—spreading the chemical and then dealing with the faster, though doomed, zoms. Everyone's best guess was that the zoms would be a problem for years. Maybe decades. There were, after all, seven billion zombies in the world. No one was dropping their guard. There would still be gates and fences and doors and fear.

It would end one day, though.

As for the infected like Chong . . . there was heartbreak there. McReady was working on a real cure, but who knew how long that would take. Or if there ever would be a cure. Until then, Chong took his pills and he lived a careful life. But he lived.

The colonel must have felt Benny's eyes on her, because she turned and looked at him. They nodded to each other.

Before leaving Sanctuary, Nix had asked the colonel not to forget the people in the Nine Towns. It was as much a challenge as a plea, and the officer had risen to it. Two days after the surrender of the reapers, the morning sky had been shaken by the thunder of helicopter rotors.

Forty of them.

Colonel Reid's people had managed to fix one of the radios,

and she'd sent an urgent call to the nearest American Nation base. Her call was passed all the way up to the commander of the army and then to the president, Sarah Fowler. Reid had begged for help to stop the reapers from destroying the Nine Towns. For help in protecting citizens of the new nation, even those who had become disenfranchised and almost forgotten. There was almost a full day of inaction as the highest ranking military advisers and the political advisers wrangled over it. But in the end, Reid's plea hit its mark. The Air Cavalry was dispatched. Had things worked out differently, those helicopters would still have arrived too late to save Mountainside, but they would have been able to save the other towns.

Instead the army's role was not combative but administrative. They helped process the tens of thousands of reapers.

That was an awkward part of this, Benny knew. Many of the reapers claimed to have sided with Saint John only out of fear for their own lives. But there were still some true believers among them. These zealots refused to lay down their arms or remove their wings. There were some clashes, a few skirmishes, but the army, backed by the Freedom Riders, won out. The surviving zealots were not imprisoned or executed—Solomon and Benny argued ferociously for this, pushing hard on the message that the time for killing was over. Instead these reapers would be transported to islands off the California coast. They would be given some simple tools, seed for planting, and materials for building shelters. As long as they wore the angel wings of the Night Church, they were barred from setting foot on the mainland.

"They'll sneak off the island and come back," said Nix as they watched the helicopter transports lift off.

Benny did not think so. What he feared—what saddened him to think about—was that those lost souls would find a different escape. Into the darkness through mutual murder and suicide.

The rest of the reapers were given a choice. They could join the construction teams who were rebuilding New Haven and Reclamation, or they could enlist in the American Nation's Rebuild Now corps and work to spread the mutagen and reclaim the zombie-occupied territories. The only other choice was to join the zealots on the islands.

Not one of them chose exile.

It would be impossible to ever identify former reapers who had killed in the name of Thanatos, but when Benny watched these new "citizens" at work and saw the passion with which some of them helped to heal the damage done . . . he thought he knew. For many, the question of redemption would be a very personal thing.

Over the weeks since the Battle of Mountainside, the American Nation sent more troops, engineers, medical teams, and others to help integrate the Nine Towns into the new country.

The war was over.

Maybe all wars were over. Just as the old world was over. The new world wasn't going to be built on a foundation of misery and pain.

Solomon Jones, head of the Freedom Riders, was appointed by President Fowler to serve as the interim governor of California. His first act was to appoint Sally Two-Knives as his lieutenant. Benny wondered how that would look in some future history book.

Someone snapped fingers under his nose, and he realized that people had been speaking to him while his mind wandered. He turned to Chong. "What?"

"I *said* the new Zombie Cards come out tomorrow."

"Big whoop."

"We're all on them," said Morgie. "Even me."

"Let me rephrase that . . . big freaking whoop."

"We saw the proofs the other day," said Chong. "I look heroic . . . though they're still making my skin look too green."

"That's because you're a half-zee," said Morgie. Lilah punched him on the arm. Very hard.

"Owww."

"He's not a zombie," she said.

"I didn't say he was a zom, I said he was a half—"

Lilah pulled her knife and drove it into the tabletop in front of Morgie.

"Point taken," said Morgie. He turned to Riot and offered her the plate of corn. She took an ear, hiding a smile.

Benny noted that Riot seemed to smile at everything Morgie said and did. And he seemed to find whatever she did endlessly fascinating. Benny smiled too as he spread butter on an ear of roasted corn.

"What are you smiling at?" asked Nix.

"Nothing," he said. "Just smiling."

Nix pushed her knee against his. But it was under the table, where nobody but Benny knew about it.

Benny took a bite of the corn and chewed as he thought about all that had happened. Next Tuesday would make one year since he'd agreed to apprentice with Tom. It seemed impossible that so little time had passed. A year.

He thought about the kid he'd been. The Benny of one year ago had been so mired in assumptions and inflexible opinions, few of which were valid. That Benny had hated Tom, and believed him to be a coward.

Tom. A coward.

Benny smiled and shook his head.

A year ago Nix's mother had been alive. A year ago Benny, Chong, and Morgie idolized Charlie Pink-eye and the Motor City Hammer. A year ago none of them had ever set foot outside the gates. A year ago zoms were the most frightening thing Benny could even imagine.

So much had happened since.

So much.

Pain and loss. Heartache and blood. Tears and death.

And so, so much had been gained.

More than Benny thought was possible.

The world was not at all what he'd thought it was. And he still didn't know what else was out there. Europe, Asia, and so many other places were still unknowns, still silent and ominous places. There was a whole new world to explore. Benny wanted to explore it. Nix did too. They weren't town kids anymore. They weren't yet adults, either; Benny knew that and accepted it. That would come.

So what was he? Benny knew the answer to that question, and he knew that this answer would be a defining characteristic from now on and all through his life. For him, and for Nix, Lilah, Chong, Morgie, and Riot.

They were samurai.

And even now, as everyone celebrated peace, Benny

could feel the pull of the road. He could hear the siren call of unknown places sing to him.

He turned and saw Nix staring at him the way she often did. The way she looked at him when she was tapping into his thoughts.

She smiled and nodded to him.

He nodded back. There was no need to say anything. They both understood on a level that Benny no longer tried to define.

He looked around at all the people he knew, and at all the strangers. There was so much laughter, so many smiles. He didn't remember it ever being like this. He wished Tom were here to see it. To share it.

This was a better place. Not just this new town, but this new world. So much brighter and cleaner than the old world of rot and ruin, fire and ash.

Jonathan Maberry is a *New York Times* best-selling author, multiple Bram Stoker Award winner, and Marvel comics writer. He's the author of many novels, including *Assassin's Code*, *Dead of Night*, *Patient Zero*, *Rot & Ruin*, *Dust & Decay*, and *Flesh & Bone*. The topics of his non-fiction books range from martial arts to zombie pop culture. Since 1978 he has sold more than 1,200 magazine feature articles, 3,000 columns, two plays, greeting cards, song lyrics, poetry, and textbooks. Jonathan continues to teach the celebrated Experimental Writing for Teens class, which he created. He founded the Writers Coffeehouse, cofounded the Liars Club, and is a frequent speaker at schools and libraries, as well as a keynote speaker and guest of honor at major writers' and genre conferences. Jonathan lives in Bucks County, Pennsylvania, with his wife, Sara, and their son, Sam. Visit him online at jonathanmaberry.com and on Twitter (@jonathanmaberry) and Facebook.